If You Leave

To learn more about her, visit her website:

Also by Courtney Cole

The Beautifully Broken series
Book 1: If You Stay
Book 3: Before We Fall

About the author

Courtney Cole is a novelist who lives near Lake Michigan, USA, with her family and her pet iPad. Her favorite place in the world is on the shore with her toes in the water. If she's not there, you can find her wearing cashmere socks and staring dreamily out of her office window.

To learn more about her, visit her website:
www.courtneycolewrites.com.

If You Leave

The Beautifully Broken Series: Book 2

COURTNEY COLE

HODDER

Originally published as an ebook
First published in the USA in 2014 by Forever
An imprint of Grand Central Publishing
A division of Hachette Books USA
First published in Great Britain in 2014 by Hodder & Stoughton
An Hachette UK Company

1

A CIP catalogue record for this title is available from the British Library.

Paperback ISBN 978 1 444 78574 6
Ebook ISBN 978 1 444 78575 3

Printed and bound by Clays Ltd, St Ives plc

Hodder & Stoughton policy is to use papers that are natural, renewable
and recyclable products and made from wood grown in sustainable forests.
The logging and manufacturing processes are expected to conform
to the environmental regulations of the country of origin.

Hodder & Stoughton Ltd
338 Euston Road
London NW1 3BH

www.hodder.co.uk

*To anyone who knows what it's like to be broken and
to everyone who is stronger because of it.*

Acknowledgments

I spent a lot of time secluded in my office while I wrote this book. So I have to thank my family for putting up with me. For never complaining about eating out so much. And for not making fun of me (too much) when I forget to shower or eat or when time gets away from me. I'm blessed that you're so supportive and I love you so much.

Amy Pierpont, my rock star editor from Forever. Oh my Lord. I don't know what I would've done without you during this book. Thank you for being patient through the four revisions and for not killing me whenever I added new stuff. And thank you for being awesome and for your amazing insight.

To Lt. Col. (Ret) Gerritt Peck and SPC Desiree DeCoteau. Thank you both SO freaking much for answering all my questions about life in the military and Afghanistan. I know you're both busy, so it meant so much that you were willing to take the time to answer everything I asked. You're both heroes.

To my BFF and partner in crime M. Leighton. I have to thank her in each and every book because she practically holds my hand when I write. If I have a problem or a question, if I'm stuck, if I'm neurotic, if I'm unsure...I call M. And she talks me off the ledge or drops whatever she's doing to take a look at the scene and give me her input. She's crazy awesome. And someday, hopefully, we'll live in the same area—next door to each other with adjoining wine cellars.

To my dream agent, Catherine Drayton. You're amazing and I still find myself in shock sometimes when I see your name in my in-box or on my phone. Thank you for taking a chance on this rural farm girl.

To my talented and amazing PR/marketing team... Kelly Simmon from Inkslinger PR and the amazing ladies at Hachette: Jessica, Marissa, Jane and Tanisha. You guys are simply the best.

And to the bloggers and readers who read my work. Each of you is awesome. And I appreciate each of you more than you'll ever know. Thank you so much for all that you do, for reading my books, for your kind notes and e-mails and Facebook posts and tweets. You're the reason I get to do what I do and I will be eternally grateful.

The world breaks everyone, and afterward, some are strong at the broken places.

—Ernest Hemingway

If You Leave

Chapter One

Kabul, Afghanistan

It's the smell of blood that tells me I'm dreaming.

Or awake.

At this point in my life, it could be either one.

Either way, the smell fills up my nostrils and sticks inside my nose; rusty, metallic and sweet. I know from experience that if I'm sleeping, it'll still be there when I wake up. A pungent reminder of a night I'll never get away from.

It's a hell that I'll never escape.

Even as I squirm, as I try to wake, a noise penetrates my consciousness, a noise that doesn't belong in this dream. I know that because I've relived the same nightmare a hundred times. This new sound and sensation don't belong.

It's the unmistakable crunch of bone in my hand.

My eyes snap open and I look around, registering several things at once.

I am in a whorehouse in Kabul, the same one I always use. The girl's black hair is grasped tightly in my fingers, wrapped around my left hand. With my right, I clutch her limp hand, her broken fingers splayed at unnatural angles.

I immediately release her fingers and she stares at me, pressing her other hand to her mouth to contain a scream. Tears flood her eyes and spill down her crushed cheek. The blood turns her tears red and I realize something. The smell of blood wasn't coming from my dream. It was coming from her.

Jesus.

There is blood everywhere, spewing from her nose and her eye, from the entire side of her shattered face, dripping onto her naked olive skin and staining the yellowed sheets of the bed. I gasp and instinctively back away from her in horror, my gut tightening in shock.

"What the fuck?" I manage to choke.

When I move, she cradles her broken hand.

The hand that I broke.

Sweat forms immediately on my brow and my heart pounds wildly. *I did this to her. I did this to her.* What the fuck have I done? I'm panicked and shaken, but at the same time, my training kicks in and I pull myself together.

"I'm sorry," I tell her quickly, gathering my wits and stepping toward her, reaching out to assess her injuries. She flinches away, fear apparent in her wild eyes as she turns her shoulders away from me, as if to absorb another blow. My gut sinks at her response, at the knowledge that she is terrified of me.

At the sick realization that she has a reason to be.

I swallow hard, the thick taste of self-revulsion pooling in my mouth.

"Please," I tell her raggedly, holding my hand out. "Let me see. I won't hurt you again."

The prostitute, a slender girl named Niki, trembles but forces herself to remain still as I feel her arms and legs. She sucks in a breath when I get too close to her broken hand, but rigidly allows me to examine everything else. It's almost odd. I've fucked this girl twenty different ways to Sunday, but right now she's as distant as a stranger. Because she's terrified.

Of me.

"I'm so sorry," I tell her, glancing away from her stiff blood-spattered shoulders. "I won't come here anymore. I was asleep. I didn't know what I was doing. I won't ever hurt you again, Niki. I'm sorry."

One of her eyes is swollen shut, but the other one widens at my words and she grabs me with her good hand. Her fingers are cold and they shake.

"No," she whispers. "If you stay away, they will beat me for being unpleasing to you. Please. Do not stay away, soldier."

I stare at her, aghast. "*I* just beat you," I tell her slowly. "I didn't mean to, but that's not an excuse. *I just beat you.*"

Niki shakes her head, flinching as the movement causes her pain. Guilt floods through me. I hurt an innocent woman. Jesus Christ. I'm a monster.

"You were sleeping," Niki says adamantly. "You have night-mares when you sleep. It wasn't you. It was the bad thing."

"The bad thing?" I ask uncertainly, my eyes frozen on her bloody face. She nods.

"It chases you," she answers solemnly in her thick Afghan accent. "It is different for everyone, but it chases us all. The bad thing caught you."

The bad thing caught me.

I swallow hard, trying to dislodge the fucking lump that has formed in my throat.

"I'm sorry, Niki," I tell her again. "Maybe the bad thing did catch me. I swear I'll make it right."

She looks at me curiously, her body tense with pain, but stays motionless as I wrap a sheet around her shoulders and quickly get dressed.

I'm out the door and down the hall within a minute. I ignore the moans and shrieks and thumping noises coming from the other dark, tiny rooms as I make my way down the battered hallway to the office. I know the man in charge sits in there, because I pay him every time I visit Niki.

He looks up at me in surprise when I walk in, but I don't hesitate. I toss all the money that I have in my wallet onto his desk; all the strange-looking foreign money that is equivalent to hundreds and hundreds of US dollars.

"The girl has pleased me," I tell him quietly. "I will be returning to the United States, but I'll miss her. She should be rewarded. Also, she needs a doctor. She's hurt."

The man stares up at me, his dark gaze gleaming at the sight of the large pile of money. He nods curtly without speaking, clearly unworried about the bloody girl down the hall as he snakes out dark fingers to scrape the bills toward him.

"She needs a doctor," I tell him firmly, gritting the words from between my teeth. "Now."

I slam my fist down on his table, hard, right in the middle of the money.

He looks up at me and wordlessly picks up the phone. He mutters words into it that I can't understand, then hangs up.

"It is done," he says shortly, returning his attention to the papers on his desk.

Without another word I slip out into the darkened streets of Kabul, making my way back to my camp outside of town. After I'm back in my tent, I mechanically begin folding things neatly into my knapsack. When my fingers brush against my satellite phone, I pick it up, then punch numbers into it.

"Colonel?" I say when he answers. "You're gonna need to send another XO out here. I'm coming in."

The colonel doesn't ask why. He knows me well enough to trust my judgment calls. If I say I'm coming in from the field, he trusts that there's a good reason. And of course there is. This is the only life I've ever wanted. Only something monumental would force me to walk away from it.

The bad thing caught you.

I've never retreated in my life. I've never backed away from a fight and I've never cowered in fear. Ever. That's not who I am. But I've been in combat long enough to know that when something unbeatable chases you, you do the only thing you can do.

You run.

Chapter Two

Eight Months Later
Chicago

Madison

The music in this club is so loud that it literally thumps in my chest, rattling into my rib cage. What the hell do people see in places like this? I cough from the fog-maker's smoke, then strain my neck as I try to find my friend Jacey among the hundreds of sweaty people crammed in this room.

The last I saw, she'd disappeared into a dark corner with her loser boyfriend.

"Have you seen my friend? The blonde in the tight red shirt?" I yell to the random guy who has been intently watching me like a creeper for ten minutes. He smiles a piranha grin and inches toward me.

"No," he yells back. "But we don't need her for what I have in mind."

Gross.

"Not now, not ever," I answer coldly, turning my back on him to search the crush of people on the dance floor. I seriously just want to go home.

How I let Jacey talk me into coming into the city to celebrate her birthday is far, far beyond me right now. I'm supposed to finally meet her brother tonight, but Jacey disappeared with her boyfriend over an hour ago and I haven't seen them since. My feet hurt, I'm exhausted from working sixty hours this week and I need something to eat before I stab someone's eye out.

Knowing my limitations, I make my way through the bar and onto the sidewalk out front. I've got to get out of here. I'm the one who drove us, but I'm sure Jacey can get a ride home with Peter if she needs to. Her boyfriend can't hold down a job, but at least he can drive.

I pull my phone out. *I'm leaving. Can you catch a ride home with Peter?*

As soon as I send the text, I realize that she's not going to be able to hear it. So who knows when she'll see it? With a sigh, I decide I have to hunt for her. At least for a few minutes. It wouldn't be right to just leave her here.

"If I wanted to have public sex with my boyfriend, where would I be?" I muse aloud, trying to think like Jacey as I walk around to the side of the club. Jacey is pathetically bad about PDA. She doesn't give a flying eff what people think about her. It's one thing that I both admire about her and get annoyed at.

As I get farther and farther away from the sidewalk and into the shadows, it seems more and more like someplace Jacey and Peter might be getting it on against the building. But at the same time, it also seems like the perfect place to get mugged. It makes me instantly nervous and I glance around quickly.

I'm in an alley now, a narrow wet street that is littered with trash and graffiti. My heels click on the glistening asphalt and I take a deep breath, enjoying the fresh air as the inky darkness swallows me.

Thank God I'm out of that club. That's my main thought as I walk farther into the darkness, but even still, I reach into my purse and grip my little can of pepper-spray. It doesn't hurt to be prepared.

There's nobody here. That much is apparent as I take in the dirty building, the heaping trash bins and the empty shadows. Well, I'm hoping the shadows are empty, anyway. They seem to be. And I seem to be all alone. While that's comforting on the one hand, it's frustrating on the other.

"Jacey, where the fuck are you?" I mutter.

Just as I'm getting ready to give up and head back into the club, I catch sight of something that snags my attention and I stop.

A guy is leaning against the building a little ways from me, half in the darkness, half in the light. Normally that wouldn't give me pause, especially since I'm in an alley alone. But something about his posture intrigues me, something that I can't quite put my finger on.

I peer at him more closely.

His long legs are crossed gracefully in front of him as he leans against the building. And holy cow, he's big. He's got to be a few inches over six feet tall with a broad chest and wide shoulders that narrow into a slender waist.

It's chilly outside, but he's not wearing a jacket, only a snug black T-shirt and a pair of perfectly fitting jeans. There isn't a trace of fat on him. He's lean and muscled, with short darkish hair. From the side his features are chiseled and from what I can tell, he's got just the barest hint of stubble along his strong jaw. That's an instant turn-on for me. It seems so rugged.

And this guy...he definitely seems rugged. Everything about

him screams strength and power. That's an instant turn-on for me too. I decide that this is what intrigues me. He's like power personified. He holds himself with purpose.

As I watch, he lights up a cigarette and takes a drag, releasing the smoke slowly into the night. His lips are full and masculine and he's got a cleft in his chin. He's undeniably sexy. Normally I would stay far away from someone like him, someone sinfully sexy but so . . . forceful. A guy like that is trouble. That's for sure.

But I didn't come to the club tonight to run away.

I came here to hook up. To blow off my responsibilities and be reckless for a night. To act my age. To be someone I'm not.

I eye the guy again.

Normally I would run away from him.

But maybe . . . just tonight . . . I won't.

I don't have to be me tonight. I can be anyone I want to be because he'll never see me again.

Just for tonight.

I hesitate, trying to decide what to do.

Then, almost as though my feet have a mind of their own, I take a step toward him. And then another.

❧

Gabriel

My cigarette burns red in the dark as I take a nice long drag. I suck in the city air and the nicotine, then exhale the toxic waste. I know that smokes are bad for me, that they're shit for my lungs, but I don't particularly care right now.

From inside the club, I can feel the bass thumping against the wall, vibrating my spine. Inside, women are mindlessly mashing together on the dance floor in time to those drums, waiting for guys like me to take them home and fuck them.

I don't care about that either. I had to get some fresh air, to get away from the claustrophobic club smoke and sweat before I fucking exploded.

If I were a normal person, I'd be nervous in a dark Chicago alley by myself. I'm not a normal person, though, and the shit I saw in Afghanistan rendered my ability to feel fear impotent.

But not the rest of me.

I shift my weight and adjust the boys and my semi-hard dick. I'd have to be inhuman to not be horny after watching the half-dressed drunk girls rub themselves on anyone who might buy them a drink. I should feel bad about that, but I don't.

Before my tour overseas, I wouldn't have been caught dead with any of them. But after being overseas for three years, my penis isn't listening to reason anymore. It knows what I need.

I sigh and adjust the constraining crotch of my jeans again, before taking another deep breath, then another. My dick starts to calm down and my claustrophobic feelings begin to fade. Thank God. One of the many things I brought home was claustrophobia, and it's not even the predictable kind where I'm afraid of small spaces. It's the random kind that can strike at the strangest times, like in the middle of a crowd.

Fuck it.

I toss down the cigarette and grind it out with my heel, then pull out another, lighting it up. It's a bad habit I brought back with me, along with a couple tattoos and the tendency to wake up in a cold sweat from crazy-ass nightmares.

"You know those will kill you, right?"

I startle to attention, my head snapping around to find the soft voice in the dark.

A woman steps closer and I can't believe that I didn't see her approach.

Fucking hell.

We're the only two people in an isolated alley. How could I have missed her? My senses have seriously dulled since I've been back stateside. She's a tall, willowy bombshell, the kind of woman who stands out in a crowd, let alone an abandoned street.

Blonde hair falls halfway down her back and wide eyes stare at me. Her full lips are pursed, as though she's trying to decide if it's safe to be out here. And it's not, especially for a woman who looks like she does.

"Don't you know walking alone in a dark Chicago alley is more dangerous than a cigarette?"

I gaze at her levelly as I take another drag on my smoke.

She doesn't look afraid at all as she shrugs.

"Either of those things has to be better than being crushed to death in there."

She gestures toward the closed club door in disdain. I examine her again. She's wearing the right clothes to be here...tight pink leather pants, a cream-colored halter top, equally tight, and a pair of extremely high glittery heels. As I examine her, I notice that she's not wearing a bra under her light-colored shirt. Somehow that looks out of place on her, as though she doesn't fit the slutty clothes.

The problem is, the slutty clothes definitely fit *her*, in all the right places. My dick lurches back to life as my gaze skims over her curved hips and tight ass.

"In that case, want one?" I offer her the pack.

She looks surprised, then chuckles, shaking her head.

"No, thanks. I'm already in the alley alone. I think that's enough of a risk tonight."

I grin back as I tuck the smokes into my pocket. "But you're not alone now. I'm here."

She eyes me and I can see now that her eyes are blue.

"Somehow," she says thoughtfully, "I doubt I'm any safer."

I smile. "Somehow, I think you're right."

The funny thing is, she doesn't look worried. In fact, she steps closer and leans against the filthy brick wall beside me. Even under the yellowed dingy streetlight, she looks flawless.

"You're going to get dirty," I point out. She looks up at me innocently, her blue eyes wide.

"I like getting dirty sometimes."

And then she grins a wicked grin.

I feel like I've been sucker-punched as all the air whooshes out of my body. A suggestive grin like that on this runway model is too much for my logical thought processes to overcome. My good sense has apparently been hijacked by my hormones.

Tossing the smoke down on the sidewalk, I grind the heel of my boot into it. I don't know what the fuck I'm doing, but I don't much care at this point. I'm horny and she's gorgeous. That's a perfect arrangement if I ever saw one. The air between us practically crackles with sexual attraction.

I look down at her and as I do, I let myself lean into her. She's soft and she smells even softer.

"I'm Gabriel."

"I'm Madison," she answers. She hasn't looked away from me

even once. She's definitely into me, although God knows why. I'm as different from her as I can be.

"Why are you here, Madison?" I ask. "You seem a little out of place."

She suddenly looks self-conscious. "A friend talked me into coming. She thought I needed a night in the big city. But I really wish I was home instead. I'm tired and these heels hurt."

I smile. Her shoes do look painful as hell. I've never understood why women wear shit like that.

"So you don't live here?"

She shakes her head and as she does, her scent seems to envelop us, blocking out the pungent city smells. Her nearness is intoxicating and I brace myself against it so I don't get sucked in any further.

"No. I'm from a little lake town, just an hour or so from here. But it seems like a world away. I'm not much of a big-city girl. Not anymore, anyway."

I actually wouldn't have guessed that. She's got that perfectly put-together look that big-city girls have, that perfectly confident attitude.

She nudges me, her slender shoulder bumping mine. "Why are you here? You don't look like you fit here either. Not here at this club, anyway."

I cock an eyebrow. "Oh?"

The Underground is a trendy Chicago hot spot. And she's right. I don't fit in here. I fit in a Humvee in the hills of Afghanistan. Except I don't. Not anymore.

Madison notices my expression and flushes.

"No offense. But you're not wearing skinny jeans and hipster glasses. You seem more like … the football-playing type. Or the outdoors type, maybe."

I smile down at her. "No offense taken. And I *am* more of the outdoors type."

The gun-toting soldier type, to be exact, but I don't say that.

Madison looks relieved. "I thought so. So what are you doing in the middle of the city?"

"What makes you think I don't live here? Can't I enjoy the outdoors but still live in the city? Or am I too uncool for that?" I raise my eyebrow again.

She flushes yet again. "I'm sorry. I guess I just assumed. Where do you live?"

I grin. "Here. Just call me a fish out of water."

She shakes her head and swats at me, but I easily catch her wrist and pull her to me instead. It's a ballsy move, but I'm feeling cocky. She doesn't resist, which both pleases and surprises me.

She presses against me, looking into my eyes. She looks expectant and nervous, confident yet hesitant. Her tits are smashed against me, making it hard to form coherent thoughts, hard to examine our differences or even her motives. Her softness is the perfect contrast to my hardness. That's all I can think about.

"To answer your question, I'm here at the club because my little sister thought I should come out and meet someone. To quote her, I'm 'getting mean as hell and need a piece of ass.' "

Madison laughs, a low and husky sound.

"Do you? Need a piece of ass?"

She sounds anxious. And interested.

I hold her gaze.

"More than you can imagine."

I slide my hands from her back down to her ass, cupping it, squeezing it.

"And I like yours," I add. I'm being cocky again, but she seems to like it.

She practically purrs as she leans into me even closer, her nose almost touching mine. Her lips hover so close that I can feel them.

She slides her hands down to my ass, gripping it in her fingers.

"Yours will do."

The air hangs heavy between us, charged and electric. Our eyes are locked and we each pause, waiting for the other to make a move.

The anticipation is killing me.

I take a breath.

Then she takes one.

Her lips graze mine and her mouth smells like mint. And then before I can think another agonizing thought, she covers my mouth with her own.

Finally.

Her tongue slips into my mouth and she tastes like Heaven, like an icy drink of water at the end of a hot day in the desert. Our tongues tangle together and her lips consume mine. I find myself instantly rock-hard and she notices.

She smiles against my lips.

"I think you liked that."

"What gave me away?" I ask with a grin, wedging myself even tighter against her.

Madison grins back and kisses me again. The second kiss is just as consuming as the first. She seems a little bit desperate, a little bit vulnerable. And a whole lot sexy.

She slides her hands back up my spine, wrapping her arms

around my neck. As she does, I run my palms along her sides, feeling the skin of her back beneath my fingers.

"Remember when I told you that my feet hurt? I'd like to take my shoes off."

I stare down at her. "So take them off."

"At your place," she adds.

I inhale sharply as I grip her hips even tighter.

"You don't have to say that twice."

And she doesn't. I grab her hand and practically drag her toward the street, hailing a taxi.

In less than a minute we have tumbled into the back seat of a cab and we're speeding toward my apartment.

Madison kisses my neck, tugging at my ear with her teeth as her hands skim my chest. "How far away do you live?"

"Not very," I manage to say. I'm actually proud of myself for being able to speak at this point, since her hand has made its way down to my throbbing crotch. I arch my hips so that I am planted more firmly in her hand.

She licks my neck.

"You taste good," she whispers.

I can't take it. I wish she were wearing a skirt, but she's not. So instead I cup my hand between her legs, moving my thumb in circles against the outside of her pants. She moves against me, moaning.

I thrust my hand into the front of her pants, finding her panties completely soaked.

I slip one finger in.

And then two.

Then I withdraw them both and slowly rake them into my mouth. Her eyes widen, exhaling a tiny sigh as her fingers clutch me.

"Are you drunk?" I ask her. I don't know why, but it feels like the right thing to do, to make sure that she's not. *Please say no*, I silently urge her as her fingers spin circles around my nipple.

"No."

Thank Christ. I don't ask again. Instead I lift her onto my lap and rock her against my body. The friction is both satisfying and frustrating.

Her eyes widen as I thrust against her through her clothes and she reaches her hand down to skim it over my throbbing dick.

"You're enormous," she breathes, her eyes widening in both apprehension and appreciation.

I grin.

"When we get to my house, I'm going to fuck you with that," I tell her in her ear. "And you're going to like it."

Her teeth graze my lip, her hips firmly planted against mine. "You're pretty sure of yourself, aren't you?"

I smile against her throat before I bite at it.

"Very sure. In fact, let's make a deal. If you don't end up screaming my name within the hour, I'll buy you breakfast in the morning."

She pauses, looking into my eyes. "Sounds like I win either way."

"You do," I manage to say before I plunge my tongue into her mouth again.

In between panting kisses, Madison manages to ask a question.

"I've never done this before. How do I know you're not a crazy person?" she asks in a near whisper.

"You don't," I answer, as I pull up her shirt and suck at her bare nipple, my fingers splayed around her slender rib cage. She arches against me and gasps. "But I won't hurt you." I pause and look up at her. "And somehow, I get the feeling that you need this as much as I do. Am I right?"

Madison catches her breath and nods.

"I do."

I don't answer and I don't ask why. I just wrap my arms around her shoulders and kiss her again.

I'm inhaling her feminine scent, sucking it down, when I'm startled by the squeal of tires. Before I can even see where it's coming from, instinct raises the hair on the back of my neck. I shove Madison onto the floor of the taxi and duck down on top of her.

The impact is shockingly violent.

There is a crunch of shrieking metal as the door next to me is bashed in and our taxi is flung in a spin across the narrow city street, slamming to a stop against the wall of a nearby building. The car rocks to and fro for a moment, then it is still.

We're stunned as we sit for a scant second, trying to wrap our minds around what just happened. Steam and smoke begin to pour out from under the hood of the taxi and the driver stumbles from his seat, opening the door next to Madison.

"Quick, get out," he says in a heavy Indian accent. "Hurry."

I all but shove Madison out ahead of me and then pull her away from the crumpled car. There's a hissing sound coming from the engine, then a strange crackle. I know what it means. I know from the acrid scent of gasoline that's stinging my nose.

"Move," I snap to Madison, and her heels click loudly on the pavement as we rush to the curb on the other side of the street. We turn when we reach the sidewalk, just in time to see the cabbie duck for cover as the front end of the cab bursts into flames.

"Oh my God," Madison breathes, leaning into my arm,

shielding her face from the waves of heat that roll over us even from this distance.

As I watch the orange flames licking the black night, as the heated breeze brushes across my face, it triggers a response in me.

I feel the now-familiar anxiety coming on and my gut clenches tighter than a vise grip. I can feel my throat begin to close up as it prevents me from getting a full breath.

Fuck.

"I've got to get out of here," I mutter as my chest tightens. Sweat pours down my temples and I wipe at it, squinting as the salt stings my eyes. Madison stares up at me, her eyes filled with concern.

"Are you OK?" she asks, her fingers trembling as they curl around my arm. "We can't leave. I'm pretty sure the police will want to talk to us."

She gestures toward the crowd forming, to where cop cars have already begun to congregate. I can see uniformed officers milling about, a couple of them headed our way. Heat from the fire and from my own anxiety begins to overwhelm me.

"I've got to get out of here," I mutter again. Her fingers are too tight now, along with everything else...my shirt, my waistband, my shoes. Everything bears down on me in blurs and smells and sounds. I can't take it. I'm going to fucking explode. Or implode. I yank my arm from her grasp and stalk away.

The last thing I see before everything turns black is the astonished look on Madison's face, backlit by the red-and-orange glow of the taxi fire.

The bad thing caught you.

Chapter Three

Madison

For a brief moment I wonder if the shock of the taxi accident has gotten to me or if I've somehow fallen down the rabbit hole.

The guy standing in front of me has completely melted down, going from ultra-cocky and excruciatingly sexy to a complete panicky mess in literally thirty seconds.

I don't even know what to do with him.

I put my hand on his arm, only to have him shake it off. There's a wild look in his eye as he spins in a circle, hunting for a way out, his gaze darting around the perimeter of skyscrapers that surround us.

"I've got to get out of here," he mumbles for the third time. His eyes have a glazed-over look to them that I've never seen before. He starts to walk away and I grab his arm again. There's no way I can let him walk off in this state. I don't know him, but I feel a responsibility not to do that.

"Wait," I tell him quietly. "We're got to give our names to the police and then we can go. Do you have an ID with you?"

He fumbles in his back pocket and hands me his wallet before he sits on the curb, staring off into space, into the flames of the burning cab. After a minute he closes his eyes tightly and drops his head into his hands, as if to shut everything out.

What the hell?

I watch him hesitantly for just a second before I trot off to give the nearest policeman our IDs. The cop asks me for my contact information, then glances over at Gabriel.

"Is he all right? Does he need an ambulance?"

I turn and look. Gabriel is now leaning forward, his head resting on his knees, his eyes still closed.

"I don't think he's hurt," I answer, even though I honestly have no clue. "I think he just drank too much. We were taking the taxi home from the Underground."

"Smart," the cop tells me. "There's too much drunk driving out there. Good to call a cab."

"Except for when the cab explodes," I mumble as I put my driver's license back in my purse. The cop smiles wryly.

"Yeah. Good point. At least no one was hurt."

I eye Gabriel uncertainly as I head back toward him. I'm not too sure about that. He's still got his eyes closed, but his foot is tapping wildly against the pavement.

When I reach him, I kneel down in front of him.

"Gabriel, did you hit your head in the crash?"

Because that would make sense. Maybe. Would a concussion cause someone to freak out like this?

Gabriel looks up at me. "I don't know. I don't think so. I need to go home." He doesn't even sound like himself now. He's speaking in a strange monotone, completely unlike the husky sexy voice he had before.

It's freaking me out.

I sigh. Because I can't leave him here.

"Where do you live?"

He just stares at me.

I realize that I'm still holding his wallet, so I open it up and look at his driver's license. His address isn't that far away. We're actually within walking distance. Thank God. I don't want to get into another cab anytime soon.

Reaching down, I tug on Gabriel's muscled arm.

"Come on," I tell him. "I'm walking you home."

He comes with me without protest, pulling at his collar.

"I can't breathe," he mutters to me. I look up at him. His collar isn't too tight.

"You're going to be OK," I assure him.

Although I'm not sure of that myself.

I hold on to his arm, although I don't know why. After we've walked a couple of blocks, Gabriel starts muttering incoherent words under his breath. I can't understand him, but when I ask him to repeat them, he just looks at me.

This is *seriously* freaking me out. I highly doubt I should be walking anywhere alone with this guy. Why in the world didn't I just tell the cop to deal with him? I'm clearly not equipped to handle this situation.

"Is there anyone I can call for you?" I ask him, hoping that there is. He just looks at me again, almost like he doesn't understand.

When I look into his eyes, they are vacant and glassy.

Like he's not there.

I gulp hard.

Within a minute we've reached his building and I've never been so happy. A doorman recognizes Gabriel and greets him by name.

"He's not himself," I say by way of explanation, because I'm honestly not sure what to say. "I'm walking him to his condo. Can you tell me his condo number?"

The doorman is actually kind enough to walk us up to the condo and then unlock the door for me with his master keys. I smile at him.

"Thank you," I tell him simply as I walk Gabriel through the door. Gabriel isn't speaking at all by this point.

The doorman looks at us.

"If you need anything else, let me know," he tells me, staring at Gabriel curiously before he takes his leave.

That's interesting. He's obviously not used to seeing Gabriel like this, so maybe it really was an injury in the accident. Maybe he *did* hit his head. For a second I wonder if I should call an ambulance.

But Gabriel is already walking back toward his bedroom, mumbling. I can see his neatly made bed through the open door. I follow along at his heels and almost run into him when he abruptly stops and slams his fist into the wall. His movement is strong and unexpected and packs enormous power. So much power that he shakes the entire hallway and leaves a hole in the wall.

I gasp and freeze when he turns to me. Fear floods every part of me, every last nook and cranny of me. Because as Gabriel turns his face, a small illogical part of me almost expects to see someone else. Someone terrifying.

My father.

My heart pounds in my ears and memories from long ago flit through my head. Fists and blood and arguments and fear.

But of course Gabriel isn't my father. And so I force my breathing to slow and my heart to calm down, even as I balance lightly on the balls of my feet, poised to run if I have to. I swallow as Gabriel looks at me.

"I hate this," he tells me. His cheeks are flushed, his eyes are slightly glazed and his hand is still curled into a fist at his side, his knuckles scraped. I eye it and take a step back, because I know what can happen with a fist.

"You hate what?"

Emotion fills his eyes, something dark, something pained. "I hate the way it controls me."

I definitely feel panicked now. "What controls you?"

But he doesn't answer. He just walks into his room and drops onto his bed. He's calm now, quiet. As though he didn't just punch a hole in the wall.

As though he didn't just tell me that something controls him.

What the fuck is wrong with him?

Ignoring my still-racing heart, I bend in front of him. *I can do this.*

"Does your head hurt?" I ask him. When he shakes his head, I look into his eyes. His pupils seem the same size. I heard somewhere that if you have a concussion, it makes the sizes of your pupils uneven.

Physically he seems fine. No bumps, no scrapes, no bruises. I stare down at him uncertainly. He stares back, but it's like he's not even seeing me.

I sigh, long and loud.

"Let's get your shirt and jeans off, at least," I finally tell him. "Then I'm going to go."

He stands up obediently and unbuttons his pants, letting them drop to the floor. When he sits back down, I strip his shirt off over his head, then fold down the covers on his bed.

He immediately drops back into it, curling onto his side and closing his eyes.

As I cover him up, I can't help but glance at his body. It's sculpted and cut, and it's apparent that he works out. A lot. He has the body of a triathlete. Or Olympian. Or Greek god, maybe. He's got a tattoo on his bicep, a skull wearing a beret over a pair of crossed swords. Words are scrolled above and below it. "Death Before Dishonor."

Hmm. Where would he get that? Is he a marine, maybe? He doesn't have a marine haircut, though.

I sigh again. This whole turn of events is so unfortunate. If I was gonna have a one-night stand, this was clearly the guy to do it with. He's freaking hot.

At this exact moment he moans and thrashes, throwing off the covers as he mutters into his pillow.

He's also apparently crazy because *something controls him*. God. Just my luck. I meet a hot guy who hears voices or some shit. *Or* he hit his head and he's just delirious.

I shake my head as I pick up the covers and pull them back up over him.

I take in his clenched jaw and furrowed brow. One part of me wants to call an ambulance to be on the safe side. But another part of me thinks it's not my place to do that, especially since I don't know if he needs it. I don't even know if he has insurance.

I honestly just don't know what to do.

Finally I decide that I'll hang around for just a little while, to see if he gets any worse.

It's the least I can do. I wouldn't feel right otherwise. If he wakes up and acts dangerous, I can be out of here in half a minute.

I find the bathroom so that I can pee and it is surprisingly clean for a guy's bathroom. It's decorated in various shades of gray, even a gray-tiled floor. There's no evidence whatsoever of a woman's touch, so he must be unattached. Or at the very least unmarried. At least he's not a scumbag like the married guys who troll the clubs for a piece of ass.

Out of curiosity I open the medicine cabinet. Q-tips, razor, razor blades, shaving cream, and a bottle of sleeping pills with his name on them. There's nothing that would suggest that he's crazy. There's no psychotropic prescription pills or anything.

That's good, right?

I walk back out into the dining area, looking around with interest. Everything is neat, modern, masculine. On one wall is a mahogany case, as tall as I am. It's so shallow that it can't hold much, so it piques my interest. I open it and suck in my breath at the neatly lined-up guns facing me.

Holy shit. Is he expecting WWIII? Who in the world would have this many guns? He's crazy after all. As I'm backing away from it, unreasonably afraid of the guns, a certificate catches my eye. It's lying on a short stack of paper at the end of the black-and-white granite kitchen counter.

I stop and look at it and find that it is actually a diploma, issued a few years ago by the United States Army Ranger School, and it's got his name on it.

Gabriel is a Ranger. Or he *was* one. One or the other. Either way, that explains the amazingly cut body. And the tattoo. And the guns. *Thank God.* I feel an incredible amount of relief right now…apparently I'm not in the home of a psychopath.

Unless he was kicked out for being crazy, which seems like a real possibility at the moment.

Yikes. I'm suddenly incredibly uncomfortable being here.

I walk quickly back down to his bedroom, which is decorated just like the rest of his house—gray tones, dark wood, masculine.

He's still sleeping and he's no longer muttering. I stare down at him for a second, watching him breathe.

He seems fine now.

Fine enough for me to leave him alone without feeling guilty, anyway.

Before I can rethink it I'm out the door, down the stairs and on the street again, breathing in the cool night air. When the doorman waves at me, I walk over to him.

"Gabriel isn't feeling well," I tell him. "I think he'll be OK, but maybe someone should check on him later. If you know anyone to call, that would be great."

The doorman nods and assures me that he'll take care of it.

His assurance makes me feel slightly better, but I still feel like I've been bitch-slapped by tonight. It's all been so bizarre.

But that's OK. It's over now. I just have to make my way back to the club, get my car, and then leave all this weirdness behind me. In a few minutes the crazy hot guy will be a distant memory.

Gabriel

I wake up in a cold sweat.

I'm not sure where I am.

This isn't unusual, so I force my breathing to slow, to regulate. I need to gain my bearings.

I glance around, at the gray walls of my stark bedroom, at the white ceiling, at the familiar ceiling fan with the blades that look like large wicker leaves.

I'm in my apartment. In my bed. One glance at the clock tells me that four hours have passed since the last time I was conscious.

The problem is, I have no idea how I fucking got here.

My hands are shaky as I reach for the glass of water on my bedside table, swirling the water inside the glass as I force myself to calm, as I try *not* to remember the nightmare that woke me. I take a gulp and force the blurs of reds and blacks out of my head, even though I know from experience they are unwilling to go.

Darkness and blood.

These are two things that will apparently always haunt me. I doubt I'll ever get a full night's rest, or that I'll ever feel comfortable in the dark again.

I slump against the pillows, then startle as I remember Madison.

The beautiful girl from the club.

We were on our way here when we were in a car accident. I hold up my hands and look at them, barely able to see them in the dim light streaming through the window. I seem to be fine, nothing on my body hurts, so apparently we weren't injured. Or *I* wasn't, at least.

I honestly don't know about Madison. There's no possible way I can because I don't even know how I made it home. I hope she's all right. But I don't fucking know. Everything is a black void. All I know for sure is that I'm alone now.

I left Madison there, standing next to the twisted, burning wreck of our taxi. Even though I can't recall much else, I remember the stricken look on her face as she realized that I was leaving.

I'm not sure if I'm ashamed of myself or relieved. She was pretty fucking amazing. And pretty fucking hot. But there's no way she should get mixed up with someone like me, even for only one night. *Especially* for only one night. I might look normal, but I'm far from it.

I think back to Madison's question in the cab.

How do I know you're not a crazy person?

I almost smile grimly in the dark.

I'm not crazy... exactly. The army doctors say I just need time. They call it PTSD. Posttraumatic stress disorder. I call it something else entirely: fucked up.

Chapter Four

Madison

I open my bleary eyes, not exactly sure what woke me from my dead sleep.

The lake crashes against the shore outside, but that's not it. I'm used to that sound since I hear it every night. The rain is slanting against my bedroom windows, but that's not it either. As I gaze at the ceiling, my phone buzzes, vibrating from my nightstand with a text message.

Ah, that's it. Mystery solved.

I rub my eyes, glare at the clock (which surely must be wrong because there's no way it's that late), then grab the stupid phone.

Where are u? Where did you go last night?

Staring at the words, I cringe with guilt.

Craaaaaap.

Jacey. The friend I left at the Underground last night, the friend who just happens to work for me. She's the best waitress I've got, mainly because she's just the right mix of charm and flirtation. She's also the best friend I've got, mainly because I don't get close to that many people.

I never found her last night and then I completely forgot about her...because I was distracted. My distraction flashes through my head, a vision of Gabriel's face and muscled body, and my cheeks flush. I quickly put him out of my mind and turn back to my phone.

I'm a bad friend, I text her back simply. *I'm sorry.*

Where did you go????

Apparently I'm not going to get off that easily. I sigh.

Remember when u said I needed to get laid? Well, I almost did. But didn't. So I came home alone instead. Did you just go home with Peter? I would've called, but I knew you wouldn't hear your phone.

Gabriel's face pops unbidden into my head again. The look on his face while we watched that taxi burn was indescribable. Tortured, almost. But that sounds stupid to say.

Obviously I was in shock too. It's not every day that you get nailed in an intersection and then your taxi explodes into flames. So of course I was disturbed.

But not to the degree that Gabriel was. For some reason my heart twinges just thinking about it, but I ignore it. I don't know him and there's no use wondering what the hell was wrong with him. He's irrelevant now. I force him out of my thoughts and wait for Jacey to reply.

It only takes her a second.

You should definitely be sorry. I was almost worried. And why didn't u get some??? Any man would give his left nut to take you home. I'm pretty sure I hate you for that.

I have to smile. Jacey wasn't worried. I'm sure of it. She probably didn't even realize I was gone until it was time to go home.

Long story, I answer.

One beat passes and then she replies.

K. My brother never showed up last night, but he's coming to the Hill tonight to bring me my bday gift. You can meet him then.

I smile, which hurts my pounding head. I'm glad she mentioned it. I'd forgotten it was her birthday. Maybe I really am a bad friend.

Fine, I tell her. *You're not going to let up until I meet him, I know. And I'm bringing you a birthday cupcake.*

One pause, then an answer.

My diet doesn't thank you. But I do!

I toss my phone onto the foot of the bed and settle back into my pillow for a second. My head doesn't hurt because of drinking. I only had one drink last night. It's pounding because of lack of sleep. I didn't get in until four thirty a.m. And that's very unlike me. I glance at the clock again.

Nine a.m.

Normally I would already be at my restaurant, the Hill, by now. But I'm dying from sleep deprivation. If I don't consume a massive amount of caffeine, I might murder someone later.

I throw the covers back on my little double bed, the same one that I had all through high school. I barely spare a glance at the walls covered in old posters and high school news articles. I inherited my childhood home a couple of years ago. One of these days I need to get off my ass and clean this room out.

I'm not going to worry about it today, though.

Today I just need coffee.

I pad down the long hall to the kitchen, where I start the coffee and make a frozen burrito. I sit eating it in my underwear, something I can do since I live alone. My eating habits are shit, which is ironic since I own a restaurant, something else I inherited.

After two cups of coffee loaded with sugar and cream, I finally feel human again. I take a quick shower, twist my hair into a sloppy bun and throw on a pair of capris, a polo and a sweater before I grab one more cup of coffee on my way out the door.

I button my sweater up as I jab at the button that lowers the top on my convertible, my one luxury. Driving with the wind in my hair is the only freedom I really get to experience and since the spring rain has stopped for a minute, I can ride with the top down today.

I shift into gear and back out of my driveway, starting down the narrow road that winds along Lake Michigan. It's a fun little road and I used to love driving it, back before it killed my parents.

Today the morning sun is bright and the ground is wet from rain. As the light rebounds from the misty surface of the lake and directly onto the glass of my windshield, I squint while I reach for the volume on my car stereo. The ridged knob slides in my fingers as I crank it up.

I almost sigh aloud. That's better. There's nothing like coffee and loud music to jar me from sleepiness. I punch at the button to change the satellite radio station as I glance up into the sun.

The light is in my eyes, bright and sharp.

I blink, but before I can really refocus, I realize exactly where I am. I'm coming up way too fast on a hairpin curve.

Fuck.

I gasp and yank on the wheel, spilling hot coffee between my legs as my car veers sharply from the road. Everything seems to happen in slow motion as my car careens into the ditch, skidding sideways at an unnatural angle toward the beach below.

I'm almost frozen, blinded by the sun and completely at the mercy of Newton's laws of motion as my car slides through the mud, the wet grass hitting it in a thumping hiss as the bottom of the hill rushes to meet me.

I'm at such an unnatural angle and skidding so fast that I'm afraid for a second that the car is going to roll, but it doesn't. Instead it slams to an unceremonious stop at the bottom, the wheels halfway buried in the wet sand of the beach. I'm flustered as I try to take deep breaths, yet somehow remain breathless as I sit frozen in shock.

Holy shit. What the hell just happened? Was I seriously in my second car accident in as many days?

My hands shake as I look around. I didn't hit anyone or anything.

I'm not hurt.

I'm not hurt.

I chant this silently to myself as I look around. I'm at the bottom of the incline leading up to the road, in the middle of rocks and grass and sand. I'm so stupid. I've driven this road a thousand times. I knew better.

Even though my hands are shaking and I can't breathe, everything's fine. I'm fine. My car is fine. I'm not my parents. Unlike them, I didn't die. There is no broken glass or blood. *I'm fine.*

I think.

I open the door and step directly down into calf-deep mud.

Hell. I cringe as I pull my foot back up, glancing at my mud-covered paisley Jimmy Choo wedge. Shoes are my weakness and this one, which had been practically brand-new, is now ruined.

Effffff.

As if that's not bad enough, I'm surrounded by mud, a result of last night's thunderstorm. I can't get out to check my car, but from where I can see, the left front wheel is bent under. I have no idea if it's even drivable.

With a scowl I press the accelerator and attempt to drive back up the incline, but my car won't budge. The bent wheel won't even turn.

I'm stuck. Not just stuck, but firmly and completely stuck.

"Fuck."

My head drops to my steering wheel as my fingers reach for my cell phone.

~

When my sister comes to my rescue twenty minutes later, she rushes to get to me, picking her way down the wet hill. Her descent isn't graceful.

"I'm fine, Mila. Go back up!" I lean out my window and call out to her. "You're going to fall and break something, preggo!"

She scowls at me as she walks toward the car, stopping where the mud pools start.

"Oh, God. Not you too. Pax will barely let me lift a finger to do anything. You're a woman. You should know better. I'm pregnant, not an invalid."

I shake my head as I take off my shoes and grab my purse. As carefully as I can, I step from the car, instantly sinking ankle-deep in the mud. I slam my car door closed hard.

"Your husband just wants to take care of you," I remind her grumpily as I slog through the mud toward her.

At seven months pregnant, Mila has that mythical glow about her that few pregnant women actually get. In fact, pregnancy truly agrees with her. She's always been gorgeous, but now she literally glows. Her long dark hair is lush and shiny, her cheeks pink and flushed, and her skin flawless.

"I can't believe you look so good," I grumble as I eye her tiny baby bump. "It's sickening. You've barely gained any weight at all."

She holds out her hand to help me over a rock and laughs.

"What? You want me to look hideous?"

"Maybe," I answer with a mock scowl as we carefully make our way to the top of the hill to where Mila's car awaits. "It's not fair that you're prettier than me even while you're pregnant. Big sisters are always supposed to be hotter. It's a law of nature. I didn't make the rules, Mila, but we should definitely follow them. Try to gain a few pounds."

She laughs again and rolls her eyes as we buckle ourselves in.

"You're crazy, Mad. You're the model in our family. The only things I have that you don't are bigger boobs. And you can't have those."

"Whatever," I mutter as I flip the visor down and look at myself. "I'm not a model anymore."

I have mud splatters on my forehead. And mud caked almost up to my knees. It drips onto the floor and I sigh.

"I'm sorry. You're going to have to get this thing detailed now," I tell her apologetically. "I'll pay for it."

"It's fine," she assures me, serious now. "I'm just glad you're all right. How the hell did this even happen, Maddy? You know how dangerous this road is."

Of course I know.

I feel guilty at the worried strain in her voice. I feel guilty that she had to come here, to this particular curve of all places.

"I'm OK," I answer. "I'm sorry, Mi. I didn't mean to worry you."

She glances at me. "I know. Just be more careful. I almost had a heart attack."

Her and me both.

I lean my head back against my seat, still shaky from sliding down the hill. The aftereffects of the adrenaline rush aren't being kind to me. My heart is still pounding, my hands and legs still shaking. I stare at the ground from my window and the vehicle is so tall, it's a long way down.

"I still can't believe Pax made you get this thing," I chuckle, trying to lighten the mood. "It's so . . . not you." Mila rolls her eyes.

"I know. The minute he found out I was pregnant, he went out and bought the safest vehicle he could find. This thing is practically bulletproof. It might actually be a tank in disguise."

"You handle everything so much better than I do," I tell her. "I would hate being controlled like that."

Mila laughs again, shaking her head.

"I'm not being controlled. When you're married, sometimes you have to compromise. And this wasn't that big of a deal. Yes, my little car got better gas mileage, but it makes Pax happy to think that I'm safer. And besides, I can fit more of my art supplies in here anyway. So there's an upside."

"You know you don't have to lug art supplies around anymore," I tell her, one eyebrow raised. "You don't have to keep your art shop. Since Pax is taking over his grandpa's company soon, you'd never have to work again if you didn't want to."

Mila rolls her eyes as she turns onto a city street. The big SUV barely even shudders as she runs over a piece of leftover winter ice.

"And *you* know I've got to create art. If I don't have an outlet for it, I'll go insane."

"You're insane already," I answer. "For agreeing to move to Connecticut."

She glances at me. "I know. I don't want to go either. But that's where Alexander Holdings' headquarters are. Pax can't take over for his grandpa from here. And his grandpa really wants to retire. So it's something Pax has to do. I've got to support that."

I sigh. "Another one of those marriage compromises?"

She nods.

I sigh again. "I've decided that your marriage isn't really working for me. You're going to have to get divorced."

Mila bursts out laughing. "Can't. We have a prenup. I can't get rich that way."

This makes me laugh. Mila is the furthest thing from a gold digger I've ever seen. And I personally know there wasn't a prenup.

I feel the onset of a tension headache, stemming from my stupid car accident and my stupid lack of sleep. I rub at my forehead before the stupid tension wrinkles become permanent. I scowl because everything is starting to feel stupid this morning.

Mila notices.

"Why are you in such a bad mood?" she asks curiously. "You weren't hurt. I'm sure you've called a tow truck. You'll have your car back in a bit. No harm, no foul."

I adjust the radio and then settle back into my seat, watching the scenery as Mila turns onto the lakefront drive that houses our restaurant.

"I don't know," I admit. "I guess I just woke up on the wrong side of the bed. I didn't sleep well last night." I don't bother telling her why, because she'd just be immediately and insanely interested. She's been wanting me to go out for months and I don't want to tell her what a bust it was.

"Well, cheer up," Mila tells me as she pulls into the parking lot of the Hill. "It's a beautiful day. Life is good."

"Yeah," I answer grumpily. "Life is good."

"And you're lucky," she prompts me. "You could've been hurt and you weren't. You know as well as I do that that road is dangerous." She's serious now and I know why. I can practically see the memories in her eyes... of our parents' twisted car, their funeral, the overwhelming horrible grief.

I gulp, then nod.

"Yeah, I was lucky. Are you coming in?"

She shakes her head. "Can't. I've got a doctor's appointment and then I have to get back to my shop. I'll catch up with you later. I think we're coming here for dinner."

"'K. I'll save a table for you."

"Perfect. Thanks! Talk to you tonight."

Mila waves as she backs the giant black SUV out. I wave back limply. God, I'm going to miss her when she moves. It's only she and I now. We don't have any other relatives. Well, we have Pax. So it's just the three of us.

I sigh, but put it out of my mind. They aren't moving until summer. I'll worry about it when the time comes.

For now, I head into the little stucco Italian bistro on the shoreline where I've spent every waking hour for the past couple of years. The Hill was my parents' dream, not mine. They worked day and night for years to make it a success and when they died, Mila and I couldn't bear the thought of closing it.

But I swear to God. Some days, I get so pissed off that I gave up my life for this... that I'm confined to a little lakeside town, living someone else's dream. There are days when it sucks the lifeblood out of me and I feel so much older than I am.

And some days I feel so much younger...because I don't always have the answers to every problem that I face.

I have no fricking idea how to run a business. My business degree is a piece of paper. It didn't prepare me for a business loan, running a staff, or ordering massive amounts of food. But I can never say that out loud, because as a business owner and a big sister, I'm always expected to have answers.

The right ones.

No one needs to know that I really don't know shit—that I drift along in life without any real answers. No one needs to know that there are times when I seriously hate how things turned out, and that I'm powerless to change it.

I sigh and head inside.

The Hill might seem like a prison sometimes, but it's a prison that pays the bills.

∾

One of the worst things about running a business is all the freaking paperwork and red tape. Sometimes I actually have nightmares that I'm drowning in a sea of paper.

Today I barricade myself behind a wall of it, barely lifting my head until Tony, the bartender who has been with our family since my parents opened the place, pokes his unruly head into my office.

"Madison, did you get your car all taken care of?"

I barely glance up from yesterday's tickets, which I'm tallying. "Yeah. They're towing it in and bringing me a loaner to use for the next couple of days."

Tony nods. "Good. They'll get you squared away. For now, though, you've got to come eat. I mean it. The dinner rush is going to start soon. You're going to waste away to nothing and your father will haunt me until the end of time if I don't take care of you."

I shake my head as I look away from the schedule for next week and into Tony's concerned face. At forty, he really doesn't look a day over thirty. But I'll never tell him that. As a fiery Italian, he has an ego that's already big enough.

"My father wouldn't be the one haunting you about my eating habits," I tell him. "It would be my mother. And I don't think you want to mess with her."

He laughs and agrees.

"For sure. Your mother was a force to be reckoned with. The only one who could really control her was your dad."

I pause for a moment, my fingers frozen on my desk. Tony's eyes are gleaming with amusement and I know it's because he has no idea exactly how my father controlled my mother. No one knew.

No one except me and Mila. I swallow hard and smile at Tony, forcing the ugly thoughts out of my head. My parents are dead. There is no reason to think about the past.

"I'll be there in a minute," I tell him. "I promise."

He lifts a bushy black eyebrow. "You'd better be. Jacey just clocked in and I made her favorite cherry tarts for her birthday. As far as she's concerned, it was your idea. You've at least got to come have one with her."

"Crap," I mutter. I look up to meet Tony's accusing stare. "In my defense, I was going to get her cupcakes on the way to work, but then I almost drove my car into the lake. So I think I get a pass. Don't judge."

I turn my nose up and he almost grins, but doesn't because he has a cranky image to uphold.

He turns and saunters away, muttering something about women drivers and whipping me to within an inch of my life if I don't do what I'm told. I can do nothing but follow him, laughing. He'd never harm a hair on my head and woe to anyone who ever did, because he'd break their kneecaps (mainly because he thinks that's what an Italian should do).

He leads me to the outdoor patio, which is situated on the beach directly behind the Hill. Stringed lights and lanterns crisscross over our heads, and soon the honeysuckle on the trellises will start to bloom. At night it's magically romantic out here, particularly with the majestic view of Lake Michigan and the sweet scent of the honeysuckle. Tourists love it and so do I.

Right now a tray of Tony's famous tarts and a birthday card with Jacey's name on it sit on a table, along with three salads.

I turn to him in appreciation. "Thank you, Tony. You know I love you."

He grins now and wraps a meaty paw around my shoulder, squeezing it.

"I know you're busy," he tells me gruffly. "It's not a big deal."

But it is. He was hired on years ago as the bartender, but since my parents died, he's helped me in so many different ways. He still tends bar, but he helps me keep everything else in line. He even oversees the cooks and makes special desserts from time to time. I would be lost without him and both of us know it.

The evening breeze is blowing the hair off my face when Jacey bursts through the doors, her brown eyes sparkling in anticipation.

"It's a perfect day to have a birthday," she announces, and like always, I have to admire her.

Jacey looks at life with childlike wonderment, something I've always loved about her. She can make even the most boring thing fun.

We've been friends since we were teenagers. She used to spend the summers here with her grandparents and one day she breezed into the Hill with them for lunch and breezed out with a summer job. She's been with us every summer since then. She's fun, she's carefree, and even though it's gotten her into trouble from time to time, she's a refreshing change from the mundane.

I cherish that even more now that I am the queen of mundane.

"Happy birthday," I tell her as Tony hands her the card. She grins and opens it, finding a hundred-dollar gift certificate from Tony and me for a massage in town. I mouth *Thank you* to Tony as Jacey throws her arms around my neck.

"Thank you," she squeals. "You have no idea how stressed out I've been. I need this."

She releases me and hugs Tony, then digs into her tarts, inhaling three of them before she glances at her watch.

"We've gotta hurry," she tells us. "We're booked solid tonight. You're probably going to have to help out on the floor, Maddy, which is fine because you definitely look comfortable enough. You're taking business casual to a whole new level." Jacey looks at my clothes curiously and I sigh.

"When don't I help out on the floor?" I demand. "I'm out there every day. I have the blisters to prove it. And I'm dressed like this because I got all muddy on my way to work and had to change into my gym clothes."

Jacey grins, her eyes sparkling. "Well, with bike shorts and a little bitty T like that, I'm sure the guys will be leaving you big tips. So there's a plus."

I groan and swat at her before I turn to follow her inside, but Tony snags my elbow and points at my salad.

"Eat."

I glance at him and from the look on his face I know it's useless to argue. I bend and shovel five bites into my mouth.

"Good?" I ask with my mouth full as I wipe at it with a napkin.

He gives me a dubious look and I take two more bites before I scoop up my plate.

"I'll eat the rest later," I promise him. He shakes his head.

"No, you won't," he sighs. "You'll go home and eat a frozen burrito."

He can't see me grinning as he follows me inside, which is probably a good thing. I absolutely hate being told what to do, which is probably a result of watching my father boss my mother around with his fist for years, but I don't mind Tony's fussing.

For all Tony's gruffness, he's got a heart of gold, and he tries his hardest to watch out for both Mila and me. He's the closest thing to family that we have now.

As we walk back into the dining room, we are just in time to meet Mila and Pax coming in the front doors. Pax holds Mila's elbow as she trips over the doormat.

I have to laugh at the stricken expression on his face. I think Pax would pick Mila up and carry her for the next four months if he thought he could get away with it. He's been more than a little overprotective lately. And as I stare at his tough exterior, it's so hard to believe that it's true, but it is.

My brother-in-law is like a rock-hard, tattooed sex god or

something. Seriously, the guy exudes sex appeal. My first thought when I first met him was *Holy shit, he's trouble*. And he really was.

Pax grins at me now, his hazel eyes twinkling.

"See something you like, Mad?" he teases. And I realize that I've been staring. I grin back, not at all chagrined.

"Yes, surprisingly enough. I do like you, little brother. Who would've thunk it?" Being the protective older sister, I told Mila to stay away from Pax, and of course that made her even more attracted to him. He had that bad-boy thing going on, that cocky attitude and dangerous demeanor that Mila couldn't resist. Pax's issues had issues, and he and Mila went through hell and high water together, but they stuck it out.

Pax shakes his head. "Yeah, it's hard to believe you ever misjudged this awesomeness."

I roll my eyes and lead them to a table, chatting with them while they get settled. Pax pulls out Mila's chair and drops her napkin onto her lap for her.

"Are you going to chew her food for her too, or…?" I raise my eyebrow but Pax just grins.

"Happy wife, happy life," he rattles off as he sits down. "It's something I live by."

"And you're very good at it," Mila commends him, but her eyes are frozen with interest on something behind me. "Maddy, isn't that Ethan Eldridge?"

I turn to see my hostess, Julie, seating our old childhood friend at a small table by the window.

"Holy crap," I answer. "I think it is. I haven't seen him since he went off to med school. He never came home for the summers. His mom used to come in here and complain about it."

"He looks *good*," Mila says, pointing out the obvious. I stare at him, taking in his blond hair and blue eyes, and his lanky, lean frame. "You should go talk to him. That's your job, anyway. You need to make him feel welcome."

I scowl at her. "I'm not going over there and flirting with him. It's not happening."

"I didn't say *flirt*," Mila answers innocently. "I said *talk*. He always had a thing for you, though. And you do need a social life."

I'm just debating whether to stab her in the eye with a fork when Ethan glances up and notices me. He gives me an excited wave.

"Hell," I mutter, as Mila crows triumphantly. "I'll be back to deal with you in a minute."

I can hear her laughing as I make my way over to Ethan.

"Madison." He smiles, reminding me exactly how gorgeous his smile is. "I was hoping you'd be here."

"I'm always here," I tell him wryly. "I think I practically live here. Are you back for good? I thought I'd heard that you were coming back to the ob-gyn department at the clinic."

He smiles again and I briefly wonder why I don't feel a reaction. Is it because I've known him so long?

"Yeah, that's where I'm at. If you ever want to switch from Dr. Hall to me, I'm sure I can make your yearly exams much more pleasant for you." He waggles his eyebrows in the ridiculous way I remember, and for a minute he seems just like the kid I knew in high school.

I roll my eyes.

"Oh, yeah, that's just what I want. The guy who vomited up his chocolate milk on me in kindergarten doing my pap smear. Besides, you're not even a real doctor yet, are you? And I've had Dr. Hall for years. So…it's not gonna happen. Your hands aren't getting anywhere near this." I gesture toward my downstairs area and he shakes his head. "It's good to see you, though. It's been forever."

"I *am* a real doctor. I'm a resident doctor. That counts, you little brat. I can even prescribe medicine and shit. But whatever. It's good to see you too. You look fantastic, exactly the same as you did the day we graduated high school."

I grin at his compliment. "Thanks, Ethan. I've been feeling old lately, so that's good to hear. You look pretty good too."

He throws his most charming smile at me. "We need to sit down and catch up sometime soon, Mad. I've missed you."

I stare down at him, trying to see him in the way any other female would.

He's tall, at least six-two, blond and blue-eyed. He looks like a descendent of Vikings or something. Well, without the muscles of a Viking. We'd make gorgeous babies together, if I'm honest. But I've known him since preschool, which means that I know all the dumbass stuff he did between then and now. I still vividly remember him eating a grasshopper on a dare in fourth grade. His tongue isn't getting anywhere near mine, doctor or not.

He winks and I shake my head. I'm just getting ready to tell him how terrifying it is that people are putting their health in his hands when the restaurant door opens, letting a slice of sunlight in to shine across the floor. I follow the light to the man who just walked in from the rain. He's sliding his cell phone into the pocket of his jacket.

He looks up and his eyes meet mine and there's no way in hell.

No effing way in hell.

My heart is slamming a million miles an hour in my chest.

Because it's Gabriel.

Chapter Five

Gabriel

You've got to be fucking kidding me. The universe obviously has a strange sense of humor. After lusting after this girl last night and wondering what happened to her all day today, I'm now standing face-to-face with her? What are the odds of that?

Pretty fucking small.

Yet there she is.

Madison stares at me in shock as she stands next to a guy dressed in fancy jeans and a button-up shirt. The guy is clearly a candy-ass, but he's not my concern.

I'm totally fixated on Madison: her wide eyes, her mouth slightly open.

That's exactly how I feel. But unlike her, I manage to keep the surprise off my face.

I'm trying to process the crazy coincidence of us meeting like this, the second meeting in two days, when I see my sister emerge from a back hall, carrying a large tray of drinks. As Jacey glances up at me, everything suddenly clicks together and makes perfect sense.

Jacey mentioned that she was going to bring a friend with her to the club last night.

And Jacey has told me about her boss before, a supposedly cool girl who had to grow up way too soon for reasons that I don't remember right now. What I do remember is that she called her Maddy.

Maddy is Madison.

Jacey is the common thread, the root of this unholy coincidence. Of course.

I shake my head and watch while Jacey sets her tray down and bounds across the room to grab me in a bear hug.

"Gabriel!" she squeals. "It's about time you got here. I've missed your ugly face."

I can't help but hug her back, even though I'm annoyed about the whole Madison thing. I almost feel like Jacey finagled all of this on purpose, but I know that can't be right. There's no way she could've arranged our meeting behind the club.

I can feel Madison's cool stare, but I refuse to look up and meet it because I can't tell if she's annoyed or intrigued that I've intruded upon her life.

For the life of me, I can't remember much after that fucking taxi accident last night. It was a total blackout, the first one I've had in months.

I don't remember what I said to her, I don't remember how I acted around her, I can't remember shit. I do have strange little flashes of Madison tucking me into bed, but I don't know if those are real memories or if my mind was just playing tricks on me. You never know with me, not when I'm in that fucked-up state.

But if it was real, I hate that she saw me like that. It's humiliating, which is as good a reason as any to ignore her.

"Hey, Sis," I murmur into Jacey's blonde hair. "Happy birthday! You smell like spaghetti."

She rolls her eyes and lets go of me, turning to Madison.

"Maddy, you've got to come and finally meet my brother."

Madison looks stricken, but she manages to put one foot in front of the other, leaving the candy-ass's side to stand reluctantly in front of me.

Even though I'm uncomfortable about this myself, I fight the urge to laugh at the distinct expression of discomfort on her gorgeous face. No matter what else she might be feeling, it's clear she's not sure how to handle this situation, just as it's clear that she's not used to not being in control. She has no idea what to say to me. At all.

It's pretty fucking funny.

"This is my brother Gabriel." Jacey looks up at me proudly. "He just got back from Afghanistan a few months ago and he's hardly made the time to come see his poor little sister. Gabriel, this is my friend—and boss—Madison. You've heard all about her."

Madison's blue eyes are frozen on me, a question gleaming in them.

What the fuck?

I can hear it just as clearly as if she'd said the words. And it makes me wonder again just how much she saw last night. It puts me on the defensive and I smirk, just to prove that none of it matters.

When Madison sees it, her eyes harden even more.

Jacey stares from Madison to me.

"Um. Aren't you going to say anything? 'Nice to meet you,' maybe? What's wrong with you two? Did I miss something?"

Madison finally blinks and breaks our gaze, glancing at Jacey.

"It's, uh, nice to meet you." She looks uncertain of what to say next so I clear my throat.

I don't see the point in mentioning what happened last night. Or what almost happened. Mentioning any part of it would open a can of worms that I don't want to discuss.

Madison looks grateful for a moment before her face closes up and she turns cool once again. For some reason, I'm guessing that's her normal persona . . . cool and collected.

It seems very her.

Or maybe she's being cold because she's mad that I left her at the accident? I internally flinch. I hate that I did that. It was a dick thing to do. But I wasn't myself. If she's judging me for that, fuck her. She doesn't know shit.

I grin widely to show her that she's not always in control.

Because that's very me.

"It's nice to formally meet you, Madison. I've heard a lot about you. Some of it was even good."

Jacey gasps and punches me, but I ignore her quick protests about how everything was good and how she'd never say anything bad about Madison. I even ignore her whining about how my arm hurt her hand.

Instead I glance down and notice the way Madison's chest fills out her snug T-shirt, and I briefly flash back to the way her nipples tasted in my mouth, pink and sweet. My groin tightens and I quickly return my attention to the present as Madison slides her slender hand into mine.

"It's a pleasure," she answers coolly. "And Jacey, don't worry. I know you only say good things about me. Your brother was just joking, I'm sure."

I swallow a snort, but Jacey looks appeased.

"Sorry, Maddy," she mutters. "My brother didn't used to be so rude. He's still adjusting from being overseas."

Anger flashes through me, quick and hot, but I tamp it down. I meant to be a little rude. I can't get mad for being called out on it.

"I'm sure I'll be back to normal soon," I agree with her smoothly before I change the subject. "Do you have a table for me? We're gonna need a table for three. Brand's coming too."

Jacey's face lights up at the mention of our childhood friend.

"Thank God! I haven't seen him in at least a month. You both suck at coming to see me. You should be ashamed of yourselves." She turns to Madison. "Can I give them the window table in the corner?"

Madison nods.

"Of course. It was nice to meet you, Gabriel. I hope you enjoy your meal."

She abruptly turns and joins a couple at a different table. Not that I'm going to show it, but I'm a little flabbergasted at the change in her. This cool, unflappable woman is nothing like the hot-blooded chick I met last night. I find myself staring at her tight ass for a minute, wondering how such a small ass fits such a big stick in it. I'm chuckling at the thought as Jacey leads me to my table.

"I'll bring you a beer," Jacey tells me as she hands me a menu and eyes the wrapped gift that I set on the table next to me. "What will Brand want?"

"A beer is fine," I tell her as I look over the food selection. "Thanks, Sis."

She nods as she leaves and I glance around.

The restaurant is nice, although Madison doesn't seem like the kind of person who would own a restaurant. At least she didn't seem that way last night. Today, though, who knows? I think about it for a second, and vaguely remember Jacey telling me that Maddy inherited it from her parents. That would make more sense.

Turning slightly, I find her in my periphery. Her light blonde hair is easy to find. Whereas last night she was dressed like a runway model, today she's wearing workout clothes—tiny tight shorts, a tiny shirt that leaves nothing to the imagination and tennis shoes. It's strange as fuck. It's like she's done a complete about-face.

So who is the real Madison? The sexy siren who wanted to go home with me last night or this tightly wound business owner?

Maybe she's tightly wound during the day and a siren in the sack?

It seems like something that I should make it my mission to find out.

She's sitting with her little group now: a gorgeous dark-haired woman and a muscular tattooed guy. She's also purposely not looking at me, I can tell. Her shoulders are angled away from me and she's laughing at everything her companions say, as if to show me what a good time she's having.

And no, I'm not egotistical for thinking that her behavior revolves around me. At this moment, her behavior is revolving around me. She's as acutely aware of where I am in this room as I am of her. Every so often I can see her sneaking sideways glances at me. She's probably wondering about the real me, just like I'm wondering about the real her. If she saw much of my episode last night, if it was bad, then she's probably trying to figure me out right this minute.

Since I can't remember what happened last night, there's only one thing I can do.

Fuck with her.

Prove to her that I'm not a pussy. Stare at her until she squirms in her seat, as she remembers exactly what we almost did last night, what she begged me to do. Show her that she doesn't have the upper hand with me just because I can't remember what I did.

Grinning to myself, I switch seats so that I'm squarely facing her. And then I pointedly stare at her.

This should prove entertaining.

Madison

What the hell?

My cheeks flush hotly as I feel Gabriel's stare burning into me from across the room. How in the name of all that is holy did I not notice that his last name was the same as Jacey's when I looked at his driver's license last night? That accident must've shaken me up even more than I realized. And why the hell is he staring at me? He's acting like nothing happened last night at all, like he didn't totally lose his shit. What am I supposed to do with that?

Even though he's very obviously trying to draw my attention, there's no way in hell that I'm going to acknowledge it. I'd rather die before I give him the satisfaction of looking at him. Instead I concentrate even more on appearing like I'm having one hell of a good time.

I pick up my wineglass and take another sip, before I smile broadly at my brother-in-law.

"So, how do you like working for your grandpa? How often are you going to have to go to Hartford this summer?"

Pax pauses mid-bite and thinks about my question. As he does, he absently rubs my sister's back with his free hand.

"At first I wondered what the hell I'd gotten myself into. There was no way I wanted to be surrounded by suits and ties every day. But then I settled in and found my place. I don't have to wear a suit and tie because I own the fucking company. I'm still proving myself to my grandpa, but I think I'm gonna like it."

"Good," I answer. "But I'm not going to like it when you guys move away."

Mila rolls her eyes. "Mad, we've been through this a hundred times. It's a two-hour plane ride. You can come see me and I'll come see you. It's not like we're never going to see each other again. And hopefully you'll be dating someone soon, so that will distract you. We've gotta figure out something to do with your personal life."

I raise an eyebrow. "Oh, *we* do, huh? You're going to have input on that?"

Mila laughs and pats Pax's leg. "I'm good at relationships, apparently. I can help you with yours."

"I don't have a relationship," I remind her. "That was your whole point."

She rolls her eyes again.

"Fine. We're going to start with an easy one. Ethan Eldridge. I know for a fact that he's single. I bumped into his mom at the library the other day. She said he's been lonely because a lot of his old friends have moved away. So there you go. You can start by dating Ethan. He'll be good practice."

I hold up a spoon. "And it doesn't matter to you that this spoon has more of a personality than he does?"

Pax bursts out laughing, looking over at Ethan before he glances at his wife.

"She has a point. Madison needs someone who can give her a run for her money. That guy...er, he doesn't seem quite up to it."

Mila gives her husband a skeptical look. "Maybe. But Maddy has always picked guys that are too overbearing, too controlling. And then it ends in a disaster and Maddy's pissed off at the world and at the male species in general. Maybe she needs to try out a guy like Ethan."

We all glance discreetly in Ethan's direction, to find him scrolling quietly through his cell phone. He's wearing a preppy watch, a preppy shirt, perfectly fitted khakis. He's so neat and tidy that even his nails are buffed and cut to a neat square. Very neutral, very bland and vanilla.

Bland and vanilla just aren't me.

Pax turns back around, shaking his head. "I don't think he's got it in him to handle Maddy."

I raise my eyebrows. "He can't *handle* me?"

Pax quickly backtracks. "That's not exactly what I meant. You're...shall we say...a little fierce. You need a guy with balls. You don't need a guy whose balls are in your purse. Just sayin'."

"Ha, so says the guy whose balls are in Mila's handbag as we speak."

Mila laughs as I give Pax an icy stare. He ignores it *and* my comment, while he chews on a piece of bread, totally unaffected by my glare or my accusation that my sister owns his testicles. I guess he's secure enough in his manhood to not care.

Turning my head slightly, I can see Gabriel's dark shape from the corner of my eye and I almost flush again.

Throughout this entire conversation, his smoldering stare has burned holes into me. It's so potent that it almost feels like it's actually touching me. Finally I'm unable to resist and I glance at him.

He stares back at me, his eyes stormy and dark.

What the hell is he thinking? Is he remembering the accident? Or is he remembering how scorchingly hot last night was *before* the accident? I stare at his mouth and I can't help but remember how it tasted last night before his meltdown.

Smoky, minty... like a man. I gulp.

And then I die. Because with his gaze still connected to mine, he very purposefully slips his finger into his mouth, then pulls it out slowly, sucking it.

Just like he sucked the taste of me off his fingers last night.

Oh. My. God.

My cheeks explode into flame and his dark, dark eyes glimmer with amusement. I stare at him as I realize that he's fucking with me. He's purposely trying to remind me of last night.

The corner of his lip twitches and I know.

I know that he thinks he won whatever little game he's been playing.

Eff him. Willing the color to drain away from my face, I give Gabriel my iciest stare, lift my nose into the air and turn back around to find Mila watching the interaction.

"Who's that?" she asks with extreme interest. I shrug.

"Jacey's brother. I just met him."

Mila raises her eyebrow. "You just met him?" She stares at me. "That seems doubtful. You keep staring at each other. You know him. Spill."

I scowl at my sister. "Why do you have to know me so well? I met him last night at a club in Chicago."

Mila chokes on her drink of water. "Seriously? You met him at a *club*?"

And without any shame at all, she spins around in her seat to stare at him.

Gabriel stares back at her with interest, then cocks an eyebrow at me. He's sprawled out in his seat, his long legs casually relaxed. None of this is affecting him in the same way it is affecting me. It's like he doesn't care that what happened last night was disconcerting as hell. That pisses me off.

"Turn around," I hiss at Mila, yanking on her arm. "God. Do you have to be so obvious?"

"I can't help it," she says, without turning around. "How can I not look at the guy who has you all worked up?"

"I am not worked up," I answer between my teeth, tugging on her arm harder. "Don't make me manhandle a pregnant woman because then Pax will kill me. Just turn around. *God*."

She finally does as I ask, but she looks at me strangely. "What the hell, Maddy? Why are you so upset? It's just Jacey's brother, right?"

There is a knowingness to her tone that makes me want to smack my sister, even if she *is* pregnant.

"Yes," I answer firmly, ignoring her tone and resisting my urge to inflict bodily harm. "He's just Jacey's brother."

"Well, in that case, I should go introduce myself. I mean, Jacey *is* our employee. It's only polite."

And with that, Mila is out of her seat and across the room before

I can stop her. She moves surprisingly fast for a pregnant girl. I'm left staring with my mouth open. Pax reaches over and snaps it closed.

"She got you, Mad."

I look at him. "Pax, I swear to God. One of these days I'm going to kill her. It's gonna happen."

Pax just laughs, entirely unconcerned.

"Whatever. If you were going to kill her, you would have done it a long time ago. But you didn't. Instead you protected her like a mama bear. So I have a hard time believing that you would ever harm a hair on her head. And now I've gotta go take a piss. Can you behave yourself out here alone? And by that, I mean can you stay out here without killing anyone?"

I shake my head and follow him.

"I'm not staying out here," I mutter when he looks back at me in surprise.

"Well, you're not coming with me," he grins. "It's big, but I can hold it myself."

It takes me half a second to realize what he meant, and what *it* is. I feel myself blush in spite of myself.

"God, I'm surrounded by imbeciles."

I roll my eyes one more time for good measure, then stalk back to my office. I can hear my brother-in-law laughing as I go, just as I can feel Gabriel's dark gaze tracking every move I make. It's freaking unnerving and I'm pissed at myself that I let him get to me like this.

I'm barely in my office for ten minutes before Jacey finds me. She barges in without knocking, as she always does, adjusting her blonde ponytail before she drops into a chair in front of my desk.

"Maddy, what the hell? You and my brother are staring at each other like you're food on an all-you-can-eat buffet. What the hell is going on?"

Her large brown eyes are curious as she waits for me to answer.

I start to speak, close my mouth, then try again.

"Last night... Gabriel..."

But it doesn't want to come out. I don't want to tell her that I almost hooked up with her brother. It doesn't feel right. This feels like dangerous territory. Isn't it against a code somewhere to not date your friend's brother? Especially when something strange seems to be going on with him? If she doesn't already know about it, I certainly don't want to be the one to give her the bad news.

Jacey knows me well, however, and her eyes glitter and then narrow as she looks at me.

"Go on. What about last night?" Brief pause, then her eyes light up. "Oh. My. God. Did you meet Gabe last night in Chicago? He was supposed to meet us but didn't because there was some problem with his taxi. But you disappeared too. Did you meet my brother last night, Madison? There's no way... right?"

I swallow hard and look away.

"Oh my God!" Jacey crows, jumping from her chair and dancing around in a weird circle, like an awkward little bird. "You hooked up with my brother!"

I stare at her warily. "Almost. Is that weird?"

She looks at me like I have two heads.

"Are you crazy? I've wanted you guys to date for years. But when we were teenagers, he never wanted to come into town in the summers. He was going through a shy stage or some shit. And then he went overseas. You're perfect for each other. You just don't know it yet. The real question is why *didn't* you hook up last night? You never explained."

I roll my eyes and glance at the clock. It's just shy of seven, prime dinner rush.

"Don't get too excited. It was a late night, it was a club...and we just got a little carried away. And then we were in an accident in the taxi and it killed the mood. Since you were the one who talked me into trying to hook up with someone, the whole thing is your fault, if you think about it."

Jacey ignores that last part as her brow furrows.

"An accident? Gabe told me this morning that there was a problem with his taxi. He didn't say anything about an accident. Was anyone hurt?"

I shake my head. "No. Some guy just ran a red light and T-boned us in the intersection. The taxi was totaled, but nobody was hurt. It totally killed the mood, though."

And so did walking a strangely incoherent man home to his apartment and leaving before he could murder me and hang my skin in his kitchen cabinet or something.

I so want to ask Jacey about Gabriel's weird behavior, but I hesitate. Her face is completely frozen now, as she looks utterly concerned about her brother. I don't want to give her even more to worry about.

"Holy shit," she breathes. "I owe Gabe an apology. I thought he was just making up an excuse for ditching me. You guys could've been hurt."

I don't tell her that he actually was ditching her when we got in the accident.

"Yeah, I guess so. But we weren't. Just shaken up."

Him more than me. But again, I don't mention that part.

Jacey shakes her head and sighs. "I swear to God, that man

attracts dangerous situations. A normal person runs away from danger and Gabe runs straight for it. Always has. No one was surprised when he joined the Army Rangers, but I'm definitely surprised that he's lived this long."

This is the perfect opportunity to get more information about Gabe. I stare at my friend, trying to decide how best to go about it.

"I don't remember you telling me that he was a Ranger before," I tell her carefully. Jacey stares at me.

"Do you listen to me at all?" she demands. I flush. Truthfully, I tune her out sometimes. She tends to chatter aimlessly. A lot.

"Gabe's been overseas with the Rangers for the last three years," she continues. "It's all he ever wanted to do. It's why I've been so worried about him. He was in combat and Rangers do some scary shit. But then something happened and he resigned his commission. And he came home. So did his best friend, Brand. Now they're starting a business together, but I don't understand any of it. It's so not them. They're Rangers to the bone."

She's quiet now, subdued. I hesitate to ask, but I can't help it.

"What happened?"

She shrugs and looks me in the eye. "Your guess is as good as mine. He won't talk to me about it. But it fucked him up. I know he has problems sleeping and he's just not himself. Like, he gets mad easier and shit."

I must look horrified or something because Jacey rushes to continue.

"Not like super mad or anything. He just gets annoyed easily now. That's not like him. But I know that he'll go back to normal eventually. Probably soon. I've done some reading on guys who come home from combat. Apparently this stuff is normal. It will go away."

This stuff is definitely not *normal*. Not what I saw last night, anyway. But I don't say that. From what Jacey is saying, it's clear she has no idea what's going on with him.

It fucked him up. She did get that part right.

Something twinges in my chest, something soft, something I usually keep hidden away. It must be my heart, but it's hard to say. It's been so long since I acknowledged that part of me. But the idea of a wounded soldier who came home damaged like that gets to me.

For a second I picture Gabriel in fatigues, sweaty and dangerous in the desert. It suits him, actually. But then I picture him injured and maybe even alone and for whatever reason, I hate the thought. I swallow hard, then change the subject to lighten the mood.

"I'm sorry, Jace. That's terrible. But if that's true and he's some badass alpha guy, then there's no way he's right for me. I don't like guys who are adrenaline junkies or whatever. And I definitely don't like guys who lose their tempers easily."

She scowls. "That's not what I said. He doesn't lose his temper easily. He's just . . . more easily annoyed. I think he's just adjusting to civilian life. It's not a big deal, Mad. You should give him a chance."

I already did.

I push away the thought of Gabriel's hand between my legs last night in the taxi, while the taxi driver was right in the front seat. I sort of liked that adrenaline junkie side of him last night. I can't lie. Not to myself.

When I fail to answer, Jacey rolls her eyes. "What the hell has happened to my old friend? The one who liked to take chances and steal gin from her parents' liquor cabinet and sneak out of her bedroom window to go to beach parties? You know, the Madison who didn't do things like leave her BFF at the club? I hope she comes back soon because I need a partner in crime again. I want the old Madison back. And when she comes back, she can date my brother."

Her words practically stab me in the heart because I feel old. I feel boring. I feel like someone I'm not. And she's totally calling me on it. So I do what I always do when I'm cornered. I hide behind a wall.

I roll my eyes. "Whatever. That Madison isn't coming back. It's called growing up. You should try it. And shouldn't you be checking on your tables? Julie is probably going nuts without you."

Jacey stares down her nose at me. "Fine. You can get rid of me right now, but trust me, I'm gonna come back to this conversation. You're going to tell me every detail about your 'almost' one-night stand with my brother and we're going to discuss how you should date him."

With that, Jacey flounces out of my office. I try to turn my focus back to my never-ending paperwork, but I can't help going back to her words.

A retired Army Ranger. That makes such perfect sense.

Disciplined. Rigid. Dangerous. That all fits the description of a Ranger, at least in my limited experience. And even though I haven't seen evidence of it in his actions, I can see all of that in his eyes.

He doesn't seem very old, though. He can't be much older than me, so it must've been something really bad that made him retire so young.

I decide that Gabriel Vincent is an enigma.

A blatantly arrogant enigma.

A scorchingly sexy, dangerous-as-hell enigma.

An enigma with a rippling six-pack and smoldering eyes.

Against my better judgment, I creep back down the hall and

peek around the corner at him. Jacey's got her arms wrapped around his shoulders, laughing down at something he said. While he chuckles with her, he's relaxed and warm, much as he was with me last night before the taxi incident.

Across the table from him, his friend laughs at the two of them. Brand, I think Jacey called him. He's built like a brick wall and drop-dead sexy as hell. Blond, blue-eyed, crooked grin. He looks like a real-life Thor. Holy shit—is this what Rangers look like? If so, they're definitely our country's finest.

But when I look at Brand, even as gorgeous as he is, the blood in my veins doesn't catch fire like it does when I look at Gabriel.

Gabriel fascinates the hell out of me. When he's in a room, he owns it, completely and totally. The memory of him sticking his finger in his mouth from across the room causes my eyes to flutter closed.

The stuff Jacey told me about him coming out of the Rangers early only made my curiosity worse. I want to know more about him, yet at the same time I know I should run far away from him.

Because there's one thing I know about myself. Try as I might to stay away from powerful, strong guys, guys who command a room, guys who might hurt me...I am totally and completely attracted to those guys. I'm attracted to the very things that might hurt me the most.

It is glaringly obvious that Gabriel is all of those things.

And more.

Chapter Six

Gabriel

Madison disappeared into a hallway an hour ago and she hasn't been back out since. She hasn't even been back out to sit with her sister, Mila, the chick who introduced herself to me. That makes me think Maddy might be hiding from me, which is a thought that makes me smile. I don't know why...sadistic, I guess. But if she's so coolly put together, the way she's acting tonight, then the thought that I rattled her is funny as hell.

I glance back over Mila's way. She's laughing and trying to force-feed her husband a strawberry. Pax, I think she told me. What the hell kind of name is that?

He's a big dude and rough-looking, but then I guess he'd have to be with a name like that. It looks like he's been domesticated, but it's just as apparent that it wasn't always that way. He's got that look in his eyes. That lean and mean look that doesn't just go away.

Mila laughs again and as she glances up, her eyes meet mine for a second and I think about what she said to me.

Maddy might seem like a bitch, but I promise you that she's not.

Why the hell would she say that? Maddy doesn't seem like a

bitch to me, but then again, I think I know why she's acting so cold. I know, sort of, what happened last night. No one else here does. They must all think she's snubbing me for no reason.

The sound of Jacey's cajoling brings my attention back to the present, where my sister is practically sitting in Brand's lap as she tries to coerce him into telling her stories from combat.

Brand shoots me another desperate look over her head, so I take pity and rescue him. Brand might be an incredible hulk of muscle, but Jacey's always turned him into knots. He just thinks that no one knows that.

"Jace, you know he can't talk about that. That shit's all classified. And you don't have the security clearance level to hear it."

Jacey glares at me. "I don't have a security clearance at all."

I smile at her. "That's my point. Give the guy a break. Besides, I'm sure we should probably leave. We're taking up a table."

"Don't go yet," Jace whines, picking up another bite of her cake. "I've missed you guys. A lot. And I hardly ever get to see you, even now that you've been home for months. Don't you find that weird?" She pauses, takes another bite, then turns to me. "Just have one more cup of coffee," she tells me bossily. "I'll even make it decaf."

She scoots off Brand's lap and darts off for the kitchen before I can even answer.

Brand grins at me. "Some things never change. Jacey's still got you wrapped around her little finger."

I shake my head. "Whatever. She was sitting on *your* lap. Seriously, though. You know I feel bad for her. She always thinks our dad is going to change—that he'll miraculously take an interest in her and then when he doesn't, she's devastated. She's never gonna learn."

"So you're always gonna be there to take his place," Brand adds. "And do the shit he doesn't. I know you, dude. And I respect the hell out of that. I do. I'm sure Jacey does too, even if she doesn't show it."

"My sister's tougher than she looks," I answer thoughtfully, watching as she stops to talk to some guy who just walked in the restaurant. "She tries not to get all gushy and shit, but I know she appreciates you too."

Brand follows my gaze to Jacey, freezing on the guy who is standing with her. Something about the guy seems off. He's wearing dirty work clothes and he's muscled and stout. Clearly he does some sort of manual labor. He's also clearly pissed.

"Who's that?" Brand asks with sharp interest. I shake my head.

"No clue."

I can't hear what they're saying, but they seem to be in a heated discussion and the guy's face turns red. Jacey shakes her head, rolls her eyes and turns to walk away.

And then the guy grabs her arm.

The second he touches her, anger flashes through me, red and hot. Like lightning, Brand and I both shove back from the table, lunging to our feet. I reach my sister in a few strides, with Brand right beside me.

"If you want to keep your hand, I suggest you let go of my sister," I say calmly. There's no need to raise my voice. I know how intimidating I am. And standing together, Brand and I are like a wall. We tower over this little punk.

He looks up at us and I can see fear in his eyes, even if he doesn't want to show it. He takes his time, but he makes a show of slowly and exaggeratedly releasing Jacey's arm, then holding his empty hand in the air.

"That's better," Brand tells him. "I would suggest you not do that again."

"Fuck off," the guy spits angrily. "This isn't your business."

"Jared, just leave," Jacey interjects. "Seriously. You need to go."

Jared smiles. "This is a public place. I need some dinner. And I want you to serve me."

"No fucking way," Jacey tells him. "Get out. Now. I'm sick of your shit."

"What the hell is going on?" I demand. "Who is this guy and why is he bothering you?"

But before she can answer, Madison emerges from the back hall. When she spots Jared, her eyes widen and she looks startled, then she masks it. She calmly approaches us.

"What's going on?" she asks Jacey quietly.

"Jared won't leave," Jacey answers.

"I'm just getting ready to help him out," I tell Madison. The guy smiles.

"Try it," he dares me. "Just try it."

He turns to me, his slitted eyes challenging me, even though I can see the fear in them. He's cockier than he is smart and, if I'm not mistaken, a little drunk too. I scoff at him.

"You're not worth my time. Just leave before you embarrass yourself. Or before I embarrass you."

Jared stares up at me.

"I know who you are," he scowls. "Jacey told me all about her big war-hero brother. Well, dumbass, you aren't overseas now. And you're not a hero here. So back the fuck off."

I ignore the anger that flashes through me quick and hot. Out of the corner of my eye, I see Pax stand up from his table. Mila puts her hand on his arm, as if to urge him to stay put. I smile. She must realize what I already know. I've got this. I don't need assistance.

"I don't need to be a hero to handle a little pussy like you," I answer him, maintaining my calm. "Get the fuck out of here."

Jared doesn't move. So I move him.

Grabbing his elbow, I drag him toward the door. He struggles against me, but even though he's strong, he's much smaller than I am.

"I'm going to call the police," Madison tells him as she tags along at my heels. "Just go, Jared."

"You're both whores," he spits at her, struggling in my grip to turn and look at her. "I haven't done anything to you. You need to mind your own fucking business."

"Jacey *is* my business," Madison answers coolly, stepping around us to open the door for me. "Stop harassing her. We're calling the police this time."

This time? I glare over my shoulder at Jacey, who has the good grace to look sheepish. This is the first I've heard of someone harassing her.

Spinning, I slam the punk against the doorjamb. Behind me I hear Madison suck in her breath, but I ignore it. This asshole's back makes a satisfying thunk against the wood and I dig my fingers into his collarbone.

"Call my sister a whore again, and you won't have any teeth left," I warn him. "Got it?" He squirms and I release him, shoving him hard toward the parking lot. "Get the fuck out of here."

He spits on the ground, then starts to walk away. "Good thing you had your buddies to help you," he calls back to me. "Next time you won't be so lucky."

He gets into his car and I glance over my shoulder. Both Brand and Madison's brother-in-law are standing behind me, as if I need backup for this pathetic piece of shit. I shake my head.

"Oh, trust me. I won't need help. And there better not be a next time."

The guy flips me off and spins out, squealing his tires as he tears out of the parking lot. I turn around to find Madison facing me, her hands on her hips.

"Was that really necessary?" she asks. "I was going to call the cops. Violence really wasn't appropriate. I have customers here."

I stare at her in shock. "I thought you'd be happy that I removed him from your dining room."

"You thought wrong. I had the situation under control."

I'm astounded now. "Oh, really? And how exactly were you controlling it? By threatening to call the police? Assholes like that don't listen to reason, Madison. You have to speak in the language that they understand."

"Well, I'm sure you're fluent in asshole-speak." Madison stares at me icily for a moment longer, then spins around and stalks off.

I don't give myself enough time to ponder the fact that the kitten has claws before I whirl around, pinning Jacey with my glare.

"What the fuck was this?"

Jacey shrugs. Over her shoulder I see Madison walking her brother-in-law back to his table, then turning her head to talk with her sister. But instead of thinking about what they might be saying, I return my focus to my current problem.

Jacey.

"He's an ex-boyfriend who can't take no for an answer," she

answers. "He's just an asshole who takes rejection very personally. Not that big of a deal."

"He sort of is," Madison says from behind me. I glance at her, surprised that she came back after her little show of theatrics. She looks at me, her pretty face drawn. "His behavior could be a big deal, I mean. He practically attacked my little sister last year. And he's been bothering Jacey for a while. At least a month. I keep telling her to call the police but she won't. I figured I should tell you that. Maybe you can get her to see reason."

She ruined her dramatic exit to come back and tell me something to help Jacey? Interesting.

"Madison, God." Jacey snaps. "I don't need the police involved in this. It's embarrassing. Jared is an asshole and he's annoying, but he's not really going to do anything. Most of the time he just texts me . . . sends me pictures of his naked junk and shit."

Madison stares at her. "Jacey, he's already doing something. Not only is he still harassing you, but he's here in my place of business creating a scene." She lowers her voice now and dips her head closer to Jacey, as if what she's getting ready to say is for Jacey's ears only. But I can still hear it.

"Jace, my dad had that kind of temper. It doesn't get better. Those kind of guys are bullies who will intimidate you until you push back, until you make him see that he can't treat you like that. *That you won't let him treat you like that.* You have to step up and do something."

I'm still now as I watch her. She doesn't know it, but she just showed me something about herself, something that makes her vulnerable. Some*one*.

But I can't think about that right now. Right now I have to deal with my sister.

"We're going to talk," I tell Jacey, taking her by the elbow and guiding her back to the table. "What exactly happened when you broke up with that guy?"

Jacey shakes her head. "Nothing out of the ordinary. I told him that it wasn't working and he didn't like it. He texts me nonstop, drives by the cottage, calls and hangs up...it's frustrating, but he'll get over it."

Brand stares at her. "Little hotheads like him sometimes don't just 'get over' something. He's clearly got a problem. I'm going to need his name and address."

I glance at my friend. After serving in the Rangers with him, I know exactly what he's capable of.

"Stand down, soldier," I mutter to him. "This is civilian life. We aren't going to pay the asshole a visit. Not yet, anyway." I turn to my sister. "I'm not leaving you here alone. When is Gran coming back from Florida?"

Our grandparents have owned a cottage here in Angel Bay since before I was born. We stayed here with them every summer when we were kids, but then our grandfather died and our gran hasn't been the same. Jacey still spends summers here to keep Gran company, but for at least the past year, Gran has been in Florida most of the time anyway.

Jacey cringes. "You won't believe this but I don't know when she'll be back. I think she met someone in her retirement village." She watches my face and nods. "I know. I don't like to think about it either. But you know, Grandpa's been gone for years now. I suppose she's lonely."

"Oh, God," Brand mutters, swigging his beer. "Geriatric sex. I'm out. Where's the bathroom?"

Jacey points him in the right direction and then she drops into his vacant seat. I stare at her, waiting for her to give me an explanation. After a couple of minutes of silence, I just flat out ask.

"Why didn't you tell me about that guy?" I ask her, serious now. "You should have."

She drops her eyes and stares at the empty beer bottle that Brand left behind.

"Because I can handle it on my own," she tells me with a sigh. "I don't need to have my big brother swoop in and save me."

I sigh too. "I know you don't," I reply. "But maybe your big brother *wants* to swoop in and save you. It's sort of what I do."

She laughs at that. "Oh, great. So you retire from the army and I'm going to have to let you save me all the time so that you get your hero fix?"

"Something like that," I answer absently. In my head I'm thinking about my schedule. "I think I can stay here for a while," I tell her. "Brand and I have to pitch our new body armor to the Pentagon in a couple of months, but until then I'm free."

"Unless I find another investor in the meantime," Brand interjects as he grabs another chair and comes back to the table. "But even then, you can get to the meeting just as easily from here as you could from your condo."

I nod and Jacey stares at us.

"I don't understand your new business," she admits. "You're selling body armor to the government, right? Why don't they make their own body armor?"

"They do," Brand explains. "But it's not good enough because the good stuff has always been too expensive. Gabe and I want to design better armor that the government can buy for every soldier. If we can do it, and if we can get the army to buy it, then no one will ever have to go through what we went through."

Jacey grumbles, "And I have no idea what you went through because you won't tell me."

Brand and I both are silent and Jacey sighs. "I know, I know. You'll talk to me about it when you're ready."

"It's not you, Jacey. It's just not something we like to talk about to *anyone*," Brand offers. "Think about the most horrible thing you could possibly think of. The bloodiest, scariest thing...your worst nightmare. Then picture it happening to you...picture it becoming your reality, a nightmare that you can't wake up from. Trust me, you wouldn't want to talk about it either."

Jacey looks stricken and she puts a hand on my arm as she stares at us both.

"Fine. I get it. But seriously, if either one of you ever want to talk about it, I'm here. And I have two ears to listen with."

I pat her hand. "Thanks, Jace. But back to the matter at hand. I'm going to stay with you for a while. No arguments."

Jacey groans, but finally nods. "Fine. I guess it would be nice to have you around anyway. I miss you. And you know, Gran's been after you to come and bug-bomb her basement for spiders ever since you got home. This will give you an opportunity."

She grins and it's my turn to groan. "Crap. I forgot. I don't know much about bug-bombing, but between Brand and me, we'll figure it out."

Brand yelps. "How the hell did I figure into this? The only thing I know about spiders is that I stay away from them."

"I'll pay you in beer," I offer.

"Done," he quickly agrees.

I turn back to Jacey. "Now, about this Jared guy. What's he like? I want to get a handle on him."

Jacey thinks on that. "Well, he isn't the most stable person. I should've listened to Maddy. She tried to tell me what he did with Mila. But when I asked him about it, he said he'd been drunk and wasn't himself and I believed him. The problem is, he's drunk *all* the time and so he gets ugly. But if you're at the house, I bet he'll leave me alone. No one in their right mind, drunk or not, would mess with you. Your bicep is as big as my thigh."

I picture Mila, the sister who introduced herself to me earlier. The sweet, charming sister who clearly wouldn't hurt a fly. If that asshole would fuck with a chick like that, he wouldn't hesitate to fuck with my feisty sister.

"You have to take unbalanced little fucks like him seriously, Jace. And somehow, I doubt your little boy toy is intimidating enough to help much. But I'll be here now and hopefully Jared will just stay away and the problem will be taken care of."

"OK." Jacey sighs. "But don't rag on Peter. He's in a band. He doesn't need to be intimidating. He's a creative."

I roll my eyes and she grins.

"I'd better get my side work done so that Maddy doesn't freak out. She pretty much stays until the last person is ready to go. When will you be at the cottage?"

"I'll drive home and pack a bag and then be back tonight. It might be late, but I'll be here."

"'K." She drops a kiss on my forehead as she walks past. "You're the best big brother I have. Thank you for my birthday watch. It's gorgeous." She stares at her wrist, at the glittering gold watch I brought her.

"I'm the only big brother you have," I answer. "And you're welcome."

She starts to walk away, then stops, glancing back at me. "Hey, Ethan Eldridge is asking Maddy out. You'd better get over there and take care of that."

My head snaps up, only for me to find Madison talking to the candy-ass she was with earlier. I can't hear what they're saying, but Jacey can.

"You missed out." She shakes her head. "She just said yes."

Why does that annoy me so much? Maddy looks up and catches my gaze, her cheeks flushing. Why do I bother *her* so much? What the hell did I do last night?

"I don't own her, Jace," I finally answer. "She can date whoever she wants."

"But I want her to date *you*," Jacey says. "You don't even know how perfect you are for each other." I just roll my eyes and turn back to Brand.

We watch Jacey walk off and then Brand looks at me.

"You're going to fuck him up, right?"

I know he's not talking about the candy-ass who just asked Madison out. He's talking about the little asshole giving my sister a hard time. I stare at Brand levelly over the rim of my beer bottle.

"Yep. If he comes anywhere near her."

Brand nods in satisfaction. "Fucking prick. Jacey's gotta stop dating those losers."

"I know," I agree. "She's got to stop dating so many guys, period. She needs to be more discriminating. Jesus."

Brand looks at me, his expression suddenly serious.

"You know, it might help you to be here. It's a good place for you to try and get back on your feet, to get healthy again, you know?"

A knot forms in my throat and I ignore it. I nod wordlessly as I stare out the window. I don't like talking about this shit, not even with Brand.

"I know what it's like," he reminds me. "Everyone's got demons. You and I just happen to share ours. And dude, it's not your fault. And it's not my fault. We got served a shit sandwich that night. You've got to stop blaming yourself for it. Mad Dog wouldn't want that."

"Mad Dog can't want anything," I tell him grimly. "He's dead. And if I hadn't been distracted..."

"No," Brand interrupts. "No. Just stop right there. There's no way we could've known what was going on. Not you, and not me either. You've got to deal with this and move on, Gabe. Trust me, I know."

I stare at him for a minute before I finally nod. He's got a point. It really might help me to be here. And he does know what he's talking about. When we first came back from overseas, Brand signed up for extensive PTSD therapy, while I opted out. For one thing, I think therapy's a bunch of bullshit. For another, they can't fix me like they fixed Brand. What happened wasn't his fault. It was mine.

"Fine," I agree. "I'll try to deal with this. How's your foot?"

That night...the night that we both would like to forget, has left lasting scars on the both of us in different ways. The explosion that blew apart our Humvee broke every bone in Brand's left leg and foot, basically crushing it. The doctors had to reconstruct the entire thing and now it's more steel and screws than it is bone. Brand still walks with a barely discernible limp.

"It's getting better," he answers. "Still hurts like a bitch, but you know what they say. Pain is just weakness leaving the body."

"You're a crazy summabitch," I tell him. "You know that, right?"

"Uh-uh," he answers, shaking his head. "I passed the psych test with flying colors when we discharged. I'm certifiably sane. True story."

I roll my eyes. "Nope. You just know how to act that way. True story."

Brand laughs and throws a twenty on the table as a tip for Jacey.

"Isn't that a bit much?" I raise an eyebrow. He shrugs.

"It's her birthday. And she's always broke. That girl seriously can't manage her money. She needs to get her ass back in school so that she can get a job where she makes more of it."

I shake my head at the mere thought of my sister's fickle career plans.

"If she made more money, she'd probably just spend that too. She's changed her mind a thousand times. But she'd better figure it out soon. She can't wait tables forever."

Regardless of my harsh words, I toss a tip down too. She does need the money.

Brand hesitates before he walks away. "I mean it. Take some time off."

Jacey's nowhere to be seen, so I shoot her a text, telling her that I'll see her later tonight. I take a step for the door, and then get an idea.

Taking the extra receipt lying on the table, I scribble a note and then my cell number before I fold it over and walk it to the burly guy tending bar.

"Could you give this to Madison?" I ask him. He stares at me curiously, but holds his hand out for the note.

"Sure," he answers, questioning me with his eyes.

"Thanks," I reply, handing it to him, not offering him an answer.

I leave without looking back, climbing into my Camaro.

It's not a practical car, but I always wanted one, so when I discharged from the Rangers I bought one brand-new...sort of as a consolation prize for giving up my dream job. It's a badass car, but it's not nearly good enough to make up for the life I lost.

One single night changed my life forever.

One fucking night.

And the worst part is that even though it was my fault, if we'd been better protected, Mad Dog would still be alive and Brand's leg wouldn't have been destroyed.

None of that can be changed for us now. But if we can change it for future soldiers, we'll try like hell to make it happen. All we have to do now is finish designing the product, get another investor so that we can have prototypes made and then successfully pitch it to the Pentagon.

Easy.

I light up a cigarette as I blow down the quiet highway. Everything here in Angel Bay is quiet and uneventful; barely anything happens. This really might be what I need to get my shit straight.

And it doesn't hurt anything that this is where Madison is.

I grin at the sheer fucking coincidence of it all.

And then I grin again at the note that I left for her.

We need to finish what we started.

Chapter Seven

Madison

I grit my teeth as I think about those words, color flooding my cheeks as I let Gabriel get to me once again.

We need to finish what we started.

Who the hell does he think he is? Oh my God. He's so fucking arrogant. He thinks he can completely ignore the fact that he turned into a crazy person the other night, offer me no explanation whatsoever, stroll into my restaurant and just find me waiting to fuck him?

He's crazier than I thought he was.

I look into the mirror as I put in my earrings, the diamond studs that I wear when I want to dress up. They were the last gift that my parents gave me before they died, a college graduation present.

I study myself now. My hair is pulled into a loose chignon at the nape of my neck, I'm wearing lipstick, a little black dress, and kick-ass black strappy heels. I'm the perfect picture of a date.

And hell no. I'm not going out with Gabriel. He thinks he can come in and shove someone around in my restaurant and I'll just fall at his feet in gratitude? He's crazy. The Hill already had one bully, and he's been dead for four years. We don't need another one.

The memory of Gabriel's face as he slammed Jared against the door causes my stomach to clench. He almost seemed to like it. He liked having Jared at his mercy. I squeeze my eyes closed, then open them again, refocusing.

No more thinking about Gabriel.

Ethan is making me dinner tonight and damn it, I'm going to like it. Or at least I'm going to pretend like hell that I do. I sigh and pick up my black clutch, turning the lights off and heading out to my car.

Screw it.

Other people's perceptions don't usually bother me at all, but for some reason I really hate the idea that everyone thinks I don't have a social life. I don't have a social life because I haven't met anyone who makes me want one.

It only takes ten minutes to drive across our little town and Ethan meets me as I walk up to his door. He's wearing a light-blue V-neck sweater that complements his eyes and slim black pants that complement his ass. I should be attracted to him.

So why aren't I?

"I'd thought you'd be right on the lake," I tell him as he greets me. "I'm surprised you'd live in one of these new condos."

He smiles and takes my sweater.

"I know. But my schedule's too crazy to take care of a cottage. I'm pretty much a slave to the hospital."

I stare at him, marveling once again that people put their health (and their very fragile babies) into his large and clumsy hands. I can't help but tell him that very thing.

He laughs good-naturedly. "Oh, Maddy. You've got to get to know me again. I think you're gonna be pleasantly surprised."

As we walk into his condo, I have to admit that I *am* pleasantly surprised by it. Everything is so sleek and modern; and everything is neat and clean. It's not what I was expecting, based on the guy Ethan used to be. As hard as it is for me to imagine it, maybe he really has grown up.

"This is gorgeous," I tell him as I turn around, taking it all in. "A very grown-up condo."

He chuckles. "It suits the grown-up man who lives in it."

I stare at him. "Touché. All right. I admit it. I'm going to have to try and see you in a different light, not like the boy who ate a grasshopper."

He rolls his eyes. "Seriously. Am I never going to live that down? I was ten years old! A lot changes in fifteen years, Madison."

We laugh and he sits me down on a sleek sofa while he pours me a glass of wine. "I hope you like red," he says as he hands it to me. "We're having veal so I paired it with a nice merlot."

"That's perfect," I tell him as our fingers touch. "And very grown-up. I love merlot."

He grins, then excuses himself to go check on the food. The delicious smells coming from the kitchen make my mouth water.

"It's such a surprise to find out that you can cook too," I call across the room. The condo is an open design, so I can see everything he's doing. He chuckles as he closes up the oven and then comes around the kitchen bar top with the bottle of wine.

"I'm good with my hands," he tells me suggestively as he sits next to me. "Trust me." I have to smile.

"OK. You really have changed. You weren't this flirty in high school."

Ethan stares at me, surprised. "I was too! Just not with you.

You scared the shit out of me. I wanted to ask you out for four years straight, but I was afraid you'd crush me if I ever did. You were out of my league."

I'm the surprised one now. "Out of your league? You know that everyone called you Ken, right? As in *Ken doll*...because you were so perfect?"

He's interested now, staring at me intently. "Tell me more about this," he grins.

I laugh and we chat and suddenly everything feels like old times again, just like when he used to come to my house with groups of our friends and hang out for bonfires on the beach.

The problem is, it feels just like old times. I don't feel any chemistry with him now, just like I didn't back then.

"So, what do you do for fun, Ethan?" I ask politely, sipping at my wine. He mimics the motion, sipping his.

"I don't really have time for much," he admits. "My time is pretty much all taken up by the hospital. If I'm home, then I'm sleeping or watching TV for a minute. I have very little free time."

"Yet you're spending an evening with me," I point out. Ethan grins.

"See? You should feel flattered."

I practically sigh aloud as I ignore the way he keeps edging closer to me. It's apparent that he's not having the lack-of-chemistry problem that I'm having.

To make matters worse, he's probably used to women at the clinic throwing themselves at him for the simple reason that he's a good-looking doctor. He's not used to rejection because those nurses and nurse's aides and patients...they don't care that he's boring as hell and just lives to work. All they see is the "MD" on his name tag.

They don't care that he lacks a spark. They don't care that he'd never slide his hand between their legs in a taxi. They don't care that he would never fuck their mouths with his tongue while the cab driver sneaks glances in the rearview mirror. My cheeks explode into flame.

Fuck. Why am I thinking about Gabriel again?

And worse, why do thoughts of him turn me on so freaking much?

I'm almost relieved when dinner is finally ready, when I can step away from Ethan, when I can stop pretending to be interested in what he's saying. When I can stop pretending that I'm not thinking about someone else.

Instead I can distract myself by eating. I've never been so happy to see a plate of steaming veal Marsala in my life.

"This is really good," I tell him as I take another bite. "I'm impressed."

He grins. "Good. That was my goal. I really can't make anything else."

I burst out laughing. "Really?"

He shakes his head. "No. I can. I just wanted you to laugh. You're too serious, Mad. You might look like her, but you're not the girl I remember from school."

I feel my cheeks flush with color as I reach for my wineglass. How many times have I heard that very thing since my parents died? What the hell do people expect? Mila and I were orphaned, for God's sake. We had to grow up in a hurry and that meant getting serious. I had to watch out for my sister, take over the restaurant, assume the business loan... none of those things were easy.

I don't say any of that, though, because none of it is Ethan's fault... or his business.

"Well, things changed after my parents died," I simply say.

He nods thoughtfully. "I figured that was it. My mom said that you pretty much shouldered everything yourself. You let Mila do her own thing while you came home and took over the restaurant. That was nice of you."

I shake my head. "It wasn't that big of a deal," I protest. "I majored in business so that when I got too old to model, I'd have a fallback plan. So it made sense that I should take over the Hill. Neither of us wanted to sell it and Mila would have taken it over if I'd asked her to."

"But you didn't ask her," Ethan pointed out. "You came home to run it."

"Yes," I answer. "I did. Mila never wanted anything to do with business. She's always been artsy. That was always her dream. And her dreams shouldn't die just because our parents did."

Ethan stares at me and then pours me another glass of wine. "I was at school when I heard about your parents, Maddy. I didn't really know what to do. But I am really sorry about what happened to them. And about what's happened to you because of it. I understand that you don't want Mila to give up her dreams... and I respect that. But what about your own? Running the Hill wasn't your dream. It was theirs."

"No, it wasn't," I admit grudgingly. "What's the deal, Ethan? Are you trying to make me think I should be unsatisfied?" I smile, to try to lighten the tone, but I still ask the question. Because seriously—what the hell?

Ethan immediately shakes his head.

"Of course not. You just don't seem as happy as you used to be. And I'm just trying to figure out why. I didn't mean to offend you."

"Well, things change and I'm not the girl you remember," I point out. "And you didn't offend me."

But he kind of did.

I sip at the rest of my wine and we chat for a bit more over dessert, about old times. About high school and college, and old friends that we have in common. And then out of the blue, Ethan looks at me seriously.

"I know this is probably a stupid question since you're here tonight, but are you dating anyone? I mean, seriously seeing someone?"

I'm taken aback by his question and stare at him stupidly for a second.

"Of course not," I finally manage to say. "If I was, I'm sure he wouldn't be too happy about the fact that I'm here on a date with you."

Ethan grins and seems relieved. "OK. Good. I just wasn't sure if you were considering this a date or not, or if you just thought we were catching up. I just wanted to check."

I have to laugh. "I actually thought we were just catching up, but Mila insisted it was a date. So I'm glad that's cleared up."

"Well, you look beautiful and I'm not ready to say good night," Ethan announces. "Want to go for a walk on the beach? It's not raining for the first time in days. We should take advantage of it. I can drive us there and you can leave your heels in the car."

"Good plan," I tell him. "Because there's no way in hell these heels are getting anywhere near the sand. I had to eat frozen burritos for a month for these."

He chuckles, not knowing that I eat frozen burritos anyway. As he helps me shrug into my sweater, he dips his head and inhales. "You smell fantastic."

"Thank you," I murmur. The compliment was nice, but I'm rethinking my decision to extend our date.

I can't help but wonder if there's something wrong with me because I'm still not attracted to him, even though he's Mr. Perfect now.

I climb into his BMW and he closes my door, a perfect gentleman. We're at the beach in just a couple of minutes.

As Ethan pulls into a space, I gaze out across the water.

"It seems so majestic, doesn't it?" I ask Ethan softly. "So big. It makes me feel so small."

"I don't know about that," he replies as he opens my door. "But it's definitely windy."

I roll my eyes at his lack of appreciation for the beauty around us and follow him down the narrow path to the shore. Wild grass blows on either side of the hard-packed trail. To our left the water crashes into the shore. To our right the sand dunes roll, rugged and beautiful.

"I love it here." I sigh and I grasp Ethan's arm.

I mean, it's supposed to be a date. I can touch the guy, right? The wind is chilly and his arm is warm. It's not a crime to absorb some of his heat.

I don't even let my mind wander to the guy I'd really like to be touching. And I wouldn't just be touching him to stay warm, either. The mere thought of how I'd like to touch him makes my cheeks flush yet again as in my head, Gabriel winks at me.

Why the hell is he stuck in my head?

"I like it here too," Ethan answers, bringing me back to my present company. "I thought about staying in the city to do my residency but I really just wanted to come home. It was a nice surprise to find you still here. You always seemed destined for something bigger than here, you know?"

He smiles down at me with white teeth a supermodel would be envious of. I really, really, really wish that my heart would flutter or my hormones would react. But they don't. Nothing. Nada.

Hell. I'm such a dating failure.

"Well, it was definitely hard getting used to being back here. It's so small."

Ethan laughs at that, but thankfully lets the conversation thread go. I'm grateful because his small talk is annoyingly bland.

We continue walking and chatting and I continue holding on to his arm.

He appears to be genuinely interested in all the things I tell him about the Hill, although I can't say the same for myself about his tales from the clinic. How can someone so gorgeous be so freaking boring?

"So, yeah, I was freaked out when I first gave someone a catheter. I mean, seriously. Who really wants to pick up another man's penis and insert a hose into it? Thank God that's usually the nurses' job." Ethan continues to tell me his medical tales and I continue to tune them out. Because *seriously*. I don't want to hear about him playing with another man's junk.

As I concentrate on *not* listening, a figure takes shape in the near distance, jogging toward us. Out of idle curiosity, I keep an eye on the jogger as he draws closer and closer, and then almost gasp when I finally realize who it is.

Gabriel.

No freaking way. It's like the universe is determined to keep bringing me into his path.

My mouth instantly goes dry as his stormy eyes lock on my face.
We need to finish what we started.

I feel my cheeks flush and as they do, he smirks ... like he knows exactly what I'm thinking.

He's shirtless and the muscles in his chest and abdomen flex with every movement. His dark hair is mussed and damp, so it's obvious he's been running for a while.

Sweet Mary. Why is it that an entire evening with Ethan leaves me cold but one freaking glance from this guy sets my blood on fire?

The man is built. His arms are cut, his abs are a rock-hard washboard and he's got that perfect V running down into the waistband of his shorts. I try to pretend that I don't notice, but I can tell from his smirk that he knows that I did.

I ignore it. Instead I ponder the way he seems so lean and efficient. Every movement is smooth and deliberate. And powerful. I've always heard that Special Forces turn their soldiers into trained killers. I don't know about that, but holy crap, he looks lethal.

I can't seem to look away and as he jogs past, he glances at me sideways.

He also splashes through a tiny pool of water, which splatters Ethan's pants in muddy droplets.

"Hey, dude," Ethan protests, turning to glare after Gabriel. "Watch what you're doing."

I'm surprised that Ethan would say anything at all because it was clearly an accident, but I'm equally surprised when Gabriel stops, turns and walks back to us, sweat glistening on his brow. *Hell.*

"What did you say?" he asks incredulously. Apparently he's surprised too.

Ethan seems hesitant now that he's face-to-face with Gabe.

"I said watch it," he says, quieter now. "You got mud on my pants."

"Did I now?" Gabe rolls his eyes. "I apologize. I apologize that you're a candy-ass who doesn't like to get dirty."

Ethan practically sputters as he steps toward Gabriel and I have no clue what to do.

"Whatcha gonna do, candy-ass?" Gabriel taunts him, leaning forward mockingly. "Anything?"

Gabriel raises an eyebrow, waiting, and I shake my head, disappointed that he would react like this. Disappointed, but not surprised. He did punch a hole in his wall, for God's sake, then turned around and slammed Jared into a wall. It's clear what kind of guy he is . . . someone who has a temper problem. Before I can stop myself, I speak up for Ethan.

"What the hell, Gabriel? You splashed mud on him. This is your fault, not his. Why are you being such a dick about it?"

The way he looks at me, with almost an offended expression, makes me wonder . . . is this overreaction about me? Is he annoyed that Ethan is here with me? His face closes up, though, and I decide that that can't be right.

"Come find me if you get tired of having a girl fight your battles," Gabriel tells Ethan. "And I'll be happy to buy you another pair of candy-ass pants."

He starts to walk away, then turns back around, his eyes locking on mine. His dark gaze is intense as he stares into my eyes, then at my mouth.

What's he thinking? Why the hell is he acting like what happened the other night was normal? Like any of this is normal?

It's not normal.

Doesn't he care that I helped him? I took a chance, a risk, by walking a strange man home because I just couldn't leave him there alone. And now he just wants to pretend that none of it happened.

He just keeps staring at my lips with a gaze that says, *It doesn't matter. None of that matters, Maddy.*

And for a minute it really doesn't because he's staring at my mouth like he wants to devour it and that's all I can think about.

Self-consciously, I drag my teeth across my bottom lip. In reaction, the corner of his tilts up and I get a glimpse of his white teeth, his pink tongue.

The same tongue that has licked and sucked my nipples.

My heart slams in my chest and he smiles, just slightly.

He knows what I'm thinking.

I take a breath. He takes a step.

He takes another one, dipping his head toward my ear, close enough that Ethan can't hear, close enough that his lips graze my cheek.

"Think about me, Maddy."

My heart stops. Before I can respond, he grins cockily and spins around, jogging past us without looking back.

"What a dick," Ethan mutters. "Who is that guy? What did he say to you?"

"Jacey's brother," I answer, fighting an incredible urge to look over my shoulder, to watch him jog away. "I don't know why he's still here. I think he lives in Chicago."

I *know* he lives in Chicago. But obviously I don't mention that or how I know that. And I definitely don't tell him what Gabriel said.

"Well, we can hope that he goes home soon," Ethan grumbles.

"We don't need assholes like that here. This town is too small for that. It's bad enough that we have Pax Tate."

His head snaps up as he remembers that Pax is my brother-in-law, as he realizes that he just stuck his foot in his mouth.

"God, I'm sorry. I didn't mean it like that. It's just that ever since he moved here a few years ago, we all knew to steer clear of him. We knew that if we bumped into him on a bad day, he would be a total asshole."

"What do you care?" I demand. "You were hardly ever home to bump into him. And he's not an asshole anymore."

"That's what they say," Ethan says, seemingly unconvinced. His tone, his words... everything about him right now is annoying me. He has no right to judge Pax. Not by a long shot.

And yes, Gabriel overreacted. He could've kept on jogging and pretended that he didn't hear Ethan. But Ethan didn't need to say anything in the first place. So what if he got some water splashed on his pants?

He really *is* a candy-ass.

And Gabe so clearly is *not*.

My mood toward Ethan has definitely been dampened even more than it already was and I remain quiet as he and I walk back to his car.

After he drives me back to his place, I tell him that I'm tired and that I should really head home rather than come inside for a drink. I can tell he's disappointed, but he handles it smoothly.

"That's all right, Maddy. I've been up since four a.m., so I'm wiped too. But this was fun. We should do it again soon."

There is an awkward pause as I stand next to my car.

I can tell he's contemplating kissing me and I dread the thought.

Don't, I silently instruct him. But instead of expecting him to read my mind, I solve the problem by raising myself up on my tiptoes and kissing his cheek.

"Sure," I murmur.

Ethan stares down at me as the top of my car lowers.

"I'll call you this week, OK?"

I nod and get into my car, and as I drive away, I mentally examine myself.

I hate candy-ass guys but I also hate bullies. My father was a bully. I didn't like it then and I don't like it now.

Even bullies who are sexy as hell. *Especially* bullies who are sexy as hell, because they just draw me in toward something that I need to stay far away from. Because Mila was right the other night—I do tend to pick the wrong guys. I tend to be *attracted* to the wrong guys.

Honestly, I'm starting to think that there is no one out there for me. I don't like the guys I should, and the guys I like are bad for me. Maybe I'm destined to be alone.

When I walk into my empty house, it only emphasizes that fact.

I'm alone.

I kick off my shoes, drop my purse on a table in the foyer and collapse into a chair in the living room with a bottle of wine.

Just the bottle, no glass.

I dangle my legs over the side of the chair as I think about the evening.

Thoughts of Ethan make me cringe. Besides annoying me with his judgment of Pax, Ethan just lacks something. A spark, a passion. I can't put my finger on it, but whatever it is, I doubt he's ever going to make me feel the way I want someone to make me feel.

But Gabriel does.

One smoldering look from him sends my pulse racing, bully or not.

We need to finish what we started.

Fuck. What is wrong with me? Why am I so stuck on someone I shouldn't want... but do?

All I know is Gabriel has that certain kind of confidence. The kind that turns my stomach inside out. And there's something else about him, too... something intriguing. I don't even know him, but there's something in his eyes, something dark and haunted that draws me to him.

I ponder that for a minute; ponder what he might have seen in Afghanistan that was so terrible that it scarred him inside. What turned him into a panicky mess the night of the taxi accident?

Because he doesn't seem like the kind of guy who panics.

In my head I see him jogging on the beach again, all huge and strong and disciplined. Judging by how sweaty he was, I bet he'd been jogging for miles and yet he was still going, just like a machine. He's clearly a force to be reckoned with.

Yet something has the power to bring him to his knees. It's a puzzle.

My eyes flutter closed as I picture Gabriel's rippling muscles, glistening with a light sheen of sweat. I picture him crawling up and over me, rubbing against me, his fingers stroking me.

Oh my God. My eyes snap open and my cheeks flush as I realize I just drifted into a fantasy about Gabriel. He's a guy that is made of everything that scares me.

He will hurt you.

I know that.

Yet at the same time, I know he's a guy who can turn me on in one second flat.

What the eff is wrong with me?

❧

"Madison, there is something wrong with you," Jacey sighs, shaking her head as she sifts through a rack of spring blouses. "Seriously. I know some girls who would give their left ovary to date Ethan Eldridge and you're standing here complaining that he doesn't do it for you? Let's recap, shall we? He's gorgeous, he's a doctor, and did I mention that he's a gorgeous freaking doctor?"

I roll my eyes as I pull out a pink tunic and examine it. It would look perfect with my gray skinny jeans so I drape it over my arm.

"He's a resident doctor and he *is* good-looking. But I've just known him too long. I want the butterflies…that fluttery feeling that you get when you meet someone amazing. And besides, why are you on Team Ethan so hard right now? I thought you wanted me to date your brother."

I stare pointedly at her and she doesn't even have the grace to look sheepish.

She simply stares back at me. "Because he was sort of rude yesterday, not exactly a great first impression. I just figured you wouldn't want to give him a chance."

Actually, Gabe made one hell of a first impression.

I smile as I think of him outside the club that night. He was so cocky and sexy in the alley behind the club, grabbing my wrist and pulling me to him. My heart speeds up just thinking about it.

I shouldn't like that shit…that alpha, ultra-confident bad-boy shit. But I do. I can't help it.

"He didn't make a bad first impression," I tell Jacey. "It was the second impression that sucked."

Jacey crows when she sees the expression on my face.

"I knew it! I knew you liked him. Maddy, I promise you, he's perfect for you. Just give him another chance. Puh-leeeease! It will be easy for you too. He's going to stay here with me for a while because of Jared. Big Brother Gabriel is going to fight my battles for me."

Jacey hands me a blue peasant blouse to try on. "He'll be with me for at least a couple of weeks. I'm sure he'll be into the Hill a lot to eat. He doesn't really cook."

I look up at her. "You know we have a delivery service. He won't even have to come in. We can deliver meals right to his door."

Jacey laughs. "Whatever. You know you want to see him. I can tell."

Heaven help me, I do. But I'd never admit it to her. To admit my infatuation to her would make it real. And I can't make it real or act on it because it's not good for me. At all.

So instead I just shake my head.

"I don't need to see him. And he's not into me anyway, so it's all a moot point."

That's a lie, but I figure it might shut Jacey down.

But no.

Jacey glances up at me, even more interested now.

"You don't think he's into you?" Her eyes gleam. "Because I can find out for you."

"Oh my God," I groan. "We're not in fourth grade. Leave it alone, Jace."

"Whatever," Jacey mutters. "But if you change your mind, I'll give you his number and you can call him yourself."

I can tell that she's not sure whether I'm telling the truth or not about not wanting to see her brother. And to be honest, I'm not sure either.

Because even though I know I shouldn't, I find myself thinking about him all the time. I think about his husky voice in my ear and his hand between my legs in that taxi. I think about his dark, dark gaze and how it sets my skin on fire from across the room.

But even more telling than my runaway thoughts is one interesting thing.

I haven't thrown his number away. It's neatly folded and tucked inside my purse, along with the accompanying message.

We need to finish what we started.

Chapter Eight

Gabriel

The night is so fucking black that I can't even see my hand in front of my face. I groan, try to move, then give up. I try to hear, try to see, try to move the rest of my body...but fail on all counts. The shadows move around me and I'm too weak to care. I don't feel anything and I think that's odd. I should be in fucking pain and for a second I'm panicked that I'm paralyzed.

I calm down when I realize I'm probably just in shock. I groan again, trying to get up, but I realize it's not happening.

And then I smell it.

Blood.

Brand and Mad Dog are out there and I've got to see if they're alive. The smell of blood is strong in the breeze, as well as burning metal, hissing gas and dust. Fuck. It takes me a minute, but I finally manage to flip onto my belly and drag myself by my elbows.

I'm definitely not paralyzed and fuck, the pain has arrived. My head is screaming, but I've got to find my friends.

Inch by painful inch, I pull myself through the carnage-riddled dust. A twisted piece of our Humvee is lodged in the ground to my left, and I can smell melting rubber as a tire burns to my right.

And then, through the smoke, I see a face on the side of the road, bloody and mud-spattered. My heart hammers as I try like hell to get to it, to see if it's Brand or Mad Dog...until I arrive and find that it's neither.

The girl's eyes are wide and open. And lifeless.

She stares at me, blaming me.

I remember everything and the memories slam into me like a freight train.

It's all my fault.

The pain in my head intensifies, like a million shards of glass, and everything fades to black.

I wake up in a cold sweat, my sheets drenched with my terror, my throat bone dry.

I lie still for a minute, sucking in coarse breaths of air as I try to force myself to calm down. The dream is so fucking real, though, as if every memory from that night is permanently imprinted in my mind. Which, of course, it is. I'm never going to be free of it.

I reach for a glass of water to soothe my parched throat, only to find that I don't have a nightstand here. I'd forgotten.

I pull myself into a sitting position, running a hand through my hair, before I get out of bed and make my way to the kitchen in the dark. I'm still unnerved by my fucking dream, and even the shadows cast in this dark and familiar kitchen make me uneasy. The luminescent microwave clock tells me that it's five thirty a.m. The sun should be coming up soon.

I grab a bottle of water and slump into a chair at the kitchen table, gazing absently outside. Jacey's car isn't in the driveway, which means she didn't come home last night. That's a fact that pisses me off.

Yes, she's an adult. Yes, normally she could stay over at her boy-friend's without a problem. But shit. I'm here so that she feels safe. If she doesn't even bother to come home, there's no sense in me being here.

I drink the water, then drink one more bottle. My mouth is still dry when I'm finished. The night terrors always affect me in a very physical way…headaches, sweat, shortness of breath. It's like I'm actually back in Afghanistan, actually reliving that night over and over. It's a pain in the ass.

I toss the bottles into the recycling bin and head to the bath-room. I know there's no way I'm going back to sleep now. I turn the water on and I'm waiting for it to heat up when I hear the back door quietly open.

Jacey.

I fling open the bathroom door and storm down the hallway to find her creeping quietly through the kitchen.

"Welcome home," I say grimly as I flip on the light. She blinks in the brightness, then grins at me.

"Hey, big brother," she says, as she trips on a rug. "I didn't mean to wake you up."

She's obviously drunk.

"You do realize that you're supposed to be at work in a few hours," I point out. She doesn't seem concerned.

"I'll be fine," she slurs. "Don't worry about it, I'm a big girl. What's your problem?"

"My problem would be lost on you at this particular moment," I tell her. "But trust me, we'll be talking about it later. If you ever drive home drunk again, you won't need Jared to manhandle you. I'll kick your little ass myself. Go sleep it off. We'll talk when you're coherent."

"Whatever," she mutters as she wobbles down the hall. "Shows how much you know. Jared's still messing with me. He's been texting me all night. Said he's going to teach you a lesson." She kicks off one of her heels, then throws the other down the hallway in frustration.

"Don't trip on my shoe," she calls helpfully over her shoulder.

I shake my head as I follow her, stooping to pick up the offending shoe. I toss it into her bedroom as I head to the shower, stewing the entire time over my sister's dumbass ex-boyfriend and her irresponsibility. If he's been texting her all night, why the fuck didn't she call and tell me?

But there's no use trying to talk about it with her right now. It won't do any good because she wouldn't remember the conversation in the morning. I grit my teeth and try to find things to distract myself with. I clean my boots, rig the bug bombs for the spiders in the basement, and clean out my car.

Unfortunately, though, four hours later I find myself insanely restless. Jacey is still snoring in her room, although I know she'll have to get up soon if she's going to make it to work by eleven.

I've answered some work e-mails, touched base with Brand on the phone and gone for a thirty-minute run on the beach.

Luckily, this time I didn't run into the candy-ass that Madison was with last night. For the life of me, I can't figure out what she sees in someone like that. She actually took his side when he bitched at me for getting his fucking pants wet.

There's no logical reason that I can think of that she would prefer that guy over me.

I pointedly ignore the one thing that it might be...the thing that I'm hoping like hell it's not. She might be totally turned off by me because of what she saw that night in Chicago. She might have seen too much and now she thinks I'm crazy. Or a pussy.

Neither of those things is good but the problem is I have no idea what she's thinking. She wants me. I can tell. But she's icy as hell too.

I shake my head.

I'm gonna have to stop trying to figure women out, because they make no fucking sense. I'm definitely not going to sit here stewing over it, but I have nothing left to do. So I do the only thing that makes sense to me.

I head out to find a gym. Lifting weights always burns restless energy. Besides, I can't stop working out just because I'm no longer in the army.

It doesn't take me long to find the gym since Angel Bay only has one. That actually doesn't surprise me in a town this small. In fact, I'm surprised that it has one at all.

I'm signed up as a member and headed back to the weight room within a few minutes. This gym is old-school, nothing fancy. The walls are white and covered with inspirational posters.

NO PAIN, NO GAIN.

YOU MISS 100% OF THE SHOTS YOU DON'T TAKE.

CLEAR YOUR MIND OF "CAN'T."

THE ONLY WAY TO FINISH IS TO START.

All true, all cliché.

But whatever. Cliché or not, this is the kind of place I like. There's no coffee bar, lounge area or girls dressed to the nines. This is a gym meant for people to work out in. Those fancy places in the city make me want to punch a hole in the wall. I don't go to the gym to pick women up. I go to work out.

I do fifty curls with the twenty-pound weight before switching to the other arm. As I breathe out through my mouth, slowly and evenly, I notice Madison's brother-in-law across the room on the hip sled. Seeing someone familiar shouldn't surprise me since this town is so fucking small. I can't go anywhere without bumping into someone.

He catches my gaze and after a few minutes makes his way over to me, holding out a sweaty hand.

"I'm Pax Tate. My wife Mila introduced herself to you the other night. I'm not as social as she is, so I didn't interrupt your dinner." The way he's grinning, it's clear Madison's sister has this guy wrapped around her finger.

I chuckle at the memory. "It was no problem. I get the feeling that Angel Bay doesn't get many new people. She was curious. And thanks for stepping up with Jared. I didn't get a chance to say anything to you that night."

Pax rolls his eyes. "Mila thought you might need some backup. I was pretty sure you had it under control. And yeah, she's curious. More about you and her sister, but whatever. Women." He rolls his eyes again. "I could use a spotter for the bench. You got a second?"

"Sure." I get up and follow him to the bench, waiting until he is situated on his back before lifting the three-hundred-pound-laden bar off the rungs and handing it to him.

"Why is Mila fascinated with Madison and me?" I ask as I count his reps. He's strong and in shape. He does fifteen with no problem before setting the bar back into the holder.

"Because Maddy doesn't date. You're the first person she's shown any interest in for a long time. And trust me, Mila is fascinated with that."

"By 'showing interest,' do you mean that she absolutely refused to even look at me the other day in the restaurant? Until she bitched at me for being too rough with Jared, that is."

Pax looks at me as we switch places and he hands me the bar. As I bench the weight, I explain how we met and how she definitely didn't want anyone to hear about it at the Hill, especially her sister. He bursts out laughing.

"That does sound like Madison. She wouldn't want to give Mila any ammunition. Was she mad that you dared to show up at her restaurant or what?"

I nod, hooking the bar into the rungs again, then pausing to catch my breath. "Apparently."

"Typical Madison," Pax chuckles. "But deep down she's sweet, once you get past her outer bitchiness. I heard her bitch at you for the Jared thing. I probably shouldn't say anything, but she's got hangups with that shit so don't take it personally. Mila and Madison's dad used to knock their mom around so she's got a thing about any kind of violence at all."

I stare at him for a minute, thinking back to the other night at the Hill when she told Jacey that her dad had a temper like Jared's.

"Shit," I mutter aloud. "Seriously?"

Pax nods. "Seriously."

I think of Madison, of how she's so confident and strong, and I can't picture her involved in an abusive relationship of any sort.

"Did their dad hit them, or just their mom?"

Pax shakes his head as we switch places so he can do his second set. "He never laid a hand on Mila. But I can't say for sure about Maddy. It's not exactly something we sit down and talk about."

Pax stops talking as he runs out of breath while he's benching. I let this conversation go. It's not my business and I can see that he's not that comfortable talking about it anyway.

When we switch places for my second set, Pax changes the subject.

"So are you sticking around for a while? What do you do?"

I explain my situation, why I'm here and the fledgling company I co-own. Pax seems particularly interested in DefenseTech.

"Advanced body armor? That's badass...makes me think of Batman. You know, my family's company is looking to diversify and invest in something new. This honestly sounds like something I might be interested in. I've got a tight schedule this week, but let's hook up and talk next week."

I'm beyond surprised that an opportunity like this would fall into my lap, but I try not to act like it. When I tell Brand, he's going to shit. I keep my face calm.

"Sure, that sounds great. I'll give you a call later in the week to set it up."

Pax nods. "Remind me to give you my card before you go."

We switch places and I do my second set.

"What exactly was going on the other night with Jared? I forgot to ask. He's an asshat, by the way."

"I agree," I tell him. "Apparently he's been giving my little sister a hard time because she broke up with him. After the other night, I figured I'd scared him into leaving her alone. But Jacey told me this morning that he was harassing her all night last night."

Pax thinks about that for a minute, almost hesitantly.

"He's probably too stupid to be scared, to be honest. He's got more attitude than brains. I know that for a fact. I stomped him into the ground when he went after Mila, but he wouldn't stay down. I think it's his pride, to be honest. If someone attacks his pride, he gets crazy. And in his eyes, your sister attacked his pride by breaking up with him. And then you embarrassed him at the Hill."

I nod. I'm sure he's right.

Pax continues. "So in all honesty, you might want to watch your back. He's an unbalanced dumbass. But he's a *predictable* unbalanced dumbass. He goes to the Bear's Den downtown every day for lunch—and then he hangs out there pretty much every night. I don't suppose you're in the mood for a hamburger, are you?"

I stare at him in surprise at the abrupt change of topic. "Uh, I guess. I could always eat a burger."

Pax grins. "Good. Because the Bear's Den makes the best burgers in town."

I grin back, handing the bar to him.

"Oh. In that case, I'm starving."

We hit the showers and as we're getting dressed, I say, "So I heard you broke Jared's hand that night."

Pax grins. "I should've broken both of them," he says, yanking a gray T-shirt down over his heavily muscled torso. "That prick seriously needs to learn a lesson."

"Agreed," I tell him as I grab my bag. I follow him out to his car, a mint-condition 1968 black Dodge Charger.

"Sweet car," I tell him in appreciation. "I have a new Camaro, but I tell ya, I've always loved these classics."

Pax looks up and grins proudly. "Thanks. I've had it for years. It takes a lot of maintenance and breaks down more often than it runs, but I fucking love these pipes. Get in. I'll drive."

The Bear's Den is almost close enough to walk to, but it's a hell of a lot more fun in the Charger. Pax revs the engine as we drive downtown, turning the heads of people on the sidewalk. He doesn't even look at them as he pulls into a parking spot and we head into the darkened bar. I glance around, but don't spot anyone vaguely familiar.

"He's not here yet," Pax confirms. "But let's order our food and wait. Trust me, he'll be here. That fucking loser practically lives here."

We each order a burger and a beer, sitting down in a back booth. I watch the door as we talk. Pax asks me questions about being a Ranger and I answer them as best I can.

"It was something I always knew I wanted to do," I tell him. "From the time I was a kid."

"Then why did you retire so young?" Pax asks curiously.

It's a question that I ought to be used to because everyone asks it. I ought to have a canned answer ready, but I don't. So each time someone asks, it hits me in the gut and I flounder for a second, trying to decide what to say.

"People don't realize what it's really like over there," I tell him. "It's fucking brutal. I can handle brutal, but one night, shit got really fucking real and a good friend died in the process. Brand and I came out of it alive, but it totally messed us up."

"Dude." Pax looks at me seriously and somewhat uncomfortably. "I'm sorry. I didn't know. I respect the hell out of what you did as a Ranger. I know you probably don't want to talk about it and

God knows I hate to talk about shit, but I'm always up for a beer if you want one."

I smile and gulp my beer. "Thanks. I hate to talk about shit too. I mean, what the hell's the point? People can't understand when they haven't lived through something like that."

Pax stares at me again, then looks down at his hand. He's got a jagged scar on his thumb in the shape of an X and I stare at it too, wondering about its significance.

"You'd be surprised at what people understand."

He takes another swig of his beer, then looks at the door in satisfaction.

"Look who just walked in."

I glance up to find Jared swaggering into the bar. His clothes are sweaty and dirty and it's obvious that he's on his lunch break.

He orders, then makes his way to the bathroom, presumably to wash up. Pax jerks his head in that direction as he gets up.

"I'll watch the door," he says quietly. "Unless you need me?"

I chuckle. "No, I've got it."

I follow Pax to the bathroom. When we get there, he stands to the side and lets me pass. The bartender meets my gaze for just a moment, but then looks away. He's not going to interfere.

An almost euphoric feeling comes over me as I enter the bathroom and look around. The rush of adrenaline pulsing through me right now is an old welcome friend. I haven't felt like this since I left the Rangers.

I wait patiently behind him while the dumbass uses the urinal and then washes his hands. When he turns around at the sink, I bury my fingers in his neck and slam him hard against the bathroom stall.

"What the fuck?" he manages to say, his face registering surprise. And fear. Good, because he *should* fear me.

At his words I clench my hand tighter into his trachea, hard enough that he can no longer speak, hard enough that I can feel the cartilage rings in his windpipe. He struggles to swallow against the pads of my fingers and I smile.

"Quit talking," I tell him. "And listen. I thought I told you to leave my sister alone. If you keep harassing her, I *will* fuck you up. If I see you lurking around her house, parked on our street or anywhere within a mile radius of her, I will rip your spine out and feed it to you, bone by bone. You must be too stupid to understand English, because I already told you once. This is twice. I won't tell you a third time. I don't like dumbasses. I especially don't like dumbasses who fuck with my sister."

I jerk my knee up into his gut and he grunts, his eyes shooting daggers at me.

"I'm not fucking around. Leave her alone. Got it?"

He nods and I release him. He immediately rubs at his neck and glares at me again.

"Your sister is a lying whore," he snarls. "I haven't seen her since the other night."

Without missing a beat, I slam his face into the lip of the sink. As I yank him back up by the hair, his mouth gushes stringy red saliva.

"You're a fucking prick," he rasps, spitting out a bloody tooth.

I nod. "I know. But I warned you what would happen if you called my sister a whore again. Leave her the fuck alone. This is the last time I tell you."

I turn to leave, and Jared lunges at me from behind. I easily grab his arm and throw him over my head and into the wall. He slides to the ground, heaving as he glares up at me.

"Don't fuck with me again," I tell him. "And don't fuck with Jacey."

"Fuck you," he mutters, but I ignore it.

I walk out and leave him on the bathroom floor.

Pax looks at me. "Taken care of?"

I nod. "For now. If he tries anything else, I'll fuck him up for real. He might be a slow learner, but he's gotta learn sometime."

Pax shakes his head. "What a dumbass. Did he come at you? I heard the crash."

"Yep. From behind."

Pax shakes his head again.

"Fucking pussy," he mutters. "He's a waste of oxygen."

He focuses on his phone, then looks at me. "Mila just texted me. Her art shop is just down the street. She locked her keys in her car. Do you mind if we stop there on the way back to your car?"

"Of course not," I tell him. We toss some bills down to cover our lunches and walk back out into the sunshine. Mila's shop is literally fifty paces from the Bear's Den and her face lights up when we walk in and she sees her husband.

She's standing on a stepladder wearing a paint smock, hanging a painting on a thin steel cord. Pax immediately grumbles and heads for her, holding her legs to steady her.

"Mila, for fuck's sake. Get the hell off the ladder. You're going to break your neck."

She just smiles and shakes her head as she climbs down, ignoring his extended hand.

"Pax. Seriously. I'm pregnant, not sick or crippled. It's OK." She turns to me, rolling her eyes good-naturedly. "Well, well. Gabriel. It's so nice to see you again." She looks from Pax to me curiously. "This is strange. Why are you two together?"

Pax grins. "What? Am I so unlikable that I can't make friends?"

Mila laughs. "You're not unlikable. You're overprotective. And of course you can make friends. You're charming. You just don't realize it."

He waggles his eyebrows. "Oh, I realize it, baby."

Mila giggles and turns to me. "Thank you, guys, for coming to unlock my car. I have pregnancy brain. I'm so forgetful. No one told me that it would affect my memory too."

It's Pax's turn to roll his eyes.

"Babe, let's just face it. Your memory was never good. You can blame heartburn on the baby, gas on the baby, weight gain on the baby... but you really can't blame your bad memory on the poor thing."

Mila blushes and slaps at his arm. "Pax, seriously. I don't have gas. I'm a delicate flower."

He rolls his eyes again. "Whatever you say, sweet. You fart with the best of 'em in your sleep. Just sayin'."

"Oh my God." Mila blushes darker. "I'm going to pretend you didn't just say that in front of someone." She turns to me again. "Just keep in mind that I'm pregnant, Gabe. It does horrible things to the body." She grins charmingly. "What brings you back to Angel Bay? I thought you lived in Chicago."

I decide that small-town people have no compunction whatsoever about asking nosy questions and that I shouldn't be annoyed. It would be impossible to be annoyed with Mila Tate anyway. She's as genuine a person as I've ever met.

"No, I'm here to stay for a while. Jacey's having a problem with an ex-boyfriend and I'm here as her security detail."

"Yeah, babe. Jared Markson is still fucking with them, even after that scene at the Hill the other night. I told Gabriel how you aren't a fan of the guy either," Pax says as he wraps an arm around his wife. "And I told him why."

Mila raises an eyebrow. "So you told him that you broke Jared's hand?"

Pax grins smugly. "Yep. And how I wish I'd broken them both."

"That might have made things easier," I answer wryly. "But whatever. I'll take care of it. He'll wish he hadn't messed with Jacey, I can promise you that."

"Well, just be careful," Mila cautions me, her face concerned. "He used to be a pretty decent guy, back in high school. But he's got a problem with alcohol and it makes him mean. He's not worth you getting hurt or into trouble. Trust me on that."

I smile at her. "Don't worry. I won't get hurt. And I won't get caught."

Pax grins at me. "That's what I'm talking about. If you need help, let me know. I'm still holding a grudge."

While Mila asks us to not personally get involved with Jared, to call the police instead, the bells over the shop door jingle and we all turn to find Madison walking in.

She looks drop-dead gorgeous in a slim skirt that hugs her swaying hips, and knee-high tan boots.

She's smoking hot. And surprised as hell to find me here. She's got that deer-caught-in-the-headlights look and I have to chuckle at it.

"Hey, Madison," I can't help but say. "It's so nice to see you."

I'm taunting her and she knows it. I can see her face freeze up, then relax as she consciously makes the effort to hide her surprise. It's an effort that amuses me.

"It's so nice to see you too," she tells me as she strolls through the shop toward us. "Are you an art collector? Or an artist? My sister sells art *and* art supplies, so either way, you're in the right place."

"Oh, I'm just out for lunch with Pax," I tell her. "And Mila locked her keys in her car, so Pax came to save the day."

Madison glances at Mila. "Pregnancy brain?"

Pax rolls his eyes at me. "It's a conspiracy. There's no such thing."

I chuckle as Mila protests, but she abruptly stops and sniffs at the air.

"Something smells good." She continues to sniff toward Madison.

Madison shakes her head and hands Mila a bag. "You've seriously got the nose of a bloodhound now. It's soup. Tony said to eat it all or he will come over here and spoon-feed it to you. He said it doesn't matter if your morning sickness is back or not, you've still got to eat. And he's right."

Mila takes it and glances at me. "Tony is the bartender at the Hill. He's been with us forever and he's a little protective of my sister and me."

"You could say that," Pax says under his breath. To me he says, "He threatened to break my kneecaps if I ever mistreated Mila."

I smile because Tony seems like my kind of guy.

"I'm sorry," I tell Mila. "I've gotta respect that, though."

Mila rolls her eyes. "Men." But she obediently pulls out the Styrofoam container of soup and sniffs at it. "Eating this will be such a hardship." She grins and spoons some into her mouth. "Very hard."

Mila continues eating while Pax goes outside to unlock her SUV. While he does, I can't help but stare at Madison discreetly.

I've never seen such a beautiful woman in person before. She seems like she stepped right out of the pages of a magazine. I can't tell if she knows how gorgeous she is. Most women know and use it to their every advantage. But Madison doesn't seem to play that card. She seems to rely on her prickly personality instead.

Unfortunately she notices my covert gaze and the corner of her mouth turns up.

"See something you like?" she asks quietly. I grin back.

"I was just noticing the difference between you and your sister. You don't look a lot alike. Mila's small and dark, and you're tall and pale."

When Madison's cheeks flush, I realize that I could've used more tact. She might be self-conscious about the fact that she's bigger than her sister. Women are weird about that shit. But honestly, she's taller. She's willowy, like a model.

"No offense," I tell her. "It was just an observation."

"None taken," she lies. I know it's a lie by the way her cheeks are still stained pink. In fact, the flush has spread down to her chest.

I'm saved by the bells on the door, though, as Pax returns, tossing Mila's keys to her.

"All fixed," he tells her. "Good thing I have an extra key. You're good to go, pregnant brain."

She shakes her head, but thanks him. "There is one more thing before you go," she mentions. "Could you move some boxes for me in the back? Supplies came this morning."

Pax stares at her in surprise. "Good lord. Have all of my lectures finally paid off? Thank you for not trying to move them yourself, for once."

Mila smiles gently, but as they walk away she turns and mouths *Overprotective* as she points to Pax's back. Madison grins.

"He *is* overprotective," she tells me as the other two disappear into a back room. "But it's sweet. I never thought Pax had it in him when I first met him. He's like a different person. He had sort of a shitty childhood, but he's going to be a great dad. Speaking of him, though, I didn't realize that you were friends."

"We ran into each other at the gym this morning. And then we had a little run-in with Jared over lunch. Pax had my back again, which I appreciate. He's a stand-up guy," I answer. "I should've asked him if he served. He seems like that kind of guy."

Madison practically chokes. "Served? As in the *military*? Um, no. Pax used to be kind of messed up. The military wasn't something that would have appealed to him."

I eye her. "Messed up?"

Madison stares at me, her blue eyes very dark and instantly troubled.

"Yeah. When he was seven, his mom was killed in front of him. It messed him up pretty bad. For years he couldn't even remember exactly what happened. That's how bad it was. I thought he was beyond saving, but Mila didn't give up. She sees the good in people better than I do. And she was right. Pax came through it just fine. Eventually."

I stare at her in horror. His own mother was killed in front of him? I thought *I'd* seen some shit.

"Damn," I answer. "That's terrible. That scar on his hand... was that part of it?"

Madison nods. "Yeah." She suddenly looks uncomfortable. "I'm sorry. This is his story to tell. I don't feel like I should talk about it."

I nod slowly. "That's fine. He might share it himself sometime over a beer."

Madison actually looks guilty as she curls into a red chair. "He might, and if he does, good for him. He got counseling last year when all of his memories came to light. But I'm a big believer that you can't talk things out too much. The more the better."

I cringe at that as I take the chair next to her, because I strongly disagree. I don't see the point in talking about shit. People can't fix what happened to you.

"Let's change the subject," I suggest. "How's your boyfriend? Did he get his candy-ass pants cleaned?"

She stares at me solemnly, but the corner of her lip is twitching again, making me wonder why. Is she glad I asked about that guy? Is this a game of cat and mouse?

"What makes you think Ethan is my boyfriend?" she counters, a question with a question. Classic deflection.

Now it's my lip that's twitching, but not from amusement. I hate games.

"Well, the two of you seemed pretty cozy the other night. I felt bad about jogging right through the middle of your date," I finally answer.

She stares into my eyes and I see the blatant question there.

Do you want to play?

I stare back with an answer.

Yes.

Madison leans back in her chair, her eyes pointedly on my face, the air charged around us. The attraction between us is potent, yet we're sitting here talking about her date with another guy.

We're definitely playing now. Only right now I'm not sure who is the cat and who is the mouse.

"Oh, don't feel bad," she says smoothly. "Ethan and I are very old friends. It wasn't a bother at all. Until you stopped and pushed him around, that is."

I snort. "Your candy-ass boyfriend started it. And I didn't lay one finger on him. If I wanted to push him around, you'd both know it."

Madison doesn't react to that, her face is a perfect expressionless mask.

"Were you dating Ethan when we met at the club?" I ask curiously. Madison doesn't seem like the type to cheat, but then what the hell do I know? My training is in military tactics. I honestly don't know shit about the inner workings of the female mind.

She flushes again, probably thinking back to that night and how she was so very willing to go home with me.

Thinking about it actually stirs my dick to life and I shift in my seat, picturing the way her nipple tasted in my mouth and how her soft lips felt against mine. The simple thought makes me hard and I shift my hand so that it's covering my telltale crotch.

"Of course not," Madison answers quickly, her slender hand fluttering up to push her hair behind her ear. "I wouldn't do that."

"I didn't think so," I tell her. "I just thought I'd ask."

"Why? Looking out for Ethan's best interests?" she asks me sharply. I stare down at her, my eyes frozen on hers... unwavering.

"No... my own. You aren't really into Ethan. You're into me."

I drop my hand now, until it rests softly on the edge of her knee, my knuckles barely grazing her thigh.

I am sure that she wants me, although I'm not sure exactly why.

It was there the other night even when she was with Ethan. It's in her eyes, in the way she finds me wherever I'm at in the room. It's crackling in the air between us.

She wants me. And I want her.

Fucking her would be like harnessing a raging summer storm. And some weird part of me wants to make up for melting down on her that first night, to prove that I'm not a weak-ass pussy.

There is a pregnant pause before Madison bursts out laughing, not exactly the response I had been expecting.

"You're pretty sure of yourself, aren't you?" she answers.

"Always." I dismiss her words. "But you know it's true. You're into me and you have been since you met me. We'd be able to get someplace if you'd just admit it."

"And what place, exactly, are we trying to get to?" She laughs again, but there is something in her eyes that tells me I'm right. Something about the way she turns her body toward me, in the way her hands can't be still when she's talking to me. She's on edge around me.

Yet she still leaves my hand on her thigh. The heat from her radiates into my palm and I itch to move it upward.

But I don't. I leave it still as I stare into her eyes.

I want her to ask me for it. Eventually she will say my name and ask me to fuck her.

It's all part of the game.

She grows serious now, turning to face me head on in her seat.

"What I will admit is that ever since that first night, I've been curious about something."

"Oh?" I raise an eyebrow, ignoring my trepidation, ignoring the way my heart starts to pound. This is it. I'm going to see what she knows. What she *saw*. And from the unsettled look on her face, it wasn't good.

Madison actually looks nervous, but she lifts her chin and looks me in the eye anyway.

"It's been driving me crazy trying to figure it out because everything I've seen of you since then doesn't match. You totally lost your shit, Gabriel. What happened?"

Fuck. *You totally lost your shit, Gabriel.*

I yank my hand away and try to pretend that I'm normal. That it was no big deal. It sucks the air out of me because I hate that she saw it. It makes me feel weak. That's something I'm not. And it *is* a big deal.

She's waiting for an answer, her stare unwavering.

Do you want to play? Yes or no?

I shake my head. *I only like to play when I have the upper hand.*

So I try to deflect by being vague.

"It's a long story. Let's just say that everyone has demons and I haven't shown mine who's boss yet."

Madison stares at me for a moment more and then she speaks. Her tone is soft now, sympathetic almost. It makes me cringe. I don't want her fucking sympathy.

Jesus.

"Well, that's not really the explanation I was hoping for, but whatever. Maybe someday you'll tell me. And if there's one thing I learned from Pax, it's that everyone has demons. I have no doubt that you can whip your demon's ass."

She smiles another sympathetic smile and I can't take it anymore. I hate that she thinks I need her pity. So I do what I do best. I deflect by being an ass.

"I'm glad that you're so understanding," I tell her. "Maybe you'll give me a second chance."

She raises a slender eyebrow. "A second chance? For what?"

I grin. "To show you my bedroom."

My cocky words don't have the effect I thought they would.

Sexual tension flares between us like a live wire and Madison laughs again, a genuine and sexy laugh.

Leaning up toward me, she lays a hand on *my* thigh, moving her fingers ever so slightly upward as she murmurs into my ear.

"I've already seen your bedroom. How do you think you got home that night?"

Fuck. I can't breathe as I stare into her blue eyes.

"Did I hurt you?" I ask quickly, before I can think about what I'm saying. All I can think about is the hole I found in my hallway the next morning.

Maddy's head snaps up, her blue eyes widening.

"No, of course not," she answers in surprise. "You were just out of it. You seemed to have a little issue with your wall. It offended you somehow and you punched the crap out of it. But you didn't lay a finger on me. Why?"

I relax, my shoulders settling back to where they should be. *Thank God.*

"I didn't mean that like it sounded." I attempt to cover. "I meant in the taxi, when I dropped down on top of you..."

My fumbling attempts are interrupted by Mila and Pax's return.

Thank you, God.

Madison smiles up at her sister and almost imperceptibly moves away from me.

The moment between us is over but I have more questions than I know what to do with. Did she put me to bed? What did I say to her? This whole time I've tried to pretend it doesn't matter. I've tried to tell *myself* that it doesn't matter.

But it does.

What did I do?

I don't fucking know.

She looks at me, amusement in her eyes. She likes that I'm puzzled. She likes thinking she has the upper hand. *She likes playing this game.*

Whatever she witnessed that night, she thinks it gives her an edge. She thinks she's the cat in this conversation.

Fuck that.

I turn to Pax. "Hey, dude. You about ready? I've got a date tonight. I should get going."

I turn to smirk at Madison, but the look on her face deflates me. For just a second, before she closes up again, she looks crushed and I fucking hate that I did that. I only meant to take the upper hand again. I didn't mean to actually hurt her.

Before I can add that my date is with my friend Brand, Madison gets up and turns her back on me in dismissal as she makes a pointed effort of asking Mila about a piece of art on the wall.

I sigh as I follow Pax to the door.

Sometimes being the cat isn't as fun as it should be.

Chapter Nine

Madison

Oh my God. What. A. Fucking. Prick.

My thoughts form in time with my feet as they pound against the packed sand of the beach. I tossed and turned all night because of that egotistical asshole and here I am out running at seven a.m. This is so unlike me. I don't go running. I don't feel the need to burn off nervous or frustrated energy.

I don't.

Yet here I am. Because I can't get that cocky grin out of my head or the way he so casually told me that I was into him, then turned around and mentioned that he had a date. As if I care who he dates or who he fucks.

And he was so surprised that I walked him home. How the hell did he think he got home? Does he truly not remember it at all? Is that why he hasn't mentioned it?

If that's the case, what in the hell is wrong with him?

Did I hurt you?

What a strange thing to ask. His rushed explanation didn't hold water because we hadn't been talking about the taxi crash at all. We were talking about me being in his bedroom.

Did I hurt you?

Did I hurt you?

I can't get his question, sudden and anxious, out of my head.

My feet fall hard, one after the other, as I slam them into the ground. The crisp spring air stings my throat as I suck it into my lungs, trying to breathe, but at the same time enjoying the discomfort. It distracts me from the pissed-off feelings coursing through me. I hate feeling affected like this. I hate that he affected me like this.

Because I do care who he dates. And who he fucks. I don't know why; all I know is that I do.

Effffff.

The sun is beautiful at this time of day and regardless of my pissed-off state, I can't help but appreciate it. The lake is calm this morning, tranquil and silent. There isn't even a breeze to stir the grass on the dunes above me. It's like God is giving me a break, letting me get my thoughts together.

The problem is, I can't make sense of my thoughts. I can't make sense of why I'm attracted to a guy who has an ego bigger than the state of Michigan and who clearly has two tons of personal baggage.

Everyone has baggage, though, my inner voice tells me. *Even you.*

Screw that. My baggage doesn't come close to his. My parents died. End of story. Well, maybe I have a few trust issues because of their relationship. But who wouldn't in my shoes? Well, maybe not Mila. But that's just because she didn't see as much as I did. I shielded her from it.

Seriously. It's no wonder that I suck at relationships.

But my issues are nowhere near the level of Gabriel's. I don't know exactly what he's dealing with, but it's far worse than anything I've known. I can see it in his eyes. And of course there was that question. *Did I hurt you?*

My phone buzzes, interrupting my thoughts, and I reach into the pocket of my hoodie, stooping over to breathe as I read it.

I have a free morning. Want to get breakfast?

Ethan.

I feel a stab of guilt. I've ignored a few of his texts this week or just barely responded. I can't keep ignoring them; it's rude and he doesn't deserve that. At the very least I should tell him in person that we can't date. Or maybe I'm wrong about the whole thing. Maybe I should try going out with him one more time.

Sure. I'm jogging, let me change my clothes and take a quick shower, I answer. It takes him two seconds to reply.

Perfect. I'll pick you up in 30.

I jog home and quickly shower and dress. Ethan picks me up in thirty minutes on the dot. He looks like a model in *GQ* magazine this morning, wearing khaki shorts, a button-up and a hundred-watt grin.

"Morning, gorgeous," he greets me when I open the door. "I was thinking we could go to that little café on the beach in Oval Cove. Sound good?"

"That actually does," I admit as I grab my purse. "I haven't been there in forever."

"I'll have to stop and get gas first," Ethan says as we walk to his car. "But then we're outta here."

I have to smile. Yes, he's vanilla. He's bland. He's even boring. But I know him. And he knows me. There's definitely comfort in familiarity.

And he'd never play dumbass games that would hurt me on purpose. I know that.

Maybe I shouldn't dismiss him so quickly.

We chat as Ethan drives down the road to a gas station. Bland, yet safe conversation. *How many babies have you delivered this week? Four? That's incredible. I still can't get over the fact that you're a doctor.* He laughs and I laugh and there is absolutely no chemistry.

But I'm not giving up yet.

Maybe we could be one of those couples who grow into love. And who cares about the chemistry? There are people out there in arranged marriages. They've got it way worse than this.

As Ethan pulls into the gas station, I'm distracted by wondering if arranged marriages are still actually a thing.

And then I'm distracted by my bladder, which is apparently as small as a peanut. Using a gas station bathroom is disgusting, but a girl's gotta do what a girl's gotta do. I find it surprisingly clean, though. Thank God. I still wag my butt above the toilet, refusing to touch the seat, just in case.

As I make my way back outside, I pause at the doors, staring through the glass.

Jared Markson is at the pump next to Ethan's, filling up his work truck. *Ugh.* After the other night, he's the last person I want to see.

I stare at the bulldog set of his jaw, at the way he almost seems dirty even before his workday has begun, and I shake my head. I can't imagine what Jacey ever saw in that guy. He was a jerk even back in high school. Some things never change.

With a sigh I glance over at Ethan. Oblivious to Jared, he's filling up his BMW, talking on his phone and glancing at his watch.

Some things definitely don't change.

Ethan is perfunctory and efficient. Perfect for a doctor, but probably not the best qualities in bed.

I remember Gabriel slipping his fingers into me and then licking them. Holy shit. My cheeks ignite. *Where did that come from?*

I shake the thoughts from my head and push open the door, walking toward Ethan's car, but of course Jared catches sight of me and turns. His top lip is split and scabbed over, but that doesn't stop it from spreading into a leer and exposing chew-stained teeth, one of which is missing.

Gross.

"Madison," he calls. "You can tell your slut of a friend to stop lying about me."

What the hell? I can't imagine what he's talking about but I would rather die than ask. I continue walking, trying to ignore him.

"Mad-dddyyy," he calls mockingly.

He steps around the concrete island and approaches me. Ethan looks up now, distracted from his phone call by Jared's loud voice. Surprisingly, though, he stays put, leaning against his car and watching curiously rather than hanging up his phone.

Geez. Thanks for the backup, Ethan.

With a sigh I turn to Jared.

"What?" I demand. "I'm not in the mood for you, Jared."

"I said, tell your slut of a friend to stop lying about me." Jared enunciates every word slowly and loudly, as if I'm dumb. I glare at him as I start walking again.

"I don't know what you're talking about and I don't care."

Jared's hiss halts my steps. "Jacey was right about you, you know. You're a spoiled bitch. You have no idea what the real world is like. You've had everything handed to you your whole life."

I freeze, anger flooding through me until my vision almost blurs at the corners of my eyes.

"Jacey would never say that," I snap. "Because she knows better."

Jared skirts around me and gets in my face, invading my personal space like an annoying ankle-biting dog. "But she did. And she was right."

"You know better than that," I tell him icily, knowing full well that he's lying just to get under my skin. "Do you consider having my parents killed in a head-on crash with an eighteen-wheeler 'having everything handed to me'? Or did I have something handed to me when I had to come home from New York and live my life next to worthless fucks like you?"

"No one is making you stay here," Jared snarls. "And in fact, I'd like it better if you left. But before you go, tell your slut friend to lay off the bullshit. If I wanted to fuck with her, I would. Until then, I would appreciate it if she didn't lie."

"I'm not your messenger," I snap. "And neither of us are interested in anything you have to say."

He grabs my arm and I whirl around.

"Get your fucking hand off of me."

Out of the corner of my eye, I see Ethan take one step and then stop. He's not on his phone anymore, but he still doesn't come to help. Jared grins at me, close enough that I can smell his rancid morning breath.

"Are you going to make me, princess?"

I open my mouth to answer, but someone else answers first, a husky and familiar voice.

"No, but I'd be happy to."

Without even turning around, I recognize that deep voice, the rich timbre, the steady tone.

Gabriel.

Unconsciously my body relaxes ever so slightly in relief, as though I've been waiting for him to arrive and didn't even know it.

I exhale slowly, turning to find Gabriel standing on the pavement with two breakfast burritos in his hand. His other hand is flexing as it dangles by his thigh. He's staring at Jared with unflinching precision.

His gaze is undeniably lethal.

It's frightening in its intensity.

"For fuck's sake," Jared mutters under his breath. Looking up at Gabriel, he says, "There's no problem here, man. I was just explaining that to Madison."

"No, you weren't," I answer firmly, stepping out of his grasp. "You wanted me to take Jacey a message."

"And that is?" Gabriel raises an eyebrow.

Jared doesn't answer, so I do.

"He wanted me to tell her to stop lying. And he called her a slut."

I couldn't help but add that last part on. Jared so deserves it and he's so obviously scared of Gabriel.

Gabriel calmly sets his breakfast down on the roof of his car and approaches us. His gaze hasn't moved from Jared. It's like watching a lion and its prey. It's fascinating to witness.

I step back.

Gabriel steps forward.

Jared turns around.

"Fuck this," he mutters. "That bitch isn't worth it."

He bolts for his truck and peels out from the parking lot.

Gabriel stands still, watching him go. Then he turns to me.

"Are you all right?" he asks quietly, his dark eyes flitting over me, checking for damage. I nod, noticing the way Gabriel is dressed in workout clothes, the way his T-shirt clings to his broad chest, the fabric skimming over his chiseled abs. I swallow.

Suddenly this doesn't seem like a game anymore. Gabriel is serious and concerned, strong and lethal.

And I want him.

I want him.

I want him.

I swallow, dropping my gaze before he can see the truth.

"I'm fine. Jared is just an ass. He's always had a temper problem."

"Maddy!" Ethan calls, coming forward now that it's safe. "Are you all right?"

No thanks to you, I think, utterly disappointed in everything about him. His candy-ass clothes, his bland personality, his ability to stand aside and watch Jared harass me.

I hate violence and I hate bullies, but standing up for someone smaller or weaker is something different entirely.

And Ethan didn't do it.

Resentment wells up in me. Seriously. He was ten yards away. He could've stepped up to help, but he didn't. What kind of man does that?

"I'm fine," I sigh, fighting the urge to be a bitch, fighting the urge to tell him what a pussy he is. "Gabriel stepped in."

I turn abruptly, blocking Ethan from my sight. It might be rude, but I'm pissed.

All I want to look at now is Gabriel. I want to revel in the fact that he stood up for me. He stepped in when he didn't have to.

No one's ever done that for me before.

"Thank you," I tell Gabe simply. "You didn't have to do that."

"I didn't?" he asks doubtfully. "I'm not going to watch something like that without stepping in. You were holding your own like a champ, but once he put his hands on you, it was game over."

I nod, suddenly feeling a little choked up.

Gabriel is night and Ethan is day. And all of a sudden I see the beauty in that.

Yeah, Ethan is a doctor who is trained to save lives. But he doesn't have it in him to stand up to someone if he needs to. And even though I should probably respect that about him since I hate violence, I just can't. I need someone who can walk a thin line—someone who isn't a bully, someone who isn't violent, but someone who has the ability to summon up all the fury of hell if he needs to protect someone.

Someone like Gabriel.

Gabriel has been trained to protect people at all costs, even if the cost is his own life. He's not a violent bully. *He's a protector.*

For some reason, even though I should've seen it before, this knowledge slams into my chest and leaves me dumbfounded. The idea that I need a protector makes me feel weak. But the idea that I just had a protector makes me feel strong.

Invincible.

I only savor the feeling for a minute before I shake it away. Needing someone like that makes you weak. You can't count on other people to be there. You can only count on yourself.

Myself.

Ethan walks into my periphery again and I shove my annoyance with him away. Now isn't the time. I don't know why I ever thought, even for a minute, that he and I could work.

"Maddy, I'm sorry," he says hesitantly, staring from Gabriel to me. I can see that he's very uncomfortable standing next to Gabriel, but he doesn't address it. "I've got to go. A patient is fully dilated and ready to deliver. Can we get a rain check on breakfast?"

I nod quickly, almost relieved. I almost feel guilty for being pissed that he didn't step up, but I don't. He stood over there looking on even after he hung up his phone. He could definitely have done something then.

But he didn't.

Because he's a candy-ass.

"Of course," I tell him. "Not a problem."

I stand still, waiting for him to leave, and he looks at me uncertainly again.

"Maddy, I'm your ride."

Oh.

In the heat of the moment I'd forgotten. And Gabe's intoxicating nearness isn't helping either. I inhale his power and his strength with every breath I take. It's distracting.

I flush and take a step away from him. My foot doesn't seem to want to comply, but I force it.

"Right," I say sheepishly. "I came with you."

Gabe smiles, like he knows exactly why I'm distracted. Like he can see the comparison I've been drawing between him and Ethan. Like he can see how much he wins that comparison.

"I can take you," he offers. "I mean, if the doctor has an emergency."

Ethan looks uncertain for a split second, then nods. "That would be great. I really should go. Maddy?"

Ethan looks at me, expecting me to agree. And there's really nothing else I can do, not without seeming like an utter bitch.

But the idea of Gabe and me . . . sitting within the small confines of a car again. The mere thought almost makes me twitch, because all I can do is think of the last time.

When Gabe licked his fingers clean.

Warmth spreads into my panties.

I can't help it.

Gabriel's dark gaze is on me, potent and powerful, and I swear to God he's remembering too. His lip actually twitches, trying to fight off a smile.

The man can affect me without saying a word, especially now that I've decided I was wrong about him. I was so, so wrong.

He's a protector.

That makes it even harder to fight off this attraction.

You don't need protecting anymore, I remind myself. *You're all grown up—strong and independent. No one can hurt you now.* But that doesn't matter. None of that matters. All that matters is how Gabriel is making me feel right now.

Safe.

My fingers tremble so I clench them into fists. He makes me self-conscious, like he can see right into my thoughts.

I swallow hard and try to act nonchalant, as though he doesn't affect me at all.

"That would be fine," I finally manage to say. "Thank you, Gabriel."

"I'd give you a ride anytime," he answers and I look at him sharply. His double entendre hasn't been missed. At least not by me. Ethan is oblivious.

"Thank you," Ethan tells Gabriel grudgingly. He starts to walk away, then calls over his shoulder, "I'll call you soon, Maddy."

I don't even answer.

Gabe looks at me, amusement in his dark eyes. "What the hell do you see in that guy?"

"I . . . er . . ." and then I can't help but dissolve into a giggle.

The memory of Ethan standing helplessly to the side, watching while Jared puffed out his chest like a rooster, suddenly makes me laugh. I'm no longer even mad about it. It's just so ridiculous.

"I don't know," I finally manage. "He's been a friend for a long time. He was probably just afraid. Fighting isn't really his thing."

"He's a candy-ass," Gabriel answers simply. "Fear is a choice."

What an interesting thing to say. I'm sure that, for him, fear *is* a choice. It's how he's been trained. He's hard and strong and he's not afraid of anything.

Except for one thing. The thing that brought him to his knees that night in Chicago.

His secret.

We walk to his car and I slide into the passenger seat, clicking my seat belt. I don't know what it is about guys and hot rods, and I'll probably never understand it.

As Gabe pulls out of the parking lot, he glances at me.

"I'm sorry about your parents."

Crap.

"You overheard that?" I ask, not looking him in the eye. I hate talking about this with people. I hate the sympathy in their eyes and trying to figure out what to do with it.

He nods.

"Yeah. I was standing right behind you." But then he drops it.

I don't know whether he's just not interested enough to ask questions or whether he's uncomfortable talking about stuff like that, but either way I'm grateful. If I never talk about my parents dying again, that would be just fine with me.

"What was Jared saying about my sister?" Gabe asks as he turns onto the main road. I shake my head.

"He said she was lying about him and wanted me to tell her to stop. I have no clue what he was talking about."

Gabriel looks thoughtful. "I don't know either. But he ran like the pussy he is. You know, he grabbed you. I'm sure the gas station probably has a surveillance camera. You could press charges if you want to. Teach the little shit a lesson."

"I might," I answer. "I keep thinking that he'll get tired of messing with Jacey, that he'll just go away, but he hasn't so far. Maybe we really should call the police. On the other hand, if I do, that might really piss him off and he'll never stop. I grew up with him. He's always gonna be an asshole."

"You don't need to be intimidated by him," Gabriel says firmly. "That's why I'm here, so that he can't shove you guys around. He's a schoolyard bully that needs to grow up. But don't underestimate him."

I nod slowly. "Let's change the subject. I've had enough of Jared for the day."

Gabe finally smiles, a slow smile that spreads along his lips.

"OK. First you can tell me which way to turn, then you can tell me the real reason you're fucking around with doctor boy."

I roll my eyes. "Left. And I told you the real reason. He's been a friend for a long time."

Gabriel's the one rolling his eyes now.

"He doesn't think he's just your friend," Gabe points out as he turns down my road. "You should put him out of his misery."

"And why would I do that?" I demand. "You don't know what I'm going to do."

"No," Gabriel concedes. "But I know what you want. You want me."

"Oh, geez. Are we back to that?" I shake my head, but his words cause a rush of warmth to spread through me. I *do* want him, asshole cockiness and all.

"Jacey thinks you should date me," Gabriel announces as he turns into my drive.

I put my hand on the car handle. "You don't want to date me," I tell him. "You want to fuck me. There's a big difference."

He shrugs. "Tomato, tomahto."

A thrill shoots through me and I can't help but smile as I open the door.

"To be honest, I rarely do what your sister suggests. She's insane."

"Yes, she is," Gabriel agrees. "About most things. The verdict is still out on this particular thing, though."

"Oh, really?" I ask, my eyebrow cocked.

"Yup. Maybe we should do a little research. You know, just to see. Let's have dinner on Saturday night."

And with that, just like that, the game is back on.

He stares at me, waiting for me to accept.

Do you want to play? Yes or no?

He apparently thinks there's no way I would decline. I have to avoid looking at his totally cut body so that I can. I have to put the image of him standing up for me out of my mind.

Because there's something about him that I don't know.

Something secret.

Something that made him freak the fuck out, turning this strong protector into a violent incoherent guy who has panic attacks and punches walls. And I have no idea what that *something* is.

I shake my head.

"You're so cocky," I tell him. "So fricking cocky. I would've thought that you would be too busy with your other dates. But it doesn't matter. I can't on Saturday. Sorry."

I have no plans whatsoever, but he doesn't need to know that. If he can throw his dates in my face, I can throw mine in his. Even if mine are imaginary.

Gabriel looks stunned and then realization clouds his face as he remembers that he told me he had a date last night. He starts to say something, but I cut him off as I spin around and head for my house. With every step I feel his dark gaze hitting me between the shoulder blades.

I ignore it.

But one thing I can't ignore is that everything about that man makes my knees weak. I can't ignore the look in his eyes: that dark, dark look that says, *Don't worry. No one will hurt you on my watch.* I can't ignore the way one look from him sets my blood on fire.

And I can't ignore the biggest thing of all, the heavy question that sits on my chest all the time, even though I've only just acknowledged it.

I know he has a secret that has the ability to turn him into everything that I'm afraid of.

The question is, are all the good things I know about him enough to make me see past it?

Chapter Ten

Work seems particularly monotonous today. I've placed next month's food order, drunk four cups of coffee, and I have a caffeine buzz when I follow up with Jacey and make sure that she's up in time to come to work.

She's made a habit lately of coming home from the clubs in the early-morning hours, then oversleeping for work. That was one thing when we were teenagers, but we're not kids anymore. It's time to grow up.

"Yes," Jacey sighs into the phone. "I'm up. I'm showered. I'll be there shortly. You didn't need to check on me. And what did you do to my brother this morning? He said he gave you a ride, but he was mean as hell when he came home."

"Nothing. I just told him I couldn't go out with him on Saturday."

"God," Jacey grumbles. "Why can't you just hook up already? You know you both want to and you'll both be happier when you do."

I'm starting to think she's right, but I don't say that.

"Whatever. I'll have your paycheck ready when you get here."

"'K. I'll be there soon."

We hang up and I stare forlornly at the papers balanced precariously in stacks on my desk. I decide to take a quick break and run out to the dining room to stretch my legs. As I enter, Tony calls for me from the bar.

"Hey, Maddy. Your sister just called and wanted to know if you'd bring her out some soup on your way home. Pax is in Hartford for a week and she's not feeling that well today. She really didn't sound good. Maybe you should take it to her right now."

I'm instantly concerned. Mila isn't one to complain, not ever. She could be on her deathbed and she wouldn't whine.

"Seriously?" I ask Tony as I lean against the bar. "What's wrong with her, did she say? Is it morning sickness still or something else?"

He shakes his giant head. "She didn't say. She just said she feels sicker than usual and that she's going to stay in bed today."

"Well, hell," I mutter. "That's not like her. I hope she doesn't have the flu. If you box something up I'll run it out to her right now."

"Already done." Tony grins, handing me a large carryout sack. "There are saltines in there too. They might settle her stomach."

It's not a problem to make a food run to my sister. Her house is only a few minutes away, perched on the edge of the bluffs by the lake. It was Pax's before they got married and it's a gorgeous home.

I knock on the door and when Mila finally answers it I'm even more concerned. Her face has a grayish pallor to it, her normally bright eyes dull, and she's still in her nightgown.

"What the hell?" I exclaim as I follow her into the house. "What's wrong with you? Is your morning sickness worse? That's not normal, right? Shouldn't you be over that by now?"

"I don't know," she groans. "I had the worst stomachache last night, so I was up all night long. I barely slept."

I gently push her onto a barstool and begin unloading her lunch. "When did Pax leave?"

Mila drops her head onto her crossed arms. "Yesterday. Don't tell him that I'm sick or he'll come straight home. He's got meetings with his grandpa this week."

I stare at her uncertainly. "I don't know, Mi. You look pretty bad."

"That's exactly why I don't want him to come home, Madison. Have a heart. It's just a stomach bug. He doesn't need to be here, listening to me every time I'm in the bathroom. Seriously. How embarrassing."

I sigh. "Fine. I won't call him yet. But you've got to promise to get some rest. Is there anything else I can bring you?"

She shakes her head. "Nope. I'm just going to finish eating this and then curl up and sleep."

"I'll sit with you for a bit."

Mila manages a smile. "You're as overprotective as Pax is."

I don't even bother to answer, because I know she's right.

"So, how's life?" she asks quietly in between bites. "How was your date with Ethan?"

I roll my eyes. "That's probably the last time I listen to your advice about my love life. It was dry, boring, vanilla...all the things that Ethan is."

"Awww. Poor Ethan," Mila answers sympathetically. "He can't help it."

"I know," I answer ruefully. And I do.

"This soup is good," Mila says, blowing on another spoonful as she changes the subject. "Can you tell Tony thank you for me?"

Mila sticks another bite in her mouth and, as she does, I hear the muted buzz of my cell phone in my purse. I slide it out and am startled to see the text message it displays.

This is Gabriel. I have to tell you something.

The mere sight of his name on my phone causes my pulse to race and I stare at it. This catches Mila's attention and she pauses, watching me, interested now.

I answer, *How did you get my number? Let's start with that.*

I grin and Mila raises an eyebrow.

"Who is it?" she asks curiously.

"No one," I tell her. She rolls her eyes but returns to her soup, her forehead in her hand.

My phone buzzes.

From Jacey, obviously.

I answer, *Jacey talks a lot.*

It takes him one second to reply, *Hell yes, she does.*

I feel a little breathless as I type, *What did you need to tell me?*

There is a moment, and then, *My date the other night was with Brand.*

The amount of relief that floods my body as I read those words is incredible. I feel lighter than I have for days. But I can't tell him that. Instead I say *Is that supposed to matter to me?*

Gabriel's cockiness knows no bounds, because he answers without hesitation.

It matters to you.

I smile a little, because it does. But before I can answer, he sends a second text.

And it matters to me that I misled you about it. I'm sorry about that.

I pause, astonished by his apology. He doesn't seem like someone who would readily apologize. He's too self-assured, too commanding, like my father. And one thing I learned from my father is that people like him don't apologize often.

Even still, Gabriel did.

If I concentrate hard enough, I can almost hear Gabe's husky voice saying the words. It sends warmth gushing through me and I see flashes of him in my head . . . escorting Jared out of the Hill, stepping in when Jared grabbed me at the gas station.

In actuality, my father was more like Jared. And Gabriel is nothing like that. Is it possible that I misjudged him on every level?

Maybe he's nothing like my father at all.

The thought sends a knot into my throat as I answer his text.

It's okay.

I don't know why *it's okay*, I just know that all of a sudden, it is.

And then he says something that sends my heart into my throat.

Just so you know, the next date I go on will be with you.

I stare at the words, unable to keep from smiling, even as my fingers shake. Mila stares at me once again, her curiosity apparent.

So you're threatening me now? I answer, and I have to giggle just a little.

This game I'm playing with him is the most fun I've had in a while. Mila grows annoyed with my lack of explanation and rolls her eyes, muttering something about how stubborn I am. And then Gabriel's answering text comes through.

No, it's a promise.

I know we're just bantering back and forth, but those four words make my legs tremble. Gabriel is so strong, so assured. So secure. He makes me feel like I can depend on him. It's a thought that I know will freak me out later when I can really think about it.

Well, we DO have something we need to finish, I quickly type before I can talk myself out of it.

A thrill rushes through me as I slip my phone back into my purse and turn to Mila's waiting gaze.

"And that was?" She lifts an eyebrow.

"Gabriel," I sigh. "Jacey's brother."

"Oh, I know who Gabriel is," Mila laughs. "What's going on?"

So I tell her just a little, how an entire date with Ethan can leave me cold, but one single glance from Gabriel can set my blood on fire. One stupid text can leave me weak-kneed.

As sick as Mila looks, she laughs again.

"Oh my God. You have no idea how happy this makes me. Don't look so miserable, Mad. This is awesome!"

"Then why does it feel so scary?" I grumble.

Mila nods sagely. "Because it *is* scary. When I was first with Pax, I was terrified. I mean, he was so messed up, but I still loved him. He's who I'm meant to be with. And look how it all turned out, look how happy we are now. It was all worth it. I know that Gabriel has some baggage. I can see it on him. And I'm sure you can see it on him. But whatever Gabriel's stuff is, I'm sure you can work through it. And it will be worth it."

"You think?" I raise an eyebrow and my sister nods again.

"I *know.*"

"We'll see," I answer firmly. "I don't want to wind up curled up on my bed crying about him when he loses his temper with me one too many times. I'm never going to be Mom, Mila."

Mila looks away, at the wall, at the floor. I know that she doesn't remember nearly as much stuff as I do about our parents' problems. If Mom was crying, I took Mila outside to play. If Mom and Dad were screaming, I'd take Mila to the beach. She didn't see as much as I did, even though she knows it happened.

"I know," she finally answers in a small voice. "Dad had some anger issues. But Gabriel isn't Dad. And you aren't Mom. Trust me, you should give Gabriel a chance. My gut is telling me that he'd be good for you."

I stare at my sister, at her tired face, at her skinny arms.

"I'm sorry, Sis. I've been sitting here boring you with my drama and you need to go rest. You really do look awful. Come on, let's get you to bed."

I reach to help her from her stool, but she pauses, a strange look on her face.

"Ow," she mumbles, her hand falling to her abdomen, pressing tightly. I'm startled as I stare at her stricken face.

"What is it?" I ask anxiously.

"I don't know," she answers quietly. "I'm crampy."

She's crampy? I sit still, frozen, as she rubs her belly. Then, as she slides from her stool, she's the one who stands frozen, her eyes wide.

"What?" I ask nervously.

And then I see it. Blood drips in a crimson stream down one of her bare legs and onto the floor. I gasp and grab her, pulling her into a chair, making her sit.

"Are you OK? Are you in pain?"

I flutter around like a crazy person, not sure what to do. Mila is calmer than I am as she sits hunched over in the chair.

"I'm going to get some clothes on, then can you drive me to the doctor?"

I nod, then run up the stairs to her room, taking them two at a time.

"I'll grab your clothes," I call over my shoulder. "You stay right there. Maybe you should call your doctor."

I can hear her speaking on the phone as I rifle through her drawers and find a pair of yoga pants and a T-shirt. When I come running back down the stairs, she is hanging up the phone. Her face is grim and pale.

"What did they say?" I ask anxiously as I hand her the clothing.

"They said to come straight in."

Mila inhales sharply and I grab her. "Are you OK?"

"I don't know," she murmurs as she pulls the clothes on. "The cramps just got worse. All of a sudden."

Even I know that this shouldn't be happening. Pregnant women shouldn't be crampy. And there definitely shouldn't be blood involved.

I'm beyond panicked now and I don't know what to do. Now I know how Pax feels, because if I could carry Mila out to the car, I so would.

Pax.

"I should call Pax," I tell her quickly, in relief. Pax will know what to do.

But Mila immediately shakes her head.

"It might be nothing," she says quickly. "Let's just wait until we know. I don't want to worry him."

But her face gives her away.

She's terrified and she thinks something is really wrong. I gulp as I get her settled into the front seat of my car and then I practically break land-speed records getting her to the doctor. I gulp again when I help her out of the car and see the blood smeared on the seat.

Fuck.

To the doctor's credit, she gets Mila right in without a wait at all. I help Mila change into the horrible paper gown, then hold her hand as the doctor does a sonogram.

"Mmmhmmm," Dr. Hall muses as she runs the ball of the sonogram wand over my sister's belly, to and fro. "Mmmhmm."

"What is it?" Mila asks anxiously, her green eyes wide and scared. "Do you see anything? Is there a heartbeat?"

The doctor looks up at her. "Yes, there's a heartbeat," she assures her. "And it's strong. What I am seeing, though, is cause for concern."

"Oh, God," Mila breathes. "What is it?" Her fingers clutch mine a little tighter.

The doctor stares at the computer screen and then points to a round, dark mass just to the side of the fetus. "See that area right there? That black area?" Mila and I both nod.

"That is what's called a subchorionic hemorrhage. In plain English, it's a blood pool that is forming between the placenta and your uterine wall. Sometimes it's a result of a serious injury, but more often than not it just happens. We don't know the cause."

"What does it mean?" Mila whispers. "Is the baby going to be all right?"

The doctor's face is serious. "It means that if the blood pool continues to grow, it could cause your placenta to break away from the uterus, in what is called placental abruption. That could be fatal for your baby and life-threatening for you."

"Oh my God," I can't help but gasp. It comes out before I even think about it. Mila swallows hard.

"What can we do about it?"

"Well, if it were a small pool of blood, I wouldn't be so worried, but it's fairly substantial already. We need to keep it stabilized and prevent it from growing. The best way we can do that is to keep you off your feet. You're going to require complete bed rest. You can only get up to go to the bathroom. No sex, no walking, limited movement."

The doctor pauses, allowing that to sink in.

"What's the prognosis?" I manage to ask.

"Good question. I'd say from the size of this bleed that Mila has a fifty to sixty percent chance of preterm labor. The real risk with this situation, though, is hemorrhage. It happens so suddenly that it's hard to control, which makes it dangerous. So, Mila, I'm going to put you in the hospital overnight, so that I can give you some fluids. You're dehydrated. And then after that, complete bed rest at home and we'll hope for the best."

Mila nods, the shock apparent on her pale face.

I feel her hand get even colder as I clutch it within mine.

"Don't worry," I tell her. "It's going to be all right, Mila. Everything is going to be fine."

I glare at the doctor, all but daring her to say otherwise. It's irrational, I know. It's not Dr. Hall's fault at all, but I'm annoyed at her matter-of-fact manner. This is my sister we're talking about, and she needs reassurance.

After the doctor leaves, with instructions for us to go straight to the hospital, I help Mila to her feet and then help her get her clothes on. I look into her face.

"I mean it, Mila. Everything will be fine. I'm going to call Pax as soon as we get you settled into the hospital and I know he'll be here soon."

She nods now, not arguing. Her limp acceptance of this situation rips my heart out. My little sister has been my responsibility for years now and knowing that I can't protect her from this is too terrible to bear.

"It will be fine," I insist once again as I bundle her into my car. She leans her face on the car window and doesn't reply. I swallow a lump in my throat as I start the car and head for the hospital. This can't be happening. Mila and Pax almost lost each other a couple of times this past year. They can't lose their baby too.

When we arrive at the hospital, a nurse brings out a wheelchair and they wheel Mila on up while I fill out her paperwork and call Pax. He answers on the second ring, probably concerned when he sees my number. I never call him when he's out of town.

"Madison?"

"Hi, Pax. There's a problem. You need to come home."

I quickly fill him in and he practically hangs up on me in his haste to make arrangements to fly home. He texts me ten minutes later.

I'm taking the company jet. I'll be there in three hours. Tell Mila I'm coming.

The lump forms in my throat again, but I swallow it as I head upstairs to Mila's room. When I arrive I find her attached to all kinds of wires and monitors, and she has an IV stuck in her arm. She seems so small amid all the tubes.

"Hey," I tell her softly as I walk in. Her big green eyes stare at me.

"Hey. Thanks for calling Pax," she tells me quietly. "He texted that he's on his way."

"Of course he is," I tell her. "He wouldn't be anywhere other than here, I can tell you that."

"I know," Mila answers, closing her eyes. "I'm so sleepy. I'm going to take a nap while I wait, OK?"

I nod. "OK. I'll sit right here until Pax arrives."

Mila nods without opening her eyes and I pick up her hand. It's freezing cold, so I pull her blankets up a little tighter and then settle into the chair next to her.

I watch her sleep for a while, holding her hand tight. Her breathing is rhythmic, her chest moving slowly up and down as she takes little peaceful breaths. She seems calm in sleep and I'm glad. She deserves a break from reality right now.

After a while, when I feel pretty sure that she isn't going to wake up anytime soon, I rush down to the gift shop and grab some magazines. On my way back, while I wait for the elevator, I glance to the side and notice a tiny family huddled together in the ER waiting room. A dad, a mom, a son.

They are sitting hunched together like they are facing the world together, each face streaked with tears. I stare at them for a minute, unable to look away, until the mom looks up at me and meets my gaze. There is such utter pain in her eyes that it makes my heart hurt. Something horrible has happened to them and I know that feeling.

Unbidden, memories from the day my parents died come back to me, flooding through me as I stand limply in front of the steel doors of the elevator.

Mila's phone call, her sobbing voice.

Me, standing in New York City as my world crashed down.

Flying home.

Picking out caskets.

Choosing flowers.

Hymns.

Verses.

The overwhelming grief that made it so hard to function, so hard to even swallow or breathe.

The guilt.

The guilt.

The guilt.

Knowing that I hated my father for hurting my mother, but still loving him anyway.

Feeling like I was abandoning my mother for loving him, but then remembering that she loved him too. Passionately and completely.

Which is why she stayed.

That day, that one day, changed me forever. It taught me that everything you love, every*one* you love, even if you love them and hate them at the same time, can be taken away in a moment and there isn't anything you can do to change it.

It made me helpless. Powerless. And I hate that feeling with every ounce of my being.

"Miss?"

A hesitant voice breaks into my thoughts and I look up, startled, to find a woman holding the elevator for me.

"Do you need to go up?" she asks, her kind eyes flitting over my face. I nod, unable to speak because somehow that fucking lump is back in my throat. The same lump that was there when we buried my parents.

I step quickly into the elevator, leaning against the back wall as I try to breathe deep, to swallow.

Mila's not going to die. I'm completely overreacting. Yet I can't stop my feet from practically flying down the hall to get to her, to make sure she's all right, to make sure something catastrophic didn't happen to her while I was gone.

Because I left her. I left her back then when I moved to New York and I left her now.

But when I throw open the door, she's still sleeping peacefully, curled on her side, her hand cupped to her face.

My stomach tightens. I can't lose Mila. She's been through too much not to have a happy ending. And if I lost her now, I don't know what it would do to me.

I know that much is true.

I collapse into the chair next to her and drop the magazines onto the floor. I'm content to sit here and stew in my worry.

Minutes turn into hours and before I know it, Pax bursts into the room.

I glance at the clock. It's barely eight p.m. He's thirty minutes early. I have no idea how he managed to make it so fast, considering he had to drive from the airport in Chicago to Angel Bay. He must've broken some land-speed records of his own.

"How is she?" he asks worriedly as he pulls up the chair on the other side of the bed. "I got here as fast as I could." His handsome face is ashen as he takes in the full picture of his wife, small and pale in the bed. "Oh my God. I can't believe this. What did the doctor say? What caused this?"

I explain what the doctor said, and with every word Pax's face gets paler and paler.

"This could actually threaten her life?" he finally whispers.

I nod. "If the placenta ruptures from the side of her uterus, yes. That's why she's got to stay in bed. The more she stands up, the more the force of gravity will pull on the weight of her uterus and could cause the abruption. She's got to have complete rest."

"Don't worry," Pax says firmly. "She won't be moving. Not until the baby is born."

"It's going to be a long couple months," I tell him. "But between us, we've got to keep her still."

"If we have to tie her down, we will," he says. At his words, Mila opens her eyes.

"That won't be necessary," she says softly, smiling at her husband. "I'll stay in bed. And everything will be OK. Madison already promised."

"Oh, because Madison's in control of that?" Pax smiles back at his wife, bending to kiss her forehead.

My stomach tightens again at their obvious tenderness for each other. It's practically palpable. I've never seen anyone love each other as much as they do, and while I'm happy for Mila, it makes me feel so very alone.

"You know she'd never let anything hurt me." Mila nods, grinning. "Seriously, I have faith. Everything is going to be fine."

"You're right," Pax agrees. "You're going to be fine. And the baby is too."

They curl up together with Pax half on the bed and half on his chair, his arms encircling Mila as if to protect her from the world.

Pax is a protector. Mila's protector.

It's a sight that causes that freaking lump to immediately form back in my throat, both because it's heartwarming and because I'd like to have what they have . . . a pure and perfect love for each other.

And someone to protect me from everything that might hurt me.

Someone like Gabe.

Oh my God. I've got to get out of here before I embarrass myself.

I stand up and they both look up at me, their cheeks pink and warm from being cuddled together.

"I'm going to head home and shower since Pax is here now. I want to wash off the hospital smell. If you guys need anything, just give me a call. I'll come out to the house tomorrow to check on you, Mi." I bend down and kiss her cheek. "I love you. You're going to be fine."

"I know," she tells me confidently. "I love you too."

I walk through the hospital woodenly as all my emotions come down on me, the fear that Mila could lose her baby, the worry for Mila herself...and the overwhelming loneliness that encompasses me right now.

I don't even realize until I've reached my car that tears are streaming down my cheeks.

Chapter Eleven

My house has never seemed so empty or quiet.

And I have never been quite so alone.

Jacey is covering for me at the Hill because there was no way that I could've left Mila to go to work. But now, as I sit all alone on my patio with a bottle of wine, I wish that Jacey were here with me instead. I'm stuck here by myself, with only my worries for company.

They're bad freaking company.

I take a sip of wine and stare at the sky, watching the storm clouds roll in, heavy and dark.

I stare at my wineglass and remember when my mother bought it, and decide that I need to buy my own freaking glassware.

I stare at the sand behind the house, noticing the way it's packed down, hard and damp.

I glance back at my watch and find that's it's only been one minute since the last time I looked at it.

I'm pathetic. I'm sitting here wallowing in my fear and worry and misery and it's ridiculous. I can't keep doing this tonight.

Just as I'm getting up to find something else to do to keep my mind occupied, my doorbell rings. For one split second, I'm panicked that it is bad news about Mila. And then I realize that's stupid. If something happened, Pax would call. Not send someone.

I open the door and am startled to find Gabriel standing in front of me.

He's strikingly sexy in his ever-present snug T-shirt and I somehow feel a marked sense of relief just at the mere sight of him.

He grins at me, holding up a silver tube of my lipstick.

"You left this in my car. I figured it must've rolled out of your purse. Since it's not really my color, I figured I should return it."

I reach for it and he deposits it in my hand, and when he does, the warmth of his hand transfers to my own. It's the touch I've been thinking about for days: his strength, his power.

He smiles at me and I try to smile back, but I suddenly can't.

My stomach clenches and a tear runs down my cheek.

Then another.

Gabe's face sobers up and his eyes are veiled as he looks at me, assessing me.

"Are you all right?" Gabe asks, concerned as he stares at me, as his eyes search for what is wrong. He takes a step toward me, then stops. "Are you?" he repeats hesitantly.

I stand limply in front of him, an empty shell, but I nod.

"Yes. Maybe. I don't know. Would you like a glass of wine? I really don't want to be alone." My eyes burn, but I manage to get the words out.

Gabe looks at me, his stormy eyes focused on my face.

"Of course," he finally answers. He doesn't even say that he prefers beer and I know that he does.

He takes my arm as I lead him through the house to the terrace. His hand is gentle, and strong, and warm on my elbow. I revel in the feel of it, in the warmth of his fingers, and I hate the coldness when he pulls it away. But we're on the terrace now, so he steps back, watching me, hesitant.

He's waiting.

He doesn't know what I want.

It's lightly raining now, but neither of us acknowledges it. I pour him a glass of wine and hand it to him with shaking fingers. I see the crimson liquid splash upward against the side of the glass, sliding back down into a pool. In my head I see the crimson blood running down Mila's legs and I cringe, squeezing my eyes shut, trying to block it out.

"Maddy," he says uncertainly, his voice deep and husky. "What happened? What's wrong?"

I open my eyes and am distracted by the shape of his mouth, by the slant, by the full but firm lips. The lips I've thought about for days. The lips that licked me from his fingers.

I swallow, then I lift my fingers and trace his lips, sliding my fingertips over the softness. He stands still, completely still, as he waits to see what I'm going to do. As his dark eyes find mine, I decide that for this moment, I don't care what his issues are.

This isn't a game anymore, if it ever really was.

"Maddy," he murmurs quietly, but firmer this time, his eyes frozen on mine even as he remains still. "Tell me what's wrong with you."

"I've just had a bad day. And I need you to make it good again."

He stares at me in shock. I can't blame him.

Confusion fills Gabriel's eyes as he stands there facing me, not sure of what to do.

So I show him.

Reaching up, I press my lips softly to his, tentative at first, enjoying the taste of salt that lingers there, loving the way his chest is so rock-solid beneath my fingers.

The kiss is so soft, so gentle; barely there. But the intensity of having wanted it for days makes it fierce. His lips ignite a fire that flashes through my mouth and down into my chest and buries itself between my legs.

It roars to life there, burning bright, the flames licking up into the rest of me.

Gabriel's strong arms automatically close around me as I deepen the kiss, plunging my tongue desperately into his mouth, tangling with his. I glance up and his dark eyes are open, staring into mine.

"Are you sure you're OK?" he asks against my lips, almost desperately. I nod.

"I am now."

My voice is a whisper and he groans, kissing me again, pulling me closer.

My hands are everywhere, running over his hard chest, his chiseled waist, his toned backside. Our mouths are hot and wet and open, our breath panting.

The friction from his warm skin against my fingertips is delicious and for a minute I remember that night in the taxi, how his dark eyes burned for me then, how he licked his fingers. That mere memory turns my knees weak yet again, just like it does every time I think of it.

I grasp his hand and shove it between my legs, but my pants are in the way. I step out of them as I push my wet hair out of my face and he reaches down, ripping my panties away from my body...ridding us of the barrier between him and me.

He stands there, the shredding tatters of my underwear dangling from his fingers, then he flicks them away and they fall onto the wet ground at our feet.

I'm throbbing now as I stand facing him, waiting for him to touch me, the heat between my legs almost more than I can take.

Every nerve ending waits for him.

I hold my breath.

The rain pours down.

And then he touches me. His fingers, so long, slide into me and suddenly I find myself balanced on the palm of his hand, like everything in my being is tied to him. Waiting for him.

It's been waiting for him forever.

He slips farther inside and everything in me moans. My eyes flicker up and catch his; his are hooded and dark as his eyelashes flutter down.

I run my fingers along his waistband.

"Is this OK?" I whisper, my lids lifting to meet his gaze, watching the rain run off his face.

"Hell, yes," he mutters, guiding my hand to his hard crotch. It strains against my hand, pulsing and hot, and need for him flows in me everywhere, hot and rough and impatient.

I know that I need him to put the fire out.

I shove his shorts down and discard them to the side. It doesn't matter to me that we're outdoors. Nothing matters now but this.

This heat, this need; this blur of colors and feelings. This explosion of things that I can't control, can't even name.

Gripping him in my hand, I slide him easily in my fingers, wet from the rain. He's as enormous as I remember, slick and hot and pulsing.

He's hard for me.

He wants me.

He groans again, grabbing my face and pulling me to him, crushing my lips with his own, hard and yet soft.

I nip at his neck, dragging my teeth along the curve of his shoulder, aching to have him fill me up already, but knowing that we should wait. I want to drag it out, to prolong this exquisite agony of waiting for it.

Of waiting for him.

He stands naked in front of me now, tall and proud, and he's so fucking beautiful.

Around us the rain pours down and the thunder rumbles, the electricity in the sky colliding with our energy. It's a heady combination and I drop to my knees, taking him into my mouth. He's huge and hard, and I move my lips up his length, letting him slide in past my teeth, down my throat.

"Fuck, Madison," Gabriel groans, his fingers buried in my hair, guiding my speed. "God, that feels so good."

I slide him in and out for a few minutes more, until he pushes me away, grabbing at my shirt and almost ripping it off. The raging heat from our bodies pressed together pools between my legs.

"I want you," I murmur to him. "Right now."

"I want to ask why you've changed your mind," Gabriel says roughly, dipping his head to trail his lips along my neck. "But it doesn't matter right now. I want to be inside you, Madison. I'm finally going to fuck you and you're going to like it."

He pulls on my hand, urging me back toward the house, but I plant my heels.

"Here," I tell him simply. "Right here, in the rain. I want you right now."

Gabriel looks sharply at me, but he doesn't argue. He simply eases me onto the large stone table behind us. It's cold and wet, but it doesn't matter.

Nothing matters but this.

His body covers mine, rubbing against every inch of me, bringing every nerve ending singing to life. He hovers above me now, just as I've imagined him hovering above me, waiting to enter me.

Reality is even better than my imagination.

I grasp at his back as he slides his fingers into me again, my muscles flexing as he moves. Everything around us ceases to matter; the wind, the rain...it all fades away and all that I can see is him.

"God, you're so wet," he rasps into my ear. "And so fucking tight."

He fingers me softly, then harder. And then he withdraws his fingers. Before I can protest at his absence, I hear a wrapper crinkle and then he slips into me, hard and full.

I gasp, then hold on as he thrusts into me.

I needed this so much.

I needed *him* and I didn't even realize it.

My legs wrap around him, pulling him to me, as close as he can possibly get.

Intimate feelings, strange and foreign feelings, threaten to overwhelm me as I clutch him to me, as I absorb his warmth, his vitality, his scent.

Everything about this moment is exactly what I need, even if I can't define what I'm feeling, or why I'm feeling it. All my sadness, all my worry, all my fear culminate and explode in this moment. It makes everything blurry, makes everything happen so fast. I just want to take and take and take...everything he has to give.

Gabriel reaches between us and, using his thumb, brings me to climax a scant moment later.

"God, you're beautiful," he tells me raggedly, still thrusting into me, filling me up. His strength is apparent as he moves against me, every muscle flexing with every movement.

He pulls my leg up and over his shoulder, deepening his penetration. I call out, scratching into him, holding tight; and then he shudders with his own release a minute later.

He collapses onto me, holding me close as we recover.

"Holy shit," he finally says, after a few minutes. "That was incredible."

My chest almost hurts from the feeling of completion that is filling it. I reach out and slide my fingers along Gabe's jawline, along the stubble that always lingers there and turns me on.

"It was," I agree. "Except for the rain. I didn't care about it a few minutes ago, but now..." My voice trails off as my teeth start to chatter.

Gabriel sits up and then stands, pulling me to my feet. He hands me my clothes, then gets dressed himself.

"Come on," he tells me, grabbing my hand and pulling me into the house.

"What are we doing?" I ask curiously.

"Taking a hot shower. That rain is fucking cold."

We tumble through the door and I lead him to the bathroom, stopping only to let the shower water get hot. Gabriel turns to me and helps me into the shower, and then lathers up his hands, running them over my back.

"You're so beautiful," he whispers into my ear. "You have no idea how much I think about you."

He does? That thought makes my heart race.

Gabriel drops to his knees and lathers his hands again, paying close attention to my thighs, then to the crevices behind my knees. When his soapy hands slip to the apex of my thighs, I inhale sharply and watch him smile.

"Do you like that?" he asks knowingly. He rinses his hand, then slips a finger into me. I nod and another finger slips in. I squeeze my eyes shut.

"Open your eyes, Maddy," he tells me. "I want to see you when I do this."

The idea of being vulnerable right now while I'm so exposed makes me nervous, but Gabe doesn't give me the time to think about it. He pushes me back onto the ledge of the shower, and then, while I watch, he detaches the shower nozzle. He rinses away the water, then holds the nozzle between my legs.

"What...the...hell..." I murmur in amazement as waves of pleasure ripple through me, buoying me up, teetering me on the edge of another orgasm.

I close my eyes again, allowing myself to give in to the pleasure, to the sinfully good sensations stemming from the water hitting me at just the right angle. I'm self-conscious and nervous that Gabe is watching me, but it feels so freaking good that I can't help but to just let him do it. If I protested, he might stop. And there's no way I want that.

"That's it, sweetheart," he murmurs into my neck. "Let yourself go. Relax."

So I do. I just focus on the building waves of my orgasm. And just when I am grabbing at the shower wall, almost ready to come, Gabriel pulls the shower nozzle away and replaces it with his tongue.

"Holy fuck," I practically scream, as I shudder against him. My legs go weak with the strength of my orgasm and I hold tight to Gabriel so my knees don't give out.

His face is clouded, his eyes slightly unfocused as he pulls me up and flips me over. I see him reach for his wallet and there is another rustle of foil. Then without another word he slips inside me from behind, thrusting harder and harder.

Even though I already came once, the sensations start building again. He wraps his hand around and moves his fingers against me too. I moan, my hands slipping down the wet wall in front of me, my cheek resting against the wall.

"Your ass is amazing," Gabriel murmurs, his lips resting against my shoulders. "Tell me what you want, Madison. Tell me."

I breathe in, then breathe out, slowing down the moment.

"I want you to come," I finally tell him, loving how he fills me up. "I want to know you like it."

He groans as he thrusts again. "Oh, trust me. I fucking love it."

"So come then," I tell him. "Show me how much you love it. I want to feel it."

He moves his hands to my hips now, clutching tightly there, his fingers digging into my skin as he moves. Rhythmically, he moves with me until he finally sucks in a breath and pulses into me. I can feel the heat spreading into the condom and I close my eyes, enjoying it.

We stay that way with the water beating down on us for several minutes, before Gabriel straightens up and rinses us off. We step out of the shower and as I'm drying off, Gabriel looks at me.

"I could use some coffee. Can I go make some?"

I nod. "Of course. The kitchen is...well, you know where it is. We came in through the kitchen door."

Gabriel ducks out and I join him in the kitchen after I've gotten dressed. He's still shirtless, maneuvering about the kitchen with ease. The smell of coffee percolating is already filling the air and I watch as Gabriel finds two cups, filling them both. He sips at one, then dumps sugar and cream in the other, simply assuming that I want it. And he's right. That's exactly how I take it.

He sets a cup in front of me and then sits down across from me at the table.

The air between us has cleared, the frenzied sexual tension is gone. The need, however, remains...only it's quiet now, latent.

Waiting.

Gabe stares at me. "Are you going to tell me what that was all about?"

I think about my poor sister, huddled in her bed back at the hospital. I think about the possibility that I could lose her. I think about the fact that I'm always afraid and the only time I've *not* been afraid in as long as I remember was a few minutes ago when I was wrapped in his arms. I think of all of that.

As I do, my eyes well up again, against my will. I hate to cry. And I've never been a crier. Until today, apparently.

"I've just had a bad day," I manage to say without crying. But my throat is hot and tight, and I know that if I keep talking, I'm going to lose it.

"Apparently," Gabriel replies drily, thoughtfully. "And did I manage to make it better?"

I give him a weak smile and then sip at my coffee. I don't answer because I think he already knows.

"Is this decaf?" I ask instead.

He nods. "Yeah. I didn't know if it'd be hard for you to sleep otherwise."

It's surprisingly thoughtful, something that just closes my throat up even more.

"Thank you," I utter, before a tear escapes.

Gabriel looks at me in alarm. "Madison, I swear to God. Just tell me what is wrong. Seriously."

I sigh and stare at my hands, then slowly look back up at him. Where should I begin? I decide to start with the only thing I can easily explain.

"My sister might lose her baby." The mere words are terrifying and they catch in my throat. "And if she's not careful, she could die, too."

"Jesus," Gabriel mutters.

I nod shakily. "She and Pax have been through so much and now they have this to deal with. It's not fair."

Gabriel looks at me seriously, his eyes softening.

"I'm so sorry," he says quietly. "I'm not going to tell you all the bullshit about life not being fair. I'm sure you know that already. What I will say is that I'm sure your sister will be OK. She's strong and I'm sure she'll do whatever the doctors tell her to do."

I nod limply. "She will. It's just... you don't understand. Our parents died when she was a senior in college. I had just graduated. All of a sudden, it was just the two of us and it was so hard. I grew up in a hurry. I had to be the rock in our little family. Everything was always all right because I made it that way... but I can't fix this for her. It's out of my hands and I hate it."

My vision blurs as my eyes well up with hot tears, and one drips onto my thumb.

Gabriel reaches across the table and wipes my thumb off before enclosing my hand within his. His is large and rough and I imagine it got that way from his being a soldier.

"It's OK to cry," he tells me. "Even the strongest do it."

I break down at his words, at the soft expression on his hardened face. My head drops to the table and I weep uncontrollably.

At some point Gabriel rounds the table and kneels in front of me, pulling me against his chest. His strong hands pat my back and stroke my arms and I cry until there's nothing left.

I can hear him speaking to me, telling me that I can't fix everything all the time, that I'm just a person like anyone else. But his words don't even matter.

It's his voice that gives me comfort; his calm, husky, soothing voice. I wish I could wrap myself up in it and stay that way forever.

But even his voice can't stop my endless flow of tears.

I'm not sure if I'm only crying for Mila's current situation, or if I'm crying for everything that's happened in the past couple of years, for everything that I haven't allowed myself to cry for. Even at our parents' funeral I only cried once. I wanted to be the strong one, the one Mila could lean on. It feels so effing good to let it all go now.

I feel utterly drained when I finally look up at Gabe.

"Thanks for letting me cry on you," I tell him weakly. I'm embarrassed, but he smiles.

"Jacey tells me that sometimes a woman just needs a good cry." He shrugs. "Now, I should also admit that she cries at the drop of a hat, say if her coffee isn't hot enough. But still, it makes sense. Crying is cleansing. You should try it more often."

I roll my eyes, but I do feel remarkably cleansed, not that I'd ever admit it. I'm a strong person. I've always prided myself on that strength. I'm not about to become weak now. I lean my face against Gabriel's chest again.

I stare at the wall, at the shadows that move there, and I know that I just don't want to be alone tonight. I don't want Gabriel to leave. He's so very strong and I just want to absorb all that strength, to replenish my own.

The thought of him leaving me after the emotional mess I've been tonight... it makes me feel panicky inside, deep inside a place where I've never looked.

"I know this seems sudden and clingy," I mumble against his warm skin, "but can you stay? I want to sleep next to you tonight. I don't want to be alone."

Gabriel tenses up, his muscles coiled against me. Staying with me is obviously something that he doesn't want to do. My breath catches in my throat and heat burns up my cheeks.

"Never mind," I say quickly, pushing away from him. "That was stupid. You don't need to stay."

He gazes at me and brushes a piece of my hair away from my face. "It's not that I don't want to. It's just... there's shit you don't know about me. I can't stay. But I'll stay until you go to sleep. How about that?"

I find myself nodding when my pride really wants to tell him to just go if he doesn't want to be here. But something in his face, something vulnerable in his eyes, makes me really hear what he's saying. He's not rejecting me. It's something deeper than that.

There's shit you don't know about me.

After we turn off the lights in the kitchen and climb under the covers of my bed, I turn and snuggle into Gabriel's chest, enjoying the way his arms hold me close. I can hear the beat of his heart against my ear and the sound soothes me.

"Tell me about the shit I don't know," I say quietly. "Because I'd like to know it."

Gabriel is quiet for a moment and just when I think that he must be trying to decide how to tell me, he declines.

"Maddy, I just can't."

I can tell from his firm tone that he means it. He's not going to talk about it. I can't even be mad about that because I can also hear something else in his voice…something hurt, something tired, something resigned. Something that doesn't have anything to do with me.

Something secret.

It makes me wrap my arm tighter around his side, pulling him closer.

"If you ever want to tell me, you can," I tell him quietly. "I won't judge. I promise that I'll try not to even ask probing questions. I'll just listen."

I've known all along that he has a secret, something that has the power to drop him to his knees. He *thinks* that it's a secret, anyway. But I've seen it. I know how it affects him.

It's what *caused* the secret that I'm afraid of. I'm afraid of anything that can decimate a person like Gabriel.

I feel his lips moving against my hair.

"Thanks, Maddy. Maybe someday."

But don't count on it.

He doesn't say that, but I'm sure he's thinking it. I would bet any amount of money that he's never planning on talking about it, that he's going to keep everything buried as far down as he can for as long as he can. I know that's dangerous. You can't do that with something so big. If you do, it will explode.

And then what will happen? If it affects him as violently as it does right now, what will happen when it explodes?

I close my eyes again. I can't answer that question. It's so important and so scary, but I don't have it in me to think about it tonight.

So instead I inhale him, enjoying his masculine smell. I know I'll never forget his scent now; it smells like the outdoors, like musk and cedar. Like everything strong and good in the world. It's delicious.

But I can't sleep. Even though I'm warm and safe with Gabriel, I'm restless and I know the reason why. Because I know that the second I fall asleep, he's going to leave.

"If you leave, I won't be able to sleep," I tell him. "So I think we're just going to have to lie here together, both of us awake until morning."

He chuckles again, tightening his hold on me. "Somehow, Maddy, I feel like you won't be a pleasant person to be around if you don't get any sleep."

I start to protest, but then can't even deny it.

"Fine, you're right," I grumble. "I'm a bitch when I don't sleep."

"Thought so," Gabriel answers smugly. "But that's OK. I like your bitchiness."

I jab him in the ribs and he laughs, while I snuggle back into the crook of his arm. I lie still for a minute, just savoring his nearness before I feel the need to share something.

"You're not the person I thought you were."

Gabriel startles, then his words are quiet. "And what kind of person am I?"

My answer is immediate. "You're someone who won't hurt me."

I hope.

Gabriel is silent for a moment, then he exhales a ragged breath. "I would never hurt you on purpose, Maddy. Did you think that I would?"

I hesitate. "I, um. I thought you were a different kind of person. I thought you were a bully and I seriously hate bullies."

Gabe lets that sink in. "Pax told me a little bit about your father. Is that why you hate bullies so much?"

I freeze, my hand unmoving on Gabriel's chest. I can't believe that Pax would tell someone. I'm not mad, just taken aback. It's not something any of us talk about.

I have a brief flash of my father's fist hovering above my mother's face, droplets of blood on her dress, and I force the taste of fear out of my mouth.

Even the memory of fear tastes bad.

"I guess," I finally answer. "I loved my dad. But he had an anger problem."

Gabe's question is hesitant, yet his words are strong. He sounds pissed, but like he's reining it in. "Did he ever hit you?"

My heart squeezes in my chest and I don't want to answer. I don't want to admit it out loud, but at the same time I don't want to lie. Not to Gabe.

"Only once. But once was enough."

It's enough that I close my eyes and stilt my words and it's very obvious that I don't want to talk about it. Gabe takes the hint and holds me closer, his strong arms incredibly gentle.

"It's OK. You don't have to tell me about it. I'm not like that, Maddy. I won't ever hit you. That's not me."

I relax now, letting my body soften against his.

"I know," I tell him honestly. "I'm not worried about that. I was more worried that you would be controlling like him, violent when you're angry. I can't take that kind of man. But that's not you. I know that now."

He doesn't ask why I would think that and I'm grateful. Because then I don't have to explain that I search for my father's traits in every man.

I don't have to explain how it makes me weak, how always being afraid of those traits gives me a vulnerability. A vulnerability that I don't want.

I close my eyes again, reveling in the comfort that Gabe brings me, surprised by it, actually. I never expected to find someone who affects me the way Gabriel does. It's like an unexpected gift.

Gabe seems tense though, his body stiff, and I figure it's because I scared the shit out of him by talking about my feelings... by sharing some of my past with him. I gently shake him.

"It's all right," I tell him softly, teasingly. "I'm done talking about deep stuff. I just wanted you to know that I misjudged you and that I'm sorry for it."

He relaxes, his hard body slumping against me. "You don't need to apologize. Everyone judges people when they meet them. It's normal."

It only takes me a couple of seconds to respond to that.

"What did you think about me?"

Gabe thinks about it for a minute. "I thought you were drop-dead fucking gorgeous and I couldn't figure out why you wanted to go home with me. You didn't seem like the kind of girl for a one-night stand. But I thanked God for my good fortune anyway."

I'm OK with that answer. It's not deep, but it's such a man answer. At least he's honest.

"I'm not the kind of girl for a one-night stand," I admit. "That was your sister's idea. She thought I needed to hook up and blow off some stress. But I met you instead. And that might've been a really good thing. I'm not trying to get serious or anything so don't get worked up, but what are we doing here, Gabe? What is this? You and I have been playing cat and mouse since we first saw each other. But I'm tired of playing games."

He's quiet for a second, then bends to press a kiss on the top of my head.

"This is you and me, Madison. This is just you and me. We might be fucked up in some ways, but like Jacey says, we're good people. We'll figure it out. Everything will be fine."

I nod and count his breaths, then listen to his heartbeat for a while. I count the steady beats and while I do, I can't help but ponder how everyone has issues. Some are more horrible than others, and so often, people just walk around with their painful secrets buried deep down inside because they are so ashamed of them.

Just when I'm almost asleep, I ask one last question.

"Is everyone in the world broken, Gabriel?" Even to my own ears, my whisper itself sounds broken in the velvety night. I can feel the weight of Gabriel's gaze as he stares down at me in the dark.

"I think so," he finally answers. "In their own way."

He pulls me close, kissing me softly on the mouth, before I settle back into his side. Before long sleepiness does overtake me and I slip into the oblivion that only sleep can offer.

When I wake up, the sunlight is streaming through my windows, and Gabriel is gone.

Chapter Twelve

I sit up and stretch, basking like a sated cat in the sunlight pouring across my bed. I'm warm and perfectly comfortable. Except for the fact that Gabriel isn't here. But that's no surprise. He told me he couldn't stay.

There's shit you don't know about me.

That may be true, but I'm not going to worry about it right now. I've put that away because it doesn't matter today. Gabriel is gone and last night was amazing.

I stretch and throw the covers back, picking up Gabe's pillow and holding it to my nose. It smells like man, musky and outdoorsy. Like him. I inhale it, then toss it back in place.

As I move, I realize that I'm a little sore *down there*. But that's not a surprise. I haven't had sex in quite a while—and last night was...er...vigorous. My cheeks flush as I remember Gabriel bending me onto the table outside. I'd better remember to wipe that thing down before I use it next.

I pad into the bathroom and brush my teeth as I wait for the shower to heat up. Staring at the water, I can't help but remember Gabriel bending me over in the shower as well. I blush harder.

Pretty soon I won't be able to go anywhere in my house without blushing. If I'm lucky. I have to smile at that, picturing Gabe and me christening every room in the house. It's an interesting thought and as I daydream about it, I dance around my bathroom singing "I Love Rock and Roll" at the top of my lungs.

I can't help it. I feel so happy today that dancing like a lunatic seems to be the logical thing to do, sore crotch or not. I feel lighter and happier than I've felt in a long time.

He did that.

Just as I'm spinning around by the shower door, I catch a glimpse of someone big and dark in the bathroom doorway. A shadow.

I startle, then freeze as I realize who the shadow belongs to.

Gabe leans casually against the doorjamb, his eyes glinting with amusement.

"Good morning," he says glibly. "I see someone's in a good mood."

He's here.

My heart practically sings, but just as quickly almost dies from embarrassment when I realize that he just witnessed my personal little karaoke/dance party.

My face explodes into a thousand shades of red and I turn so I can spit my toothpaste into the sink.

"What are you doing here?" I stammer. "I thought you weren't staying."

He grins again. "I wasn't going to. Did you know you're cute when you dance in the bathroom in your underwear? You can't hold a tune, though."

I shake my head and grin back. I might as well laugh at myself, right?

"Don't worry. I won't quit my day job, I'm just in a good mood."

Gabe stares at me wryly. "Well, you might not be in a good mood for long," he tells me. "The road's flooded. That's why I'm still here. We can't get out."

I stare at him blankly. "What? You've gotta be kidding. The last time that road flooded was years ago."

Gabe shrugs. "I don't know about that, but it's flooded today. It's been raining for two weeks straight. It's not that big of a shock. But it boils down to the fact that we're not going anywhere."

We're stuck here. Gabe and me.

Together.

As I think of the possibilities, I grin broadly.

"There are worse things," I announce, thinking about my daydream of christening every room. I smile impishly at him. "I can think of some things to do."

Gabe rolls his eyes. "Judging from that grin, I'm afraid to ask."

I'm about to respond when a distracting thought suddenly occurs to me that makes me panic.

"Mila. I've got to call and see how she's doing. I won't be able to get to the hospital."

I rush to my cell phone and drop onto my bed as I call the hospital, my foot bouncing nervously as I wait.

I had put her out of my mind last night when Gabe and I were...together. I had been so focused on my own pain, my own fear, that I lost myself in him.

How could I have done that? What kind of person am I?

After I'm transferred to Mila's room, Pax answers the phone on the second ring.

"How's Mila?" I ask by way of greeting.

"Good morning to you too," Pax replies. "She's fine. Calm down, Maddy. I can tell by your voice that you're freaking out. Mila slept through the night, they gave her fluids and they're releasing her today. She's going straight home to bed. And if you see her up at any point, you have my permission to beat her."

"I don't need your permission," I grumble. "I knew her first. But I don't know if you'll be able to get home. My road is flooded. I don't know about yours. I can't even get out."

"Ours is fine," Pax answers. "But I'm sorry that you're stuck. Don't sit there and stew about it. There's nothing you can do about it anyway."

"I'll try not to," I promise, as I eye Gabe. He stands in front of me, his muscled torso at eye level. To be honest, it's hard to think about anything but his exquisite body for the time being. It's a little distracting. "Is Mila awake?"

"Yeah, but the nurse is giving her a sponge bath. I'll have her call you when we get home."

We hang up and I turn to Gabe. "I've just got to make a couple more calls and then we can figure out what we're going to do. I wonder how long the road will be closed?"

Gabe shrugs. "It's hard to say. Do you have anything to eat?"

"I have a year's supply of frozen burritos," I tell him. "And maybe some rice."

"So we won't starve," Gabe points out. "We'll be fine. I'm going to go call Jacey while you make your calls. I'll need to get Brand to stay with her while I'm stuck here."

He ducks out of the room and I call Tony. His part of town wasn't flooded at all, so he'll be able to get to the Hill.

"And I saw on the news that it's only on your side," Tony tells me. "So the Hill will be fine. I'll call you if we need anything, not that you'll be able to do anything about it."

"Haha," I grumble. He chuckles, then hangs up.

I throw some clothes on, a T-shirt and shorts, and find Gabriel in the kitchen, looking through the fridge.

"You weren't kidding," he says. "You practically do have a year's supply of frozen burritos."

"I told you." I shrug. "I already know the irony of owning a restaurant and not being able to cook. You don't have to tell me."

"OK, I won't," he chuckles as he turns around. "I'm making some coffee. I figure you might need it. It took you forever to fall asleep last night."

I sniff at the freshly brewed coffee smell and glance at Gabe in appreciation.

"If I didn't love you before, I do now," I tell him jokingly. If I didn't know better, I'd think that his knuckles just turned white as he gripped his coffee cup harder. But that can't be right. I was just joking. Surely he knows that. I snatch a coffee cup from the rack and pour myself a cup.

"What should we do?" I ask dubiously. "We're going to get awfully bored if we're stuck here long."

Gabriel lifts an eyebrow. "Seriously? We're in a nice house on the edge of Lake Michigan. We'll find something to do."

I look around doubtfully. "You think this house is nice?" In my head I picture Pax and Mila's palatial beach-side mansion. This place is a shack compared to theirs.

"Of course," Gabriel answers. "You don't?"

I shrug. "I don't know. It was my parents'. I guess I haven't given it much thought. When they died, Mila and I inherited it. Mila didn't want it because she had a little apartment over her shop, so she let me have the house. I keep thinking that I need to renovate or something, to make it mine, but I haven't gotten around to it."

"You'll get there," Gabriel tells me knowingly. "When you're ready."

If that ever happens. It's been four years.

But I don't want to think about that.

"I want to go outside and look at the flooding," I tell him as I push away from the table. "How close is it to the house?"

"Not very, at least not right now. Have you ever seen it get close?" Gabe asks as we walk out the front door. I nod.

"Once. Years ago. I think we still have those sandbags stacked in the basement."

I suck in my breath as I step out on the front porch and take in the scene in front of me. There's water everywhere.

Fast-moving water has completely covered my road, the kind you can't drive through or it will carry your car away. The murky water is also lapping at the front edge of my lawn, watery fingers that are even now trying to grab at more ground, moving quickly toward absorbing everything between the road and my house.

"Holy shit," I breathe.

"Where did you say those sandbags were?" Gabe looks down at me. "We're gonna need them. That water has moved at least three feet toward your yard since I looked at it fifteen minutes ago."

"The basement," I tell him as I spin on my heel and dart toward the basement door. I jog down the steps and find everything just as my parents left it in my dad's dark underground workshop. The sandbags line the very back wall, at least twenty rows of them.

"There was a bad flood ten years ago or so," I tell Gabe as I grab one and haul it back toward the stairs. It's heavy—probably fifty pounds, but Gabe grabs four of them easily. "Dad kept the sandbags in case we ever needed them again. They were a pain in the butt to fill up the first time. He figured we didn't need to do it twice."

"Smart." Gabe nods. He acts like lugging two hundred pounds up the stairs is no problem at all. As we burst out the front door again, Gabe heads farther out than I would have expected.

Glancing over his shoulder, he tells me, "We've got to stack them a ways out. If we don't and the water seeps through, it can actually cause more damage to your house by trapping the water."

"That makes sense. How did you know that?" I ask curiously as I follow him, dropping the sandbag into place on the ground, starting a line. He shakes his head.

"I know stuff," he answers wryly, as he lines his bags up with mine. "I'm smart like that."

I don't comment on that. Instead I wonder about what kinds of things he must've done when he was a Ranger as we head back into the basement for more bags.

We end up making more trips than I can count. With each trip the stairs seem a little steeper and the yard seems just a little farther from the house.

By the time we carry the last bags out and stack them around the perimeter, the wall of bags is four feet high. The water has crept forward by another two feet, and my arms and legs are shaking like leaves.

Even though I'm covered in a layer of sand and dirt, I drop onto the couch, flopping onto my back.

"Holy crap. I couldn't carry one more bag if I tried," I moan.

"I don't know how you carried so many. You carried four times as many as I did, and you're not bothered at all."

"That's because I'm a badass," Gabriel says lightly, picking up one of my arms and rubbing at it. "You really *are* shaking."

"I knoooowww," I groan. "Carrying one bag is fine. Carrying a hundred starts to get to a person."

Gabriel shakes his head a little, but doesn't stop rubbing my arm. The warmth of his hand feels good against my skin. I flip onto my side, looking him in the eye.

"Do you think it'll keep the water out?" Even as I ask, I'm not sure that I care. If this house is destroyed by water damage, I'll get a brand-new one with the insurance money. One that doesn't carry bad memories in it.

Gabriel nods. "It should. Temporarily, I mean. I can't imagine the water will stay up very long."

"OK," I murmur. As long as we don't have to worry about the house being flooded while we're in it, I'm good. And with Gabe's hands on me, I'm *really* good.

"Thank you for helping me," I tell him quietly. "You didn't have to do that."

He lifts a dark eyebrow. "And how would you have carried all of those bags by yourself? You've got spaghetti arms."

I sputter and he laughs.

"You're welcome," he continues, ignoring my indignation. "It wasn't a problem."

"My own personal hero," I declare, smiling into his eyes. His expression turns a little cloudy, but he doesn't say anything.

He simply says, "It's what I do."

Once again I find myself thinking about Gabe in combat gear, dusty and hot, running with a rifle to rescue someone. But that's where my daydream ends, because I don't know *exactly* what he did as a Ranger.

So I ask.

Gabe tenses, then relaxes, almost like he's forcing himself to.

"A little of everything," he tells me. "We did some search and rescue, some recon, some surveillance. Our team was a specialized unit. But unfortunately, most of what we did was classified. I can't talk about it. It drives Jacey crazy."

"I bet." I smile, thinking of Jacey's inquisitive nature. "I'm sure it kills her. Speaking of her, is everything all right over there? Is the water near your grandparents' house? We were so busy with my house that I forgot to ask you about yours."

He shakes his head. "Nope. No water. They're fine. Brand's going to stay with Jacey until I get there just to make sure Jared doesn't try anything. I think he's probably done harassing her now, but you never know."

I remember Jared's terrified expression at the gas station a few days earlier. "I think he's probably intimidated now," I agree. "But like you said, you never know. He's a dumbass. And if Brand doesn't mind being there, it's probably a good idea."

"Brand doesn't mind."

"Well, good." I get off the couch and stare down at Gabe. "I'm covered in sand. I'm going to take a quick shower. Help yourself to anything you need; just make yourself at home."

"If you play your cards right, I'll give you a massage when you get out," Gabriel offers. "You got a big workout carrying those bags. We should probably rub the lactic acid out of your muscles so you don't get sore."

"Wow, that sounds so . . . clinical." I laugh. "But hey, it's a massage, so I'll take it."

I walk down the hall and I can feel his stormy gaze watching me as I go. I don't know what he's thinking, but it seems as dark as he is.

~

Gabriel

What the fuck am I doing?

Obviously I can't help being here, but why the fuck am I acting like a domesticated pussy-whipped idiot? Jesus. I'm not pussy-whipped.

Madison is pussy. Pure and simple.

She doesn't mean anything to me.

I don't care how many times her eyes turn soft when she looks at me, when they're normally jaded and worldly. I don't care how many times she calls me her own personal hero. I don't care that she's damaged on the inside, in a way that reminds me of Jacey—and of the damage that my father did to her. But Madison's damage is far, far worse than Jacey's.

And it's not my job to fix her.

I can't even fix myself.

I go through two cups of coffee while I wait for her on the sofa, as her "quick" shower turns into half an hour. But when she comes out dressed only in a T-shirt and panties, I'm wide awake without the aid of caffeine. I can see the outline of her perky nipples through her shirt and all my previous arguments about how little she means to me go out the window.

Especially when she looks at me with those soft eyes. Eyes that aren't soft for many people. It clenches my stomach into a fucking knot.

You can't trust me. But obviously I can't say that.

"Hey," I say instead. "Feel better?"

She nods. "Yeah. I stood under the hot water for a while. I'm sorry to keep you waiting."

"It's OK," I tell her. "Seeing your nipples was worth the wait."

She smiles, her cheeks flushing. "Where do you want me?"

"Under me on the bed."

Madison startles, but then I laugh. "Under my hands. I just meant under my hands."

She smiles back at me, but tugs me to my feet.

"OK. I'll lie on my bed. Then we'll both be comfortable. I have to tell you something, though." She pauses and blushes, which immediately piques my interest. This ought to be good. "I'm pretty sore. Down *there*, I mean. So..."

I interrupt. "Don't worry. I can rub that too." At her look of utter chagrin, I burst out laughing. "It'll be fine, Maddy. I won't try anything. We'll be fine on the bed. I mean, if you can control *yourself*."

She turns around and walks down the hall. "I'm not the one who needs that talk. The little man there needs that talk."

As soon as I realize that she's talking about my dick, I bristle.

"Hey, never, in any situation, should you call him 'little man.' The word *little* should never be used in conjunction with my penis."

She laughs as she walks into her room and sits on her bed.

"Whatever. I don't think you really need to be reassured about your big size, army man. It's the reason I'm in the shape I'm in, and you know it." She's smiling, and I can tell she's sufficiently impressed.

"That's better," I grumble as I settle onto her bed. "You can use that word all you want."

A wicked gleam shines in her eyes and she flips onto all fours, crawling up over me.

"*Big* army man. I love your *big* muscles." She trails her fingers along my biceps, up and over the contours, following the line of my neck. She turns my face toward her and touches her lips to mine. She tastes like honey. "And I love your *big*... ego."

I roll my eyes, but hold her tight to me, my tongue tangling with hers again.

"What else do you love of mine?" I ask softly, dipping my head to kiss her neck.

"I love your *big* sense of humor," she whispers, her hands trailing over my shoulders. "And your *big* smile, when you choose to use it."

"And?" I whisper back.

Her eyes meet mine and hers are so fucking blue. She kisses me again and then sits on me, wedging her hips tight against my crotch. My dick is rigid against her, rock-hard and straining against my underwear.

"I love..." she whispers, her lips touching mine. "Your *big cock*."

I almost choke when she says the word. Not only does she say it, she places extreme emphasis on it. It seems so strange coming from her lips. But she's feisty. I knew that. And Christ, I love that about her.

But she means nothing, right? My own thoughts taunt me and I gulp as her hand drops down to my lap and her fingers rub the length of me.

I groan.

"You've got to stop," I manage to say. "Seriously. Before you kill me. If you don't want to fuck me, you've got to stop."

She laughs lightly and hops off.

"That was a fun game," she says, her eyes twinkling. "What do you want to play next?"

I drop a pillow onto my head and take deep breaths.

"You're a female devil," I tell her. "Seriously evil."

She only laughs harder. "You're the one who made me sore," she reminds me. "So just remember that."

A thought occurs to me.

"Turnabout is fair play, you little demon. On your belly. Now."

Good-naturedly she flops onto her belly and I straddle her slender form. I bend down and whisper into her ear.

"Oh, sweetheart. It's not going to be that easy. I'm giving you a massage. You're going to have to take your shirt off."

Without saying anything or even looking at me, she strips her shirt off and tosses it to the side. She's not wearing a bra. Suddenly I can't decide if my punishment for her is going to be harder on her or on me.

She means nothing.

She means nothing.

I remind myself of that as my hands span the width of her back and I rub her muscles soothingly, her skin soft beneath my fingers.

My dick doesn't get that memo about how little she means to me and how little she affects me. Because each touch makes me a little harder and with each stroke my dick presses more and more into her ass. Fucking traitorous appendage.

I know Madison's acutely aware of it, but she doesn't point it out. She simply remains relaxed, facedown on the bed.

I move down to her feet and pick one up, rubbing every inch of it before I continue up her leg, up and over her knee and onward up to her thigh. I knead, pull and rub every inch of her. Up to her neck, down to the small of her back. Her breaths are coming in small little pants now and I smile. She's not as unaffected as she would have me believe.

And why does her body have to be so fucking perfect?

I slide my hands around her hips and pull her up just a little, as my fingers slide to the juncture of her thighs.

She inhales sharply and I smile again.

Leaning forward, I whisper into her ear, "Don't worry. I'll be gentle."

And then I bury my fingers slowly inside her, moving in circles as I slide them in and out. I kiss between her shoulder blades as my fingers fuck her. Within minutes her body tightens up and she moans. When she falls limply back against the bed, she turns to me, her cheeks flushed.

"What was that for?" she asks, her eyes slightly glassy. "You know I can't have sex with you right now."

She reaches for me, pulling me to her before she buries her face into my chest.

"I know," I say. "But since I've massaged it for you, maybe tonight?"

She giggles and nestles into me even tighter. "Maybe. If you play your cards right. For now, though, God, I'm tired from those stupid sandbags. Let's take a nap." She closes her eyes, but after a minute opens them again with a random question.

"Do you miss the Rangers? What rank were you?"

"Every day." My answer is immediate. "It's all I ever wanted to be. And I was good at it. I was a first lieutenant when I discharged."

"Wasn't there a way that you could've stayed in?" she asks, opening her eyes and looking up at me. "Somehow?"

I pause, stricken, but try not to show it. It's a question that I asked myself a hundred times before I made the decision to resign.

"No," I finally answer. "There wasn't a way. If there was, I would've done it."

"Are you happy doing what you're doing now?" she asks curiously.

I nod. "Yeah. I'm happy doing what we're doing because we're going to help other soldiers. Brand and I went through something shitty. And if other soldiers don't have to go through that because of our armor, it'll make me real fucking happy."

She nods. "The thing you went through . . . is that part of the shit you don't want to talk about?"

I nod. "Yeah."

Surprisingly, she lets it go. I stare down at her.

"What about you? Jacey told me that once upon a time, you were going to be a model or something. Are you happy here in Angel Bay?"

She's quiet and I know I struck a nerve.

Finally she shrugs.

"That wasn't meant to be," she says carefully. "Sometimes shit happens, and all we can do is our best. This is my best."

I stare down at the gorgeous woman curled into my side. I might be obtuse about women but even I can hear the resignation in her voice.

"You don't have to stay here, you know," I point out. "You don't have to live this life if it isn't what you want. It's clear you don't want to be here."

Madison blinks, staring off into the distance. I'm not sure, but it seems like she might be trying not to cry.

"It *is* what I want," she finally answers. "I wanted to be near Mila. And even though she's leaving soon, Angel Bay is home. The restaurant is here and running it is my responsibility. And besides, you're here now."

You're here now.

My chest tightens and my stomach tenses up. Because I wanted to fuck her without strings, without worrying that I'd hurt her. Because I know that I will. She seems tough, but it's obvious that on the inside she's fragile. It's only a matter of time until I fuck up and she needs to know that.

"Maddy, me being here might not be a good thing," I tell her. "That shit that you don't know? It's pretty ugly."

She nods, her hair brushing my chest.

"I figured it was," she agrees. "Or else you wouldn't hate talking about it. But it doesn't matter. All that matters is that you're a good person on the inside, Gabe. That's why I'm so glad I figured out what you're really like. On the outside, you're this cocky badass with a secret. But on the inside, you're good. I don't have to worry about you hurting me anymore."

She falls silent and I rub her arm as she fades into sleep. After a half hour or so, her breathing evens out and I know she is definitely asleep. That's when I finally answer her.

"Yes, you do," I whisper, before I carefully disentangle my limbs from hers and crawl out of the bed.

Chapter Thirteen

Madison

I wake up from my nap, finding myself alone. I sigh, then stretch. A glance at my clock tells me that I've been asleep for an hour and a half. I rarely nap at all, so I must've been exhausted.

As my head clears I remember the flood. I leap from the bed and race to the living room windows, staring outside.

The water has made its way up to the wall of sandbags, and is lapping against it. For now, the sandbags are doing their job.

"It's going to be fine," Gabriel says from behind me. "It's holding nice and tight. As long as the water goes down in the next couple of days, it should be good."

I turn around. Like always, I think I could stare at him forever. He's not perfect in a male-model kind of way. He's perfect in a rugged, sexy-as-hell kind of way. Masculine. Powerful. Strong.

"What?" he asks curiously as I stare. I shake my head.

"Nothing. Did you find things to do while I took a nap?"

Gabe nods as we head into the kitchen. "Yeah. I got turned around a few times. A few minutes ago, I think I found my way into your parents' room."

My gut immediately clenches, a stupid and extreme reaction to something so simple. I keep their door closed for a reason but obviously Gabe didn't mean to intrude.

"No big deal," I tell him airily, pretending to be casual. "No harm done. Did you close the door when you came out?"

Please have closed the door. I don't want to see in there.

Gabriel stares at me, curiosity in his dark eyes, like he can see through me.

"Yeah, I did. Maddy, their room looks like it must've looked the day they died. Your dad's boots are still by the door, caked in mud."

He pauses, staring at me. I stare back. "And?"

Gabe shrugs. "It's not my business. I was just curious. I wasn't judging."

I know he wasn't. Just as I know it's weird that I've left their room untouched. But grief does weird things to a person. So does guilt. I honestly just wanted to close their door and not think about it. Or them.

"I know it's weird," I tell him. "I can't explain it. Even to myself, really."

Even though it's been four years.

Gabe stares at me again, his dark eyes softening. I see sympathy in them. "Want to go for a walk on the beach?" he asks.

I nod. I throw a pair of shorts on and we make our way out my back door and down the path and spill out onto the beach. The air is cool and I can feel the moisture in it—both from the lake and from the flooding around us.

Overhead, sea gulls circle and cry.

In front of us, Lake Michigan crashes hard against the shore, disturbed by the recent storms. I know that if we walked down to the nearest public beach, the red flags would be flying...a symbol that the current is dangerous.

"Why didn't I ever see you in the summers?" I ask Gabe. "Jacey said you didn't come into town because you were shy. But that doesn't seem right."

He shrugs, looking out at the water. "I don't know. I spent a lot of time with our grandfather, fishing and stuff. Jacey and Gran were the ones who came into town."

"That makes sense," I answer. "But I wish I would've met you back then."

Gabriel laughs. "I think you would've been underwhelmed. I was so dead set on joining the military that it was all I could think about."

And you gave that up for some reason that you won't talk about.

That idea, that notion, makes me crazily sad.

"Well, it's for the best. I was sort of a wild child. You probably wouldn't have liked me anyway."

"I doubt that," he answers, and as he does, he picks up my hand and holds it. That simple little thing sends my heart ricocheting off my rib cage. It seems so intimate.

To keep from saying something stupid about it, I start chattering about my escapades, the way I used to be, the trouble I used to get into with my parents, especially my dad.

When Gabe looks at me seriously, I quickly regret mentioning that last part.

"I can't stand it when a man takes his anger out on a woman," Gabe tells me. "So I'm afraid I don't really have an open mind when I hear about your dad. I'm sorry."

I tense up, then remember that Pax told him about my dad. I

don't know how much, but probably enough. I stare at the wet sand as we walk, unable to meet Gabe's gaze.

"I know. But the world isn't always black and white. There's a million different shades of gray. I doubt that's something you've had to deal with in the Rangers. I'm sure everything is either right or wrong for you. But for normal people, there's a whole lot of space between the two."

"Are you defending your dad?" Gabe raises an eyebrow. "Seriously?"

The blood rushes into my head and I swallow hard. "No. It's just... you don't understand."

"Then help me to," Gabe implores me. "Seriously. I'd like to wrap my head around your rationale. It's clearly something that has messed you up, even still. Yet you still defend him. You still keep his boots untouched by his bedroom door, almost like you're hoping that he'll come back. I don't mean to be a dick and I don't mean to pry. But Jacey does this same shit with our dad. He doesn't hit her, but he disappoints her time and again and she always hopes for more. I don't understand it. If someone has shown you their true colors, chances are they aren't changing. Why do you hope for more? Why do you hold your dad's memory in a sacred place when he fucked you up?"

My breath is frozen as I stop in my tracks and stare at Gabriel.

"I don't hold my dad's memory in a sacred place. It's complicated. I loved my parents. And I hated them. And I miss them. And I don't want to think about them. All of that combines into something that I don't know how to deal with."

Gabe stares at me, unflinching. "How you can love someone who hurt you like that?"

I sigh raggedly. It's a question I've wondered about a million times.

"That's complicated too. But my dad was a good person... until he got mad. And when he got mad, he totally lost his shit. Like, Dr. Jekyll and Mr. Hyde. Honestly, it's one of the reasons why it unnerved me so much that first night with you in Chicago. You were like night and day too. Calm and cocky, then you lost your shit. I thought you might be like my father."

Gabe looks aghast. "Holy fuck, Madison. I didn't know your father, but I can guarantee you that I'm nothing like him."

I nod. "I know. But you were so different, like you just flipped a switch that night and then you punched a wall out of nowhere. After growing up with my father, it was terrifying."

Gabe looks uncomfortable, almost embarrassed.

"I'm sorry," he finally says. "I wish I could explain. But it's complicated."

"So you should understand how things aren't always black and white," I answer, feeling a little satisfaction at the conflicted look on his face. He looks unsure now. Unsettled.

"Tell me more about your parents," he replies, redirecting me, avoiding my statement. "Pax told me a little, but not much."

"When you grow up with someone like my father, someone who is wonderful most of the time, but a complete ass a quarter of the time, it messes with your head. You start thinking that it's normal, or that you deserve it, or in our case, sometimes I wondered if my mom deserved it. But deep down, I always knew she didn't. And then I'd get mad at her for staying... even though I loved him at the same time."

"It sounds like it really messed with your head," Gabe says quietly. "But you always knew it wasn't your fault, right?"

I step over a piece of driftwood and then stare out at the water, thinking about the one time that I didn't. "Usually," I answer. "Except for once. The one time he hit me."

"Let's sit," Gabe suggests, guiding me by the elbow to a big piece of driftwood. "I'd like to hear this. What made a grown man hit a kid?"

My eyes start to burn as I think about it and I swallow hard. Blurry memories start coming back to me, memories that I've purposely not thought about in years.

"I wasn't a kid," I correct him. "I was seventeen. My dad came home from the Hill pissed off about something from work and my mom wasn't home. I had no idea where she was but my dad thought I was lying for her. When he got mad like that, there was no reasoning with him.

"He asked me over and over where she was and I told him over and over that I didn't know. And then he just backhanded me. Hard. I went flying backward onto the couch. It felt like my entire face had exploded, it hurt that much. But that really wasn't the worst of it."

I pause, and wipe away a tear that has broken rank and fallen down my cheek.

Gabe's hand has clenched tightly around my own, tightly enough that his knuckles are white.

"What was the worst of it?" he asks.

His voice is grave and I can't bring myself to look him in the eyes. I'm afraid the expression I find there will send me over the edge and I'll break down again.

"He stood over me, screaming that I was a worthless whore like my mom. That I was lying for her because I was just like her. That I'd never be anything but a whore."

Gabe sucks in his breath and holds it. "And you thought that was your fault?"

I finally bring myself to look up at him. "Not exactly. But it's why I left for New York at the first opportunity. To get away. And *that's* my fault. I've felt guilty about that ever since. I left Mila and I left my mom...I left both of them here to deal with his shit."

"Mila was at college, though, right?" Gabe asks quietly. "And your mom chose to stay. That was her decision, not yours. You had to look out for yourself."

"Mila went to a college just an hour away. She drove back and forth. She still lived at home."

I'm silent now, staring at my feet, staring at the water, staring at the sky. Finally Gabe takes his finger and turns my face toward him.

"There's nothing to feel guilty about, Maddy. You didn't do anything wrong. He did."

"I feel guilty for everything," I blurt out. "I feel guilty for hating him, I feel guilty for loving him. I feel guilty for hating my mom for staying. I feel guilty for leaving her. I feel like nothing I will ever do will make up for any of it."

I take a deep shaky breath and Gabe stares at me.

"That's why you're here now," he says quietly, his thumb stroking mine. "You gave up your life in New York to make up for it, didn't you?"

It's something that I've never consciously admitted, but I know he's right. It's a thought that pisses me off. Everything about it pisses me off. And it pisses me off that he pointed it out.

"What does everyone want from me?" I demand suddenly, anger clouding my vision. "You, Ethan, Mila, Jacey...everyone is always telling me how unhappy I should be. How I act old, how I act boring, how I'm not myself. Of course I'm not myself. I had to give up everything to come back here and live my parents' life! Do you think I wanted this?"

I can feel my pulse beating in my temples as furious waves pass through me over and over.

Gabe stares at me, but not in surprise. It's like he's been expecting me to get pissed.

"Why are you looking at me like that?" I ask again, my voice shrill. "What do you want from me?"

Gabriel shakes his head, still calm. "I don't want anything from you. I just realized that you gave everything up. And I can relate to that. That's all. I know how you feel."

I suck in a breath, thinking about that. He did give everything up, but his situation was different.

"You don't know how I feel," I tell him. "You don't."

He stares at me silently, taking that in. "Maybe I don't know *exactly* how you feel. But I know what it's like to live a life you don't want. Do you trust me?"

I look at him, startled. Where did that come from?

"Yes," I answer uncertainly.

He smiles, a gentle, beautiful smile. "Good. Because I want you to hear me out without getting pissed and defensive."

The way he says that puts me on edge, because I'm sure I'm not going to like it. I can just tell from his tone of voice.

But before I can say that, he continues.

"We did some scary shit in the Rangers, and because of that, I know what fear looks like. You're afraid, Maddy. You're afraid to tackle your demons. And until you do, you're always going to be hung up in the past.

"The good news is that fear is a choice. You can stand in front of it, punch it in the face and get on with life."

I stare at him sharply. "You mean like you have? No offense, Gabe. But you shouldn't really be preaching at me about dealing with my shit. Not when you haven't dealt with your own."

He stares at me, his eyes hardening, then softening. As if he caught himself getting pissed and stopped it.

"You and I are two different people with two different issues. And we're talking about you right now. I'm trying to help you. Do you want my help or not?"

I don't know.

I stare at him uncertainly, my thoughts wavering. He stares back, unafraid of speaking his mind, unafraid of pissing me off, unafraid of everything.

"I don't know," I finally answer honestly. "I just don't know."

Gabe smiles patiently as he slides off the driftwood and pulls me to my feet.

"Trust me, you do."

As I stare at him, at his strong hands, his chiseled jaw, his wide shoulders, I know that he knows what he's talking about. He knows what it's like to be terrified of something, but to do it anyway. Just because he's got one thing that he can't deal with doesn't mean that he didn't face fear a million other times in the Rangers. And I do trust him.

"OK," I murmur. "What do you have in mind?"

We walk back to the house and down the hallway to the bedrooms, Gabriel's hand on my arm, both to guide me and to hold me in place when we stand staring at my parents' closed door.

"I've changed my mind," I announce as the wood door yawns in front of me. I try to turn around. "I don't want to do this."

Gabe holds me in place.

"Yes, you do. And you can do it. Fear is a choice, Maddy. Choose not to be afraid. You can start today. You don't like your life now? Change it. Start by facing this room."

I take a ragged breath back in and turn around.

In my head I picture my father when he was angry, face red, veins popping out in his temples, as he stormed through this door to find my mother. Then I picture him when he wasn't angry. Calm, loving, patient.

Dr. Jekyll and Mr. Hyde. I've always had to carefully screen what I remember so that I don't get upset. And I'm really tired of being held an emotional prisoner to memories.

I turn the doorknob and open the door.

It is still and silent in here, almost like a mausoleum. I sniff at the stale air, glancing at the walls covered in pale-pink flowered wall-paper. The room is clearly a female's domain, as well it should be, as often as my mother secluded herself in here.

Mila has been in here a couple of times since they died, but other than that, this room is untouched. I take a step inside, looking at my dad's boots by the door, their dirty clothes in their basket, my mom's makeup scattered across her vanity. I take another step, then another, until I find myself sitting cross-legged on their bed. My fingers shake as I try not to think about where I am.

Instead I stare into space, thinking back to the day they died.

"I was in Times Square when they died," I tell Gabe softly. "I lived in New York. I hadn't been there very long. But anyway, I was with a group of girls from the modeling agency when Mila called me. She was so hysterical that I couldn't tell what she was saying for a minute. But I'll never forget the feeling of standing in the middle of such a crowded place and suddenly feeling so very alone."

They're gone, Mad, Mila had sobbed. *They're just gone.*

"And for a second, just a second, all I felt was relief. I would never have to deal with their twisted drama again. But I pushed that horrible feeling aside and did what needed to be done. I was on a plane within hours and I never went back to New York. My roommate boxed up my stuff and sent it to me and I never looked back."

Until now.

"I'm sorry," Gabriel whispers, rubbing my back with one hand and pulling me to him with the other. "But in your situation, it was normal to feel all kinds of things, not just grief."

I nod. "My head knows that. But my heart thinks there's something wrong with me."

I slide from the bed and start sifting through my mom's trinket drawer. A large drawer in the top of her dresser houses anything she was sentimental about. Old pictures, random pieces of jewelry, love notes from my dad.

I pick one up, the handwriting bold and scrawled even as it is faded and old.

My love,

I hate being away from you. Every minute seems like an hour, every hour seems like a day. In only three days, we'll be married and our lives can truly begin.

I hope you like the flowers.

All my love,
Kent

My eyes well up at the thought that they were once so happy, without issues or drama, without abuse or fights. I can hardly remember a time when my father's temper wasn't hanging over our heads.

"My mom used to tiptoe around my dad's temper. She tried so hard to make sure he never got angry because she didn't want to deal with the repercussions. We learned to do the same thing."

I hand the letter to Gabe and pick up another one.

Nan,

I'm so sorry about last night. I'm sorry I lost my temper. It's just that the thought of you leaving me makes me crazy.

If you leave, I'll be nothing.

Please forgive me.

All my love,
Forever,
Kent

A tear streaks hotly down my cheek and I furiously wipe it away before I throw the entire drawer across the room, as hard as I can. It slams into the wall and everything in it explodes in a cloud of junk on the floor.

"Fuck you, Dad," I tell him as though he were standing right next to me. "Fuck you, fuck you, *fuck you.*"

Gabe picks up the letter and looks at it, then stares at me. "Your mom almost left him?"

I nod, not even caring that the tears are flowing freely now.

"A hundred times. But she never did. She would tell us to pack a suitcase and to go get in the car, so we would. But we'd wait out there for hours because they'd scream and fight and then make up. And all the while, she'd forget that we were out in the car waiting. Waiting for her to be strong and change our lives. But she never did. And I hated her for that."

I'm practically screaming now. As Gabe watches in astonishment, I rip open their closet door and start yanking clothing from the hangers and drawers, throwing each piece into a huge pile on the floor of the bedroom. I throw her shoes, his work shirts, his ball caps, her underwear.

Everything goes.

Everything.

After a while I glance at the pile. It's enormous.

"You forgot these," Gabe says quietly, holding a stack of old greeting cards held together with a rubber band. I gesture toward the pile.

"Throw it on."

He tosses it and we both watch as it slides down the mountainous heap.

Gabe looks at me. "I didn't think you'd throw all of this out in one fell swoop. You've got balls, Maddy."

"But what the hell am I going to do with all this stuff?" I mutter. The answer comes to me immediately and it's the only thing that makes sense. I look at Gabe.

"Bonfire."

A strange light shines in Gabe's eyes and he nods enthusiastically.

"That's perfect. Let's carry this stuff out down to the beach and burn it all."

We lug every last piece of the pile down to the damp beach. As we do, I remember all the bonfires Mila and I had down here over the years with our friends. In fact, Ethan came to many of them with us. We'd sit out here in the dark and make s'mores, go swimming and cuddle up around the fire with whatever boyfriend we had at the time.

This bonfire is very different.

For one, it's broad daylight.

For two, it's burning in effigy.

I turn to Gabe, throwing him a book of matches and a bottle of lighter fluid.

"I'm going to burn everything about my parents that hurt me, everything that caused me issues. My mom might not have been strong enough to deal with it," I tell him. "But I am. Fuck this."

Gabe nods, satisfied and pleased by my attitude. "This is exactly what I meant, Maddy. Fear is a choice."

He tosses a pair of my dad's shoes on the pile.

"That's your dad leaving after every fight, after every time he hit your mom," Gabe announces. Even though he wasn't there, it's as if he can see right into my life and knows what happened. Because that's exactly what my dad did. He left every time, leaving Mom at home to cry.

Leaving me at home to console her.

I glance at Gabe in appreciation, then throw a handful of mom's clothing and belts onto the pile. "That's for every time I saw my mom's bloody nose drip onto her dress…after Dad hit her."

Gabe nods and we take turns adding things to the mountain of memories.

Screamed words between my parents, a blurred memory of my mother curled up crying, an image of my dad slapping her…all of it goes onto the heap, piled like the rubbish that it is.

Dried flowers from her closet—sent as an apology for hitting her—go onto the pile as well. His apology wasn't fucking good enough.

So I'm going to burn it now.

Broken promises that he'd never hurt her again, broken promises that she'd leave him if he did…all go onto the pile. There are a lot of them.

When there's nothing left to add, I watch as Gabe squirts lighter fluid all over the pile, then turns to me, holding out a match.

"You do it," he tells me solemnly. "You deserve to do it."

I stare at the giant mountain and sniff at the acrid smell of lighter fluid as I realize that it symbolizes a monster, a monster that I have allowed to control my life for far too long.

It's because of my parents that I'm afraid to get involved with anyone, it's because of them that I'm afraid any relationship I get into will hurt me, like my dad hurt my mom. Even though my father loved me, he damaged me so much more than he ever knew.

I don't deserve that.

I toss the match and watch as the entire pile explodes into flame. The heat singes my hair, washing over me, and I take a step back. Gabe pulls me to his chest and together we watch my bad memories burn.

It is surprisingly cathartic.

I watch the dark smoke curling and wisping into the white sky, carrying the toxic memories away with it. I try to imagine that everything that has lain heavily on my heart for years is floating away… far, far away from me. It's not my burden to bear. It was theirs and they aren't here anymore.

They aren't here anymore.

But I am. I have my own mistakes to make...but I sure as hell won't make the same ones they did.

We sit beside the raging bonfire for at least an hour. When the fire grows dim I squirt more lighter fluid on it, causing it to rage again. I want to make sure that every bad memory has burned completely away.

"Do you feel better?" Gabe asks quietly as we walk back up to the house.

I realize that I do. I feel surprisingly lighter. I'm no therapist, but what I just did was really fucking therapeutic.

"I do," I tell him. "This was a good idea. Thank you. I'm sorry that you had to see me that way, that you had to see all of that...shit. But I thank you for making me face it. I'm sorry I got mad at you."

Gabe rubs his hand on my shoulder. "You weren't really mad at me and I knew that. I'm just glad it helped," he tells me.

We heat up some frozen burritos and rice, then sit curled up on the couch until bedtime. After we crawl into bed, Gabe holds me until I go to sleep, but he leaves me afterward.

I know this because he wakes me up in the night, tossing and turning and mumbling on the couch. He calls out for Brand. He mumbles incoherently. *This* is the Gabe I saw that first night. *This* is the Gabe he wants to hide from me. *This* is the Gabe he doesn't want to face.

I watch him for a while before covering him up and padding back to bed. There's nothing else I can do. He gave me the push I needed to face my demons...because I was ready to do it. That's the difference between him and me.

He's clearly not ready to face his own. I just wonder if he ever will be. And if he's not, what does that mean for me? Or for *us*?

It's not something I have an answer to, so eventually I give up thinking about it and slip into a fitful sleep.

When we wake in the morning, the water has gone down. I'm not very happy about it. On the one hand, I'll be able to go see Mila.

But on the other, this little bubble that I've been in with Gabe will burst and we'll have to go back to reality. The problem is, I'm not sure that we're ready for it.

Chapter Fourteen

Gabriel

What the fuck is happening?

My thoughts are a swirling mess as I work out at the gym. I can't believe this is happening to me. I don't get attached to women. Ever. I fuck them and I like fucking them. But attached?

No fucking way.

Why then am I all tied up in knots about Madison? It's an exercise in fucking futility because I can't stay with her. I'm too fucked up and she doesn't even know the half of it. It's not right.

But holy shit, it feels right.

Is everyone in the world broken, Gabriel?

I swallow hard as I punch the punching bag harder. Yes, everyone is broken, but I'm the most broken of them all.

Bile rises in my throat and I swallow it down. She has no idea what a monster I am. And if she knew, she would probably kick me in the balls and run hard in the other direction.

As well she should.

You're someone who won't hurt me.

Christ. The memory of her words has a visceral effect on me, tightening my gut. What the fuck am I doing here? Why am I fucking with her? It's not right.

It's not right.

But when I held her last night, everything felt right in the world. And when I think about walking away from her, everything feels like shit. Am I really selfish enough to want to keep her with me, even though I'm not fit to be with anyone?

The bad thing caught you.

I slug at the bag harder, hard enough that my shoulders strain from the effort.

The bad thing caught you.

I slug at the bag until I can't slug at it anymore, until my shoulders are weak and my arm feels like rubber.

The bad thing caught you.

I slump to the floor, leaning against the wall as I catch my breath.

The bad thing didn't catch me.

I'm the bad thing.

I hit the showers, then pick up the phone and call Jacey.

"Hey, Sis. Want to go shooting?"

"Sure. Meet me there in an hour?"

"Yup."

I taught her to target shoot when we were both still in high school, back when I was still wet behind the ears. I thought that being a Ranger would be the pinnacle of my life. It would make me a man.

I had no idea that it would break me.

I swing by the house and pile a Colt AR-15 and several boxes of ammo into my trunk before I head in the direction of the shooting range.

Over the years Jacey and I have spent hundreds of hours blowing holes in targets, just clearing our thoughts. The repetition of shooting is comforting and familiar. It's one thing that we can do together, one thing that we both enjoy.

When I arrive at the range, Jacey is already there and unloading her shit, including her pink fucking nine-millimeter that I always tease her about. She turns to me as I approach, her blonde hair pulled out of her face so she can see.

"So, what's wrong?"

I glance at her as I set my bag down.

"What the fuck? Do you think I have ovaries now? That I'm going to talk about my feelings and shit?"

Jacey grins. "Nope. We're going to blow some shit to pieces. And then we can talk about your feelings and shit."

I shake my head and put my orange foam earplugs in.

For the next two hours we blow the paper targets to smithereens. It's amazingly satisfying to blow holes through the center of the target, time after time. When Jacey is finally out of ammo and I'm damn close, she turns to me, pulling one of her earplugs out.

"You want some dinner?"

I nod. "Yup."

We head to the little burger place down the road, where Jace practically orders a side of beef along with a margarita. I stare at her incredulously as I place what seems like a small order now: a double quarter pounder, onion rings and a beer.

"Have you not eaten in a month?" I ask her as we slide into a cracked vinyl booth.

"It's 'that' time of the month, Gabe," she tells me with a grin. "I could eat two cows and a calf too."

Ugh. "TMI, Jace. Seriously."

She just laughs.

"Why are we here, Gabe? Seriously. I know something's wrong. You might as well just tell me, or you can let me badger it out of you. Either way is fine with me."

I roll my eyes. She'd actually enjoy the badgering part.

"I fucked up, Jace," I finally admit. "Big time."

She raises a blonde eyebrow. "What happened?"

I sigh and swig my beer, enjoying the cold bite of it as it slides down my throat.

"Madison."

Jacey instantly narrows her eyes. "What did you do? I swear I'll castrate you if you hurt her. I mean it. I don't want to see your junk, but I'll do it."

I shake my head, staring at the table, swirling my beer in the glass.

"I haven't yet. But I'm going to."

Jacey's puzzled now. It's apparent as she looks at me in confusion. "I'm not following you. If you haven't hurt her yet, then you don't have to do it."

Our food arrives and Jacey dives into hers, eating with more gusto than I've ever seen a chick eat with.

"You don't understand," I finally tell her with a sigh. "I'm fucked up. When you look at me, you see your big brother, same ol' Gabe. But I'm not that guy anymore. That thing that happened to Brand and me... it seriously fucked me up. Maddy doesn't deserve someone like me."

Jacey stops chewing and looks at me. "Why don't you let Maddy decide that?" she suggests. "Have you told her what happened to you?"

I shake my head. "No."

Jacey tilts her head, examining me. "How bad is it? Seriously, how bad can it be? I know you, Gabe. You're a good person, through and through. I would never have wanted to set you up with Maddy if you weren't."

"But that's what you don't get, Jacey," I answer. "I'm not good through and through anymore. I'm just not."

"Did you kill someone while you were in the Rangers?" she asks curiously. "Is that it? Because that's dumbass, Gabe. Obviously you had to know that you would kill someone if you joined the Army and went to Afghanistan."

I shake my head. "That's not it. And yes, I've killed people."

"It's worse than that?" Jacey is incredulous. "Then maybe I don't want to know."

I level a gaze at her. "Trust me, you don't. But I have a problem now and I don't know what to do. I didn't mean to get so close to Madison. I really didn't. I thought we'd hook up a few times and then I'd go back home. But..."

"But you really like her, don't you?" Jacey asks knowingly. "I told you a long time ago that you were perfect for each other."

I sigh. "I do like her. And she's been through a lot already. She doesn't deserve my shit. But I'm selfish enough to not want to leave just yet either."

Jacey pushes her plate away and stares at me over it, her arms crossed and a serious expression pasted on her face.

"Gabriel Joseph Vincent. Do you think you don't deserve something good in your life? Do you think that whatever happened overseas is so bad that you shouldn't ever be happy again? Because again, that's dumbass. You deserve happiness more than anyone I know. In fact, you deserve it more. Listen to me. You need to tell Maddy the truth. Just lay it out there. Let her decide for herself if you're worth it. You owe it to yourself *and* to her."

I nod, wiping my mouth and tossing the napkin on the plate.

"OK," I exhale. "Maybe you're right."

"I'm definitely right," she answers. "And for once it feels good to lecture you, instead of you lecturing me."

I roll my eyes, we pay the check and then walk out to our cars.

"Seriously, bro. She's worth it. She really is. She's tough and prickly on the outside, but she's got a heart of freaking gold."

I think back to yesterday, to standing in front of that bonfire watching her bad memories burn, and the vulnerable look on her face.

She's tough and prickly on the outside but she's fragile as hell on the inside.

And that's the part of her that I'm afraid of.

"Thanks for the advice, Sis." I kiss her on the forehead. "I'll be home later."

"And if you're not, don't worry about it," she answers. "We haven't seen Jared in a while. I think he's done messing with me now."

"We can hope," I answer as I climb back into my car. Before I start it up, I send Maddy a text.

Wanna meet me at the pier by your house after you leave work?

It only takes her a few minutes to reply.

Sure. Why?

I answer back, *I need to talk.*

A split second later she answers. *Hmmm. Ok. I'll see you around 9:30.*

I head home and shower, messing around the house for a while, until it's time to go. I leave a little early and sit on the end of the pier with my legs hanging off, throwing stones until Maddy shows up.

Even if I hadn't heard her car door slamming in the parking lot, I would feel her presence. She stares a hole between my shoulder blades as she walks down the long pier to meet me. She situates herself next to me, taking a stone from my hand and throwing it. It skips once on the surface of the water, then sinks like the stone that it is.

"So, what's up?" Maddy asks quietly. From the look on her face, I think she probably thinks that I'm going to end things with her.

"Remember when I told you that I had shit you don't know?" I ask solemnly, heaving another stone out into the water.

She pretends to think about that. "Yeah, I seem to remember something about that."

"Well, I decided you should know about it."

Maddy inhales deeply and stares at me.

"You sure?"

I shake my head. "No. But you were fucking brave yesterday. I'm not pussy enough that I can't do it too. But you might think I'm a pussy by the time I'm done talking."

Maddy sticks her chin out and looks me in the eye. "I doubt it, but there's only one way to find out."

I take a deep breath, then another. The night air is chilly and fireflies flit around us. For just a second I contemplate changing my mind. But that's not an option.

Just do it, you fucking pussy.

"OK," I begin. "You know that I was in Afghanistan with the Rangers. You know that I had to do some shitty things. But there was something, one thing that happened that fucked Brand and me up. It's why we're here, in the comfort of air-conditioned homes and eating decent food while our guys are still in the hot-as-hell desert eating MREs."

Madison stares at me, waiting.

"OK," she says. "I understand that part. And I know that if it wasn't something terrible, you wouldn't be here. I'm ready to hear it. I'm not going to judge you."

I stare at her in the dark. "I need you to know that it was the worst day of my life. I can't tell you all of it, but I want you to know what you're dealing with, OK?"

She stares at me solemnly, nodding.

I inhale, then exhale. My breath sounds ragged in the night but I ignore it. Instead I focus on the words I'm saying, focusing on each one separately so I can get through them all.

"It's hard to know where to start. Afghanistan was fucking brutal. I guess I can start with that. Hot, sweaty, smelly. Everywhere we went we had to watch over our shoulders. People hated us but pretended they didn't. It got to be a lot to take. But I could've taken it. Forever, if need be, because that was the life I chose. It was what I wanted. But one night something happened that broke me. It completely broke me, Madison."

I pause, gathering my thoughts, gathering myself before I continue. I can't even look at Madison's face. I don't want to see what she's thinking.

"One night it was so fucking hot and black, and Brand and I were doing patrols outside of Kabul with our friend Mad Dog. We were leading a four-Humvee convoy, headed to a break-apart point where we would separate in four directions. Right after we separated, a bomb went off. Our Humvee exploded into a million pieces—and it blew Mad Dog apart."

Madison sucks in her breath, silently waiting for more. I swallow.

"He was a good guy, Maddy. A real good guy. He had a wife and a little baby back home. He got his name from drinking too much cheap ass Mad Dog and he never lost at poker. Ever. He was a good friend. And I repaid him for that by making a decision that blew him into a million fucking pieces."

I stare at the water now as I pause to collect myself. Because all I can see in my head is the memory of his intestines piled outside his body in a pool of blood that looked black in the night.

All I can see in my head is everything else, everything I can't tell Madison about. The rest of the story.

Maddy breathes in, then out, and I can see that what I've told her is enough.

"I'm so sorry, Gabriel. Oh my God. It's just so horrible. I don't know what to say. I'm so sorry. You can't blame yourself, though. There's no way that was your fault."

I look at her and her gorgeous face is drawn, tightened up in horror.

"That's just it. I made a mistake. That's what happened that night. And when I came home, I went to Mad Dog's funeral. When I tried to hand his wife the flag that covered his coffin, she looked me in the eye and said, 'It should've been you.' Because it should've been. She knew the truth."

She knew all the things that I can't tell Maddy.

She knew what really happened. She'd read the army's incident report, the black-and-white words that couldn't possibly explain the *incident.*

Heat flares up in my throat, threatening to close it. I swallow, then swallow again as I try to relax, to breathe.

Just breathe, motherfucker.

Maddy wraps her arms around my shoulders and holds me tight, her breath soft on my neck.

"You can't believe that," she tells me softly, her lips grazing my ear. "You can't believe that. You're strong and good, Gabriel. It was a horrible accident. You didn't cause it."

I look at her again, a lump in my throat.

"I did cause it," I tell her. "You don't need to know how. What you need to know, though, is that I came home fucked up. The past doesn't stay in the past, Maddy. I came home with PTSD and I can't fix myself. I'm not normal anymore. And I don't think you should be with someone like me."

Maddy looks at me, her eyes glistening with unshed tears, filled with sympathy for me. I should hate that, but I'm so fucking glad not to see judgment in them that I don't. I'm so fucking glad not to see that she thinks I'm weak. Or pathetic. Or all the other things that go through my own mind.

"No, you're not normal," she tells me firmly. "You're good and strong and brave. You put your life on the line every day for people like me, so that we can sleep safely at night. You did unimaginable things, Gabe. *For people like me.* Trust me, I want to be with someone like you," she tells me. "So don't even try that shit with me."

Then her eyes widen.

"That night in Chicago. You were having flashbacks, weren't you?"

I nod, not looking at her. "It happens at fucked-up random times. I can't control it and that's the most fucked-up part. It gives me a weakness."

Maddy looks at me. "And you can't have a weakness? Even Achilles had a bad heel."

I roll my eyes. "If I remember right, Achilles died because of his heel."

"True," she acknowledges. "Gabe, you're not weak. I'm so sorry that any of this happened to you. You didn't deserve that. And I hate that you think you have to hide it. It's nothing to be ashamed of. I've heard that lots of soldiers come home with PTSD. Even the biggest and strongest like you."

I just shake my head. There's nothing I can say to make her understand how emasculating it is. How much it fucking sucks to have a weakness like this one.

"What are you doing about it?" she asks hesitantly. "What's the treatment?"

I shake my head again. "I declined treatment when I came home. I mean, I saw a shrink a couple times, but I didn't do the extensive program that Brand signed up for. It's called CPT. It stands for cognitive processing therapy or something like that. Brand told me that it fucking sucked, but still thought I should do it. I said no way in hell. I'll deal with it on my own."

"And how's that working out?" Maddy sounds doubtful.

"Shitty," I admit. "But it can't be worse than CPT."

"How long does the CPT last?" Maddy asks curiously. "Can you still do it?"

"I could," I answer carefully. "But I don't want to. It's supposed to be a week of pure hell. I've had enough of hell."

"OK," Maddy answers uncertainly. "But do you remember what you told me yesterday? You said you could see that I'm afraid to face my demons, that until I do, I'll always be hung up in the past.

Those were pretty wise words, Gabe. And I think they might apply to you too."

I shake my head. "Your past is different from mine, Maddy. People died because of me. It's not the same."

She stares at me doubtfully, but doesn't push it.

"I'm sure you know what you're doing."

I don't.

But I don't say that.

Instead I look at her again. "Do you think I'm a crazy asshole now?"

She stares at me like I'm actually crazy.

"Gabe, I saw you melt down in Chicago. Trust me, my imagination was way worse than reality. When you didn't say anything about it, I thought you might actually be crazy. But you're not."

I stand up and hold out my hand to help her up. "Do you hate me now?"

"For what?" She's incredulous. "For doing your job? For coming home devastated? For losing your friend? Um, no. I respect you even more for what you've been through."

"Maybe you're the crazy one," I mutter as we walk down the pier.

"We shouldn't rule that out," she agrees. I chuckle, a low sound in the night, before I tuck her into her car. "Meet me at my house," she suggests. "Stay with me tonight."

I tense up automatically, out of sheer habit. "I don't think so," I tell her. "I don't think I should."

"But I know what to expect, right?" she answers. "Nightmares, tossing and turning? Trust me, I've seen it already. I saw it that first night and I saw it last night. You woke me up from the couch. It's not that big a deal."

I picture that girl in Kabul. The blood running down the side of her face. She would beg to differ, I'm sure.

But that was almost a year ago. Surely I've come a long way since then.

Surely.

I finally nod. "All right. I'll meet you at your house."

Maddy grins beatifically. "Perfect. See you there."

I get into my car and sit there for a second. I can't believe I just did that. I might not have told her everything, but I told her some of it and she didn't run.

I take a shaky breath in. Then out.

Is it possible that everything might really turn out OK?

Is it possible that like Maddy, I can face what happened and move on with life?

It seems too much to hope for.

Yet that's exactly what I'm doing.

Hoping.

I start my car and follow Madison's taillights to her house. In the dark they almost seem like glowing red eyes watching me.

The bad thing caught you.

Fuck the bad thing.

Chapter Fifteen

Madison

Driving to my house, I think about what Gabriel said. And it all makes perfect sense.

No wonder he freaked out in Chicago when our taxi exploded. It was an explosion, for God's sake. It must've seemed just like the bomb in Kabul.

I swallow hard.

Hearing him talk like that, so vulnerable and hurt, touches me in a place that I've never been touched, a deep-down place where wives and mothers keep their protective instincts.

It makes me want to wrap my arms around him and hold him where I can protect him, as if I could. I know that I can't, just as I know he would never allow it. He's as alpha-male as they come.

I pull into my driveway, get out of my car and meet Gabe as he's stepping out of his Camaro. I drag his face down to mine, kissing him hard. He's surprised, but wraps his arms around my waist, pulling me closer, returning my kiss.

Finally he pulls back. "What was that for?"

I shake my head. "Just for being you."

He looks at me skeptically, but doesn't push it. He simply follows me into the house. Knowing what happened to him puts me in a sentimental mood and all I want to do is sit around and stare at him, marveling at his bravery. Or hold him tight. Or drape myself in his arms. All of these things would make me look crazy, so I don't do any of them.

Instead I suggest that we sit in the hot tub.

"You have a hot tub?" He raises an eyebrow. "How did I not know this?"

"It never came up before." I shrug.

"I don't have a swimsuit," he warns me, his dark eyebrow lifted.

I smile.

"You don't need one."

I tug him by the hand until we reach the sunken hot tub on my veranda. Gabe eyes it in surprise.

"I didn't even notice it was here that first night that we...well, I didn't see it."

I laugh as I step out of my shorts, then peel off my top. "We were a little distracted that night."

I take off my bra and then step out of my panties, standing in front of him completely nude. He eyes me in appreciation, his gaze doing a slow sweep up and down my body.

"I'm a little distracted right now," he admits, undoing his own pants and shedding his clothes.

He pulls me to him, my skin against his, his hands running up and down my backside.

"Have I ever told you that you have the sexiest ass in the world?" he asks quietly.

"No, you haven't," I chuckle. "But feel free to."

"You do," he announces against my lips. "I could keep it in my hands all day."

"Why don't you keep it in your hands over here where it's warm?" I suggest, as I move away from him and toward the hot tub.

Gabe slips out of his clothes and follows me, and true to form, he does grab my ass as I step into the steaming water.

Once I sink down in the water, I climb onto Gabe's lap.

The feeling of his skin against mine instantly turns me on and I kiss him hard. For a reason that I can't explain, I need to feel close to him tonight. I want to absorb his pain, all the pain he's been hiding. I want to take it away so he doesn't feel it anymore.

I want to drown in him. I want him to drown in me. My body and his body and nothing in between.

And there's only one way I know of that I can do that.

I slide my hand along his stiff cock, listening to the way Gabe sucks in his breath as I touch him. I love the way his voice sounds in the dark, I love the way he feels against my hand. I love the way he responds to me.

I love the way he opened himself to me.

The way he trusted me with himself.

I love the way he feels beneath me, his thighs under mine.

I kiss him again, muffling his full-throated groan with my lips, and it's like he knows my thoughts, he knows all of these things that I love about him.

And I don't even have to say it.

Without another word, I lower myself on him in the water, burying his cock deep inside me, and he throws his head back, gripping my back with his large hands.

"Don't you want a condom?" he manages to say, lifting his head and looking at me with stormy eyes. I shake my head.

"I'm on the pill. And I trust you."

"Fuck, Mad," he groans, as I lift myself up and down the length of him.

The water makes it easy to take more of him in me, to sink fully down on him. I can tell it's driving him crazy. But it's driving me crazy too. The way his skin slides against me makes me want to cry, my nerves are so feverish, my emotions so raw.

I want him to come, though. I want to absorb him into me, I want to take everything he can give me. Take and take and take. All of it.

"Come for me, Gabe," I whisper against his throat, since his head is tipped back. I kiss it slowly, licking the wetness from his skin, tasting him. "Come for me."

He groans. "You're killing me."

I laugh, a low and husky sound because I'm so turned on. "That's the point," I tell him. "I want you to come. I want to feel it."

I move faster, slipping up and down his length, until he does groan and grab at me, and I know he's coming. I feel him throb and pulse. I feel the heat of it inside me and I smile.

"Now was that so hard?" I ask with a smile as I curl onto his lap. He grins.

"No. That's the problem," he answers. "It wasn't hard at all. But you didn't come. We need to take care of that. Fair is fair."

Even as I protest and tell him that he doesn't need to, he flips me onto my back and holds me against him as he slips his fingers into me. Moving fluidly, he deftly and quickly brings me to my own climax and I come and come, twisting and writhing beneath his hand.

"You're good at that," I finally tell him when I can breathe again. He grins.

"Thank God. You're insatiable."

"Whatever," I chuckle. We lie in the hot tub until our fingers start to prune.

"I think we're going to have to drain this, sanitize it, and refill it," I mention as we climb out and wrap ourselves in towels. Gabe chuckles.

"Why? Is anyone else besides us going to be using it?"

He has a point.

We order Chinese and curl up on the sofa to eat it. We watch a movie until we're sleepy enough for bed and then it's finally my favorite time of day.

I love the night because I love snuggling against Gabe's hard chest. I love it when his arms close around me and he holds me close. I feel safe and secure, as though nothing from the real world can touch me.

And tonight he won't be leaving. He'll stay with me all night. It's a thought that makes me smile.

As I lie inside the crook of his elbow, I listen to the crickets chirping outside my window and the lake crashing against the shore, lulling me to sleep. I listen to Gabe's rhythmic breathing and the sounds of his light snore when he slips even deeper into sleep.

I don't know how long it is before I follow him.

I don't know how much time passes until I'm awakened.

But it only takes me a brief second to realize that I can't breathe.

Gabe's hands are squeezing my throat, his fingers curled around my neck like a vise grip.

I startle completely awake, thrashing against him as I try to breathe, but his arms are wiry steel bands and I can't budge them.

"Gabe," I rasp. "Gabe! It's only me. Wake up."

But the look in his dark eyes is dull, he's not awake. And he clearly thinks I'm someone else.

"Fuck you!" he screams at me, his face contorted in anger. "Why did you do it? She was just a girl. You're a fucking murderer!"

He clenches his grip tighter and I can no longer breathe at all. I push at him as hard as I can until my vision begins to tunnel and the edges turn fuzzy.

"Gabe," I gasp desperately.

My chest feels hot from lack of oxygen and my fingers and legs go numb. I can't feel my hands enough to push at him anymore. My eyelids are too heavy to hold open and I know beyond a shadow of a doubt that if I close them, I might not ever open them again. "Gabriel, please…"

I can't speak anymore. Gabe's grip on my throat is too tight.

I can't move. He's fifty times stronger than I am.

And I can't breathe.

As I close my eyes and everything goes black, I realize that this is what it's like to die.

Chapter Sixteen

Gabriel

Smoke curls around me, making it impossible to see and just as impossible to breathe. I duck my head closer to the ground as I drag myself by my elbows. The lower I get, the cleaner the air is. The smell of gasoline and burning rubber is almost suffocating and I try to take small breaths.

"Brand!" I hiss, as quietly as I can. I don't know who else is hiding in the shadows, who else is watching us, waiting to attack. "Brand!"

I still can't see, but I hear a moan, low and ragged, and I keep crawling to find it.

The darkness makes it impossible to see and the crackling fire from the burning Humvee makes it almost impossible to hear.

"Fuck," I mutter as a jagged piece of metal cuts into my thigh and wedges in deep. I reach down to pull it out, and my hand comes back bloody. I know I'm in shock because I don't feel anything, not a thing, even though I am covered in blood. I can taste it, the metallic rusty taste, dripping down my throat. I don't know how much longer I'm going to stay conscious because my vision keeps blurring in and out.

It makes me nervous that I can only hear one person. The blast was bad. And if something happened to Brand, I'll never forgive myself. I should have seen this coming. I should have acted faster. If only that little girl hadn't looked so fucking scared.

"Not Brand," I tell God. "Not him. Please."

I keep crawling through the dirt and finally the smoke breaks and the moon shines brightly enough that I can see the situation a little better. I can see Mad Dog's still form, lying a few paces away. His legs are no longer attached to his body, his intestines are hanging out of his torso. His blood seems as black as the night as it pools around him.

Fuck.

He's dead and it's my fucking fault. But I can't help him right now. I need to find Brand.

I spin to the right, hunting for him. I see nothing. I peer into the distance as far as I can see, and I'm relieved to see a slow movement from up ahead. A leg. A combat boot, army-issued. It moves again.

Brand.

Thank fuck.

I am trying to get to him when I come across the girl.

Her eyes are glassy and open.

And her head is detached from her body.

I know I pass out, because when I next open my eyes, a man is standing over me. Dressed in traditional Afghan garb, he stares down at me wordlessly and I know instinctively who he is. He sent the girl to attack us. He's not real, though. He's not real because he wasn't there that night. My mind is making him up.

But real or not real, I want to kill him for what he did.

I lunge to my feet, regardless of my pain, regardless of anything except the rage that is coursing through me. I wrap my hands around his throat.

"You motherfucker," I hiss. "She was a child. You're a fucking murderer. She didn't have to die for your fucking misguided beliefs. You're insane."

I squeeze tighter when he tries to speak.

"Fuck you!" I scream at him. I can see that my hand is covered in blood. "She was just a girl. You're a fucking murderer!"

I want to snap his neck. And I'm going to do it. But first I want him to suffer.

He needs to suffer for what he did.

I squeeze tighter, enjoying the way the life drains from his eyes, the way the breath squeezes from his helpless lungs. He deserves pain. He deserves all of it.

"Gabriel, please," he begs in a forced whisper.

I squeeze tighter and the man finally goes limp in my hands.

It's only then that I realize something.

He shouldn't have known my name.

I open my eyes to find Madison's slender neck in my hands, her eyes closed, her body limp. Shock slams into me hard and fast, and I can hardly breathe from the realization of what I've done.

Jesus Christ, I've killed Madison.

Chapter Seventeen

Madison

I'm in the dark. Floating in a pond. Or I'm at the end of a dark tunnel. Or maybe at the beginning of one. To be honest, I don't actually know where I'm at. But everything's cloudy and warm and soft and I never want to leave.

Nothing can hurt me here.

I know that. I can feel it.

But then someone shakes me, grabbing my shoulders, their fingers digging into my arms. There's harsh breathing in my ear and mumbling.

"Holyfuckholyfuckholyfuck." The words run together, panicky and fast. And I know that voice.

I'm balanced on a precipice. Because it's Gabe and he just tried to kill me. He was crazy after all.

If I open my eyes I'll be back with him. I'll have to fight for my life. And do I really want to? It's so comfortable here. It didn't hurt. It's all done.

But if I stay here, *it's all done*.

I'll never be anything.

My arms are limp and my body numb as I do the only thing I can do.

I open my eyes.

Chapter Eighteen

Gabriel

"Holyfuckholyfuckholyfuck."

Madison is limp in my arms, not moving.

"Maddy, wake up," I beg her, my fingers digging into her shoulder. "Wake up. God, please...wake up."

Please.

God.

She's limp, pale and fragile. Her eyes are closed, her lashes pressed against her cheek. She's too quiet, too still. Because God doesn't listen to me anymore.

I bend my head, listening for breath, feeling for a heartbeat.

Nothing.

But wait.

Yes, it's there, but barely.

"Maddy," I beg, one last time before I completely lose my shit. I can't breathe. I can't think. I press my lips to her forehead, saying her name against her skin. "*God, please.*" I beg one more time for her.

And just like that, she opens her eyes and stares into mine.

"Gabe?" she asks groggily, her hands cupping her throat as though the effort to speak is too much.

I drag her to my chest, holding her tightly there, clutching her as my heart races, as I try to make myself believe that I didn't kill her.

Is this real? Because I never know anymore. Not at night. Not while I'm sleeping.

"I'm so sorry," I tell her raggedly, breathing into her hair. "Jesus, I'm so sorry."

It takes me a minute to realize that she's struggling to get away, her hands fumbling against my chest. Startled, I release her and she scoots away from me, like a cornered animal.

"*What the fuck, Gabe?*" she asks wildly, her hands still gripping her throat. "What *was* that?"

As I stare into her wild eyes, I see the worst possible thing I can see. Not anger, not hate, not blame.

But fear.

Of me.

And with that, I know this is real. All of this is real. Everything.

My gut clenches into a vise grip and I swallow hard, my jaw clenching, then unclenching. I can't even answer her.

She stares at me, still panicked. "Get out!" she screeches. "Just get out."

I'm stunned, frozen in place, so she moves instead, scrambling to her feet, rushing for the bedroom door. I watch her run away and I do the only thing I can do because I can't let her leave like this.

Not when she doesn't understand.

She needs to understand.

I lunge across the room and grab her, holding her to me, preventing her from leaving. It's the only thing I can think of to do.

She struggles, spinning in my arms, hitting at my chest, kicking and clawing.

"Let go!" she screams, her fingernails raking across my face. "Let go!"

"Maddy, stop," I plead quickly, ignoring the burning slashes across my cheek. "Just stop. I'm not going to hurt you. I just want to explain. I swear to God I'm not going to hurt you."

She stops and stares up at me uncertainly.

"Let. Go," she demands again. "If you let go, I'll listen."

I immediately let go and she stands dead still in front of me.

"See?" I ask. "I promise you. I'm not going to hurt you. I just want to explain. God, please, Maddy."

Her eyes are hard, but they soften just slightly as I speak.

"What the fuck was that?" she demands. "Tell me right now."

"Maddy." But my voice breaks and I have to try again. "Maddy, that was...it's the part that I haven't told you. That was the bad thing. It caught me and no matter how much I try to get away from it, I can't. I'll never get away from it because *I'm* the bad thing now."

I'm babbling, nonsensical. But I don't know how to fix that because all I want is for her to hear me. To know what I am.

Maddy's face shudders, her eyes close, then open. "The bad thing?"

Skeptical.

Doubtful.

I try to take a breath as I nod.

"A woman in Afghanistan...afterward. She told me the bad thing had caught me. But she was wrong. *I'm the bad thing*, Maddy. And I shouldn't be anywhere near you. I tried to tell you. And now you know. I didn't mean to hurt you. Jesus Christ, I didn't mean to hurt you. This is why I wouldn't sleep with you. It happens when I sleep... the night terrors. They're so real and I'm not myself. *I'm not myself.*"

I close my eyes, hating the red burning that is behind my eyelids, hating the pressure in my throat, on my heart. Hating that I can't breathe. Hating this fucking weakness.

Hating myself.

But Maddy's cool hands are on me now and they shake as her fingers brush against my face, caressing my forehead. She ducks her head and whispers into my hair.

"It's OK, Gabe. I understand. You didn't mean to hurt me. I see that now." I know she's afraid, I can see it in the way her body is shaking, the way her eyes are hooded and guarded, the way she's ever so slightly curved away from me, like she's ready to bolt at a moment's notice if need be.

But even still, in spite of her fear, she's here.

Comforting *me.*

"You're OK," she says again, and I'm not completely sure if she's reassuring me or herself.

"But *you're* not," I tell her in anguish, eyeing the already purple marks on her throat. They're in the perfect shape of my hands. "Jesus Christ."

My head drops into my hands.

"Now do you see?" I ask her. My throat is so dry that it's hard to speak. "Do you see? This is why you can't sleep with me. *This is why you shouldn't be with me.*"

She shakes her head and pulls at me, clutching, and now I'm practically sprawled in her lap. Her breathing is quick and mine is ragged as we try to calm down, as we both try to process it.

"Tell me what happened," she says bluntly. "Tell me the rest. Please. I'm trying to stay calm here, but I'm sort of freaking out. I need to understand."

A flash of the little girl's face pops into my mind, dark-eyed and terrified. All the bodies, all the blood, the smell of the burning flesh. The smoke.

Christ.

I squeeze my eyes shut, but it's all still there. It's still haunting me and I know it always will.

I open my eyes and glance at Maddy. She waits expectantly, one hand against her throat. I gulp.

"The night that our Humvee exploded," I begin roughly. "It was so dusty, dusty as fuck. We could barely see our hands in front of our faces and the darkness didn't help anything. I was talking to Brand, keeping an eye on the horizon, when a movement caught my eye. Something made the hair on the back of my neck stand up. I knew it was something bad. And it was."

I pause for a second and the silence yawns between us.

"What was it?" Maddy whispers, her face pale, hesitant. She doesn't want to know, but yet she does. She *needs* to know and I have to tell her. She deserves that much.

I want to squeeze my eyes shut, wanting nothing more than to block the memory out, but of course I don't.

"It was a little girl. She was coming out of the shadows. I had to focus to see her face and when I did, I saw how terrified she was. And then I saw why. She had a bomb strapped to her chest."

Maddy gasps, then freezes, her hands stilled on her throat as she waits for me to continue.

"If she detonated that bomb, Maddy, I knew it would tear us

all apart. I knew that, but I hesitated anyway. I didn't want to kill a kid." I pause and swallow hard.

I can hear my tongue moving against the side of my teeth because my mouth is so dry.

"I watched her for a second—only a second—waiting to see what she would do. I was frozen, Maddy. Every bit of my training was suspended in my mind, because she was just a fucking kid. I saw her little fingers holding the detonator. I saw them shaking. And I knew she didn't want to push that button."

"What did you do?" Maddy asks woodenly, although I can see in her eyes that she already knows.

I swallow, the memories burning me.

"I watched her through the sight on my rifle. I yelled out for her to stop. And she looked up at me. Her eyes were begging me. *Begging*. Black as night and full of fear. Terror. And I knew in that second that she was more afraid of whoever strapped that bomb to her chest than she was afraid of dying. I knew she was going to do it. Her finger twitched and I pulled the trigger."

I squeeze my eyes shut, trying not to visualize my memories, trying not to remember the horrible smell in the air that night.

The blood.

"Everything exploded. Everything. I couldn't see. I couldn't feel. I couldn't think. I crawled through the smoke and the dust and when I found Mad Dog, he was dead. His legs were gone and his insides were all lying on the outside, on the ground beside him. There was so much blood. I could taste it in my mouth. I can still taste it in my mouth. Every night, over and over."

"The girl?" Maddy whispers.

"The girl...she was in pieces. I found her head. I can't get the look in her eyes out of my mind. Her eyes were still begging me to help and I couldn't. I'm never going to get away from it."

Madison stops breathing as she stares at me in horror. "Oh my God. Gabe. Why didn't you tell me about this? This is...I...it's horrible. *God*."

I close my eyes again.

When I do I see the girl's face again, frozen in that moment. Dark skin, dark eyes filled with fear as I shot her, right before everything exploded. Right before everything froze, keeping me there with her forever.

Fuck.

Maddy still looks horrified, but her fingers are moving again, brushing comfortingly against me, soothing me in spite of her horror.

"You didn't kill her, Gabe. Whoever strapped that bomb to her chest did. Not you. You did the only thing you could."

"You didn't see her face," I tell her raggedly. "But I did. Right before she exploded, she looked at me and everything froze. It was just her and me. We were connected through the lens of my rifle. She needed my help, but I shot her instead. I'll see it every night until I die. I can't forget her face."

My voice breaks and Maddy's fingers trail down my face, down my neck, over my back. Her voice spills out in broken whispers, empty words, because she can't fix me and she knows it. There's nothing she can say to fix me.

I'm the bad thing. And now she knows it.

"Gabe, this wasn't your fault. It wasn't your fault." She says it over and over and over. "Gabe... *God*."

"God didn't have anything to do with this," I tell her wearily.

"Trust me. He turned his back on that shit a long time ago. And I haven't told you everything yet."

Madison freezes, stricken, her fingers halting their movement on my back, her breath lingering on her lips in horror. "You haven't?"

I shake my head. "No. I haven't told you the worst part."

Maddy closes her eyes.

"The little girl was a distraction. They bombed my Humvee to distract us from what they really wanted us to see. They wanted us to see it, but not get there in enough time to stop it."

I close my eyes, trying not to see it all again. All the little bodies, all the mothers' bodies thrown over their children, all the blood. All the death.

I swallow.

Then swallow again, tasting the horror all over again.

"Taliban rebels wanted to intimidate a nearby village into supporting their insurgent movement. When nothing else worked, they rounded up most of the village's women and children and slaughtered them in front of the village men. They spared the boys... so that they could turn them into insurgents. Everything else was burned."

The bedroom is as quiet as a grave, the only noise being Maddy's harsh breaths. Her eyes are wide, her hands are clutched in her lap so tightly that her knuckles are white.

"Gabe," she says limply, but whatever else she was going to say dies on her lips. I stare into her eyes.

"I should've done my job and shot the little girl, Maddy. I shouldn't have hesitated. But because I did, hundreds of girls and women died that night. When that bomb went off, it signaled the insurgents that we were close, that it was time to slaughter those people. Letting that bomb go off gave them time to do it before we got to them. If only I'd shot the girl. It would've stopped the bomb...stopped the slaughter...stopped everything."

My voice breaks and my head drops into my hands. My eyes are burning so much that I can't hold them open anymore.

"They burned them, Maddy. They burned the bodies. They even burned the ones who weren't dead yet. I tasted their bodies in the air. I'll never forget that taste. Or the smell. Or the sounds of the fathers wailing. I've never heard men screaming like that. It was... brutal and inhumane and sadistic. And it was my fault."

I keep my eyes squeezed closed against the terrible memories. The sights, the smells, the sounds. The tiny blood-spattered hands. The burned flesh. The lifeless eyes. The horrible screams.

"I've never heard men screaming like that," I repeat limply.

I fight the urge to heave, even now, my stomach quaking as it rebels against me.

Maddy buries her face into my shoulder, stroking my back.

"It wasn't your fault," she finally says softly. "You had no way of knowing what was going on, Gabe."

I look at her painfully. "When you asked me if there was any way I could've stayed in the Rangers...this is why I couldn't. You can see now, right? I'm seriously fucked up. I can't trust myself anymore."

Maddy's eyes are full of pain as she looks at me helplessly. "Of course you can, Gabe. *I* trust you."

She's so focused on everything I just told her, on how sorry she feels for me, that she has forgotten what I've just done to her. I reach out and touch the bruise forming across her throat. She flinches backward, then forces herself to remain still.

"I'm a monster, Maddy," I tell her simply. "It doesn't matter if I mean to be. I *am* and that's enough."

"Don't say that," she snaps at me. "You are not. You're not."

Then why can't you look me in the eye?

I sigh. "Whatever I am, I'm a Ranger, Maddy. I'm trained to kill. And in my sleep, when I relive that night over and over, I'm like a fucking runaway train. It seems so real to me, so fucking real. We can't know what I'll do when I think I'm in a life-and-death situation."

This is why you shouldn't be with me.

She shakes her head, still not meeting my gaze.

"You might've been trained to kill, but you were also trained to protect. You're a protector, Gabe. You were protecting Mad Dog and Brand and the other three Humvees. You were protecting that little girl when you didn't want to shoot her. You won't hurt me."

"I already did," I insist, staring at the bruise on her neck. "And we have no way of knowing if I'll do it again, Madison."

My voice is anguished and rough and full of pain.

"*You won't,*" she says firmly, finally looking me in the eye. The fear is still there, even though she's trying to ignore it.

Because I taught her that fear is a choice. *Fuck.*

"We can't know that," I tell her limply. That's what I say.

You need to stay far away from me. That's what I think.

"*I* know it," she insists, her voice adamant, yet soft and scared. I have to admire her loyalty, even though it's misplaced in me.

I'm suddenly so tired, so very tired. Tired of carrying this weight. Tired of worrying about what I am or what I might do. I've already hurt Maddy and that's the worst possible thing. The only thing I can do now is make sure I never do it again.

The resolve feels good. It gives me something to focus on.

"Let's talk about this in the morning," I suggest, hating the way those words feel in my mouth. I hate lies. "I want you to rest. This is a lot to take in. And I know your throat must hurt."

I pull her close, lifting her into my arms and holding her on my lap. She's soft and beautiful and trusting, even as she's afraid.

"You're not going to stay, are you?" she mumbles. "You're going to leave just as soon as I'm asleep. You're never going to stay all night again."

She sounds saddened by this, even though I could've just killed her.

"Maddy, don't worry about this right now. Just sleep, give your throat a rest. Don't worry. I won't hurt you again."

Guilt, for the thing I'm not saying, weighs so heavily on my chest that I can barely breathe.

I won't hurt you because I'm leaving Angel Bay and I'm not coming back.

"I'm not worried," Madison answers quietly, her hand on my chest. "I'm not worried that you'll hurt me, Gabe."

But she is. I know she is.

Fear might be a choice, but *she should fear me*. I'm the most dangerous thing in the world to her. If she won't acknowledge it, then I'll have to do it for her.

You're a protector, Gabe.

She's right. I am. And even though she won't understand it, even though she'll probably never forgive me, I'm going to protect her now.

Madison takes forever to fall asleep tonight, but I don't mind. I hold her cradled in my lap for hours, long after she has fallen asleep.

I watch her, the way she turns to me instinctively, the way her body molds to mine, the soft way she breathes in the night.

My throat is hot and tight when I finally ease her onto the bed and settle her into the cool sheets. In her sleep Madison is open and trusting, unafraid. It's the way she should always be. But it's the way she'll never be able to be with me.

Because I'm the scariest thing of all. *The bad thing.* And she'll always have reason to fear me.

But not if I'm not here.

I stand above her, looking down, unable to swallow the lump that has formed in my throat. Bending, I kiss her forehead.

"I love you," I whisper.

With long determined strides, I walk from her room.

I don't look back.

Chapter Nineteen

Madison

Oh. My. God.

I'm still in shock as I pull into the Hill's parking lot, completely oblivious to the beautiful morning around me.

The sun peeks over the top of the stucco building, making it seem as though it's glowing. The scenic beauty surrounding me seems like something out of a painting, with the rolling hills along the beach and the water crashing into the sand. It's nature at its finest.

But it doesn't matter. Nothing matters but what happened last night.

As I turn off my car, I glance into the mirror, adjusting the silk scarf knotted around my neck to hide my bruise. Every time I swallow, it hurts. When I talk, my voice is hoarse. It's a nasty reminder of what happened.

I'm almost glad that Gabe wasn't there when I woke up. He's going to freak out even more when he sees the bruise.

Gabe.

I close my eyes, remembering the look on his face last night.

The terrifying look of a lethal killer. His eyes were almost black and filled with the single-minded purpose of killing me.

My heart races as I remember. *He thought I was someone else.*

He thought I was a Taliban radical.

But that doesn't make my heartbeat slow down. Or my worry disappear. Or my fear go away.

Fear is a choice, I tell myself silently.

And last night I was afraid of Gabriel.

Just like I've always been afraid of my father.

But Gabe isn't my dad.

Gabe would never hurt me on purpose. I know that. We'll just have to fix what is broken. We'll figure it out. Gabe might think it is, but I know that PTSD isn't insurmountable. He's a good man.

As I envision the twisted lethal look on his face last night, I swallow painfully and remind myself of that again. *Gabriel is a good man.*

I quickly pull my phone out and text him.

Good morning! I missed you this morning. Are you ok?

A simple good morning will do. I'm not going to lecture him via text message. We can talk about getting help for him later. Tonight, after work.

I adjust my scarf one more time, then head into the Hill.

Tony is already here and I stop to talk with him first before I head back to my office. He's picked up a lot of my slack this week and I owe him a huge thank-you. And maybe a gift card or something.

"Whatever, Madison." He waves me away as I try to thank him. "I'm only doing my job. I'll help you in whatever way you need."

He goes back to stocking the bar and I head back to my office. It seems as though there is never-ending paperwork in this business.

I check my phone only to find no answer from Gabe. He must

still be asleep, which doesn't surprise me. He was probably up all night.

I set my phone aside and bury myself in work. I don't come out for an hour, when my tiny bladder makes it necessary to take a bathroom break. Before I leave my office I check my phone again, but there's still no text from Gabe.

Hell. I really need to hear that he's OK today. Last night was so intense. I need to hear from him. And I really want to see him.

I decide to hit the bathroom and then head over to his house. This is something that deserves a calm conversation in the light of day. We need to decide what to do, how best to get him some help.

We've got to do that so we can move forward.

I'm surprised to run into Jacey in the bathroom because I hadn't realized that she was here yet. We stare at each other awkwardly for a minute.

I know I'm the one making it awkward. I haven't really come right out and told her that Gabe and I are together. And it's stupid. I need to address it, so after I wash my hands, I turn to her.

"So, your brother and I have been seeing each other," I tell her hesitantly.

She stares at me.

"I know," she answers carefully. "I'm really sorry, Maddy. Are you OK?"

I am utterly confused as I stare at her solemn, sympathetic face. Gabe told her about last night? I can hardly believe it.

"Um, yeah," I finally answer, my fingers fluttering unconsciously up to my throat. "I'm OK. It was an accident. He was asleep. He didn't mean to do it. He feels terrible, so let's not talk about it, all right? And I definitely don't want Tony to know."

Jacey stares at me blankly. "You don't want Tony to know what? What in the hell are you talking about, Madison? Gabe didn't mean to do *what*?"

Her eyes freeze on my neck, where I can safely assume that my scarf has slipped down. Her eyes widen and she grabs my arm.

"Holy *fuck*. Did my brother do that?"

I stare at her numbly, completely confused.

"If you didn't know, then what were you talking about? What are you sorry about, Jacey?"

She freezes and we stare at each other, the air between us snapping with electricity.

"We seem to have a misunderstanding here," I point out slowly, apprehension building in my chest. "What are you sorry about, Jacey?"

"Well...now I'm sorry for two things," she stutters. "I'm sorry that my brother hurt you. Holy shit, I'm sorry. I can't...he's never... I don't understand."

I look at her levelly, anxiety causing my fingers to shake.

"The second thing, Jacey." I prompt her out of her daze, terrified to hear the answer. "What is the second thing?"

Jacey stares at me and blinks, as though she's trying to blink away this situation. It's bad. It's really bad. I can see it in her eyes and I don't want to know.

I don't want to know.

But she tells me anyway.

"Gabriel left," Jacey says simply, hesitantly. "He left this morning."

I stare at Jacey, shaking my head in disbelief.

"No, he didn't," I argue numbly. "He wouldn't. He was with me last night. And he told me everything that happened to him. He wouldn't leave now."

I finger my bruise.

Don't worry. I won't hurt you again.

His words from last night echo through my head. This is the way he's not going to hurt me again... by leaving.

"Fuck," I say limply. I want to sink to the floor, to let my shaky knees give way, but I don't. Instead I walk back to my office and close the door, ignoring Jacey's questions and her pleas to talk.

"I need to be alone," I tell her through the door, before I collapse into my chair and put my head on my arms.

I feel completely empty, completely in shock. I didn't see this coming. I really didn't.

My insides are empty, cavernous and black. A void. My heart is a void. Do I have a heart after all? Was this even real? Was any of it real? I have the dazed idea that maybe I fell down the rabbit hole that first night at the club after all. Maybe... maybe... maybe... I should pull myself together.

I open my eyes and stare at the wall, my cheek pressed firmly to the cool wood of my desk.

All of it is real.

Gabriel is gone.

I am here.

And I suddenly realize that I've been scared of the wrong things all along.

Instead of worrying that Gabriel was a bully or violent or had a bad temper like my dad, I should have been afraid of him for the one thing that could hurt me the most.

For the one thing that *has* hurt me the most.

I should have been afraid of losing him.

I lift my head and wipe the tears that have streaked down my cheeks and onto my arms. I pick up my phone and try to call him. It goes straight to voice mail. I hang up.

I stare at the wall, fighting the urge to throw my phone at it.

Instead I stare at the little screen before I start typing on it.

You can't make me love you, then just leave.

I send the message, even as I realize that it's exactly what he did. He made me love him and then he left me.

He. Just. Left.

Like none of this happened. Like none of it mattered.

Like I'm nothing at all.

I add a second text.

Fuck you, Gabe.

❦

"Oh, my sweet Lord," Mila mutters, watching me check my phone for the millionth time in two days. "I'm going to freaking kill this guy myself. I'm going to get out of this bed, travel to wherever he's at, and kill him."

I stare at her miserably. I feel like a lovesick teenager, yet at the same time I feel so much more than that. I feel completely crushed, completely empty, completely jilted. Gabe hasn't even bothered to answer my texts. He hasn't called.

He told me everything, his deepest, blackest parts. He made me understand. He made my heart break for him, made me feel his pain... and then he just left.

Like I'm inconsequential, like I'm not even important enough to think twice about.

Fuck him.

That's what I keep telling my heart. But my freaking heart is so stubborn. It insists on being broken.

"Tell me what happened," Mila insists firmly when a tear streaks down my cheek. I know it unnerves her because I simply don't cry.

Not usually.

"It's complicated," I say wearily. "I don't want to get into it."

"Well, I do," Mila answers, her eyes snapping. "I need to know what happened so that I can help. When Pax left me, you made me tell you everything. Now tell me."

So I do. I go through everything, from the way I met Gabe, to the way he punched the wall that night, through my fears about the way he handled Jared... to what happened last night. When I'm finally finished, Mila is pale and wide-eyed.

"Let me see the bruise."

Her words are stark, stilted.

I untie the scarf and let it fall to the floor. Mila gasps, horrified at Gabriel's purple handprint on my neck.

"Oh my God," she breathes. I nod.

"He wasn't even awake. He didn't mean to."

Mila stares at me doubtfully. "Are you sure?"

"Of course I'm sure," I snap. "I'm not an idiot. He was asleep. His night terrors are so real that he can't even tell what's real and what's not. He thought I was someone else. He was completely wrecked by it, Mi. And now he's gone. He wanted to protect me, so he left."

I'm crying now and Mila reaches over to wrap her skinny arms around me.

"It's OK," she soothes me. "Shhhh. Go ahead and cry. It's OK. It's all going to be OK." She pats my back and I cry and cry and cry.

When I'm done she hands me a Kleenex.

"He didn't mean to do it," I repeat for good measure, staring her in the eye. She nods slowly, her face expressionless.

"I don't doubt that," she says slowly. "I can see that about him. But that doesn't change the fact that he *did* do it, Maddy. He needs some help. And if he wasn't going to get that help, then maybe it's best that he left."

My eyes burn, but I don't cry again.

"You don't understand," I mumble. "He thinks he's un-helpable."

She nods again, solemnly. "I'm sure he does. I remember that Pax was the same way. And what did you tell me?"

I turn my face, refusing to answer even though I remember very well what I said.

"What did you tell me?" Mila repeats firmly.

"I told you that he had to get help on his own, that you couldn't fix him." My voice is sullen because it seemed so very different when I was dishing out that advice rather than receiving it.

"And you were right," she tells me gently. "And I'm right now when I tell you the same thing."

"But he didn't leave to get help," I tell her limply. "He left for good, to protect me."

Mila looks pained, her hand fluttering around to pat my back again. "I know. But maybe it will all work out and maybe he'll be back. Someday. And everything will be fine. Trust me, when Pax left, I didn't think he'd ever come back. But he did."

I shake my head, changing the subject. I just can't talk about it anymore. Not if I don't want to break down again.

"I'm sorry, Mila," I tell her tiredly. "I don't mean to bring you down. You've got enough on your plate being stuck in bed. I really just came out here to help with the baby's room. It needs to be organized and I doubt Pax will know what to do with it."

Mila nods, eyeing me carefully. "Well, that part's right. Pax has no clue what to do with the baby things. But don't think you can't talk to me, Mad. Trust me, I know how you're feeling right now. If you need to talk again, I'm here."

"Thank you," I tell her softly, as I bend and kiss her cheek before I head out the door.

"Don't give up, Maddy," she calls after me. "I mean it!"

I don't answer. I just walk down the hall to the baby's room and open the door.

A flood of sunshiny yellow greets me as light from the windows hits the yellow walls. Pax hired a painter to come in and paint it yellow, per Mila's request. Since they don't want to know the sex of the baby, they had to be gender-neutral. And Mila loves the sun.

Fuck the sun. I hate the sun today.

I look around at the unopened boxes, at the baby monitors, the stacks of clothing with the tags still on, the stroller still in the box. Pax has ordered all the right supplies, he just has no idea what to do with it all.

Which is why I'm here. Hopefully it will keep my mind off my own pain.

I get to work. I put together the changing table in a logical place in the room, next to the mahogany crib. I line up all the little baby care things on the shelf next to it: the powder, the lotion, the nail clippers.

I hang the mobile over the bed, adjusting the colorful kites so that they're the right height. I put sheets on the crib mattress. I set up the baby monitor. I fluff the pillows on the rocking chair.

And then I sit in it and fold the tiny baby clothes so I can put them away.

As I stare at the tiny little undershirt in my hands, at the way it's hardly bigger than my hand, my vision blurs as tears fill my eyes.

I won't have this… not for a long time. Maybe not ever.

Gabe left me and I don't want anyone else. I can't imagine ever wanting anyone else… so a family, a baby, a husband… a happy life… it's out of my grasp.

I close my eyes and just let myself cry again, quietly in the sun… the sun that refuses to leave me alone.

I don't know how long I cry. All I know is that finally I don't have any tears left. I'm totally spent. My throat feels scratchy and hoarse and my eyes are hot.

I can't cry anymore. It's all gone.

I open my eyes to find Pax sitting across the room on the delicate white love seat.

"What the…" I'm startled. "How long have you been here?"

He stares at me, his hazel eyes troubled. "Long enough. Tell me where he is. I'm going to beat his ass."

I shake my head, staring at my hands.

"Not you too. Mila already threatened that. Not that she's actually a threat. He didn't mean to hurt me, Pax. He was asleep. Like I explained to Mila, he has PTSD. He honestly didn't know what he was doing."

Pax shakes his head. "That's not what I'm beating his ass for. I believe that he didn't mean to hurt you. He's not that kind of guy. I can tell. What I'm going to beat his ass for is leaving you like this. It's a dick thing to do."

My eyes well up again, even though I thought my tears were all gone.

One drips down my nose and onto my hand.

"I wish I'd never met him at all," I confess painfully. "I wish he had never come here. Then I wouldn't feel like this right now. I wouldn't feel like someone yanked my guts out and put them back in all the wrong places."

Pax stares at me, then crosses the room, kneeling next to me with his hand on my back.

"You don't mean that," he says gently. "You were closed off before. I don't know shit about women, but even I could see that. This is horrible, I know. But at least you're feeling something. You know?"

I stare at him incredulously. "Seriously, Pax? I would rather feel nothing at all than like this."

He nods. "I know. I'm sorry that I'm not good with this stuff. All I can tell you is that you should just concentrate on yourself right now. I'm pulling the funding for DefenseTech, so you won't even have to hear his name. Just focus on yourself. Gabe's got shit to take care of and it's not your fault."

"I know," I tell him. "I know it's not my fault. And you know what? You're right. Instead of focusing on him, I'm going to concentrate on working on myself. Lord knows there's a lot of work to be done."

Pax smiles slowly. "Well, there's not that much to do. You're pretty great, Mad. He has no idea what he gave up."

My eyes tear up again. "I don't want to think about him anymore," I whisper. "It's too hard."

Pax nods. "I know. I'm so sorry, Maddy. I honestly can't imagine what happened. Gabe's a stand-up guy. Trust me, I know assholes and he's not one. I hope that he can get his shit straightened out."

I nod silently. "That's not really my problem now," I finally answer.

"Whatever you say," Pax replies as he stands up. "I just want to see you happy, Madison. You really do deserve it. You've taken care of Mila for so long and I can't tell you how much I appreciate that. But that's my job now and you need to take care of *you*."

"Thanks, Pax. Really. I mean it. I do love you, you know. I know you don't like talking about mushy shit like this, so thank you."

He grins. "Anytime. My advice isn't always good, but it's free." At my quick look he adds, "But in this case it's good."

I roll my eyes as I stand up.

"I think I'll run to the restaurant while Mila naps. I'll be back with dinner."

Pax holds out a fist for me to bump. "Awesome. Mila will thank you. She's getting pretty damn tired of scrambled eggs, which is the only thing I can cook."

I bump his fist limply and shake my head.

"It's a good thing you're pretty," I tell him on my way out the door. I can hear him chuckling as I leave.

I don't feel like joking. I honestly don't. But maybe if I pretend that everything is normal, that everything is OK . . . maybe it will be.

Chapter Twenty

Gabriel

Fuck you, Gabe.

I stare at my phone, at the last words from Maddy.

My gut clenches with every word, more and more, over and over.

Fuck you, Gabe.

What the fuck did I do?

For two days I've been asking myself that question. And for two days I haven't had a good answer. The only thing I know is that I can't hurt Madison again and this was the only way I knew to protect her.

But God. God, it fucking sucks. All I want to do is pick up the phone and call her, to check on her . . . to explain.

You're a fucking pussy.

Because I can't. If I do, if I hear her voice, I might be tempted to forget all my misgivings and fears about hurting her and rush back to her. Not that she'd likely take me back at this point.

Fuck you, Gabe.

How I got myself into this situation, into a place where I love someone even though I know I can't have her…it's all my fault. I knew going in that I can't ever be with anyone. That I'm not whole. That I'm not normal.

That I'm a monster.

That I'm the bad thing.

I knew all of this. And I chased her anyway…because I had to fuck her, I had to harness the storm that I knew she would be.

And now I love her and everything is fucked up.

I have no one to blame but myself.

With a sigh I return my attention to this fucking interview.

Brand set up some second interviews for an assistant, one who would be based here in Denver since this is where the factory will be. He did the first interviews, so I have to do the second ones. It's only fair.

But I overslept this morning and so I had to meet this morning's candidate in my hotel room, rather than the café on the main floor.

As she talks to me, her words run together, her voice fades to the background, and I don't really give a flying fuck what she's talking about. My thoughts are in Angel Bay with a gorgeous blonde.

"So, that's about it," the girl, Alex, finishes up, smiling at me. "And I'm available to start immediately."

Sitting on the edge of the bed, I smile absently as I glance at her résumé in my hand.

"OK. Well, I know Brand has already interviewed you, so we'll talk and then one of us will get back to you."

Alex smiles again from where she's sitting at the table in my hotel room. She's young and sort of pretty. Her eye makeup is thick and dark, slightly smeared at the corners. Her red lipstick is severe. As I watch, she crosses, then uncrosses her legs.

Hello, shaved pussy. I can't believe my eyes. Did she just give me a shot of her crotch on purpose? What the hell?

"I really need this job," she tells me, her voice turning husky and suggestive. "Is there anything I can do to get it?"

Boom. She did. Fucking hell. It's like the universe is offering her to me, giving me an opportunity to take my mind off Madison.

Surely it won't be that easy.

But Alex is getting up and moving toward me, her eyes on my lips.

"I can be very persuasive," she whispers as she shoves me backward onto the bed, sliding her slim form between my legs.

"You definitely can," I agree, automatically sliding my hands up her hips. "Did you try and persuade Brand like this?"

She giggles. "No. I didn't need to. He told me that he likes me. If you like me, then I get the job."

Hell.

My conscience disappears as the blood flow is redirected from one head to the other.

"Well, you'd better show me your qualifications."

Alex bends her head, kissing me firmly. She tastes like chocolate. It's foreign, but not unpleasant. I kiss her back.

"You know, you don't have to do this," I finally tell her, and I'm actually not sure if I'm telling her or myself.

"I want to," she tells me. "Have you looked at yourself?"

So now she's appealing to my ego too. Smart girl.

She reaches down and cups my dick, making it a perfect trifecta. Hormones, ego, dick. She's got her bases covered. My body reacts like it always does. It gets hard.

I roll her over and cover her body with mine, sliding my hand up under her short skirt. I should've known something was up when she wore such a tiny skirt to an interview.

I get harder as I slip my fingers into her.

My thoughts cloud as I move toward an ending that I know will take me away from reality, from stress, from worrying about doing the right thing, *from Madison*.

When I do this, I don't have to think.

I just have to feel.

It's natural, instinctive.

Alex moans and I close my eyes. I don't want to see her. I just want to feel her. I move my fingers inside her deeper, faster. And then I shove her skirt up higher, not bothering to take it off.

She fumbles to help me, saying my name. The breathy way she says it gives me pause and I open my eyes.

She's splayed out on the rumpled hotel bed like an offering, her hair mussed.

The way she said my name reminded me of Madison.

I swallow hard, frozen above her, suspended.

"What?" she asks in confusion, opening her eyes. "What's wrong?"

She doesn't sound like Madison now. She doesn't look like her, doesn't smell like her. Because she's not Madison.

She might not be Madison, but in my head that's all I see. Maddy's grin, her blue eyes, her gorgeous body. I picture the expression on her face when she was on my lap the other night, loving, soft, understanding.

Fuck you, Gabe.

I feel the pulse in my throat as I try to swallow around it. Maddy doesn't want me. Not anymore and I can't blame her. And if there's one way to get one woman out of my head, surely it's to fuck another one.

Someone who *does* want me.

I shake my head.

"Nothing's wrong," I finally lie.

I turn my attention back to Alex and run my fingers along her side, a side that is thicker than Maddy's. I squeeze my eyes shut.

"I want it hard," she moans. "Fuck me hard, Gabe."

A sour taste pools in my mouth, but I ignore it as I drop my head and bury it in Alex's neck and unfasten my shorts. She grips my shoulders tight, pulling me to her, burying her tongue in my mouth.

She doesn't taste right.

She doesn't smell right.

And my dick knows it because all of a sudden I'm not hard anymore.

I push against her again, but it's no use. I'm not hard. I'm not going to get hard. Because all I can see in my head is Madison. I roll off and head to the shower without looking back.

I can hear Alex's confused questions behind me, but I don't care.

As the water rushes down over my head and shoulders, I crank the handle all the way over to cold.

Fuck.

I'm in seriously deep shit here.

A flash of Madison pops into my head again. Her blue eyes, soft and sincere. Her long slender legs wrapped around my hips.

You're someone who won't hurt me.

I practically groan. I have the feeling I could sleep with a thousand different women in a thousand different hollow fucks and I'd never be able to shake Maddy from my mind.

If I *can* fuck someone else, which is apparently questionable.

What is it about Madison that holds me so tight?

Everything.

I groan. Is it possible that I could be with her and not hurt her?

It's a moot question since I've already left her. But it's a question that I can't quite shake.

The idea of that kind of intimacy sends my stomach up into my throat and I lean my head against the shower wall. That kind of intimacy is terrifying.

But all of a sudden, for reasons that I can't understand and can't explain, being without it is terrifying too.

❧

After five days, I decide that I fucking hate Denver.

I fucking hate my life.

And I fucking hate myself.

I'm pretty sure all these feelings are very apparent to everyone around me because I've been a total dick.

Today, after meeting with the potential contractors at the new factory site, Alex and I came back to the table in my hotel room to look through their bids. But I don't want to be here. There's only one place I want to be and if I can't be there, then fuck everyone.

I rub at my red eyes, trying to ignore the pounding in my head. The whiskey I've been using to try to fix my bad attitude has had the exact opposite effect. Hangovers fucking blow.

Alex hands me some ibuprofen. "Here. This will help."

"Thanks," I mutter, knocking four of them back with some water.

For some reason Alex is sticking close by, she gets here early and she stays late.

It's like she took my inability to perform with her and my distance and my dickhead attitude as a personal challenge. I can't figure it out, but then again, I can't figure out women in general.

"How long do you think you'll be here?" Alex asks absently, running her finger along my back. I instinctively move away. She's been touching me at every opportunity, because she clearly believes that she's irresistible. She has no idea how much it's not working for me.

"I don't know," I answer. "As long as it takes to get everything set up, I guess."

"I don't want you to go," Alex pouts, sticking her bottom lip out. "I like having you here."

I fight the urge to roll my eyes. There's no way she *likes* the way I am. I'm onto her. She just wants to sleep with the boss.

"Well, you knew that I wasn't staying," I remind her. "It's the whole reason we needed to hire an assistant, so that you could handle day-to-day stuff for us when we're not here."

"I know," she acknowledges. "But still."

Still nothing.

I duck into the bathroom and when I come back out, Alex is standing in the middle of the room, completely nude.

"What the hell?" I mutter. Even though I don't want her, I can't exactly look away either. She's naked, for God sake. She's young and has perfect tits. Before I can even say anything, though, before I can tell her to put her clothes back on, there's a knock on the door.

"I ordered room service," Alex says helpfully.

"Well, obviously you should take your clothes off, then," I mutter wryly. *What the fuck?* I shake my head and grab the bedspread from the bed, wrapping it around her as I head for the door. I open it without even looking and am surprised as hell to find Brand standing in front of me, filling up the doorway.

He takes in the scene quickly: at the assistant standing naked behind me, the bed rumpled and seemingly used. It's pretty easy to jump to the wrong conclusion.

And he does.

"You didn't," Brand exclaims, barging on in. "Gabe, what the fuck, dude?"

"It's not what it looks like," I say by way of explanation. "And I thought you were still in Chicago."

Brand turns to Alex. "Alex, hon, could you give us a minute?"

She scrambles to put her clothes on, while Brand looks away. "I'll go down and get a coffee," she says quickly, not looking back as she darts out the door.

Brand glares at me.

"What the fuck, Gabe?" He eyes the empty bottle of whiskey on the table. "Seriously? You've been holed up here in the hotel getting drunk and banging our new assistant?"

I glance at the empty bottle. "I've only been drinking at night," I clarify. "And I'm not banging the assistant."

Brand cocks his head and I can see why he doesn't believe me, not that any of it matters.

"Whatever," I mutter. "Think what you want."

"Dude, you know that Pax Tate isn't interested in being an investor now that you fucked over his sister-in-law. We have to get serious and find a new one. We can't do that if you're drinking yourself away in this room. And Jesus, we don't need a sexual harassment suit from our assistant."

"For the last time." I grit my teeth. "I didn't fuck her. I could sue *her* for sexual harassment, for God's sake. She practically threw herself at me. Right before you got here, I went to the head and when I came out, she was standing there buck-ass naked."

Brand is interested now. "Seriously? Nice!"

I stare at him. "Nice? You were just lecturing me on banging the assistant."

He shrugs. "True. And I'm glad we don't have to worry about a harassment suit, but it's still pretty weird that you passed that shit up. What's going on, dude? If you want to be in Angel Bay with the leggy blonde, you need to just go. That would solve two problems— your bad disposition and our investor problem. If you go back, Tate would probably invest."

"So you want to whore me out for the business?" I smile grimly. He rolls his eyes.

"I hardly think it would be against your will. What the fuck are you doing, bro?"

I know he's not talking about the business now and I glare at him as I clean up the mess on the table.

"Since when do you care about the women I leave behind?" I ask.

Brand eyes me. "I don't. But I do care about you. And I hate watching you fuck up something that was making you happy."

"You don't get it," I growl as I snatch up an empty beer bottle and hurl it into the trash can. "You don't understand."

"Don't I?" Brand lifts an eyebrow. "Out of everyone in the world, I think I understand the best. For instance, I know that one of the worst things about leaving the Rangers is feeling like we quit. Even though we know we didn't quit, that we did it for a very good reason, it still feels like we were quitters. Right?"

I stare at him. "Your point?"

"My point is that I *know*, dude. I know what it's like. And I also know that if you don't fix this thing with Madison, then you're quitting again. But for real this time. Don't do it, Gabe. Clean yourself up and get your ass back to Angel Bay where it belongs."

I glance up at him as I tie my shoes. "If that's what you think, then you don't know shit. Angel Bay isn't where I belong. And me staying away from Maddy isn't quitting. It's protecting her. *From me.* Going back wouldn't be doing that very well, would it?"

Brand sighs, shaking his head. "You're one stubborn SOB, you know that?"

"Yep."

"Can you at least clean up and stop drinking your nights away?" Brand asks wearily. "You look like a hung-over frat boy. I can't believe you've been meeting with contractors like that."

I shrug. "They're gonna work for us, not the other way around. But it doesn't matter. I'm flying back to Chicago in the morning."

"Good."

We sit and look over some contracts, Brand schmoozes with Alex just to make absolutely sure that there won't be any harassment suits and I stare absently out the window through it all.

After we eat and wrap up a few last things at the table in my room, Brand heads to his own to pack, since he's taking the red-eye back to Chicago.

"I'll see you tomorrow," I tell him. "I'm flying back in the morning."

After I close the door, I turn around to find Alex has kicked off her shoes and moved from the table to the bed, where she's waiting with a come-hither look on her heavily made-up face. I have to fight the shudder that runs through me.

"I forgot to set my DVR for my favorite show," she tells me softly. "Do you mind if I watch it here? I don't want to miss it."

I want to groan, but don't. I should be polite since I'm leaving in the morning for home anyway.

"Sure," I tell her, as I drop into a chair next to the bed. "No problem."

The problem is that I fall asleep watching it.

And I wake up to the sound of Alex screaming.

"What the fuck is wrong with you?" she shrieks. I sit up and realize that I'm on the floor, dragging myself across the hotel carpet. Alex backs away from me.

"You were crawling across the floor, crying for Brand. What the fuck? Are you fucking gay or something? I'm so out of here. You're a fucking freak."

She grabs her purse and slams the hotel door on her way out.

I'm still dazed, still disoriented, so I sit for a second, rubbing my temples. I never thought it was possible, but the dreams are getting even worse, the dark-eyed, blood-spattered dreams.

They're worse because now Madison's in them too. She's lingering on the edge of the dead circle of kids and she's slipping from my grasp.

In my head I know that I need to save her, but in my heart I know that I can't. Because she's slipping toward the fire, toward the rebels, toward the danger.

But the danger is actually me.

Jesus Christ.

I'm never going to get past this.

All I want is Madison. She made everything good. She was warmth and light and understanding and trust. She was all of it. And I'll never have her again. *Fuck you, Gabe.*

It's a bleak fucking thought, and it makes it even harder to shake the nightmare.

Even after I suck down two bottles of water and have finally settled in bed, I can't get the taste of ash from my mouth. The ash from the burning bodies. My chest tightens as I try to swallow down the taste of the dead kids. But my stomach doesn't want any part of it and it lurches rebelliously. I roll to the side and heave onto the floor, retching over and over until there's nothing left.

But the taste is still there.

The ash and the blood. The bleak hopelessness. And now vomit too.

I wipe my mouth and flip onto my back, my arm across my eyes as I try to breathe, try to settle the shakiness in my legs. Try to push the visions from my head.

I'm so fucking tired of this.

So. Fucking. Tired.

Eyes black as night and full of terror stare at me from behind my eyelids and I open my eyes. I can't face her anymore. I just can't. I'm completely wrecked and I'm afraid to face what has wrecked me. I'm afraid to face any of it.

What kind of man am I?

The kind who fucks up everything and can't face shit.

I pull myself up and stumble out onto the balcony, sucking in the cold mountain air, trying to use it to force my lungs open, to inflate them. I can hear the blood pounding in my ears, rush, rush, rushing through my veins, but not air. There's no air, because I can't fucking breathe.

Breathe, motherfucker.

It's no wonder that I can't face shit, because I can't even breathe. I'm a fucking pussy.

Gripping the railing, I stare down at the traffic fifteen floors below. People are driving around, minding their own business, honking, breathing, laughing, going on with their lives, even though mine is falling apart.

Even though across the world, people are dying. They're bleeding and burning and dying. Life fucking sucks. But no one here knows that.

They have no idea what life is really like.

But I do.

I stare soundlessly down, watching the movement, watching the *life*, and it is oddly distant from me, so very far away. Up here it's quiet. Up here it's removed. Up here there's only me.

And I'm fucked up.

Like the girl's eyes, my soul is black as night and full of terror.

I grip the railing and my bicep flexes and I remember the words scrolled across my arm; a brand, a reminder. A creed.

Death before dishonor.

The words won't stop running through my head and I know why. Because I haven't been acting with honor for months, because I've been acting like a goddamned pussy who can't pull shit together. And I fucked up the only good thing I've had. I almost killed her.

It's just one more instance of dishonor to add to my list.

I stare down into the blackness.

Death before dishonor.

It would be so easy.

I know what I have to do. I know what I have to do to get it all to go away, to get it all to end, to get the terrified black eyes out of my head forever. An eye for an eye. Right?

An eye for a fucking eye.

A life for a fucking life.

I swing a leg over the railing, pulling myself onto it, sitting down. My feet dangle and I stare down again. The cars look smaller than my big toe. The fall would kill me. Surely it would kill me.

And all of this would end.

The bad thing can't catch me if the game is over.

I close my eyes, feeling the light breeze on my face, smelling the mountains. My lungs are working now, which is ironic. In a few minutes I won't need them anymore.

I'm not afraid. I'm not afraid. Fear is a choice and I'm not fucking afraid. I have a plan.

And because of my plan, I'll never hurt anyone again.

The blackness below almost looks inviting, like it's swirling around my feet, waiting to pull me down. Like once I'm a part of it, it will swallow me up and all my shit will go away.

That's what death must be like.

It's just an end.

A rest.

And God, I'm so fucking tired. I could use a rest.

I stare at it, at the tempting blackness. Every cell in my body is trained to survive. This goes against all my instincts. I close my eyes and instead of the little girl's, I see a pair of shining blue ones. Maddy.

If only I could fix it.

"What the fuck are you doing?"

Brand's startled voice breaks apart the blackness and carries out to me through the open balcony door. I glance over my shoulder. Brand is striding through my room, staring at me in shock and horror.

"What the fuck, Gabe?"

I can hear the fear in his voice. I should tell him that fear is a choice, but I don't. He already knows that.

"Stop right there, Brand," I tell him woodenly.

I can hear the lack of emotion in my voice and so he can he. Unlike anyone else, Brand can understand it. He knows what it's like to face a terrifying mission, and how we have to step away from it, dull ourselves to it, so that we can just do it.

He can see that's what I'm doing now.

He knows.

His eyes widen and I see the absolute terror in them.

"Don't, Gabe," he says quietly, stopping in the balcony doorway as I'd instructed. "Don't. You don't have to do this. We can fix everything."

I stare at him, unblinking, disbelieving. "No, we can't. That's bullshit and you know it. Everything is fucked. There's no fix for it."

"There is," Brand argues, his hands flexing.

"What are you doing here anyway?" I ask, not really caring. Not anymore.

"I forgot my wallet on the table," Brand answers. "Thank God. Gabe, think about this. Think about Jacey and Maddy. This will *kill* them. They won't be able to get over it. You're all Jacey has because your parents are shitty. Maddy already lost her parents. What do you think this will do to her? Are you thinking of her at all?"

I swallow, looking away. "She's all I think about," I mutter. "All of the time. I can't get her out of my head and it's killing me, Brand. It's killing me."

Brand stares at me and I see the determination in his eyes.

"Gabe, you chose to end things with Madison. You *quit* and

you didn't have to. All you have to do is get some help—you didn't before. But you can now, Gabe."

I don't answer, so Brand uses the silence as an opportunity to continue.

"Remember Mad Dog's funeral? Do you want them to hand your flag to your parents? Or *Jacey*? Your parents don't deserve to have your flag and it would fucking annihilate Jacey. Jesus Christ, Gabe. Get off that railing. You're not a quitter. *You're not a fucking quitter*. Come over here and we'll deal with this. We'll fix it."

"I'm too much of a pussy," I answer, my throat closing in hot and tight around my words. "I don't know how to fix it. I just don't know how. And I can't do this anymore, Brand."

Brand grits his teeth and takes a step. I eye him warningly.

"Don't."

He freezes.

"You're not a pussy," he says. "And you're not a quitter. You're a badass motherfucker. Tell me what to say to get you off the ledge, Gabe. Tell me and I'll say it. You and I have been to hell and back together. It's not going to end like this. You wouldn't let me end like this and I sure as fuck won't let you. Not after everything you've done for me."

I squeeze my eyes shut, letting the blackness seep under my eyelids. It would be so easy to let it take the rest of me too.

"Tell me that you can stop the nightmares. Tell me that you can save that little girl...that you can save all of those little girls."

Brand's breath is ragged and rough. "You know I can't save them. But I can save *you*, Gabe. Get the fuck off that balcony. We can stop your nightmares."

I'm silent as I open my eyes and stare down, past my feet, past the cars to the ground. It's a long way down, but it's there. Brand follows my gaze.

"Gabe, I don't have nightmares much anymore. I swear to Christ. Only once or twice a month. And someday I won't have any. You just need to get off that ledge and go to therapy like I did. It feels stupid and terrible and dumbass, but it helped me, Gabe. And it will help you. It's a whole hell of a lot better than this."

Better than dying.

I glance over my shoulder at him. "Because this is the easy way out?"

Brand stares at me, his eyes a steely blue, determined. "You said that you're too much of a pussy to fix it. *This* is being a pussy, Gabe. Maybe not for some people—because who am I to judge people I don't know? But I know you. And this is being a pussy for *you*. Do the hard thing and get your ass off that balcony."

I exhale, long and slow, contemplating.

I don't want to die. If I die, the bad thing wins.

Fuck that.

I take a breath, then grab Brand's outstretched hand.

Chapter Twenty-One

Madison

Gabriel isn't coming back.

I know that now. It's been a week.

Seven days.

One hundred and sixty-eight hours.

I don't know where he is and I doubt I'll ever see him again. It's a thought that I can't think about or it will crush me. It still hurts that much.

Instead I focus on pretending that I'm fine for Jacey and Tony, Mila and Pax. Today Jacey brings me a cup of hot chocolate. Because hot chocolate obviously fixes everything.

Curling up across the table from where I'm rolling flatware into napkins, she glances at me.

"I haven't heard from him either, by the way. He probably knows I'm going to bitch him out for what he did."

I glance up at her. "Can we not talk about it? Seriously. I just don't want to think about it."

"OK. That's fine," Jacey says quickly. "I just didn't want you to think that I would hide talking to him from you. I wanted you to know that he hasn't called."

I nod, folding another napkin. "Thanks, Jace. I'm sorry for being bitchy. I just…I'm not myself."

"It's OK."

We sit in silence until the door opens, sunlight flashes on the floor and then Jacey's face lights up.

"Brand!"

She jumps up and runs across the room like she hasn't seen him in a year. I suck in a breath, not sure if I'm ready to face Gabe's best friend. Seeing him will just punch me in the gut—make me remember Gabriel. As if I've forgotten.

I don't turn around, I just keep rolling the silverware, my eyes glued to the task in front of me. But I can hear their low voices and I keep my ears trained in their direction. Brand's deep voice carries through the restaurant far better than Jacey's does and I hear it easily.

"He's fine, Jace. He feels guilty, of course, for leaving you…and Madison. But he's fine. He's going to get a special kind of therapy, something designed to help victims of PTSD. I went through it back when we first came home. It sucks pretty bad, but it's effective. He's going to need your support, though."

I hear the sound of Jacey's voice, but I can't hear her words.

Brand answers whatever she said.

"I knew you'd understand. PTSD is terrible, Jace. It's something we can't control and guys like Gabe and me…well, it's hard to deal with something like that. He needs all the support you can give him. He's going to be at Walter Reed this week but he wanted me to check in on you, to make sure that Jared's still leaving you alone."

Jacey murmurs something.

"What the fuck? Why would you do that, Jacey?"

Brand seems annoyed now and I can't imagine what Jacey said to him.

"Whatever. Just don't lie to us again, Jacey. You can tell Gabriel when he's out. Don't tell him while he's there. His attention shouldn't be split. He needs to concentrate on CPT, all right?"

Jacey murmurs again.

"Trust me, Jace," Brand continues. "I've been there. I know what it's like. If Gabe has any hope of taking care of this, he's got to focus on it one hundred percent. You can support the hell out of him when he comes home."

Jacey murmurs and then they're quiet. I'm just getting ready to glance behind me to see if Brand is leaving when his voice pops up by my ear.

"Maddy?"

Fuck.

I slowly turn, looking up into Brand's blue eyes. "Hi, Brand. Good to see you."

But it's not. It's really not. Because he's here and Gabe's not. And even though that's irrational, it's how I feel.

"Hey." He looks as uncomfortable talking to me as I am listening. "I just wanted to say something, if you don't mind. Gabriel doesn't know I'm doing this, but I just wanted you to know that he's a good guy, Maddy. I know it looks like shit that he left the way he did, but I promise you . . . he didn't want to. He got it in his head that you needed protecting. *From him*. That's the reason he left."

My eyes sting as I nod.

"I figured," I tell him. "But that doesn't take away the fact that he left without saying a word. He hasn't returned my texts or calls. It's a shitty thing to do."

Brand nods. "I agree. And so does he. I think he can't trust himself to talk to you. He thinks that if he does, he'll just come back."

"And would that be so bad?" Even I hear how thin my voice is.

Brand shakes his head. "I don't think so. But Gabe is dead set on keeping you safe. He misses you like hell, though."

My eyes fill up with tears now, so I nod and look away.

"OK," I finally manage to say. "Thanks for telling me, Brand."

He puts his hand on my shoulder for a minute and then he's gone. After a second, Jacey comes back, staring at me in concern.

"Are you OK?" she asks quietly. I nod.

"Yeah. Are you?"

"Yeah. I'm glad Gabe is getting help. Want to tell me what happened to him that fucked him up so bad?"

For a minute I'm tempted. But after thinking about it for a minute I shake my head.

"I can't. That's his story to tell."

"I figured you would say that." Jacey sighs.

"What was Brand annoyed with you about?" I ask. "What aren't you supposed to tell Gabe?"

Jacey actually looks sheepish. "Um. I lied to Gabe about Jared."

I raise an eyebrow. "You what?"

"When Gabe first got here, I told him that Jared was still texting me and shit. I lied. He wasn't. He stopped bothering me after that first night that Gabe got in his face here at the restaurant."

I stare at her, aghast. "Then why in the world would you lie? The whole point was just to get Jared to leave you alone, right?"

Jacey stares at her hands on the table. "Yeah. I just... I missed my brother, you know? And I thought he'd stay longer if he thought that Jared was still messing with me. Which he did. And then he started dating you, so he stayed anyway. It all worked out."

I shake my head. "Yeah, except Gabe knocked one of Jared's teeth out because of your lie."

Jacey rolls her eyes. "Trust me, he deserved that. He's an asshole."

"I know," I murmur absently. I don't really care about Jared, to be honest. I don't care about much at all these days.

I lug the full bin of newly wrapped flatware to the sidewall and then I retreat into my office, closing the door behind me. I seriously don't want to deal with people right now.

After I work on payroll for a while, I click into my e-mail and what I see there sends my heart into my throat.

Gabriel's name in my in-box.

I'm barely breathing as I click on the message. I barely breathe as I read the words.

Dear Madison,

I'm sorry. I know you think I'm an asshole and I guess I probably am, even more so than you know. It's been killing me not to talk to you and I'm sure you probably don't want to hear from me now.

But I wanted you to know that you were right. It wasn't fair of me to expect you to face your demons when I was unwilling to face my own.

So I just wanted you to know that I'm facing them now.

I hope you're doing alright and that your throat has healed. You have no idea how much it kills me that I did that to you.

I don't know what else to say except I'm really sorry, Maddy. I really am.

                                   —Gabe

My breath seems caught in my throat as I stare at the page, at the words that Gabe has written. He signed it simply with his name. Not "Love, Gabe." He doesn't mention love anywhere, actually.

He also doesn't mention the fact that he left me without a goodbye, without an explanation...without anything. He doesn't mention how he wouldn't pick up his phone or answer a text. Or even just give me a courtesy e-mail. Even a fucking breakup e-mail would've been better than nothing.

But even now he doesn't give me an explanation.

Just a whole lot of "I'm sorry."

Yeah, well, I'm sorry too.

I'm sorry that I'm in love with someone who doesn't love me back.

Chapter Twenty~Two

Gabriel

After I'm assigned a room in Walter Reed, I sit staring at the wall.

I want to pick up my phone and call Maddy, but I can't. She never responded to my e-mail.

She doesn't want to hear from me, apparently.

As I stare at my phone, I am overwhelmed by frustration, by the idea that I've been reduced to this...It pisses me off. And when I look in the mirror that is facing me right now, it pisses me off even more to look at myself.

My anger takes over all of a sudden and I see in a blur of red. My ears roar and I punch the wall next to the mirror as hard as I can. There is a crunch as my knuckles connect with the drywall. That felt surprisingly good.

A nurse comes running and pokes her head in the door, eyeing me, then the blood dripping from my hand. She raises an eyebrow.

"Everything OK, soldier?"

I nod calmly. "Everything's fine. When's my first session going to be?"

"Just a minute. I'll get some gauze for your hand."

While she's gone I rinse my hand off in the sink, and I'm toweling it dry when she gets back. She steps into the room with her dark hair wrapped into a bun at the nape of her neck, and spotless nursing scrubs, the perfect picture of efficiency.

She sits next to me and dabs at my knuckles with iodine, then wraps then securely with gauze.

"I'm checking to see if there's a session available this evening," she tells me. "I'm not sure how much you know about CPT, but there are twelve sessions. Some like to do one session a week, others like to do one a day, and still others do two a day—one in the morning and one in the evening. I'm guessing you're a two-a-day type of a guy."

"I think I'd like to just get it over with, so however I can do it the quickest is fine with me."

She smiles again. "I'll let you know if I can get you into the evening session to kick off your week."

She leaves and I pull out my phone, clicking into my e-mail. I know Maddy hasn't answered, that she's not going to answer, but I can't help but check.

I'm surprised at the heavy weight on my chest when I see that I'm right.

She didn't answer and my stomach sinks.

I guess some part of me, deep down, thought she might. I don't know why; I guess I thought that if I did the hard thing and came here to this fucking place, she might forgive me.

But that was fucking dumb. She doesn't even know I'm here.

There's no hope left for Maddy and me.

Maddy's there and I'm here and this place is fucking hell. And that begs the question, if she doesn't care, then why the fuck am I here going through this at all?

For myself? That's a weak answer because I don't really give a flying fuck about myself anymore.

For Brand? He wants me to make it. And I owe it to him. We've invested all our money in the business. It would be a dick thing to do to leave him alone to deal with it. But at the moment that feels weak too.

Because at the moment nothing seems to matter.

Everything feels weak.

Especially me.

∾

As I sit sprawled in the folding metal chair in a circle of soldiers with PTSD, I decide that this is definitely the seventh ring of Hell. Everyone is uncomfortable as they sit in the ring, each person trying not to look at anyone else. It's tense and awkward. I immediately hate it.

The therapist sits in the middle, perched on a high stool, looking through her notes.

"We've got two new soldiers with us today," she finally says, looking up at me. "One of them is here for this evening's session. Lt. Gabriel Vincent. Welcome to the group. I'm not sure what you're expecting with CPT, but I'm sure it's nothing like you think. You are free here to be completely honest, with no fear of embarrassment or shame. Here in the safety of this room, you're going to realize that whatever it was that you faced in combat wasn't your fault. With our help, you're going to come out of this a brand-new man."

I nod, unsure of exactly what she expects me to do. I also wonder how she's able to say that nothing that happened in combat was our fault. That's bullshit. Sometimes it *is* someone's fault.

She hops off her perch and brings me a clipboard with some papers attached.

"As we do our group session, I want you to work on these work sheets. Then we'll go over your answers at the end."

I feel as though everyone is watching me as they begin their regular session and I sift through the papers on my lap. Like they're trying to figure me out or something. I try to ignore them and get through the dumbass paperwork as quickly as I can.

As I read some of the questions, I just want to roll my eyes. What the fuck?

Please explain the incident that has caused you distress and describe how that incident has made you feel.

What the fuck kind of question is that?

Obviously the incident that has brought me here made me feel like shit or I wouldn't be here in the first place. So that's what I write. Fuck it. I'm not going to sugarcoat things. She said to feel comfortable being honest, so that's what I'm going to do.

I scrawl out answers to all the other stupid questions, only half listening to what the other soldiers are saying. That is, until one voice breaks through my concentration.

A girl.

As she speaks, I realize that she is talking about being held captive by Taliban rebels. Her eyes keep finding me and she stares at me as she speaks. She's wearing a uniform, so I know she's still on active duty. Something about her seems vaguely familiar, but I can't place it.

"I was held for nine days in a dirty hovel," she says, her voice small in this big room. "We were barely fed, we were abused, and I was serially raped for a week by an entire group of Taliban rebels. I wanted to die. I didn't know if I even wanted to be rescued because I wasn't sure that I'd be strong enough to survive what had happened. But I wasn't given the choice. I *was* rescued. The Seventy-Fifth Ranger Regiment raided the compound and carried all three of us out."

The Seventy-Fifth Ranger Regiment.

Me.

I suddenly realize why her eyes are vaguely familiar. I've seen them before.

I remember her staring at me in much the same way a couple of years ago, although obviously she looked much different at the time. Her face was filthy and bloody, her fatigues tattered and torn.

I didn't have much interaction with her that day, to be honest. I certainly wasn't the one who carried her out, but my squad was there, as was Brand's.

I remember that day. It was one like many others. It wasn't my mission to retrieve the prisoners. I was in the front, breaking down the doors and eliminating the captors, while several of my men raided the facilities and carried the prisoners out.

But after we finished the raid and the dust had settled, this girl watched us all from the side, from where the medics were tending her. The other female prisoner was crying, while the male had his head buried in his bloody hands. But not this girl.

This girl kept her head high and just watched all of us as the medics took her vitals, and poked and prodded her.

She stares at me now, her eyes lucid and clear.

"Do you remember me?" she asks quietly. "I was with another nurse and a doctor when we were taken from our Humvee while we were en route to the green zone in Kabul. Your squad is the one that raided the Taliban camp and rescued us."

Several soldiers in the circle watch me with quiet interest as I curtly nod.

"Yes," I finally answer. "I remember. I've never forgotten how you kept your head held up high while the others cried."

She smiles grimly.

"It's how I kept my sanity," she tells me, her voice painfully thin. "I kept telling myself that no matter what they did to me, they couldn't take my pride. They couldn't take my right to be brave or to stare them in the eye as they raped me. They could do their worst, but the only thing I could do was respond with my best. So no matter what they did to me, I looked them in the eye. I didn't want them to think that they'd broken me."

I stare at her, at the quiet bravery in the girl's eyes, shining brightly even now. But something is there, something haunting and sad. Something that makes me ask a blunt question.

"Did they? Did they break you?"

She is quiet. In fact, the entire room is quiet. If someone dropped a pin, I'd be able to hear it. I wonder if the question is inappropriate or rude, but the therapist doesn't interrupt to say that it is.

Finally the girl nods.

"That's why I'm here. I went through some therapy right after it happened, but I didn't want to give in and do the full inpatient therapy thing. It made me feel weak, like if I did it I'd be letting them win. But I finally realized that if I let the PTSD control the rest of my life, *that* would be letting them win. If I keep seeing their faces every night when I go to sleep, *that* would be letting them win. This . . ." And she pauses, sweeping her arm in a wide circle around the room. "*This* is me winning. This is me kicking their cowardly asses."

The other soldiers erupt into applause and I am silent for a moment, watching the group. They all seem supportive and there isn't a judgmental look on anyone's face. I realize that I'm not clapping, and so I stand up, clapping hard as I stare into the girl's eyes.

When the applause finally dies down, I sit back down and the girl stands up and crosses the circle. When she gets to me, she stops in front of me.

"I never had a chance to say thank you," she tells me. "I can't believe that you're here . . . that God has somehow put you in my path so that I can thank you for what you did. You'll never know how grateful I am to you, and to your men for pulling me out of Hell that day. You saved my life."

She stands to attention and salutes me.

I can't even express the emotions that flood through me at this moment.

As a Ranger, I did my job and went back to our camp. I didn't linger to talk to anyone. Seeing this girl here like this is a reminder that my job had a purpose. And not just any purpose. While a lot of it was ugly and ruthless, we made some lives better.

We made *this* girl's life better.

Maybe I'm not such a worthless fuck after all.

I get to my feet and return her salute.

The room explodes into applause again and the quiet reverence is broken.

The rest of the session passes slowly, but finally it's time to bring it to a close and everyone straggles out. The army nurse looks as if she's going to come talk to me, but she's snagged by another of the soldiers on the way out. That's just as well. I really only want to go back to my room and go to bed.

I grab a sandwich from the vending machines and return to my room, snarfing down the dry bread and turkey.

I collapse onto the bed and stare at the ceiling for a while until I decide that I'm being pathetic, lying here doing nothing. Instead of letting the walls close in on me, I change into workout shorts. I do push-ups and sit-ups simply to get rid of restless energy. After I've done five hundred of each, I'm still restless.

I eye my laptop, trying to fight the urge to boot it up and e-mail Madison.

Fuck it. She might not want to talk to me, but I sure as hell want to talk to her.

Dear Maddy,

I'm sure you don't want to hear this, but I miss you.

Love,

Gabe

Chapter Twenty-Three

Madison

The walls of this house are closing in on me. I stare around at the pictures and furniture and colors... all things that my mother picked out. All things that aren't mine. It's time to change that. I'm not going to lie here feeling sorry for myself anymore.

I curl up on the sofa, pulling the coverlet more tightly around my waist, as I look through furniture catalogues. I need new living room furniture, bedroom furniture, kitchen furniture. Everything.

Shopping is good for keeping my mind off Gabriel. Because thinking about him is pathetic. And I'm not fucking pathetic.

I flip open my laptop and order it all, not feeling even a little guilty about spending the money. The Hill turned a profit this year. I can afford it. And I might as well use it on something to change my life, rather than more shoes.

When the phone rings, my heart leaps, because for just a second I think it might be Gabriel.

It's stupid, I know. Because even if he calls, I can't answer. There's no way I'm putting myself out there again for him to stomp on. Fuck. That.

Just the same, when I see the Hill's phone number flashing on the screen, disappointment floods through me and I close my eyes.

If I can't talk to Gabe, then I don't want to talk to anyone today. I let the call go to voice mail as I close my laptop and wander out onto the patio.

Apparently I'm pathetic after all.

I sit at the table, staring out at the lake. And even in the midst of the gorgeous views and sounds of the water, all I can do is remember the night Gabe bent me over this table.

I close my eyes and remember it... the way his lips brushed over my arched neck, the way he nipped at my shoulder, his voice in my ear, his fingers inside me. The heat of our bodies pressed together in the cold rain. The feel of him inside me as he filled me up.

I gulp, then close my eyes against the hot tears.

Don't fucking cry.

He left you.

Don't fucking cry.

I hold my eyes closed for a minute, pulling myself together... and am proud when I realize that not one tear fell.

I can do this. He didn't break me.

After a few minutes I pick up my phone and listen to the voice mail.

Hey, Maddy. This is Tony. Like I wouldn't recognize his voice. I smile. *Have you heard from Jacey? She didn't show up for work and she didn't call.*

Unfortunately that's not unusual lately. She's probably sleeping it off from the club last night or something. So I call him back and tell him that, then I click into my e-mail.

I'm breathless when I see one from Gabe.

As I read the words, my heart pounds.

He misses me.

My fingers shake as I type out a reply.

You left me. You made this choice. Now we both have to deal with it.

I stare at the hateful words and they pull at my heart, twisting it round and round. So I delete them.

I wish you hadn't left. But you did.

Tears fill my eyes as I stare at the new words, as they bleed together as my eyes fill up. Fuck it. I press the backspace hard, deleting the words.

I miss you, too.

Out of all the things I feel, this is the thing I feel the most. But I can't tell him that. Because then it would make it seem OK that he left, that he treated me like nothing. And that's *not* OK.

I delete the message, my fingers heavy as a stone as I close the laptop.

If you don't know what to say, nothing is always a good choice.

Chapter Twenty~Four

Gabriel

Do you feel that you need to be ever-alert, or always on guard?

Is your opinion of the incident based on fact?

Are you easily startled?

Brand wasn't fucking lying when he told me that this shit sucks. It sucks big donkey balls and every dumbass question that I'm asked pisses me the fuck off.

Day two is no better than day one was. In fact, it might be worse. The questions that they're asking me, both in group and in the dumbass individual therapy session, are ridiculous.

They start out talking about the seemingly innocuous questions from the work sheets, but that evolves into talking in depth about whatever incidents put us here, the things we fear the most.

It's like a sticky therapeutic web of bullshit.

I am dejected as I walk back to my room after my individual session. I don't feel like going to the cafeteria for dinner, so I'll grab something from the vending machine later.

The first thing I do after I close my bedroom door behind me is check my e-mail. As I punch my password in, I realize that I'm holding my breath . . . I want to see Maddy's name. But there's nothing but a note from Brand.

Gabe,

Day two really sucks, I remember. Hang in there. It doesn't seem like it's worth it or that it's working, I know. But trust me, it will. Just keep your chin up, bro.

—Brand

I appreciate Brand. I do. But all I wanted was to see an answer from Maddy. And the lack of one is an answer in itself.

I fucked up and I've lost her. Losing her feels every bit as bad as everything I went through in Afghanistan. Every fucking bit. And there's nothing I can do about it.

My stomach growls, so I close down my computer and venture out to the commons area where the vending machines are. I choose a sub sandwich and chips before turning around and finding Annie the army nurse behind me, holding a handful of quarters.

"So, today sucked, right?" She glances up at me. "It was day two for you, wasn't it?"

I nod, knowing that she has no fucking clue *exactly* how bad it was for me. "Yeah. It seemed pretty pointless. My friend e-mailed me and said that it will get better. Or it'll at least seem like it has a point soon."

Annie nods in agreement. "Yeah, it does. It doesn't get any easier, but it will at least make sense."

"How many sessions do you have a day?"

"Only one," she tells me as she feeds her quarters into the

machine. "I'm on light duty here at the hospital during treatment, so I have a shift that I have to work around. You?"

"Two a day," I answer. "And right now it seems pretty pathetic. But here's hoping that tomorrow will be better. 'Night, Annie."

"'Night," she calls after me.

I can feel her watching me as I walk away. Her attention makes me a little uneasy, since I don't know exactly what she wants from me. I feel like she's almost put me on a pedestal, since I was with the team that rescued her. And I sure as hell don't deserve that.

After I eat my sandwich, I open my e-mail one more time, not breathing as I look. But I release my breath on a slow exhale.

There's nothing. My in-box is empty.

Chapter Twenty-Five

Madison

I finish the call with the contractor I hired to work on my house and Tony stares at me from the chair in front of my desk.

"You using Mathis and Son?" He raises an eyebrow. "Because I know Derrick Mathis. Tell him to give you a discount."

I smile, in spite of the way I don't feel like smiling yet.

"I know him too," I remind Tony. "Trust me, he's giving me a good deal. He's painting every room in my house and laying new floor and tile, and he's doing all of that work in one week's time. Once I decided to do it, I just wanted it done. Like *now*. So he's sending in several teams to get it taken care of. I'm going to stay with Mila and Pax for a few days while it's being done."

"Good plan." Tony nods, his burly hands flipping through the work schedule. "We've gotta talk about Jacey, Mad. This is the second day in a row she hasn't called in. What the hell is up with her?"

I sigh. I texted her last night and didn't get an answer...and that always means that she's doing something she knows I wouldn't approve of.

"Well, let's find out." I sigh again as I pick up the phone. I dial her number and it rings five times. I'm just thinking it's going to voice mail when she finally answers, surprising me.

"Hey, Maddy," she says brightly, as if she hasn't been MIA for two days. "What's up?"

"You tell me," I answer sternly. "You've missed work two days in a row. What the hell, Jacey? I need you here. Business is picking up for the season and I need a full staff."

There's a pause and a rustle and a voice in the background.

A man's voice. A familiar man's voice.

"Who is that?" I demand suspiciously. "I know that's not who I think it is."

Another pause, pregnant and long.

I feel the blood boiling, up into my ears, spilling out into my cheeks, flushing them bright red.

"Jacey, what the fuck is Jared doing at your house?"

Tony snaps to attention in front of me, scowling at the phone. He holds his hands up to question Jacey's motives and I shake my head.

I have no idea, I mouth to him.

"I know," Jacey finally sighs. "I know you're mad and Gabe will be mad, but Jared came to see me the other night and he apologized for everything. He was only being an ass because he missed me so much, Mad. Deep down he's a good guy. He just needs to change some things. He really does love me."

Oh. My. God. My stomach drops into my toes and I can't even think.

"Jacey, he does not. He only cares about himself. I know you have acceptance issues. But you don't need his acceptance. He's an asshole. He'll always be an asshole. He's not going to change that. And isn't he pissed that you lied about him to Gabe? I would think he wouldn't just forget that."

Tony is standing now, a thunderous cloud above me. He can't believe this shit any more than I can.

"I apologized for that," Jacey says weakly. "He understands that I was just messed up. That I missed my brother."

My head falls back and I stare at the ceiling as I count to ten, breathing heavily.

"Mad?" Jacey asks hesitantly.

Eight.

Nine.

Ten.

I take another breath.

"Jacey, I love you. But you're seriously fucked up. If you need attention this bad, so bad that you would run right back to a psychopathic asshole, then you need some serious help. I love you. You'll always be my best friend. But you're fired. I have to have someone here that I can count on to come in when they're scheduled. When you get your head on straight, you can come back."

She protests, but I hang up on her.

Tony and I look at each other.

"I'm sorry." I shrug. "Sometimes you gotta use a little tough love. This is really stupid. I can't believe she's doing this. And I can't even tell Brand and Gabe because they're gone. I could e-mail Gabe, but I know he doesn't need this shit right now. Not while he's at Walter Reed."

I've never seen Tony as angry as he is right now, his big hands clenching into fists as he stands over me, his mouth contorted into a grimace.

"Text her and tell her to stay put. I'm going over there to talk to her. She needs a swift kick in the ass, and I'm just the person to do it," he tells me as he heads out the office door.

"Don't get into it with Jared," I call after Tony. "He's not worth it."

I jump up and run after him.

He turns and looks at me. "Don't worry. I'm only going to talk to Jacey. And to kick that little punk out of her house."

I sigh. That's what I was afraid of.

But there's nothing I can do but watch as Tony lumbers out the door.

❧

Gabriel

From what you've described to me, you killed an innocent person who was sent to kill you in a coordinated effort to kill a hundred other people. Tell me, Gabe. Do you really feel like you murdered that girl—or all those other girls and women? YOU. Not the US military, not your unit, not the girl's uncle … but YOU?

I want to punch my therapist's fucking teeth down his fucking throat. This individual session has lasted three hours today, three grueling hours.

So far, over the last three days, I've had to write about what happened, talk about what happened, and think about what happened. In depth. In a way that I haven't made myself examine it, ever.

But this morning I had a breakthrough.

I realized that one thing is the root of my issue. I can deal with the fact that Mad Dog died, even though I feel like I should've prevented it. I've seen other men die before and I had to deal with it.

What tortures me the most is the thing that gives me nightmares.

The girl.

She needed my protection and I failed her. I killed her instead of helping her. Because I couldn't figure out *how* to help in the split second that I had to make a decision.

I failed.

That's the crux of it. I wasn't trained to fail. But because I failed, people died, and I can't get past that guilt. The girl symbolizes my failure to me.

Once we make that discovery, Dr. Hart, my therapist, makes me talk about everything I know about her.

Her name was Ara Sahar. The army told me that.

She was ten years old. The army told me that too.

Her uncle was a Taliban rebel who kidnapped her and sent her to destroy my Humvee. Yet another thing the army told us.

She was terrified and needed my help. No one had to tell me that, I saw it in her eyes. And that's what I can't forgive myself for. I didn't see the other girls and women while they were still alive. But I saw Ara Sahar.

"Until you forgive yourself, you aren't going to move past this," Dr. Hart tells me solemnly. "I've seen this kind of thing a thousand times."

I stare at him with a heavy, heavy weight on my chest.

"How am I supposed to forgive myself for failing a child?" I ask him painfully. "For failing a *hundred* children? If you were me, could you? If you would've smelled them burning, could you forget that?"

Dr. Hart stares at me thoughtfully.

"If I were you, I would try to think of something, anything, I could do that would give me peace. Sometimes we just have to trick our minds into believing what we tell it. Have you ever considered writing Ara's parents a letter? Explain what happened, then ask for their forgiveness. I'm sure the army can help us figure out where to send it or tell us if her parents are even still alive."

Jesus Christ. The idea of even talking to that girl's parents sends my stomach plummeting into my shoes. I'm sure I'm the last person they want to hear from.

But maybe they do deserve an explanation. An apology.

At the very least.

I gulp.

The therapist pushes a notepad and pen toward me.

"That's your homework," he tells me.

I stare at him rigidly before I finally sigh and take the notepad.

That night, as I sit in the darkness of my room, I stare at the blank page for at least an hour before I can think of what to say. Finally, I start scrawling.

Dear Mr. and Mrs. Sahar,

You don't know me, but something I did has changed your lives...and mine.

My name is Lt. Gabriel Vincent and until recently, I was a United States Ranger. I was with the convoy that was involved in the Humvee explosion that killed your daughter.

I'm looking at the words that I just wrote and they are very black-and-white—very matter-of-fact. But in reality, what happened is far from black-and-white. I think about your daughter every day. Every day, I wish I could have stopped what happened, that I could've helped her. Every day, I hate myself for not being able to.

I don't know what to say to you except that

I'm very, very sorry. Sorrier than you'll ever know.
I doubt that I'll ever be able to forgive myself for
what happened, so I can hardly ask you for forgiveness. So I won't. But I do need for you to know
that if I could change what happened that night, I
would.

I am very sorry for your loss.

My deepest condolences,

Lt. Gabriel Vincent

US Army Rangers, Seventy-Fifth Regiment

I read and reread the letter, then finally decide that there's nothing else I can say. I fold it up and stick it back in the notepad to give
Dr. Hart tomorrow.

And then I think about Maddy. Thinking so much about forgiveness makes me think about her. Out of everyone, she's the one
I should beg forgiveness from the most. I made her trust me, then I
just left. It must've crushed her, a thought that crushes *me*.

My fingers fly across the keyboard and I don't care if I look weak
or like a pussy. I just need her to know, to really know, that I'm sorry.
Even if she can never forgive me, I want her to *know*.

Dear Maddy,

I just wrote a letter to the girl's parents . . . the Afghan girl.
And it made me realize something. I haven't asked you
to forgive me for leaving you the way I did.

I promise you, I only wanted to protect you . . . from
me. I hurt you, Maddy. I could have killed you. But when

I left you without an explanation, I know that hurt you too.

You didn't deserve to have me come into your life and stomp on it. I'm so sorry for that. I'm sorry that I offered you something that I shouldn't have—because at the time, a life with me just wasn't possible.

I'm here now at CPT, hoping...praying...that they can pick up all the wrecked pieces and put me back together again.

But it fucking sucks here. I hate it and every day I don't even know if I can stay. The therapy sort of breaks us back down so that they can build us back up, teaching us the right way to deal with shit. It's terrible.

I don't know if I'm strong enough.

I'm sorry for dumping that on you. I miss talking to you.

All I really wanted to say was that I'm sorrier than you'll ever know. And that even though I don't deserve it, I hope that you can forgive me for hurting you.

Love,
Gabe

I feel completely wiped as I close the lid of my laptop. It's like I've touched upon every emotion that I've ever had today and I decide that I have time for a nap before my last session of the day.

As I drift into sleep I see Ara Sahar's dark eyes. She's watching me curiously, but there is no blame on her face right now, which is a break from the usual.

But the nightmares still come.

Chapter Twenty-Six

Madison

As I wait for Tony to come back, I idly scroll through the Internet on my phone, avoiding the urge to check my e-mail. Something, deep down, tells me that I might find an e-mail from Gabe.

And if he keeps e-mailing me, I just don't know how long I can resist answering him.

I miss him.

I miss him.

God, I miss him.

But I can never open myself like that again. When I do I just get hurt and there's no way I'm going through this again. Ever. The Band-Aid has been ripped off now, the worst part is over. I just have to stick it out.

But I'm weak.

Not two minutes later, I check my e-mail.

And I was right. There's a message from Gabe.

My heart beats loudly in my ears as I read each painful word.

Oh my God. Reading that he thinks he's wrecked almost wrecks *me*. No matter what he did to me by leaving, I can't deny that he's strong and brave...and hearing him like this makes my heart break. Seeing that he wants my forgiveness makes my heart ache.

I hit the Reply button and hesitantly type, *You are strong enough.* That's it. No "Dear Gabe" or "Love, Madison."

My finger hesitates above the Send button, shaking. I don't know whether to send it. I don't want him to quit. He needs the help. I honestly want him to be whole again. Even if I can't be with him, he needs to be whole.

My finger twitches.

And then my phone rings, interrupting me.

Jacey's number flashes on the screen and I roll my eyes. She's the last person I want to talk to right now. Seriously. If she wants to be so stupid, I can't sit around and watch her do it.

But even still. As I glance at the phone, as I look at her name, something in me says to answer it. That I *need* to answer it.

I pick up the phone hesitantly.

And my ear is instantly filled with Jacey's screaming.

Gabriel

Screams fill my ears once again, just like they do whenever I remember that fucking night. I stare at the paper in front of me.

> *So if everything was your fault, how could you have stopped it?*
> *Let's work through this. Write down on that piece of paper every*
> *single thing you could have done to prevent Ara Sahar and Mad*
> *Dog's deaths... or the deaths of the girls and women in the vil-*
> *lage. Because the way I see it, there was never a way to save*
> *them. Try and prove me wrong.*

The blank whiteness of the paper mocks me, as my pen lingers motionless above it. I listen to the tick of the clock and I stare at my shoes. Finally I scribble out an answer.

I fucking hate this shit. The therapist is just going to tear my answers apart in the morning.

A soft rap on the door interrupts my homework, thankfully. I answer it to find the army nurse.

"Hey, soldier," she greets me with a grin, as she tosses me a cold soda. "How was your session?"

I practically growl a response as I drop back onto the bed, cracking the soda open and taking a gulp. "I hate this shit."

Annie perches in the chair, her combat boots shined to a perfect gleam.

"I know," she answers sympathetically. "You're going to hate it the whole time. But I've gotta tell you. It does help. All the questions they ask actually have a purpose. They get us thinking in ways we didn't before. I'm still having the nightmares, but they don't last all night long. I'm still jumpy, but I don't look over my shoulder as much. We might actually do this, soldier."

"I'm not a soldier anymore," I tell her as I scribble another answer onto the work sheet. She rolls her eyes.

"You know as well as I do that you'll always be a soldier. It's in your blood."

And it is.

It feels good to sit and talk with someone who gets that. Brand gets it, but we don't talk about it. Men just don't.

Annie glances at me. "Do you ever miss it?"

It's my turn to roll my eyes now. "What do you think?"

She grins. "I'd miss it like hell. When I first came back, my parents begged me to resign my commission, to come out into civilian life and be 'normal.' As if that was going to happen. I'm a soldier. I'll always be a soldier. I can't imagine turning in my boots."

It's like a sucker punch because I *did* turn in my boots.

"Everyone has to do what is best for them," I finally answer. "I had to resign because that was best for me and best for my squad."

Annie nods understandingly and I know that she does, in fact, understand. She can't possibly know what it was like to be a Ranger or to resign from the job that I dreamed my entire life of having, but she knows what it's like to be a soldier to the bone.

That kind of understanding makes it easy to relate to her. And easy for her to relate to me. She glances up at me, her hands fidgeting in her lap.

"I want to thank you again for being here," she finally says. "Not only so that I can thank you again for what you did for me, but you've reminded me of a couple things. Important things."

I raise an eyebrow. "Such as?"

Annie gets up from her chair and drops down next to me on the bed, something that puts me instantly at unease. *What the fuck*?

"You've reminded me that there are strong guys out there who know what the fuck I'm going through because you're going through it too," she says softly.

As she speaks, she slides her hand softly onto my arm. I freeze as I realize what is happening.

"I've also decided that everything happens for a reason," she continues. "What are the odds that you would be there that day in the squad that rescued me and you would be here when I come to get help?" She pauses for a brief second. "The odds are slim to none,

Gabe. I think I was meant to meet you. I really do. The question
is…what are we going to do about it?"

Before I can think about what she's doing, she's leaned into me,
pressing her lips softly to mine.

I am utterly frozen as she kisses me. I didn't see this coming, I
truly didn't. I thought we were just commiserating about our issues.

Her hands come up and clutch my back and for a moment, one
moment, I think about it. It would be so easy to slip away into that
vague place where sex takes me, to that place where nothing matters anymore. It would be the easiest thing in the world. And I need
someone. I need to be comforted by someone.

But she's not the person I need.

I've already tried this road with Alex and it didn't work.

I don't want anyone else.

I grip Annie's upper arms gently and push her away, looking
into her eyes.

"Annie, you don't want to do this," I tell her firmly. "You don't.
You're emotional because of this place. It's OK, I'm sure it happens
to everyone."

She scowls at me, then she reaches for me again.

"No, it's not this place. It's you, Gabe. I just want you. You
make me remember what I like about the world. You make everything make sense."

After knowing me for a few days? I look at her questioningly as
I hold her at arm's length.

"Annie, think about what you're saying. I can see where you
would think that we have a connection because we both have the
same shit going on. But think about that…*we have the same shit*

going on. We'd be a train wreck. We each need someone outside of this mess, someone who can keep things in perspective for us… someone to give us a reason to pull out of this. I heard you telling one of your other friends about your boyfriend at lunch the other day. You need to tell him everything that you've told me."

Annie starts crying now, big fat tears that roll down her cheeks in black streaks from her makeup. Fuck. I hate this shit. I never know what to do. I awkwardly pat at her back.

"Annie, don't cry. Everything's fine. It's fine. This is just a misunderstanding."

She continues to cry, then reaches for me, burying her head into my chest.

"I'm sorry," she sniffs. "I'm sorry that I misunderstood and wrecked everything. I'm sorry."

I pat at her again. "You didn't wreck anything, Annie. It's a misunderstanding. Our emotions are all jacked up in here. You don't have anything to apologize for."

She nods and sniffs and slips from the bed to the door.

"I'm sorry, Gabe," she sniffles again before she leaves.

I am still shaking my head as I watch her go.

What the fuck was that?

As I calm down and gather my thoughts, I realize that as uncomfortable as that situation was, it did one thing for me.

Because when Annie looked at me, accepting all my flaws, overlooking them because she wanted to sleep with me, it made me realize why I've sought out women ever since the incident.

Their acceptance comforts me.

But it's momentary.

Temporary.

For just a minute it soothes my guilt. I slip into oblivion, into a place where I'm not judged. They accept me for what I am. That's why I sought out the prostitute in Kabul, that's why I almost slept with Alex.

But I can't do this anymore. I've accepted what I did to Ara Sahar. I've accepted why I did it. And because of that, I don't need to seek out a substitute for that acceptance anymore.

I need the real thing.

Something permanent.

That's huge.

Stunned, I sit with my shoulders slumped, my hands in my lap, just thinking about it. I tried to sleep with Maddy for the very same reason I slept with everyone else. But I fell in love with her instead.

And now she's all I want.

I pick up the phone.

Chapter Twenty~Seven

Madison

Another call beeps in as I try to figure out what Jacey is screaming about, but I don't even look. All I can do is try to make sense of what she's saying.

"Jacey, slow down. I can't understand you," I tell her quickly. "Take a breath."

"OhmyGodMadison," she shrieks. "OhmyGod...ohmyGod."

She's frantic and she won't listen and it turns my hand clammy as I grip the phone.

"*What is it?*" I finally yell. "Jacey, what is going on?"

"It's Tony," she finally manages to say. "Jesus Christ. Maddy, you've got to come. We're at that curve on your street. The one... the nasty one."

The one where my parents died. My heart stops.

"Hurry up," Jacey wails. "Just get here."

I hear a siren, then I hear nothing.

I can't even feel my fingers or think as I grab my purse and rush out the door. I don't notice the drive. I don't register the red lights or stop signs or anything else. I'm on autopilot as I drive, as I distance myself from my heart so I don't feel so much of what is going on.

It's nothing bad, I tell myself as I get closer. *It's nothing bad*. He has a flat tire. He had a fender bender. He slid off the edge just like I did a few weeks ago. It's nothing bad. He's fine.

He's fine.

He's fine.

He has to be fine.

Nothing can be wrong with Tony, because he has to be fine. He holds my life together. He holds my family together and he holds the Hill together. He picks up my slack. He picked up my father's slack for years. He became my father, in a way.

He's fine.

But he's not.

He's not fine. I know it before I get there. I know it from the dead feeling in my heart. I know it as I pull up and see his truck, crumpled on the side of the road. I know it when I see the ambulance and the fire trucks and the grave looks on everyone's faces. I know it when I see the stretcher, with the still form on it, covered up with a sheet. I know it when I see the tip of his boot sticking out from under the sheet.

He's not fine.

And I'm not either.

My legs give out and I crumple to the ground. As I go down, I take in the rest of the scene. I see Jared in handcuffs, I see Jacey's tear-streaked face rushing for me. I see EMTs lunging toward me.

And then I don't see anything at all.

❧

Gabriel

Maddy didn't answer the phone.

I listen to it ring and ring, then her voice picks up on the voice mail. I listen to the entire message, savoring the sound of her voice, but when the beep comes, I can't speak. She doesn't want to talk to me. I won't force her to listen to me.

With a sigh I head down to a group session, sitting on the opposite side of the room from Annie. She tries to catch my eye a few times, but I ignore it. I'm not mad at her, but I don't want to deal with her right now. I've got enough to worry about without more drama.

Instead I focus on the paper in front of me. On answering this shit so that I can just go through it all in person in individual therapy tonight.

❧

I wish you could've prevented that incident, too. But I'm hearing a definite turnaround in the way you're speaking about it, Gabe. Instead of saying, "I should've stopped it," you're now saying, "I wish I could have stopped it." Have you noticed that? How does it feel to realize that it was out of your hands?

How does it feel? Last night was the first night in a year that I didn't have continuous nightmares.

After individual therapy last night, I crashed hard and when I woke up an hour ago, it took me a minute to realize why I felt so well rested.

Because I actually slept. It's a fucking amazing feeling. I'd forgotten what that felt like.

I also realize that my therapist was right. I think I really have shifted the blame for what happened away from me. I mean, in my head I always knew it wasn't my fault. But heads and hearts don't always agree; and my heart was guilty as hell.

It's not so guilty anymore.

Not about that, anyway.

Guilt about Maddy is still alive and well, though. But I know that can't be resolved here. It can't be resolved at all, not if she doesn't want to talk to me. Sessions today don't seem as grueling as normal, probably because I'm used to them now, but also because the end is in sight. I only have one more day, then I can leave tomorrow.

But then what?

What will I do then?

Do I have the balls to go back to Maddy, to try to explain? Because for the first time, I feel like I might really beat this. And if I can, I know that I'd never hurt her again . . .

But if she won't even talk to me, then there's no way in hell she'll listen to me try to explain.

All I know is that the void I feel without her is huge. I hadn't realized what a big part of my life she'd become until she suddenly wasn't there anymore this week. And there's no way that I want to continue like this. No fucking way.

I finish up my session and make my way back to my room, ignoring Annie's voice calling for me down the hall.

I can't deal with her right now.

I'm on the way to my laptop, to send Maddy another note, when my phone rings on the dresser.

Brand.

"Dude, I don't want to interrupt your therapy, but there's something you've got to know. When you leave in the morning, you've got to come back to Angel Bay."

Before I can protest or argue, he continues, his voice grave.

"Tony, the bartender from the Hill, is dead."

"What?" I ask, incredulously. "What happened?"

Brand sighs, long and loud. "Long story. But it involves Jacey."

I swallow hard. "What happened?"

"She apparently went back to that little fuck Jared. I don't know the details, but Tony went out to talk some sense into her and Jared ran him off the road. He died at the scene."

Like Madison's parents.

That's the only thing I can think of for a minute.

"Is Jacey all right?" I ask calmly. "Was she there?"

"Yeah, she's fine. And yes, she was there. She went with Jared to try to defuse the situation and she couldn't stop him. She's pretty shaken up, but she's fine."

"What about Jared?" My voice is wooden.

"In jail."

Pause.

"And Maddy?"

Brand's voice softens. "Jacey says that Maddy's a wreck. She won't even talk to Jacey right now. Apparently that guy was a like a father to her and she's taking it hard. She was at the scene too. You need to come home, Gabe. I think she needs you. And I know Jacey does."

"I'll be there tomorrow," I tell him. "Tell Jacey I'm coming."

"And Maddy?"

"Don't mention it to her."

"But—"

"No buts," I interrupt. "I'll be there, Brand. Just tell Jacey."

I hang up and stare at the wall.

This is going to kill Madison. I know she's devastated. I know how much she loved Tony. She's had to deal with so much loss in her life—including losing me.

This isn't fucking fair.

But *life* isn't fucking fair.

All I want to do is to grab my stuff and leave. To drive straight to Angel Bay and grab her up, and protect her from everything.

But I can't protect her from this.

Tony's dead and I can't change that.

I hit the showers and pack my shit and then drop into bed, counting down the hours until I can check out of this place and head back to where I belong.

Chapter Twenty~Eight

Madison

I'm at Tony and Maria's house all day.

They didn't have much money and what little they had was taken up by their daughter Sophia's college tuition, so as I listen to them decide how they're going to pay for the funeral, I speak up.

"I want to pay for it," I tell them as I take in their family photos, photos that include me. Maria just stares at me in shock.

Tony's been a part of my life for years.

He's family.

This is the only thing I can do for him now.

The last thing.

"It's what I want," I assure Maria as she cries in gratitude. "He was like a father to me, Maria. Mila too. He was always there when we needed him the most. It's the least I can do." My voice breaks and a lump forms in my throat and I know from experience that it's going to be weeks until I'm able to swallow it.

It's hard to swallow when your throat is full of pain.

Even though I can hardly think through my shock and grief, I help Maria make decisions, because I know that everything I'm feeling is amplified a hundred times in her. And poor Sophia is curled up in a ball on her bed, unable to process anything.

I know how it feels. I feel like I'm walking around in a haze.

But there are decisions to make.

An urn.

Crematory arrangements.

Flowers.

Hymns.

An obituary.

All the things that a funeral needs, we have to decide on. I can't even believe that I'm doing this again. First my parents…and now Tony. It's just too much. And then Jacey calls right in the middle of it. Right when I'm overwhelmed with everything.

"Please, Maddy," she begs tearfully. "I didn't mean for this to happen. I loved Tony too. I had no idea that Jared was going to do that. I thought he was different. I thought he was changing."

"Oh my God, shut up," I snap at her as I walk onto the front porch. "I can't even talk to you right now. Tony's in the morgue because of your stupid decisions. I never knew that you needed acceptance so bad that you would grovel to a scumbag like Jared. But you did. And you do. And look what happened. This is your fault, Jacey. Your fault."

I hang up on the middle of her sob and turn to find Maria staring at me, her dark eyes full of tears.

"It's not that little girl's fault," she tells me gently, her dark hair blowing in the breeze. "She makes bad decisions, but she's just young. This was Jared Markson's fault—and no one else's. Tony chose to go over there. He made that decision. You can't hold Jacey accountable, Madison."

But I can. And I do.

I'm so pissed off at the world that I can't see straight.

None of this is fair.

And as I slide my phone into my purse, I see something that I missed yesterday with everything going on.

A missed call from Gabriel.

It looks like he called right when I was talking to Jacey and he didn't leave a message.

It fucking figures.

And oddly enough, I can't feel anything about it. My entire body is numb. My mind, my heart, my limbs. I can't feel and that's good.

If I can't feel, then pain can't overtake me. I can step back and do what I need to do. And Gabriel doesn't matter right now.

Getting through the funeral tomorrow matters.

Getting past this god-awful grief matters.

Figuring out what to do with my life matters.

Because as I look around, at the lake, at the restaurant, at everything this place stands for, I think I'm tired of it.

I'm tired of it all.

Chapter Twenty-Nine

Gabriel

When I walk into the back door of my grandparents' cottage, I'm almost bowled over as Jacey launches herself into my arms.

"Thank God you're home," she cries as she buries herself in my chest. I look across the kitchen to see Brand leaning in the doorway and he looks tired. He's probably been talking Jacey down all night.

"Hey, guys," I greet them quietly as I drop my bag on the floor. "I'm sorry about Tony, Jacey. I know you were close to him."

She clings to me, her tear-streaked face turned up toward me. "I love him, Gabe. You know that, right? You know that I would never have done this on purpose."

I have to fight the urge to lecture her, to tell her how wrong it was to first lie about Jared harassing her, then actually go back to the scumbag. She's too fragile right now, I can tell. Her slender shoulders shake as she cries and Brand shakes his head at me, cautioning me.

"I know, Jace," I tell her instead. "This isn't your fault. This is Jared's fault. There's nothing we can do now but honor Tony's memory."

"But Maddy won't even talk to me," Jacey continues to cry. "She thinks it's my fault. And she's probably right. If only I hadn't gone back to Jared. If only I'd listened to everyone. They're having a memorial service in the morning and I know if I go it will upset her. But I need to go, Gabe. He was my friend too. And this is all my fault."

I pat her back and soothe her and assure her in the best way I can. In my head I'm pissed at her. But I can't make her feel even worse. It was a stupid thing to do, but Jacey doesn't have a mean bone in her body. She never meant for anyone to get hurt.

I walk her back to her room and sit her on her bed.

"You need to rest, Jacey," I instruct her. "You've got bags under your eyes. I know you haven't slept. This wasn't your fault and you'll be going to that memorial. I'll go with you, OK?"

She nods soundlessly and curls up. I pull the blanket up to her chin and close the door on my way out.

Brand is waiting for me in the kitchen.

"She'll be OK," he tells me as he tosses me a beer. "She was up all night. But she'll be OK. I know Maddy will come around. These things that happen so suddenly are always hard to take in."

I nod, knocking back the beer and crushing the can in my hand before I head out the back door.

"Where are you going?" he calls after me.

"Out," I answer, without stopping. He knows me well enough not to follow as I wend my way down to the beach.

When I reach the edge of the water, I drop onto my heels and stare out at the horizon. From this point, all you can see is the lake. It's vast and wide and makes me feel small.

It makes me feel like I'm just a fucking speck in the universe, as though all my shit is too small to worry about. Because in the scheme of things, it is.

Life goes on. Whether it's bad or good or otherwise, it goes on. And there's not anything we can do but make the best of it.

The best thing I can do is somehow fix things with Maddy. Now's not the time, because I know she's going through hell, but I know that I have to try.

One more time.

If she hates me and doesn't want to talk to me, I'll have to deal with it.

But I'll never forgive myself if I don't even try. I'm not a fucking quitter.

I can't quit at this. Not until the game is definitely over.

Not that it was ever a game at all.

Chapter Thirty

Madison

"I still don't think this is a good idea," I argue with Mila as Pax carries her down the stairs of their house and deposits her into a rented wheelchair. She glares up at me.

"I love Tony just as much as you do," she answers. "How in the world could I stay here in bed during his memorial? Seriously, Maddy. He's been there for us every time we've needed him. I'm going to be there for him now."

"Funerals are for the living, Mi," I argue again. "Tony won't know the difference."

Pax shakes his head at me. "Trust me. I argued with her all last night. Her mind's made up. She's just going to have to stay in this wheelchair and we'll bring her straight home."

I sigh in frustration. "Mila, the last thing I need today is to worry about you. It's going to be hard enough."

Mila glares at me again, her eyes red and her cheeks tear-streaked. "Maddy, today isn't about you. I'm sorry to sound rude. But today is about Tony and we should all be there. I *want* to be there."

Her words hit their mark, right in the middle of my heart. She's right. Today isn't about me and she has a right to be there too. I nod slowly.

"You're right. I'm sorry. Of course you should be there. But we'll have to bring you right back home. You can't be up very long."

She nods. "I know. I promise. I'll come straight home as soon as it's over."

Pax gets her situated in the car, then loads the wheelchair into the trunk before he turns to me.

"I don't like it either," he tells me. "But she has a point. It's important to get closure. She deserves that as much as everyone else."

I nod silently as I climb into the back seat. I'm silent as we drive to the church, silent as we unload Mila, silent as we walk into the church, silent as we find our seats in the family section next to Maria and Sophia. Maria leans over to give me a hug and we settle in on the hard wooden pews.

The overwhelming scent of funeral flowers…the lilies and mums and carnations…they smell so sweet that they make my stomach turn, and they trigger memories of my parents' funeral. Of the crying, the pain, the grief. But I block them out.

Today isn't about me.

I stare straight ahead, at the glossy black urn that holds Tony. It's so small and he was so big. I can hardly believe that he fits into it.

But he does.

I can hardly believe this happened at all. But it did. Everything really can change in a moment. Everything can end and it's out of our hands. It's depressing.

I close my eyes, listening to the haunting strains of "Amazing Grace" filtering through the speakers. I don't open my eyes again until Mila jabs me in the side.

My eyes pop open and I follow her gaze.

Gabriel is walking Jacey down the aisle, his hand on her elbow as he guides her into the church. Her face is tear-streaked and tired, but it's not her I'm focused on.

It's him.

He's here.

My heart leaps out of its dormant sleep, out of the numb confines of my chest, and lodges in my throat as I catch and hold his gaze.

His is stormy and black, as black as night, as black as always.

It doesn't stray from mine, it holds there, like an invisible ribbon is holding us together. My heart pounds hard and I feel such utter relief at seeing him. Even though I want to hate him, even though I want to be furious at him, to rage against him, all I can feel is relief.

Because he's here.

"He came," Mila whispers. I nod without saying a word, without breaking Gabe's gaze. Brand is behind him, both of them wearing their army dress uniforms. They look breathtaking as they file into a pew with Jacey, their hats in their hands as they sit staring ahead, stiff and straight and dignified.

Even though Gabe isn't looking at me now, the ribbon holding us together is still there, as strong as ever. It's like a thousand volts of electricity are rippling through the air, from him to me.

But then the service starts and I force my attention from him to where it belongs... to honor the man who became my surrogate father, better in so many ways than my real one.

"Dearly beloved, we are gathered here today to celebrate the life of Tony Romano. A husband, a father, a friend..."

My eyes well up and I press a tissue to the corners as the pastor's voice drones on. I am acutely aware of Maria sobbing silently next to me, of Pax's arm wrapped around Mila, of the flowers, of the urn, of the mourning people.

I'm acutely aware of it all, but it's still as though I'm suspended. Distant. It's like I'm watching it all through a veil.

That's what I have to do so I don't fall apart.

That's what I always do. I retreat behind a wall.

The seconds turn into minutes, then an hour. And just when I think it's over, Gabe stands up. I look at him in confusion, not sure what's going on.

But he strides to the front with purpose, a white paper in his hand.

He murmurs a few words to the pastor, then the pastor turns to us.

"Lt. Gabriel Vincent would like to say a few words."

Holy shit. My heart slams. *What the hell?*

Mila and I glance at each other briefly, but my attention is immediately and completely consumed by Gabriel. He owns the lectern, he owns the room.

He owns me.

No matter what happened or what will ever happen. He owns me. I know that now. I know it as I listen to his husky deep voice speak, as he turns to find me in the crowd, as his gaze holds mine.

Dark, stormy and black.

"I didn't know Tony all that well," he admits to the mourners. "We weren't close friends, because I didn't have time to really get to know him. But from what I saw, I know that given time, we'd have become very close. He embodied values that I hold important. Strength, integrity, honesty. Most importantly, he was loyal. He took care of those close to him in a fierce and powerful way. He took care of my sister, Jacey, which is something I'll be forever grateful for. He took care of her when I couldn't be here to do it myself."

Gabe pauses for a deep breath and I find that I can't breathe. Somehow, in just a few sentences, Gabe is managing to drill down to the core of who Tony was in a way that the pastor hasn't been able to in an hour. I can't take my eyes off him, at the way he's standing at attention, at the way he's so sincere. This isn't a show. This isn't an act. This is a display of raw gratitude. I swallow as he continues.

"I don't want to take up a lot of your time today, but I just wanted to honor Tony in my own way, to thank him for protecting my sister, and for taking care of Mila and Maddy all of these years. As you can see, I'm an Army Ranger. Or I was. And I can tell you that I've seen my share of heroes over the years. And there is one thing that I can tell you... Tony Romano was a hero. I didn't know him well, but I do know that."

He steps away from the lectern and makes his way back to his seat, striding tall and confidently. I finally catch my breath and then he looks at me, taking it away again.

His words were so beautiful that I just want to cry again. I never thought he could be so eloquent. But he was. And he said the exact perfect thing.

The ushers come to let everyone out, row by row, and I'm caught up in talking to Maria, to Sophia, to Mila and Pax and the people sitting behind us. When I turn around again, Gabriel, Brand and Jacey are gone.

I sigh.

"That was beautiful," Mila tells me knowingly, her green eyes staring into mine. "You need to go find him."

"I don't know," I tell her hesitantly. "He still left me, Mila. This doesn't change anything."

She stares at me incredulously. "Madison. He left to get help. He came back. He's here. Anyone in this room can feel how much he loves you when he looks at you. Trust me. It changes everything."

I swallow hard, all the emotions of the day threatening to overwhelm me.

"We need to get you home," I tell her, refusing to answer that. "Maria is going to spread Tony's ashes another day. There's no way you're staying for the dinner."

"Don't leave Maria," Mila tells me firmly. "You stay. I'll have Pax take me home and then he can come back and get you. She needs you."

I nod. "OK. If Pax doesn't mind."

"I don't," he reassures me from behind Mila. "Call me when you're ready."

He rolls my sister away and I thread through the masses of people to make my way downstairs to the dinner. A hand darts out and grabs me, though, pulling me into an alcove.

Jacey.

"I'm sorry, Madison," she tells me tearfully. "Please believe me. I hate it that you're upset with me. I hate it that you think it's my fault. I know it's my fault. I feel so guilty being here, but I couldn't stay away. I had to see Tony off."

A lump forms in my throat again and I can't help but hug her. Her eyes are just so sad.

"I know," I murmur into her hair. "I know that it's not your fault. You made a stupid decision, but this was Jared's fault. I was just upset the other day. I'm sorry."

"You texted to stay put, but Jared got pissed and jumped into his truck and I didn't know what else to do except go with him—to try and keep him from doing something stupid. But when he saw Tony coming around that curve, he swerved over. I don't know if he was playing chicken or what. But Tony lost control of his truck. I couldn't stop him, Maddy. I couldn't stop him."

Her voice breaks off and I murmur, "Of course you couldn't, Jacey. No one can control him."

She cries and I hold her and we stand together for what seems like forever, until a deep voice clears. I look over Jacey's shoulder to find Gabriel leaning against the wall, watching us, his gaze immediately impaling me straight through the heart.

I let go of Jacey and stand limp, and suddenly it's just Gabe and me.

The room spins around and we're alone in it, alone in the world. As if she's speaking from a fog, I hear Jacey tell me that she'll leave us alone to talk but I can't even acknowledge it. All I can do is stare at Gabriel.

He takes a step toward me, then another one, then he's close enough that I can smell his smell, the smell that is so distinctly him.

"You left me," I whisper, staring directly into his eyes. "I hated you for that."

His face is pained and he nods. "I know. I hated me for that too. I'm sorry, Madison. I'm so sorry. I didn't see any other way. But I was wrong."

I nod, stiltedly. Because I don't know what to do. Because he *was* wrong. Because the world is whirling around and around and all I want to do is launch myself into his arms, but I can't. I shouldn't.

Everything is all muddled up in my head and I can't remember how I should feel.

All I know is how I *do* feel.

I've missed him so much. All I want is him.

I'm frozen and Gabe can see that.

"Why don't we get you back to the dinner. And then maybe afterward...would you talk to me for a few minutes?"

His handsome face is hopeful and vulnerable even while it is strong. And there's nothing I can do but nod.

"Yes."

Because I have to.

Because I need you to say all the right things.

Please.

Chapter Thirty-One

Gabriel

The dinner passes excruciatingly slowly, but finally it is over. Maddy has hugged and kissed everyone she needs to hug and kiss. She's made small talk. She's comforted people. She's been comforted.

Through it all she's been very aware of where I am. She's watched me out of the corner of her eye, like she's afraid that I'm going to leave again.

Before I can give her an explanation for last time.

No fucking way. There's no way I would.

I watch as Maddy gives Jacey a hug, then hands her off to Brand. "Can you give her a ride home?" I ask him quietly. "I need to stay and talk to Madison."

He nods. "Definitely. Good luck."

"I'll need it," I mutter.

But when Maddy looks at me, it's soft. It's hopeful. It's not filled with hate or anger or fear. It's filled with hope.

And that fills *me* with hope.

I walk to her side, back to where I belong. She looks up at me.

"I don't have a car," she tells me. "Pax brought me. Would you mind giving me a ride home? We can talk there."

"Of course," I agree quickly.

I guide her through the people who are left at the dinner, out to my car, where I open her door.

As I get in my side, she looks at me. "You look really good in your uniform," she tells me. "And what you said about Tony today … well, it was beautiful."

"I meant every word," I tell her honestly.

Because I do.

As I drive she calls Pax and tells him that she doesn't need a ride. I notice that she doesn't tell him why … she doesn't tell him who is taking her home instead. But that doesn't matter right now.

All that matters is that she's giving me a chance. One chance.

And I'm sure as hell not going to blow it.

When we get to her house, she leads me out to the patio, where we sit at the table.

"Would you like wine or a beer?" she asks hesitantly, her blue eyes glued to mine. I shake my head.

"No. All I need is you, Maddy."

She sucks in her breath and even though I didn't mean to say it, I didn't mean to start with that, it makes sense now. Because it's the absolute fucking truth.

As I look at her, backlit by the sun and gorgeous as fucking hell, it's the only thing I can think of. All I need is her.

Everything starts spilling out, one word after another.

How I felt the night I left. How fucking hard it was. What I tried to do with Alex, but couldn't. How I couldn't erase Maddy from my mind no matter what I did. How I balanced on the ledge at the hotel and how Brand talked me down. The absolute utter fucking bleakness. The treatment. The therapy. How the little girl doesn't haunt me as much. How I turned Annie away.

"I missed you every single fucking minute," I tell her earnestly, honestly. Desperately. "I can't live without you. Nothing I did could get you out of my head. I was miserable every minute that I was gone."

I stare at her and she stares back and I can't read her face.

"It's like I'm not whole when I'm not with you," I tell her simply. "You're a piece of me. A big piece of me. And when you're gone, I can't function right. I'm only half a person. I'm so sorry. I know I fucked up. I acted with dishonor. I left you. But I did what I had to do to try and keep you safe. Do you understand? Do you see?"

She looks sick as she looks away.

"I can't believe you almost slept with someone else," she says limply. "I was dying here, Gabe. All I could think of was you. I would never have slept with anyone else. I just wouldn't have. I missed you too much."

"I missed you too," I interrupt. "God, I missed you. Every minute. I did a stupid thing, Maddy. I tried to do the only thing I could think of to finally get you out of my head. And it didn't work. Nothing worked. But if you give me another chance, I swear to God that I won't hurt you again. I'll never leave you. I'll never even look at someone else. You're all I want."

Without a word she gets up and walks down to the beach. She is completely silent as she stares out at the water, completely beautiful.

"Maddy?" I finally say after the minutes have ticked past. She turns to me.

"I don't know what to say," she admits. "I know I should tell you to leave. To never come back. But honestly, I don't have it in me. I'm pissed, though. I'm pissed because whoever that woman was, she touched what was mine. You were almost *inside* of her, Gabe. And *you're mine*. What am I supposed to do with that?"

I take a ragged breath. "You're supposed to put it out of your mind, Maddy. Never think about it again. Because I didn't want her. I only wanted you. In my head, it was your face I saw. Your eyes. Your smell. Your hands touching me. Please forgive me, Madison. I don't deserve you. That much is true. *But all I want is you.* And if I can't have you, then I don't want anyone."

A tear slips down her cheek and she squeezes her eyes shut. I don't know what to do. I want to grab her, to pull her to me, to never let her out of my sight again, but I don't know what she wants me to do.

After a minute she opens her eyes.

"Gabriel?" Her voice is small.

"Yes?"

"Open your arms."

So I do.

I open them wide and she folds into them, burying her face into my chest, and I do what I've wanted to do for two weeks. I hold her tight. I breathe in the smell of her hair, I run my hands over the slender expanse of her back.

I tilt her chin up and kiss her mouth, crushing her soft lips with my own.

After a breathless minute she pulls away and stares at me.

"Don't leave me again."

I nod, scooping her up into my arms, and carry her into the house.

Madison

This is real.

That's the only thing I can think of as Gabriel carries me into the house and into the bedroom. This is real and Gabriel is here.

I'm not sure what I should be feeling right now, whether I'm letting him off too easily or whether I should try to be standoffish. All I know is I can't.

Because whatever happened tortured him.

I can see that on his face and it breaks my heart.

And I know that I need him.

I look at him, and for some reason, all the leftover feelings... the being mad at him, the hurt, the fear... it all fades away. I know what's important now.

Him and me. That's it.

That's all that matters. We can sort everything else out.

"I never stopped trusting you," I tell him honestly. "Not really. When I first realized you were gone, I was pissed. And hurt. But I figured out why you left pretty quickly. And then I was pissed again. But I always trusted that you thought you were doing the right thing."

He stares at me, his rugged face pensive. "All I want is you," he tells me quietly. "I promise you. I'm so sorry I hurt you. I'm sorry that our path has been twisted and hard. But I want you to know...thinking about you gave me the strength to stick it out at CPT. In the back of my head, I always held out the hope that if I could fix *me*, then we could fix *us*."

I swallow hard. "That was in the back of my mind too. Even when I was pissed at you. Even when I hated you."

He looks at me, his eyes so stormy. "Don't hate me, Maddy. I can deal with anything else the world throws at me, but I can't deal with that. I love you. I've known it for a while and I was afraid to say it. I'm not sure that I'm fixed, but I'm sure as hell headed in the right direction. I won't ever hurt you again—I won't let it happen. I need for you to know that."

"I know," I whisper, pulling him close and clinging to him tight. "I need you, Gabe."

He swallows. "I need you, too."

"Then show me," I whisper.

Without a word he eases me backward onto the bed, covering my body with his own. I've missed his weight, the way his body slides against mine just right, pressing into me.

"I missed you," he says, right before he kisses me. His tongue delves into my mouth and he tastes like spearmint.

He kisses me soft, he kisses me hard, then he groans and fucks my mouth with his tongue, ravaging it like he can't control himself because he's missed me that much.

The air around us is desperate and hot and I want to breathe him in.

His hands are everywhere, sliding down my hips, pulling at my clothes. I help kick them away and within a minute we are both naked. The friction is delicious and I revel in the feel of his body against mine.

My hips tilt for him and he cups me there, his mouth tracing my arm.

"I love the way you smell," he tells me as he runs his lips along my shoulder, kissing my skin lightly as he makes his way back to my mouth. "I dream about that smell."

I dream about him.

About this.

I lift my legs around his hips and pull him toward me...into me.

And suddenly I feel complete. He takes all of me, right down to my fingertips, to my toes, to the innermost parts of my heart.

My hidden parts.

My secrets.

He takes it and takes it and I give it all.

Because I want him to have it.

As he slides into me I know that I never want to be without him again. It's a heady feeling and it doesn't terrify me a bit.

As he slowly thrusts into me, in and out, leisurely, slowly, he skims his hands everywhere...as though he can't stop touching me.

Like he's trying to decide if I'm real.

I look into his dark eyes. "I love you," I whisper.

He grins, a slow smile that spreads to his eyes.

"I know," he answers, before he buries his face in my neck and shudders from his release. "I love you too. God, I love you."

His words, ragged and raw, pierce my heart and send me over the edge and I follow him, shaking and arching against him, crying his name as I come.

As I lie beneath him, I know that I could die a happy death here in his arms, and we lie twisted together for what seems like forever, just listening to each other breathe.

But eventually we get hungry, so I make a tray of sliced meat, cheese and crackers and we curl up on the sofa with a bottle of wine.

"What about your nightmares?" I ask as I sip at my wine. "Are they gone?"

He shakes his head. "I've had them, but only for part of the night. It used to be a continuous thing, all night long. We can keep our fingers crossed that it lasts. Either way it's progress. For now, though, I'm going to sleep on your chaise. I don't want to take any chances just yet."

I nod, even though I don't want to. I don't want to sleep apart, but I also don't want to get strangled again. So we'll do what we have to do.

"Did you notice the house?" I ask him quietly and he looks around, only just now noticing the new paint and furniture. "I know you carried me into my old bedroom and I didn't correct you, but I've moved into the master bedroom. I've had everything changed... to make it my own."

Gabe stares at me, with something very close to admiration in his eyes. "So you've gone from not being able to open that door to moving in there in two weeks' time?"

I smile. "I've got balls, Gabe. Someone told me that once."

He smiles back. "You do have balls. Whoever told you that was brilliant."

We laugh and drop our plates in the sink, then head back to bed, where I curl up in his arms.

"Don't leave me again," I tell him before I close my eyes to sleep. "Ever."

"Don't worry," he answers quietly, dropping a kiss on the top of my head. "It's good to be home."

I look up at him, struggling to keep my eyes open after this hellishly long day. "Do you really consider Angel Bay home now?"

He brushes the hair away from my face with his strong fingers as he stares down at me.

"Maddy, I consider wherever you are home."

Chapter Thirty-Two

"We're on our way in a couple of minutes," I tell Mila, balancing the phone between my chin and my shoulder as I grab my purse from the kitchen table. "We're going to stop and get you a milkshake and then we'll be there. Please don't make it weird, OK? I'm really not comfortable bringing him out there so soon, but Pax needs me to sit with you, so..." My voice trails off because I'm not sure what to say.

"It'll be OK," Mila tells me cheerfully, before she lowers her voice. "Trust me, I understand. But just know that Pax plans on talking to Gabe."

I freeze. "*Talking* to him?"

I can practically see Mila nod. "Yeah. I told him touching isn't allowed when he talks to him."

"Well, thanks for that," I answer. "Tell him he really doesn't need to. Gabe and I have worked it out. I know why he left. He had a good reason. He's only been back for a day. I don't need for Pax to scare him off already."

I know Gabriel isn't going anywhere. But still.

"I know that he left for a good reason." Mila sighs. "And *you* know that. But Pax just wants to make sure it doesn't happen again. It's a man thing, I think."

"OK." I sigh as I hang up. Gabe looks at me from the driver's seat.

"What's wrong?" he asks as he turns the key and his Camaro fires up. I shake my head.

"Apparently, Pax wants to talk to you about what happened. I'm sorry. I could tell him not to, but it's probably best just to get it out of the way. He doesn't have much family and so he's protective over who he's got."

Gabe nods, unaffected. "That's fine," he tells me easily. "I respect that. And I deserve it. I'll listen to whatever he has to say."

I shake my head. "Men."

We grab the milkshake and are at Pax and Mila's within a few minutes.

As we walk up to the front door, Pax opens it. Apparently he's been watching for us.

"Hey, little brother," I greet him carefully. "What's going on?"

Pax is wearing his most intimidating expression as he opens the door wider, motioning for us to come in. If I were a guy, I'd be tucking my tail and running. But Gabe doesn't. He stands firmly at my side.

"Hey, Mad," Pax greets me before turning to Gabe. "Can you give us a minute? I'd like to talk to Gabe, if you don't mind."

"Actually I *do*," I tell Pax. "I'll just stick around for this. And don't forget what Mila told you. No touching allowed."

"You don't need to worry about that," Pax tells me as we head up into the living room. I glance at him.

"Oh, I think I do. I'll stay," I answer firmly.

He shrugs. "Suit yourself. It's not going to take long," he says, turning to Gabe.

"I already told you that I respect the hell out of what you did as a Ranger. Because of all the shit you had to do, it doesn't surprise me that you came home with baggage. That's fine. I don't hold that against you.

"But if you ever treat Maddy like that again—if you ever leave her high and dry or lay one finger on her in a way that I don't approve of, I will fuck you up. You might be an Army Ranger, but don't ever doubt that I can hold my own."

Gabe looks at him in the eye as they stand toe-to-toe. Pax's arm flexes at his side, but Gabe remains relaxed and still.

"I don't doubt that," Gabe answers calmly. "Any of it. Trust me, I'm not going to hurt Maddy again. I promised her and I promise you. What I did was shitty. I didn't know how else to protect her from me, so I just left. If I could do it over, I would think of another way. But I can't. What I *can* do is promise to never fuck up like that again."

Pax nods slowly. "That's all that needs to be said. I respect the hell out of you coming to Tony's funeral and speaking. That was a stand-up thing to do."

Gabe nods slowly. "Thanks. It just seemed like the right thing to do."

There is a pause and I stare at Pax.

"Are you done waving your penis around now? Because I should go see Mila and I don't want to leave you two alone unless it's safe."

He chuckles. "It's safe, Mad. She's upstairs, of course. I need to talk to Gabe a little about business before I leave. Thank you again for coming out today. I know that she doesn't need a babysitter, but I just don't like her being alone now that her due date is so close."

"Oh, I agree," I tell him. "She shouldn't be alone. It's not a big deal for me to be here."

When I walk away, I overhear Pax talking to Gabe about his armor again, something that makes me smile. I knew that he'd only withdrawn from investing because of me.

He's loyal to the bone.

I climb the stairs and poke my head in Mila's room.

"It's all over. Everyone has been adequately threatened and apparently all is well."

I hand her the milkshake.

"I'm glad," Mila answers. "I didn't want him to say anything at all, but you know how men are."

Scowling, she rolls this way and that, trying to get situated. I bend and adjust the giant pillow that she keeps behind her back.

"Better?"

She nods, but I can tell she's lying. "I can't get comfortable today," she grumbles. "My back hurts. And my hips. And my everything. It's probably because I'm getting so enormous. And because I'm stuck in this freaking bed."

I eye her tiny body. "Yeah, you're enormous. You look like a gnat with gas. Sit still and I'll do your nails. It'll keep your mind off of it."

"You can try," Mila sighs as she examines her hand. "But my discomfort refuses to be ignored."

"Well, we'll give it a shot."

I have painted her fingers and have moved on to her toes before she finally brings up Gabe. I've been waiting for it. Actually, I'm surprised it took her this long.

"So, are you going to tell me more about how it's going with Gabe?" she asks, attempting to be casual.

I smile. "It's great, actually. I know he's only been home a day, but apparently his nightmares have gotten better and things are on the right track. We're good, Mila. It's hard because so much has happened, but I'm just so happy he's back. That's all that matters right now. We'll deal with everything else."

"I know that feeling." Mila nods. "I'm sorry you had to go through all of this, Mad. But trust me, sometimes the hardest situations make for the best happily-ever-afters. I have to believe that you're gonna get yours. Gabriel has definitely put the work in."

"I know," I agree. "I keep waiting for the other shoe to drop. To find out that it's not real. That I just dreamed it—that I'm going to wake up and he's still going to be gone. But so far, so good. It's real and he's here and everything's OK."

"You'll get used to it," she tells me knowingly, glancing at my face.

I look up at her. "Used to what?"

"Used to loving someone like that, used to not waiting for it all to collapse. I know it's hard, especially after he left you like that. I know how that feels. Gabe loves you too, you know. Anyone can see it. And one of these days, you're going to realize that what you have is real. You'll learn to trust it."

"God, I hope so," I murmur, knowing exactly what she means. We slip into silence as I finish up her toes, each of us lost in our own thoughts.

After a while, after the nail polish has dried, Mila shakes her head, as if to shake the thoughts away.

"I could really use a shower," she tells me wryly. "I only get to have one once a week, you know. It's the grossest thing ever. Those sponge baths just don't do it for me."

"You do smell," I agree and she slugs me. "OK. I'll help. Let me go get your stuff ready and I'll be right back."

She nods and I make my way into her bathroom to get her shower bench ready, and line up all her bath products so she doesn't have to reach for them.

I come back and take her spindly little arm, helping her from her bed. Her muscles shake as we walk, evidence of how much they've deteriorated over the past few months of disuse. The doctor said it was normal, that she'd build them back up after the baby was born, but right now she's so clearly weak.

"You really do have chicken legs now," I tell her helpfully as she takes off her robe and I settle her on the bench. "Just like Tony always said."

Thinking of Tony makes my throat instantly tight, makes me instantly sad, and I wish I hadn't said it. I guess Mila thinks the same way because she punches me again.

"Ow," I grumble as I turn on the water nozzle and accidentally spray her in the face with it. She screeches at the cold water, grasping at me with wet hands.

"Hey," I shriek, grabbing her. "I'm sorry. Calm down before you hurt yourself. You were up entirely too much yesterday. You don't need to push your luck today."

She obediently settles down and sits still as I spray her hair with warm water and work it into a lather with shampoo. I hum aimlessly as my fingers massage her scalp, then as I rinse the soap out.

I absently space out, lost in my thoughts; thinking about Gabe, and about what he might do. Will he maybe move in with me? It's all so exciting and new and terrifying.

Suddenly Mila startles, grasping at her stomach, pulling me out of my thoughts.

"What's wrong?" I ask anxiously. "Are you in labor?"

She shakes her head, flinches as she curls over into herself.

"Ow. No, I don't think so. This isn't right," she mutters. "Labor is supposed to be a gradual thing. This…owwww." She moans, clutching at her stomach again. She glances up at me, her face suddenly pale. "Maddy, this isn't right. Something's wrong."

Shit. It's because she was up yesterday.

"Pax," I shout in panic, but I quickly realize that he won't be able to hear us from in here.

My hands are shaking so much that I can barely get her out of the shower. Somehow I manage, but just as I reach to turn the water off, she screams, loud and shrill, before she completely doubles over.

Looking down, I see that the sudsy water swirling around the drain has turned red with blood.

Within seconds it turns into more blood than I have ever seen.

Chapter Thirty-Three

Gabriel

Pax is just telling me how interested his grandfather is in DefenseTech's armor when we hear a bloodcurdling scream. I can't tell if it's Maddy or Mila, but it doesn't matter.

We both lunge to our feet and race down the hall.

As we burst into the bedroom, Maddy is pulling Mila out of the bathroom. Mila is completely naked, dripping wet and covered in blood.

"Pax," Maddy shrieks. "We need an ambulance."

I immediately pull out my phone and dial 911 but Pax shakes his head as he scoops up his unconscious wife.

"There's no time," he shouts over his shoulder as he runs down the stairs with his bloody wife in his arms.

Fuck.

Maddy rips a sheet from the bed and we follow Pax as fast we can. Mila is bleeding so much that there is a wide trail of blood on the stairs. Maddy slips in it, tumbling to the landing, smearing blood onto her clothing, her hands and her face.

I pull her up and we race to meet Pax at the car.

"Here," Maddy tells Pax, thrusting the sheet at him. "At least cover her up."

"Hurry up," he grunts, holding Mila out so that Maddy can ram the sheet down around her. "We've gotta hurry. What happened, Maddy?"

"I don't know," Maddy admits, her voice shaking. "I was giving her a shower and then she screamed. There's way too much blood."

And there is. It's gushing everywhere, dripping through the sheet and onto Pax, saturating his clothes.

"I'll drive," I offer, leaping into the driver's side door. Maddy dives into the back and Pax collapses into the passenger seat with Mila on his lap. It's tight, but in his desperation he makes it work.

"Hurry," he commands me, although there's no need. My foot is already on the floor.

The wheels on the Charger barely touch the ground as we fly toward the hospital. As I drive, Maddy calls up to Pax, "Do you know her doctor's number?"

"Of course not," Pax snaps back. "I don't know that shit. Just call 911. They can let the hospital know that we're on the way."

So Maddy does, her voice shrill as she tells the dispatcher the situation.

Mila doesn't open her eyes for the entire ten-minute drive to the hospital, regardless of Pax's pleading.

"Mila, just look at me," he begs, pushing her hair out of her face. He tries to wipe the blood from her cheek, but he only makes it worse. "Please wake up," he mutters helplessly.

There is blood everywhere.

Way too much blood.

"She's not breathing," Pax suddenly blurts, dropping his ear down to listen at her mouth. "She's not breathing. Jesus Christ."

Maddy scrambles to try to help from behind us, to try to see, just as I pull into the parking lot. Before I've even come to a stop at the curb, Pax has the door open and is laying Mila out on the sidewalk.

"Breathe, baby," he begs as he kneels and gives her a breath. "Breathe."

He's frantic and desperate and covered in Mila's blood.

"Pax," Maddy cries, pulling at his arm. "We've got to get her inside. We don't have time for this."

She pulls at him, but Pax isn't thinking clearly and he shakes her off, turning back to Mila, trying to breathe into her mouth.

He's interrupted by a team of people bursting through the doors with a gurney. Pax lunges up with Mila in his arms and thrusts her at the medical team.

"She's not breathing," he tells them in desperation. "Please—help her."

The doctors and nurses close in around Mila as they lay her out on the gurney and rush her inside.

As they do, Maddy clings helplessly to the side of the gurney. Looking down, I see that Mila's eyes are still closed and she is as pale as I've ever seen anyone. More terrifying than that, though, are the words coming out of the nurses' mouths.

She's unresponsive.

There's no pulse.

We need the paddles.

Maddy flinches as she hears them, tears running down her cheeks.

"It's going to be all right," Maddy tells her sister as the team shoves the gurney through the double doors and out of our sight. "Mila, you're going to be all right."

"Mila, I'm here!" Pax calls after her, when a nurse blocks his way. But Mila stays motionless. She couldn't hear any of it.

Fuckkkkkk.

I've never felt so helpless as when I watch them take her away. I know there's nothing I can do and from the looks of all that blood staining the sheets covering her, I'm not sure there's anything anyone can do. There's no way she's not going to die.

There's so much blood.

Hell. All of a sudden the blood reminds me too much of that night in Afghanistan and my senses threaten to overtake me: the smell of blood, the taste of fear, the feel of panic.

The smoke.

The death.

The bloody children.

I fight it off, trying to breathe.

Maddy needs me. I can't lose my shit.

I take a deep breath, sucking in the fear and releasing it on the exhale.

I suck in the panic, releasing it on the exhale.

It's a trick Dr. Hart taught me and it seems to work.

By the time Maddy collapses into my arms a minute later, turning her face into my chest, I've calmed down. I can breathe again.

I'm fine, even if Mila is not.

What the fuck? Where's the justice in that?

Maddy hides her face as if she's hiding from what is happening, hiding from the world, hiding from death. I choke as I realize something.

Loss is her greatest fear. She just lost Tony and now she might lose Mila too.

Her bad thing has caught her.

I close my arms around her. It's the only thing I can do.

❧

"She's going to be all right," Maddy says for the hundredth time as we all pace in the hospital waiting room. "She's going to be fine. I can't lose her too. I just can't. She'll be fine."

I don't even think she knows she's speaking. The words just automatically come out of her mouth at timed intervals, wooden and lifeless. I agree with her. I tell her that Mila will be fine, even though I don't believe it myself. Maddy doesn't even notice.

Pax is in his own world. They wouldn't let him back with Mila and he's like a caged lion out here. His muscles coil as he walks in tight circles. The tension in this room is palpable. I can taste the fear in the air, but no one acknowledges it.

"They're doctors," Maddy tells Pax. "They can fix her."

Pax looks up, his eyes completely stark, but doesn't answer as he paces past Maddy.

In turn, Maddy paces past me.

It's a continuous, nerve-racking cycle.

We're left out here alone, wondering what the fuck is going on. The worst thing is the not knowing. But knowing will be even worse. I feel so certain about that. Because there's no way Mila can survive.

There's no way.

And as I look at Pax and see how his face is drawn, how he's so pale, how he's pacing and flexing his hands and trying to breathe, I know he knows it too.

His bad thing has caught him too.

The very worst possible thing.

Seconds tick by. Then minutes. Then an hour. Then two. A nurse comes out a time or two to tell us that the doctors are still working, that they'll come back out when there's more news.

More time passes.

I get Pax and Madison coffee. I get them water. I go to the restroom and bring them back wet paper towels to wipe the blood from their faces. Neither of them even notices.

They are immersed in fear.

"She was so cold," Madison tells me, her voice almost emotionless. "She was so cold, Gabe."

I rub her back, I pull her close. I watch the clock.

Another half hour passes.

There's no way she survived. There's no way.

Finally a doctor emerges from the double doors. He looks exhausted.

But more than that, he looks gutted.

Shit. I suck in my breath.

Pax leaps to his feet and Maddy freezes, both waiting for the worst, praying for the best, afraid to know which it is.

"She's going to be OK," the doctor assures us, after what seems like forever. "Her placenta detached, causing her to hemorrhage. And when you handed her to us outside, she didn't have a pulse. She had lost that much blood. Her body shut down—in total shock. We managed to revive her, thankfully. It took us a while, but we were able to stop the blood flow and repair the damage." He pauses, letting that sink in.

Both Pax and Maddy look stricken.

"She really died?" Pax asks in shock.

The doctor nods. "She had no heartbeat when she arrived. But we were able to bring her back within two minutes. She's going to be fine. And she's asking to see you," he tells Pax. "You'll have to keep it short. She's exhausted."

Pax immediately starts toward the door, but pauses. "The baby?" he asks anxiously, his eyes glistening wet.

The doctor smiles. "A healthy baby girl. Since she's a couple of weeks early, she'll stay here for a few days. But everything looks good, son. Congratulations."

His words lift the cloud of fear from the room, it evaporates, and Pax smiles as he heads out the doors.

Maddy falls into me, slumping into my side with a sob.

I hold her up, then stare into her eyes.

"I told you she would be fine," I remind her. "See? I keep my promises."

She finally allows herself to smile.

"You do, don't you?" she murmurs. "I was so scared, Gabe."

"I know," I tell her softly. I hold her clutched to me for several minutes, waiting while she pulls herself back together. Finally she shoves her hair out of her face and gets up and paces.

"I can't wait to see my niece," she finally tells me. "I wonder who she looks like?"

"Well, she's got good genes," I point out. "She's going to be a looker."

Maddy collapses again, onto my lap.

"You have no idea how scared I was," she admits quietly. "I don't know what I would've done if I'd have lost Mila."

I stare at her. "I know. But you held it together so well, Maddy. I'm proud of you."

She smiles a little. "I kept reminding myself that fear is a choice, but it wasn't working out so well for me. I was too afraid."

I smile back. "I think in this situation, that's allowed," I tell her. "It was scary. But it's going to be OK. She's fine. The baby's fine. Everything is fine."

Maddy relaxes against me, nervously speculating about what the baby looks like and what they're going to name her.

"You just can't wait to buy her little shoes," I joke, trying to lift some of the lingering anxiety. Maddy smiles.

"Oh, I definitely can't wait to do that. This is going to be the best-dressed baby in the state."

We anxiously wait until Pax comes to get us and then Maddy beats us both back to Mila's room. When we arrive, Maddy is sitting next to Mila, holding her hand, telling her how scared we all were.

I glance around, but there's no baby.

I look at Madison questioningly.

"Since she was early, they had to take her to the neonatal unit," she explains. "Pax can show her to us through the window in a little bit."

Mila is pale and obviously tired, but other than that she looks good.

"You can go see her now," she tells us tiredly. "I know you want to see her, Mad."

"Are you sure?" Pax asks. "We can wait."

Mila nods. "I'm sure. Go see our daughter."

We find the neonatal unit and we all press our noses to the window. When the nurse pushes the incubator up closer to the window, Maddy coos at the tiny baby through the glass.

"She's the most beautiful thing I've ever seen," she announces, although I personally think she's red and wrinkly. "What are you naming her?"

Pax glances at Maddy.

"Madelyn Susanna Tate," he announces proudly. "After you and my mom."

Maddy goes completely still, her mouth dropping open in shock. "You're naming her after me?" she whispers. Pax grins.

"Who else would we name her after? There aren't that many derivatives of Pax."

Maddy grins widely and then turns to the baby again, talking to her through the glass.

"Listen up, Mad. You and I are going to stick together. I'm going to buy you so many pairs of shoes that your daddy will have to build a new house just to store them in. Yes, I know . . . that's a lot. But you're worth it."

I shake my head at Pax.

"I feel for you, dude," I tell him. "She's probably not exaggerating."

"Oh, I know she's not." Pax sighs. "But that's OK. My girls have me wrapped around their little fingers already. I'm man enough to admit it."

I can't help but grin at this. But I'll never fault him for it. I have a weakness too. I glance at Maddy again and decide that if I'm going to have a weakness, I'm glad it's a beautiful one.

"Madison, we should tell your sister goodbye so that she can rest," I suggest to her gently. "We can come back tomorrow. And we can even bring shoes for Madelyn, if you want."

"Oh, I want," she says firmly. She blows a kiss to the baby and we make our way back to Mila's room.

"We'll be back tomorrow, Sis." Maddy kisses Mila on the cheek. "Don't ever scare me like that again," she adds sternly. Mila smiles the gentle tired smile of a new mom, promising that she won't. Not ever.

And with that, we duck from the room.

As we drive home, I pick up Madison's hand.

"Are you OK?" I ask her solemnly. "That was intense."

She stares at me.

"That *was* intense," she agrees. "I thought I was going to have a heart attack. First there was all that blood, and then Mila passed out. I didn't know what to do. She *died*, Gabe. I still can't believe it. But having you there in that waiting room with me…you make everything all right, Gabe."

I feel choked up by her words, by the strength with which she handles everything in life. By the trust she puts in me.

As I put the car in park in the driveway, I kiss her forehead.

"I'm proud of you," I tell her quietly. "Really. You think I'm the strongest person you know, but really, it's you. You're stronger than all of us."

She rolls her eyes, but falls silent as we go inside.

We eat dinner in thoughtful silence, then sit for a little while in the living room, still quiet as Maddy lies on my lap. "We should go over to Pax and Mila's house and clean up all that blood," she tells me. "I know Pax will be staying with Mila tonight."

I nod.

"We will. But we'll do it tomorrow. You're tired tonight."

She nods and she's shivering from cold and from the shock of what happened, so I suggest a hot shower. She stays in there for half an hour.

When she finally comes out, I hold out a towel for her and envelop her in it, pulling her into my arms as I dry her off.

She still doesn't say anything and is even quieter after we collapse into bed.

"What is it?" I finally ask her, because the silence is killing me.

She sighs in the dark.

"It's just that I know how fast everything can end. My parents were gone in an instant and tonight it seemed like Mila could slip away too. And in that one instant, my heart would be broken forever, I know that—because I've been through it before. Hearts are so fragile, Gabe."

She pauses as she stares at me. I'm not sure what she's wanting me to say. But she doesn't give me a chance to reply at all before she continues.

"It reminded me of how fast I could lose you. Anything can happen and it scares the shit out of me. It scares me that you have that power over me."

She stops talking and stares at me. Her hands are shaking and I pick one up.

"Maddy, you have that same power over me. It's called loving someone. And yeah, it's scary as hell. I hate knowing that loving you makes me weak...but it makes me strong too. Loving you makes me happy in a way that nothing else ever has, and that's healthy, Madison. That's healthier than anything else in the world. It heals a lot of shit. It's even healing *me* and I'm fucked up. So before you over-think it and decide that loving me isn't worth the fear of losing me, just remember how happy you are when we're together. Fear is a choice, Maddy. But so is being happy."

"I know," she admits quietly. "My head knows that. But my

heart is scared because it knows that in a moment you could be gone. Everyone always seems to leave me, Gabe. My parents, Tony. Mila almost did. And if you leave…if *you* leave nothing will ever be OK again."

Her voice breaks and she cries, softly in the night, and it clenches my stomach into knots.

"Maddy, I know why you're scared. Anyone would be in your shoes. You've seen too much loss. But death is part of life and the fear of it can't stop us from living. That's something I learned in Afghanistan. Being ruled by fear is worse than never living at all. We're going to be fine, Maddy. You're not going to lose me, not until we're old and gray and tired. I love you."

She is quiet and still as she huddles against me, her slender hands holding tight to mine.

"Then let's make this work, no matter what. Promise me, Gabe. I know there's shit to work through. But we can do it. Because all that really matters is you and me."

Her voice is thin and anxious and I run my hands along her face, dropping them to stroke her shoulder. She trembles beneath my fingers and I hug her close. I know how much it took for her to say that, for her to commit to trying something long-term with me. It just confirms everything I've always known about her.

The girl has balls.

"Madison, everything is going to be fine," I tell her firmly. "Now that I'm back, you're stuck with me. I'm never going to leave you. Please don't worry. There's nothing to be afraid of anymore."

I can feel her smile against my chest. And then she burrows even more tightly into me. I rest my hands on her side and stare down at her in the dark.

She sniffs. "The only thing I'm afraid of is losing you."

"That's not going to happen," I answer her firmly, ignoring the ache in my chest at her words. "That's never going to happen."

I hold her until she goes to sleep, then I continue to hold her as long as I dare stay in the bed. When I finally know that I can't hold my eyes open anymore, I carefully slip away to the chair.

The chair is cold and it seems like a thousand miles away from Maddy, but I'm still here with her. That's the important thing.

I close my eyes.

Chapter Thirty~Four

Madison

I pull up to Pax and Mila's home and sit in the drive for a minute, simply enjoying the chirp of the summer crickets and the soft rustling of the breeze coming off the water. After the baby's emergency delivery, I thought it would take a while for life to get back to normal, but that hasn't been true.

Pax and Mila brought the baby home from the hospital a few days ago and everything has been fine. Mila has completely recovered, the baby is healthy and strong. We're all more resilient than I ever would have thought.

After I jog up the steps and poke my head in the door, I immediately hear the baby wailing and Pax shouting to Mila.

"I don't know what to do! She puked everywhere!"

I giggle and walk on in, taking the baby from Pax as he looks at me in relief.

"Mila's in the shower," he tells me sheepishly. "I just changed the baby, but I didn't do it right. Her diaper fell off and then she threw up."

I lay the baby down and refasten the Velcro tabs on her diaper, then strip off her little shirt.

"You almost had it," I tell him. "It just wasn't tight enough. You'll get it."

He hands me a clean shirt and I slide it onto the baby, then cradle her in my arms. Pax doesn't even bother holding out his hands for her, because he knows that while I'm here, I'm not giving her up. I hold her close and inhale the sweet baby smell, breathing deeply.

"Ahhh. I love that," I sigh. "It's the best smell in the world, aside from rain."

"Agreed," Pax says as he settles into a chair in the living room and closes his eyes. "I'm so fricking tired, Mad. Your niece was up a lot last night."

I shake my head, taking in his exhausted face. "Go ahead and rest. I'll watch the baby till Mila gets out."

"You're the best," he breathes, settling in for a nap.

I leap from my seat and hug Pax tightly, wrapping my arms around his neck.

"No, you are," I whisper to him. "You really are. Thank you for taking such good care of my sister."

"I don't know where that came from, but you're welcome." He pats my back and as he does, Mila comes in, toweling off her hair.

"Geesh, guys. Get a room." She rolls her eyes, then grins at me. "Did you come to babysit so I can take a nap?"

The hopeful tone in her voice makes me laugh. "I came to tell you something, but sure, I can stay for a while to watch the baby."

Mila looks curious. "What do you want to tell me?"

I motion to the sofa. "Can you sit?"

Mila looks worried, but does as I ask. When we're facing each other, I pick up her hands.

"Mi, I know that after Mom and Dad died, we couldn't bring

ourselves to give up the Hill. I came home to run it and I think I've done a pretty good job." I pause and she nods, hesitant. Pax looks knowing, like he's guessed what I'm going to say.

"But I can't do it anymore, Mila. I feel like I'm living someone else's life. Even though I completely renovated the cottage, it still feels like I've stepped into Mom and Dad's life and taken it over. I've got to have my own. Do you understand?"

She nods slowly. "I do. I definitely do. But what are you saying? What do you want to do?"

I take a deep breath. "I want to sell the Hill. And I want to sell the cottage. I'm thinking…and I know this might seem crazy, but I think I might want to move to Hartford and open up a restaurant there. It turns out that I'm pretty good at running one. But I just can't do it here. There's too many memories…Dad, Mom, Tony. I just…I can't. Do you hate me?"

Mila throws her arms around my neck, practically smothering me. "Of course not! You're going to move to Hartford with us? You'd do that? Oh my God. I'm so glad. I would've missed you so much."

My eyes well up. "I know. I just need a fresh start. A new life. But I don't want to do that too far away from you."

She sniffles and I sniffle and Pax throws his arms around both of us, smashing us both together.

"Everything's gonna be all right, Maddy," Mila tells me, tearfully. But they're happy tears now, thank God. "It really is."

I nod. "I know. I really think it is."

Pax finally lets go of us and they stand up.

"Are you sure you don't mind watching Madelyn for a bit?" Mila asks, covering up a yawn.

I shake my head. "Of course not. I'm going to be her favorite aunt."

"You're her *only* aunt," Pax points out. But the effect is lost because he yells it over his shoulder as they practically sprint to their bedroom to nap.

I have to chuckle at that. I've always heard stories of sleep-deprived parents, but having seen it firsthand, I know how desperate they are for sleep.

Madelyn actually falls asleep shortly after they do, which I find ironic. I hold her for a long time as she naps, just breathing in her sweet baby smell, and pondering everything that's happened over the past couple of weeks.

I miss Tony. I miss him every day. But Maria is doing OK and Sophia went back to school. They're doing as well as they can, and time will continue to heal them. And the rest of us.

Maybe everything really will be OK.

෴

On a warm summer evening, I come home from meeting with a realtor about selling the Hill to find Gabe sitting at the dining room table, a piece of paper in his hands and a strange look on his face.

"What?" I ask curiously. "What's wrong?"

He looks at me. "Do you remember me telling you that when I was in CPT, I wrote a letter to Ara Sahar's parents? It was the therapist's idea and I went along with it. I didn't really expect much to come out of it because hell—I didn't even know if her parents were still alive. But the army had it translated into Arabic and they located her parents. They answered me." He holds up the paper.

I can't read his face, it's entirely expressionless.

"Can I see it?" I ask hesitantly, almost afraid to look.

He nods, handing it to me, and I glance down at the wrinkled letter.

Dear Lieutenant Vincent,

Thank you very much for your recent letter.

At first I did not know how to respond because our hearts have been so very broken, into a million tiny pieces. But you are a soldier who came here to help people like me and children like Ara, and so I thought you must surely deserve an answer.

Even though putting this pen to this paper hurts my heart, there are several things you should know.

You should know that it wasn't your fault that my Ara was taken. My country has been torn apart by terrible things, evil things, none of which are your fault or your making. Each day, I would wake, afraid that that day would be the day when something would hurt Ara. Now that it is finally done, I no longer must worry. Nothing can harm her anymore. She's in Allah's arms now, safe and warm.

You should know that even in the midst of terrible evil, good flourishes, even still. You are good. You rose above the evil here and fought hard for good. Ara knew that. She used to watch the US soldiers pass and she would say to me, "They're here to protect us, Mama." She saw that in you. She saw that in all of you.

Lieutenant Vincent, you should know that you did not take my daughter from me. Even the evil here did not take her from me because she is not really gone. She is still my daughter and I am still her mama. Love is deathless, you see. And one day, I will be with her again. I will breathe in her hair and her sweet smell and she will smile at me and then I will be whole again. Someday.

Lieutenant Vincent, you should know that Ara does not blame you. I know that with every breath that is left in me. That is not who my daughter was, that is not who she is. She would wish you nothing but peace. Please do not weep for her. Ara is with angels. I think she is watching over you now, just as you watched over her when you were here. Even if you didn't know it, or her, you fought for her.

She knew that.

Lieutenant Vincent, you should know that you cannot hate yourself any longer. It was not your fault. You must forgive yourself.

Lieutenant Vincent, you should know that I have forgiven you.

May peace be upon you,
Pashka Sahar

My breath freezes in my throat as tears fall down my cheeks.

She doesn't blame Gabriel. Even through her veil of overwhelming grief, she has forgiven him.

In my head I picture a little Afghan girl and her grieving mother and all I can do is sit and marvel at Pashka Sahar's beautiful spirit amid all the ugliness around her. I read her words again and my heart breaks a little bit more with every word.

"She forgives you, Gabe," I tell him softly. "Now you have to forgive yourself. It's time."

Gabe opens his mouth to speak, then closes it and lowers his head onto his arms on the table.

Then he weeps.

After everything we've been through, I've never seen Gabriel cry.

It breaks my heart and everything from the past few months seems to crash down around us as I pad across the floor and pull him into my arms and onto the floor with me. I cradle him in my lap and let him cry.

I know it's not just the letter that he is crying over. It's everything. It's Ara Sahar, it's Mad Dog, it's his old life that he has lost, it's the heavy guilt that he has carried. It's all of it.

It's everything that he has never let himself properly grieve for.

"Shhhh," I soothe him, stroking his back. "It's OK. Let it go, Gabe. Even the strongest cry. A smart person told me that once."

I stroke his strong arms with my fingers, tracing each line and muscle until finally he falls silent and turns over, staring up at me.

I dip my head to press my lips against his.

"You're a hero, Gabe," I tell him. "You really are. You don't need to carry this anymore. No more guilt, no more sadness. Like Pashka said, you couldn't have prevented it. Ara wouldn't want you to carry this burden anymore."

He flips over and pulls me into his arms.

"I love you, Madison Hill," he tells me. "I've never cried before.

I should be embarrassed, but I'm not. I love you for not judging my weakness."

"You're not weak, Gabe," I answer softly. "You're far, far from weak. You're one of the reasons why normal people like me sleep well at night. It's because we can. You face danger so that we don't have to. Even little Ara knew that. You think that you're a *bad thing*, but you're not. *You protect the rest of us from bad things.* You're badass and lethal and scary, and you're as far from weak as you can get. You're a protector, Gabe. *My* protector."

He looks stunned, then satisfied. "Thank you," he says quietly.

I nod and we just sit in silence for a while.

Nothing more really needs to be said. Everything hangs in the air around us, reverent and beautiful and strong. Words aren't needed for us to feel it.

Eventually we get off the floor and drink a bottle of wine, quietly enjoying each other's presence before we finally head to bed.

As we lie in the quiet darkness, emotionally drained and tired, Gabe finally speaks.

"Maddy, I've been thinking about something. I don't want to go to Hartford with things as they are."

Every ounce of my being freezes with his words.

"You don't?" I manage to get out.

He shakes his head. "No. We've been through so much shit, Maddy. To hell and back, actually. I don't want to move to Hartford with you as my girlfriend. I want to move there with you as my wife."

The world stops again, like it has a hundred times since I met him.

I stare at him in the dark, my hand limp on his chest.

"You do?" My voice is a whisper.

"I do," he tells me. "Maddy, I know you're probably scared of marriage because of your parents'. But I can promise you that ours would be as different from theirs as night and day. I will love you every day of my life. Anything that wants to hurt you will have to come through me to do it. Fear is a choice, Maddy. Don't be afraid of this. Marry me. Please."

My answer is instant. I don't even have to think about it.

"Yes," I breathe. "I want to marry you."

"Thank God," he mutters as he pulls me to him. "I didn't know how else I was going to convince you if you said no."

I laugh, tracing my fingers along his face, his jaw, his neck.

"And you really don't mind moving to Hartford with me?" I ask, for the fourteenth time this week.

"Maddy, I would go anywhere with you."

His arms tighten around me and I hear the thrumming of his heart, solid and loud. I whisper loud enough that he can hear me over the crash of the lake outside.

"Don't leave me tonight, Gabe. Stay with me all night."

Out of habit he startles at the thought, but then he relaxes and finally nods.

A thrill runs through me at his words.

"You know what? Maybe it's time. We can't get married if we can't even sleep together, right?"

Relief floods through me.

"It's definitely time," I tell him. I relax, fitting into him perfectly. "But we're getting married either way." He chuckles and I drift toward sleep, enjoying the sense of security and love that washes over me in Gabe's arms.

As sleep overtakes me, I know that I'll never want to be anywhere else more than I want to be right here with him.

Not ever.

The night passes peacefully.

When I wake in the morning with the sun in my face, I turn to Gabe and find him watching me, his sexy dark eyes thoughtful.

"Did you dream?" I ask nervously. He grins, the slow grin that I love, the one that spreads from his lips to his eyes as he shakes his head.

"Not one nightmare. I think maybe I've kicked that demon's ass after all."

I reach for him, pulling him to me, enjoying the way his body covers mine. One thing is certainly true, this man is my own personal hero.

As I look into his eyes and see the promises that linger there, I can't help but think about another truth.

Fear really is a choice.

And we both faced ours and won.

There's nothing to be afraid of anymore.

Epilogue

One Year Later
Arlington, Virginia

Gabriel

The rows of white headstones seem to go on for miles and miles in the quiet cemetery. But only one matters right now.

The one I'm standing in front of.

Marshall Elijah Crane.

Mad Dog.

Brand bends down on one knee, wiping the slight layer of dust from the headstone. Of course it doesn't say Mad Dog. It spells out his full name and his rank in plain block letters. It doesn't say anything else about him.

It doesn't say that he was funny as shit, that he was loyal as hell or that he was scared to die, but faced it with honor anyway.

It doesn't say any of that.

"Hey, dude," Brand greets him quietly. "How's it hanging?"

I roll my eyes and Madison jabs him in the ribs.

"What?" he asks innocently. "I'm not gonna change how I talk to him just because he's dead."

I hold my hand out to Maddy and she hands me the box.

"Why didn't you tell me what you did?" she asks softly. "Why did you wait until they gave you this medal?"

"Don't feel bad," Jacey pipes up. "I didn't know either. I can't believe he didn't tell me."

I shake my head. "It wasn't relevant."

Brand chuckles wryly. "It was relevant to me."

I glance at him and suddenly, instead of seeing him standing tall and proud as he is now, I see him bloody and unconscious. His leg was blown to bits and I had no idea if there was anything else coming for us. I did the only thing I could do.

I draped him over my back and I carried him.

"Your husband carried me for two miles," Brand tells Maddy, his voice low. "After the Humvee exploded, Taliban rebels stormed in from the perimeter to kill any survivors. He pulled me out of there and carried me to safety, through the hills and the sand and the smoke. They would've killed me if he hadn't."

Maddy raises an eyebrow and leans into me. "And you never found this important to mention until now? I sounded like an idiot when the Pentagon called to invite you to the awards ceremony. A little heads-up would've been nice."

I smile. "I didn't know they were going to do that. Sorry about that."

"Why wouldn't they?" she answers incredulously, as she pushes her hair out of her face. "You're a hero, Gabe. Everyone knows it but you. For months you only focused on what you *didn't* do that night. What you should've been focusing on was what you *did*."

I stare at her, meeting her gaze. "I know," I answer.

And finally it's true. I do know. I know that I couldn't have stopped what happened that night. It wasn't my fault. The failure wasn't mine.

It's something that's taken me quite a while, but I'm at peace with it now.

Because the wheels of the government turn slowly, it wasn't until a month ago that we got the call. They wanted to honor Brand and me for that night. Brand with the Purple Heart and me with the Medal of Honor.

A medal for outstanding valor in the face of great peril, above and beyond the call of duty. That's what the president said to me today as he hung the blue ribbon around my neck.

Maddy and Jacey sat in the front row and cried.

And Mad Dog's wife was there next to them. It took her months. But time and a letter from Maddy made her understand that I would've given my life to save Mad Dog's.

And I would've.

But that's not how it happened. So I'm here today to honor his memory in the only way I can.

Kneeling, I drape the blue ribbon around the top of his headstone.

"Don't let this go to your head," I tell him.

Of course he's not here to hear me. But somehow, with the quiet reverence of this place, it seems almost possible that he is. That he's standing behind me with a bottle of Mad Dog in his hand, laughing as I leave my medal with a dead man.

But that's OK.

It belongs here.

I need to leave it behind, along with everything else that happened that night. I don't want to think about it anymore.

"You're sure you want to leave it here?" Maddy asks gently.

I nod. "I don't need a piece of metal to tell me who I am."

She smiles, gorgeous and warm, as her hand flutters down to her stomach, where our baby is just barely beginning to show.

"You feeling OK?" I ask. "It's hot. Do you need some water?"

She laughs. "I'm good, babe. Ask me again in a few months. Right now I'm fine."

Brand wraps one arm around her shoulders and the other around Jacey's. Together the four of us stand for a second, soaking in the quiet, silently paying tribute to all the fallen soldiers around us. I know that Brand is thinking the same thing I am. It could very easily have been us buried here beneath the dirt and the grass.

But it's not.

"If the baby is a boy, I want to name him Elijah," I finally say to Maddy. "Is that OK?"

Her eyes well up and she nods. "As long as his middle name is Gabriel."

Warmth floods through me. "Deal," I manage to say, lacing my fingers through hers.

"You might not want to talk about it," she tells me gently. "But our son will hear about what a hero you are. Just so you know that."

She lets go of my hand, gripping my arm instead, and I think about the words beneath her fingers.

Death before dishonor.

Mad Dog is dead and there is nothing I can do about that. He died with honor. Along with Ara Sahar and all those other women and children. But I'm still alive. So there's only one thing I can do. Live for them.

Live with honor.

"You ready?" Brand asks, glancing at me.

I nod. "Yeah."

And finally I am.

We walk away together, leaving the past behind us where it belongs.

A Note from the Author

As of the writing of this book, around 3,460 Congressional Medals of Honor have been bestowed on US military personnel who have acted with outstanding valor and courage.

The recipients of that honor deserve that recognition.

So do the thousands of military personnel doing their jobs both around this country and around the world.

And so too do the many soldiers who fought in combat and came home with PTSD, often to a debilitating degree. According to statistics, in 2012 more soldiers lost their lives by suicide (averaging one per day) than on the battlefield. That is staggering.

And heartbreaking.

Soldiers face the things that we don't want to face, things that we don't *have* to face because they do it for us. Because they face it, because they look fear in the eye, they come home scarred on the inside.

We shouldn't forget that. We shouldn't forget *them*.

There are scores of websites and groups out there, all designed to help injured soldiers and soldiers with PTSD. If you'd like to support a cause, if you'd like something to believe in, I'd highly recommend looking into one of them to become active in. One that I found during my research is the Wounded Warrior Project (www. woundedwarriorproject.org). You can start there and learn ways to help.

I have a special place in my heart for soldiers, which is one of the reasons this book came to be.

Before I quit my job in the corporate world for my dream job of writing books, I had the enormous privilege of working with a team of former military officers and soldiers. Each of them embodied the traits of the kind of person we should all aspire to be.

Honor, dignity, loyalty, bravery, discipline. These guys showed me firsthand the amazing people that soldiers are.

Also, my own grandpa served in WWII. I remember the stories my grandma would tell of not hearing from him for months (because letters were delayed). Then when she went to the movies one night, there was footage of soldiers boarding a ship bound for overseas and she saw my grandpa. She said, "I knew it was him. No one had a walk like Olen."

Those boys were boarding a ship to go fight against unknown terror, things they'd never seen the likes of before. Yet they did it with honor. They did it with dignity. All of them found out firsthand that fear is a choice. They faced fear so that everyone back home didn't have to. It gives me chills to think about.

My grandpa, who has passed away now, embodied every one of the traits I mentioned above. He was quietly dignified, strong and brave. He never talked about what happened to him in the war, because many men of that generation didn't. It was too horrible to speak of.

Things have changed, though, and soldiers are encouraged to talk about the things that scarred them. They are encouraged to deal with their internal demons...demons they acquired in the line of duty.

Demons they acquired when they were protecting *us* from harm.

This book is my way of honoring each one of them. It's a reminder that they fight for the things that people like me take for granted. Like Maddy said in the story, soldiers fight so that we can rest easily. They guard us against the things that go bump in the night.

They serve with honor so that we can live free.

They're all heroes and I'll never forget that.

I hope you won't, either.

Before We Fall

The Beautifully Broken Series: Book 3

Courtney Cole

One dark moment was all it took to turn twenty-four-year-old Dominic Kinkaide's world black. On the night of his high school graduation, a single incident changed him forever, and he became a hardened man – famous in the eyes of the world, but tortured inside. Now all he cares about is losing himself in the roles that he plays.

At twenty-three years old, Jacey Vincent doesn't realise how much her father's indifference has affected her. She tries to find acceptance in the arms of men to fill the void – a plan that has worked just fine for her, until she meets Dominic.

When jaded Dominic and strong-willed Jacey are thrown together, the combination of his secrets and her issues turns their attraction into the perfect storm. It could change their lives for good – if it doesn't tear them both apart . . .

HODDER

Read on for a taster . . .

Chapter One

Dominic

Now

I like to watch.

I know that I shouldn't, but I don't really give a shit. I like the flash of skin, the sweaty limbs, the sex smells, the *fucking* . . .

Watching makes me feel something. It's one of the only things that does.

"Some things never change, Dominic," Kira murmurs as her hand splays across my open shirt, her long brown hair moving in the breeze, tickling my chest as she watches with me. "You're just the same . . . a freak. I love that."

I don't answer because she's right. I'm a fucking freak. She knows it and I know it, and neither of us care. If anything, Kira likes it. She must, because she's stuck by me for a long time. She knows me better than anyone . . . and she definitely knows what I like.

Even though she's beautiful and familiar, I ignore her fingers as they trace across my skin, graze the tips of my nipples, and trail down to my crotch. My dick is resistant to her touch tonight and remains soft inside my pants. Not because she's not hot or sexy, because she is.

But because familiar and normal don't stir my blood. I've seen pretty much everything once and have done it twice. Normal doesn't do it for me anymore.

Forbidden things are what lift my dick. Dark things, bad things.

I stare down from the balcony, looking past the shimmering pool below, past the rippling water that sheds blue light on everything around it, at the images that waver in the night. The images of two people fucking.

Knowing that I *shouldn't* watch is what excites me about it, and so I don't take my eyes from the couple having sex next to my brother's pool.

I take another drink of whiskey, letting the fiery liquid sit in my mouth before I swallow it, letting it curl its fingers around my stomach, warming my gut.

Watching the couple, I lean against the railing, half-hidden by the shadows, enveloped by the night. It's just how I like it.

In front of me, the scene turns rough.

And my dick turns hard.

The girl's teeth sink into the guy's neck, then she whispers something unintelligible into his ear, words that hiss as she drags her teeth across his skin. Hard, aggressive, rough. I can see the red trail of pain she leaves behind from here.

"Did she just bite him?" Kira asks in amusement, her hand frozen at my waistband.

I nod. She did. And it made me hard as a rock. I love watching pain. It distracts me from my own.

The guy smiles, liking it too. He lifts her legs onto his shoulders as he thrusts into her. Hard. Then he frees one hand to grab her neck. Hard. His fingers dig into the delicate skin there, cutting into the flesh, leaving red marks that just might turn purple by morning.

But she likes it.

I can tell by the way she scratches his back and moans for more. I can tell by the way she draws him even further into herself, bucking her hips to take him even deeper. I can tell by the way she doesn't even try to take his hand away from her throat.

It always fascinates me when I see women that like getting debased, the ones who like it rough, the ones who want to be dominated or humiliated.

It doesn't make any sense, but I see it all the time, more and more, especially here at my brother's place at one of his endless parties. Around his pool, in his hot tub, on his lawn. People seem to lose their inhibitions when they pass through these gates, which doesn't make any sense, either. Most of them don't know him, not really. But it doesn't stop them from making themselves *very* at home here.

Suffice it to say I'm always entertained when I come to visit.

"Do you think they know we're watching?" Kira leans up on her tiptoes, murmuring with hot breath into my ear as she strokes my balls.

I glance back down at the couple, watching the guy's face contort and twist, and watching the girl moan and writhe beneath him. They have no clue we're here, but I have a feeling they wouldn't care even if they did.

"I think that girl served me champagne earlier!" Kira exclaims, leaning closer to look.

"You're probably right," I answer, staring at the girl's skimpy server's uniform. I briefly wonder where her boss thinks she is. Surely he has no idea that she's fucking a party guest next to the pool.

But that's not my problem.

The bulge between my legs is my problem now. It's grown thicker and heavier and I shift, easing the pressure of my jeans away from my dick. I brush my hand against the denim covering my crotch, stroking myself. Just a little. Quickly and efficiently.

I'm not going to get off right out here in the open. Because of how I make my living, I've learned not to do *anything* out in the open. The press would have a fucking field day if pictures of me jacking off leaked out.

Kira takes care of the situation for me, just as she always does when I'm in town. She pushes me backward into the shadows, where she steps out of her shorts in front of me. She's not wearing underwear.

She's right. Some things never change.

"Fuck me with your hand while you watch them," she instructs me softly, her green eyes gleaming. "Do it, Dom. And then I'll let you come on my face, the way you like to."

I reach for her. She stands limply in front of me, her head resting on my shoulder as I slide two of my fingers in and out of her. I know exactly where to touch her. She sucks in a breath and I have to smile. I know every inch of her. There are some things to be said for familiarity.

She's soaking wet, as though she's been waiting for this since I'd seen her last. She hasn't, of course. Kira and I have an arrangement of convenience. It's convenient because we know each other, we trust each other. And there are no feelings involved. She and I are the same in that way.

I can hear the girl by the pool moaning loudly and it makes my fingers move faster, working Kira harder, in time to the guy's sweaty thrusts. Kira moans with the girl by the pool and I close my eyes, listening to the fucking sounds. With my hand buried in Kira's crotch, the sounds are all I need now.

If I were decent, I'd back away from the balcony and give the couple some privacy and I'd give Kira more coverage from the shadows... just in case someone happens upon us.

But fuck that. I'm not decent. Not anymore.

After a few more minutes of rough fucking, the guy pulls out of the waitress and grasps her hard, yanking her off the chaise and forcing her down in front of him, onto her knees. I can see her skin graze the bricks, just as I can read his lips.

Suck me.

I pause as the girl shakes her head, trying to scramble away, but he holds her fast by her hair, making her take him into her mouth. Making her suck her own taste off of him.

She's definitely not into it now. She swings her arms at him frantically, but he holds her hair tightly, wrapping it around his hands, refusing to let her go.

I watch the fear wash over her face and my gut tightens in reaction.

Fuck.

Kira lifts her head as my hand stills. "What?"

Her eyes are glazed as she stares at me. I nod toward the pool, at the struggle going on down there, at the girl trying desperately to get away from the asshole's grip.

"Hell," Kira sighs. "Ignore it, Dom. It's not your problem. We're not done here."

I sigh too, because I know I can't ignore it.

This has been happening way too much. People come here and get wasted and out of control. It's not worth the trouble, but Sin keeps having the parties anyway. He says it keeps him relevant, whatever the fuck that means. I don't seem to have a problem with being *relevant*, and I don't host a single party.

I shake Kira's grip off of my wrist, gulp down the rest of my drink, and head down the stairs, ignoring her calls of protest.

It takes a minute to weave discreetly through the masses of people scattered through the house and to make my way across the lawn and onto the stones leading to the pool. But I reach the couple within two minutes, and without even pausing I grab the guy from behind, ripping him backward. He hisses as the girl's teeth scrape his dick.

It serves him right. The fucker interrupted me.

He yelps and I toss him on the ground, watching in satisfaction as he scrapes his face on the stone bricks before he rolls into the lawn.

"Get the fuck out," I snap at him. "No one gets forced against their will here."

"That bitch wanted it," he protests as he climbs to his feet. "She was asking for it."

I shake my head. "The last time I checked, no means no. It's not a new way of *asking for it*. Get the fuck out of here."

The guy looks at me again, recognizes who I am, and then stalks away without another word. I grab a pool towel and wrap it around the girl's shoulders.

Her skimpy uniform, which was barely there in the first place, is hanging around her waist now, apparently ripped in their scuffle. She seems self-conscious, but honestly, I barely notice. She's young and has perky tits, but so do thousands of other women. She doesn't do much for me. Mostly because I know she'd offer herself on a platter if I wanted her to. I briefly consider inviting her to join Kira and me, but don't. She's drunk, and even if she's too drunk to remember it, she's just been almost violated.

"You okay?" I ask gruffly. She nods, sniveling, just as another girl, a gorgeous blonde in a matching uniform, rushes up.

"Holy shit, Kaylie. What the hell happened?"

The blonde is obviously alarmed, concerned, and while Kaylie explains about the asshole, I turn to disappear back into the shadows. Regardless of my profession, I try to stay out of the spotlight when the cameras aren't rolling. Unfortunately, I only make it partway before Kaylie grabs my arm, then wraps herself around my waist.

"Thank you," she tells me shakily, her arms like thin bands, not giving me room to even squirm. I stare down at her, looking past her tear-smeared eyeliner to look into her panicky eyes.

"It's not a problem. But you need to stay out of situations like that. There won't always be someone to step in and save you."

From her shocked expression, I decide that I might've been a little too hard on her. But shit. Women have to be more careful. She can't parade around in barely any clothes, have rough sex with a stranger, and just expect him to be a gentleman. Men, by and large, aren't gentlemen. We're assholes.

Kaylie stares at me, too drunk or high to even respond. But her friend isn't so silent.

Big brown eyes snap at me angrily. "Why are you lecturing her? She was just assaulted, in case you didn't notice."

I roll my eyes.

"Is that what you call it? She was having rough sex with that asshole right out in the open. When she was supposed to be working, I might add. It looked to me like it was an incident that just got out of control. I stopped it for her. You're welcome."

Gorgeous Blonde stares at me dumbfounded. "Are you trying to insinuate that she's not a victim, that it was her fault this happened?"

I sigh. "Of course not. I'm saying that she shouldn't have been encouraging a drunk stranger to be rough with her in the first place. Good night."

I start to walk away, but apparently she's not done.

"Who the fuck do you think you are?" she demands. "You might not have heard, but you really shouldn't blame the victim."

"I'm not blaming—" I begin, but I'm interrupted by her gasp as I step fully into the light and she sees my face.

"Holy shit." She breathes. "You're Dominic fucking Kinkaide."

I can't help but smile, just a little, just enough to pull the corners of my mouth up. "Dominic will do. I tend to drop the 'fucking.' Unless of course, I'm *actually* fucking."

She smiles a breathtaking smile that should affect me. The girl is stacked, has legs that go on for miles, and she's wearing next to nothing. She should affect me. But she doesn't. Because nothing affects me anymore. I'm jaded as fuck.

"I've heard you're trouble," she announces matter-of-factly, eyeing me up and down with a slow gaze and fire in her eyes. "That's lucky, because I happen to like trouble."

"I bet you do," I answer back, trying to ignore the way she's acting now that she knows who I am. They all act like this. Every one of them. It gets monotonous. Just once, can't someone surprise me? "Nice to meet you."

I turn around and walk back toward the house, but she takes two steps and grabs my arm. I pause.

"But you didn't," she says hesitantly, a bit unsure now. "You didn't meet me. My name's Jacey."

I sigh. "Your name doesn't matter."

I keep walking, ignoring the way she sucks her breath in, the way she calls after me in agitation, the way she gives up and stops in defeat.

I might be an asshole, but I don't lie.

Her name doesn't matter.

Not to me.

I leave the entire situation behind, out of my sight and out of my mind. Within a few minutes, I'm standing in front of Kira again.

"All taken care of?" she purrs, reaching for me. I nod, burying my face between her heavy, naked tits as she unbuckles my belt. "Bind my hands with this, and come on my face."

She doesn't have to ask me twice.

"You're such a dirty girl," I whisper in her ear as I push her onto the couch and bind her hands above her head, just tight enough for the leather to bite into her flesh. Just the way she likes it.

And then I grasp my dick in my hand and fuck my fist, just the way *I* like it.

For just a second, for some strange reason, the blonde chick's face pops into my mind, her eyes wide and brown. I have no idea why, but I shake my head to clear it. I focus instead on the matter at hand.

Within another two minutes, I come on Kira's face, spurting in a cream-colored arc that spatters onto her tanned skin. She licks a drop from her lips and grins at me.

"Welcome home, lover."

"Don't call me that." I shake my head as I pull my jeans back on and collapse next to her. She rolls her eyes.

"Why? It's what we are. You always come back to me, Dom. You know that."

I unbind the belt wordlessly, tossing it onto the floor. I might always come back to her whenever I come home, but I don't fuck her. Not really. I haven't actually fucked someone in years.

"*Lover* would indicate that I bury my dick in your sweet pussy." I glance at her, then reach out to run my finger over the swell of one of her tits, then trail it downward to her crotch. She arches toward my touch. "And you know I won't do that."

I pull my hand away abruptly and Kira scowls. "Yeah, I know that. What I *don't* know is why. Dominic, you've got needs too. Watching other people fuck or jacking off and coming on my face can't be enough. Sex isn't just sex, Dom. You need all the good stuff that comes along with it."

"Oh, I do, do I?" I ask, amused now. "Like what? Like having women get attached and hoping that I'll marry them? Or worrying that I'll get some fucking disease or . . ."

"Just stop." Kira interrupts me with a glare. "*I know you*, Dom. I know why you do what you do. You don't want to get close to someone again. You don't want to give anyone that kind of power over you. But Dom . . . it's time. It's time for you to finally get over her and come back to life."

"One, don't talk about her." I instruct Kira icily, staring at her hard. "You know better than that. And two, are you insinuating that I'm not living?"

Kira sighs as she pulls her shirt on, forgoing her bra. She stuffs it into her purse and glances up at me.

"You know damn well what I'm insinuating. You've been a shell for six years, Dom. Six fucking years. That's a long time. I've been patient. I've done everything you needed. But there comes a time when a girl needs to be fucked. I've got needs, Dominic."

I have to chuckle now at the idea that I'm the only one Kira's depending on for her "needs." "Oh, yeah. Because you don't have anyone else to fulfill your needs when I'm not here?"

She glares at me. "You're a dick sometimes. I've got to work early in the morning, so I've gotta go. Call me tomorrow, okay?"

I nod even though I know I won't. I bury my face into the couch cushions, realizing I'm suddenly exhausted and just want to sleep. I don't even hear Kira leave. But I do hear when someone else comes in a few minutes later, right when I'm ready to slip into sleep.

"Dom, what the fuck? You were supposed to pull me out of the game so that I didn't lose my shirt."

I reluctantly open one eye to stare at my brother and find that he *actually* lost his shirt. He's standing in front of me bare-chested. My eyes dip down and I cringe.

He lost his pants, too.

"What the hell, Sin? Put some fucking clothes on."

My brother grins—that cocky, rakish grin that his fans love so much—as he plops himself down onto the sofa next to me, buck-ass naked, crossing his feet at the ankle on the coffee table.

"You wouldn't have to worry about it if you'd pulled me out of the poker game like I asked you to." He shrugs, picking up my glass of whiskey and drinking it all. "Those drunk chicks know how to play poker. Or I just wanted to take my clothes off. One or the other."

I glare at him. "I couldn't bail you out because I was taking care of a situation for you. Fuck, man. You've got to stop having these parties. Someone's gonna get raped or killed and they're going to sue the shit out of you."

Sin only grins, unconcerned. "If they're dead, they can't sue me."

I can't argue with that logic. Instead, I tell him what he missed, not that it bothers him much. He sees it all the time.

"Thanks for fixing it," he tells me casually, as though near-rapes are normal. I roll my eyes.

"Anytime. Now can you get some fucking clothes on?"

He waggles his dark eyebrows. "Sure. If it makes you insecure to look at my package. Not only am I older, but I'm also bigger, and that's what counts."

He's also ridiculous. He's not a centimeter bigger than I am, but I don't waste my breath telling him that.

He yanks one of my shirts out of my suitcase and pulls it over his head. Then a pair of my pants. He forgoes underwear, which means I'll have to burn those jeans.

"I forgot to ask how long you're staying," he asks as he settles back into the seat, unconcerned that he just ruined my favorite jeans. "Long enough to catch a show, I hope. It's all I've heard about for months from Duncan…how you don't even come watch your poor little brothers play."

I roll my eyes. "Poor little brothers? I think both of you are doing just fine."

Sin snorts. "Only as well as you, big bro. But whatever. We have a show coming up in Chicago next month. If you want to fly back in, we'll get you backstage passes."

I shake my head. "I'll try. Filming starts in a couple of weeks. But I'll see what I can do. I don't want to upset baby Duncan."

"What about me?"

My youngest brother saunters into my room, dropping onto the sofa next to Sin. Neither of them have any personal space issues, that's for sure, because now we're all three crammed onto the one sofa. And we're too big for that shit.

"Nothing," I assure Duncan. "I just said I didn't want to offend your ovaries by not coming to your next show. I'll try like hell to be there."

"That's the furthest thing from my mind right now," Duncan announces, cracking open the can of beer in his hand. "You can see me bang on the drums any time. What I'd like to bang tonight are the half-naked women beyond these very doors. I fucking love your house, man," he tells Sin. "Oh, and there's a chick asking for you. Said she wants to make sure you know that your brother rescued her. Or some shit."

Sin rolls his eyes, but I elbow him. "It's probably the girl from the pool. You'd better talk to her and autograph her tits or something. You need to keep her happy so that she doesn't think to call the police. You don't want that kind of press, dude. Not after Amsterdam."

The mere mention of how the tabloids had ripped Sin's band up over a wild party in Amsterdam a month ago is enough to sober the two of them up. There had been some underage girls there, groupies who had lied about their age, and if it weren't for the more lax laws in Europe, my brothers would've been screwed.

Sin nods now.

"Fine. Take me to her," he tells Duncan. To me, he hands the bottle of whiskey and says, "Do you ever get tired of being right? Jesus Christ."

"Not yet," I tell him as I gulp down a few swigs, then slide down into the sofa again, closing my eyes. "It's a burden though."

My brothers chuckle as they walk out and I relax, enjoying the way the whiskey has loosened my muscles, the way the warmth has spread to every bit of me. It helps me stay numb...and numbness is a welcome fucking thing.

When I'm numb, I feel safe enough to slip my hand into my pocket. Not for my dick, although that's normal for me, too. No, I wrap my fingers around the cool stone of the pendant that is always there, encased in a white shell and resting against my leg.

The last thing that fills my mind before I sleep is a color.

Aquamarine.